CHOICES

Carly got through the cocktail hour in a fog. She thought of Boomer. She looked at her mother and Walt, then at Cole. Was it even a matter of making a choice? Boomer had come back into her life for one night. That didn't mean it would lead to anything. She was almost twenty-five years old. Would any offer ever equal Cole's? She wouldn't have to work another day in her life if she didn't want to. She could stay in bed late, in satin sheets with a maid who brought her breakfast. She'd have an unlimited charge card and could buy anything she wanted and ...

Cole cleared his throat as he raised his wineglass. "We have come," he said, "to ask for Carly's hand in marriage."

The silence was powerful. It forced Carly to meet Cole's eyes. Then Walt said, "I don't think it's up to us. Whatever Carly wants is fine with us."

Cole was grinning. "Well," he asked, "do you want to set the date?"

Carly thought a minute. "Any day is fine with me," she said. "April is a lovely month."

"I don't know if I can wait that long." Cole downed his wine. "April it is."

"The thirtieth is a Saturday," Carly's mother said. "That will give us six weeks. Plenty of time."

"The thirtieth it is, then," Carly said.

She pushed Boomer Bannerman out of her mind.

DEEP IN THE HEART

Barbara Bickmore

Kensington Books
Kensington Publishing Corp.

http://www.kensingtonbooks.com

KENSINGTON BOOKS are published by

Kensington Publishing Corp.
850 Third Avenue
New York, NY 10022

Kensington and the K logo Reg. U.S. Pat. & TM Off.

First Kensington Hardcover Printing: June, 1996
First Kensington Paperback Printing: November, 1997
10 9 8 7 6 5 4 3 2 1

Printed in the United States of America

DEDICATED TO

the memory of my parents, Nina and Vernon Bickmore, who would not have been surprised at these past ten years,

and to Robert Mason, my friend of over thirty years, who helped set me on the straight path with this book

and
THANKS TO

Mary Ann Miller and Billy Ruth Scott, Texans who inspired and helped me along the way. A few incidents were based on their youth, but the personalities of my characters in no way are like them or based on them. Their stories fired my imagination.

Dorothy Milbank Butler, who read this and critiqued it as I went along.

PART I

1961–1968

CHAPTER 1

Not counting Brownsville and McAllen, Verity is about as far south as you can get in Texas. Small as it is, it has several claims to fame. The two largest cattle ranches in the whole country are within thirty miles—the King Ranch directly to the north and a bit east, and Sanborns, northwest. It has some of the goddamndest weather in the entire United States with summers so humid it's hard to breathe. In April, however, when the bluebonnets cover the lush countryside, newly green from spring rains, and the big spreading oaks leaf into lacy greengold, not many places are prettier.

Carly Anderson hated Verity from the first day she saw it, when she was fifteen years old, and she and her mother, Francey, pulled into town in the middle of April, 1961, a day so hot even the flies didn't move.

"This doesn't look so bad," Francey said, when they hit Verity. "I want to get as far away from Los Angeles and big city life as a girl can get."

Girl? Carly laughed to herself. Francey was almost thirty-four.

Francey pulled into a parking space in front of the soda shop. "We can at least get a lemonade," she said.

It was two in the afternoon and no one was in sight. School was still in session, and at this time of day it was too hot for people to be on the streets.

Carly's mother took the keys from the ignition and opened the door, stretching her legs. She wore short shorts, as did Carly.

Carly got out of the car reluctantly. This whole trip had been taken reluctantly. She had not wanted to leave Pasadena High, where she was in line to be a cheerleader next year, where she had a dozen good friends, and where the boys were just beginning to hang around her. Her mother told her she couldn't date on week nights, but let her stay out until midnight weekends. She'd been happy in California. She didn't know any other life. She was born there, two months after her father was killed in the war—three months before it ended. She'd cried when she left her friends, and school, and the little bungalow where she and her mother had lived for the last seven years.

Francey had hugged Carly to her and let her cry, saying in whispers, "I know, honey, but one of us has to be miserable a while. I've been miserable here for years, and it's time for me to move on. You're a kid. You'll adjust soon. I promise."

They headed east, to no place in particular. "I'll know it when I see it," Francey assured her daughter. Florida maybe. She liked the LA weather and wanted to stay where it was sunny and warm all year, so maybe the Florida Keys or Fort Myers Beach, someplace laid back, as unlike LA as possible.

They walked into the darkness of the soda shop, where an overhead fan whirred, moving the humidity around and around. Francey chose a table by the window, looking out on Verity's Main Street, over which drooped tall trees, shading the east side mornings and the west side afternoons.

The waitress, in a red-and-white checked uniform, sauntered over, checking out the Anderson women, and said, "What'll it be, y'all?"

"Lemonades," Francey answered.

"I'm tired." Francey had been driving for five days and didn't care if she ever drove again. She leaned forward, peering through the smudged window. "Look at that sign." Across the street over the door to the Blue Moon Diner, a bright blue neon sign blinked. Francey was pointing to the Help Wanted sign in the window.

"So?" asked Carly.

"So, maybe we'll just stay here a couple of months and get a little ahead financially."

Carly made a face. "Stay here?"

"Sure." Francey's voice was becoming enthusiastic. "It's a little town. That's what I want. And there's a job just beckoning me, like it's meant to be."

Carly didn't think the town looked very interesting. But then, she told herself, no place was going to look good to her. She might as well try to make the best of whatever her mother wanted. She thought her mother was the greatest person in the whole world. The universe, probably.

Francey called out to the waitress, "You got a motel in town?"

The waitress nodded. "Right down the road a piece, at the end of town. You can't miss it. Twin Oaks Motel."

Francey told her daughter, "If I'm going to apply for that job, I better wear a skirt and look decent."

"Mom, I thought you wanted to leave LA so you could stop waitressing."

"I wanted to leave LA so I could stop hoping. For more years than you've been alive I kept hoping for the right part. The only time I was offered a real lalapalooza was when I was four months pregnant with you and I had to turn it down. And I've been living on hope ever since. I want to stop hoping and live in the present, and this looks like a nice place for a kid to grow up in."

Dull place for a kid to grow up from the looks of Main Street. But they finished their drinks and drove to the Twin Oaks Motel where Francey rented a room for the night and unpacked. "Everything's so wrinkled I'll wait till morning, after I've hung this up and steamed the wrinkles out of it. Let's go walk around and see what this place looks like.''

Carly didn't like what she saw. Downtown there wasn't much more than the post office, a gas station, the First National Bank, a couple of stores, the soda shop, and the Blue Moon Diner. They walked six blocks across town to the cinema, which showed movies at one o'clock on Saturdays and at seven-thirty on Fridays and Saturdays. Down the block was the grocery store, which stayed open until six o'clock every night but Sunday, when not even the gas station opened up.

They passed a little white house with peeling paint. Francey smiled when she saw the For Rent sign. ''Looks like maybe this is meant to be,'' she said.

''Oh, Mom, that's a terrible-looking house. We never lived in anything *that* bad!''

''With a little paint and elbow grease we can fix it up real pretty. Bet they don't want much for it.''

When Francey phoned the number on the sign, she discovered the rent was forty-five dollars a month. ''We can afford that easy,'' she smiled, ''if I get a job.''

The next morning, in a V-neck red jersey, a white skirt with a slit in the side, and red sandals, Francey went to the source of the Help Wanted sign. Blue Baker had hung it in his front window two days before. When he saw her, Blue nearly dropped his teeth. She walked into the diner at seven o'clock, an hour after he'd opened and just before the rush started. She didn't say anything but, with hips sashaying, went to the window, took the sign out and placed it on the counter.

Blue and the five men scattered at the tables stared at her, their jaws slack.

Francey said to Blue, ''Try me.''

Every man in there wanted to try her, yet they each sensed they'd be no match.

''You wanna know the salary and the hours?''

''I'm sure you'll be fair,'' Francey said.

Blue handed her an apron.

"No," she said, "I have to go register my daughter in high school first."

On her first full day at Verity High School, Carly would discover that newcomers were not welcomed gracefully.

Carly wasn't like anything the tenth-grade boys had ever seen before. A robin's-egg-blue ribbon that matched her eyes exactly wound through her shining blond hair. Her ears were pierced and dangling gold earrings flashed as she tossed her head. Her blue-and-white striped cotton dress, demure on the hanger, accentuated her shapely figure. Boys thought the buttons looked as though they'd burst any minute and hoped Carly might bounce out in all her glory.

She wore white leather sandals studded with gold. All the other girls wore penny loafers.

As she stood in the doorway, she snapped her gum.

Miss Hasseldorf's first words were, "No gum chewing is permitted."

Carly, nervous at being a newcomer and reprimanded by a teacher first thing off the bat, reached out her tongue and removed the gum, walking over to put it in the wastebasket by Miss Hasseldorf's desk. She smiled dazzlingly at the teacher who, mesmerized by the young girl, stared at her before indicating an empty seat in the center middle row.

Carly sat down, opened a clean lined notebook, licked the end of her pencil, and looked up, ready to listen. There hadn't been a sound since she entered the room.

Miss Hasseldorf shook her head and blinked before returning to the equation she was writing on the board. "If you've done your homework," she said, her back to the class, "this shouldn't be difficult to solve. Who knows the answer, and can explain how you got it?" She turned to face the class.

No one raised a hand.

The teacher called on a boy slouched against the wall in the back row. "Harold?"

Harold shook his head.

She glanced around the room. "How about an answer even if you don't know how you got it?"

A pencil rolled onto the floor, and a boy bent to pick it up, staring across the room, under the desks, at Carly's long tanned legs.

"No one? Not one of you?" Exasperation was evident in Miss Hasseldorf's voice.

"Seventy-two."

The students turned en masse to stare at Carly.

Carly wished the floor would open up and swallow her. She wished she'd kept her mouth shut, but the answer had just sort of shot out.

"Do you know how you got the answer?"

Carly hesitated and Miss Hasseldorf said, "We stand when we wish to speak."

Carly stood, and the teacher thought she'd made a tactical error. Every pair of male eyes was riveted on the new girl.

Through lipstick-red lips, Carly gave a brief answer, stuttering with self-consciousness before sitting down. No one except the teacher had heard a word she'd said.

Miss Hasseldorf had taught math and after-school girls' basketball in Verity for seventeen years, and she knew that here was a girl already in trouble in this town and she also knew as Carly explained her reasoning, that the girl far surpassed any student she had.

Before noon, word was around the faculty room about the good-looking brainy girl.

Mr. Owens, the history teacher, took one look at Carly and decided it would never matter if she knew anything about Mesopotamia or the Rosetta Stone or Antietam. He could hardly keep his train of thought straight as he talked of whatever it was he was trying to remember.

Carly had no idea she'd created a stir of any kind and, when she arrived back at the motel after her first day in the new school and her mother asked, "How did you like it?," Carly shrugged and answered that the place didn't seem very friendly.

"No one asked me to lunch with them," she said, feeling more miserable than she could ever remember feeling.

Back in Pasadena her mother had been vice president of the PTA and had sung in the choir of the Methodist Church. She had found it a friendly place, and was sure Verity would be even friendlier. "I looked at that house," Francey said. "It needs a lot of work, but what else do we have to do?"

She grabbed Carly's hand and said, "Let's walk over and look. I have the key."

Carly was dismayed at what she saw.

Her eyes dancing, Francey said, "This front room can be painted white and we'll get some furniture on time. Look at these hardwood floors. We'll scrape that wood down and varnish it and it'll be truly beautiful."

The Formica on the kitchen counter was scratched, but Francey had once read in some magazine how you could fix such countertops. The stove and refrigerator looked so old, Carly asked if they worked. Instead of answering, Francey said, "That bay window in the dining room overlooks a magnolia tree. Imagine that."

"It's got two bedrooms." Francey pulled Carly down the hallway. "I thought maybe you could have the larger one because you'll need a desk, too."

Carly knew a bribe when she heard one.

That weekend they drove over to Corpus Christi and bought cheap gauzy fabric for curtains and made a down payment on a few pieces of furniture, just enough to make do until Francey began earning money.

In her years in Verity, Carly made only one friend. Zelda Marie Spencer's family had lived there for three generations. They owned a ranch four miles out of town and her father was on a first-name basis with everyone in three counties, including the Sanborns and the Klebergs, who owned the famous King Ranch.

Carly loved it when the Spencers invited her to the ranch

weekends. She and Zelda Marie would skinny-dip in the creek, and Zelda Marie taught Carly to ride a horse. They spent hours walking through the meadows, talking endlessly, giggling together, dreaming of their futures.

Weekends and most of the summer, out at the Spencers' ranch, were the only times Carly was really happy.

Francey knew Carly didn't like the town, but she still thought it was a great place for a girl to grow up. Much better than LA. And she was glad Zelda Marie had entered Carly's life.

Two events happened during Carly's first two years in Verity that forever colored her life.

Zelda Marie became pregnant and had to drop out of school to get married. Joe Bob Lovett's father, owner of the gas station, gave him a sound thrashing when Joe Bob admitted he must be the father.

The school expelled Zelda Marie—but not Joe Bob—and her parents threw a wedding and barbecue for the whole town.

It was the first time Francey had been invited to a party in the two years they'd lived in Verity.

"We only did it once," Zelda Marie wept on Carly's shoulder. "I didn't even like it."

Carly swore such a fate as being forced to marry a Joe Bob Lovett would never happen to her.

Francey Anderson was now thirty-six years old, still retained her Yankee accent, though she did say "you all" and turned just as many male heads as did her daughter.

Francey made most of Carly's clothes on her old Singer. She hadn't bought herself a new dress in almost three years, but her clothes, the ones she'd worn in Hollywood, were unique in Verity. She was still a looker, and her figure was even more voluptuous than Carly's.

She did buy enough fabric to make herself cute little ruffled aprons to wear at the diner. She also bought six pairs of dangling earrings, one with fruit hanging down, another a pair of long gold hoops, and ones that looked like silver waterfalls. She began wearing just one earring at a time, always in her left ear.

Francey might have left Hollywood, but the acting bug was still inside her. Three times a year she tried out for a part in the Verity Little Theater, and despite the fact that she had the experience all the others lacked she never got a part. She wondered if it was because Mrs. Padgett, choir director of the Baptist Church, was the director of Little Theater also. Despite the fact she wasn't a Baptist, she started going to church there Sundays and one Wednesday afternoon even walked into choir practice. Mrs. Padgett took one look at Francey with her dangling earring and her short skirts and open-toed sandals and wanted to tell her they really didn't need any more people in the choir. But once she heard that alto voice she couldn't.

Francey enjoyed her job. She earned three times as much in tips as in salary, and Blue Baker's business had never been so good. The men who came in for breakfast joked with her and, though she laughed with them, she never flirted, and not one ever had the nerve to ask her out. But more and more men came in for breakfast, and Blue's even began to fill up at the lunch hour, too.

The second happenstance to affect Carly's life was Boomer Bannerman.

She had had a soft spot for Boomer from the time she first noticed him. Boomer wasn't a student, meaning he didn't study more than he had to, but he was smart and he had a personality that charmed everyone.

He wasn't exactly handsome. When Carly first came to Verity High Boomer was a gangling awkward kid who grew seven inches in the next year, to six-two. His wavy brown hair matched his lively dark eyes. By his senior year he had filled out and weighed two hundred six stripped, with no flab. Working summers for a construction company hadn't hurt his physique. His brown eyes always seemed to dance, and he whistled while he drove the back hoe.

He never felt he was anything but part of a team on the football field, even though he scored most of the points. There wasn't a boy in school who didn't like Boomer, and not a girl who didn't have a crush on him.

Boomer's family had been around the county for close to eighty years and his father had been senator in the state legislature for longer than Boomer had been alive. When Boomer was eighteen, his father was fifty-nine. They'd lived alone together for fifteen years, ever since Boomer's mother died of polio when he was three.

Boomer's daddy spent a part of the year in Austin legislating and the other half in Verity, arranging wills and deeds of property and once even a divorce, managing to talk to everyone in the county personally at least once a year. Not a thing happened in his whole precinct that Earl Bannerman didn't know about.

But Boomer didn't become the captain of the Verity Panthers due to the senator's influence. He was greased lightning on a football field.

Boomer began to pay attention to Carly when they were thrown together four nights a week for rehearsals of the senior class play.

Though Boomer and his friends had discussed Carly Anderson's anatomy in detail, Boomer had never tried to date her. He stared at her in classes when he thought she wasn't looking, but all the boys did that. He listened when she answered questions—questions that no one else could answer—and felt an inner pride that always surprised him.

He liked the sound of her voice, sure of itself yet with a little-girl quality. He liked the sound of her laughter, and the way she waved her hands in the air when she was excited and how she bit her bottom lip when she was thinking.

Once in a while, she'd feel him staring at her and she'd turn to meet his eyes, giving him a dazzling smile. He never saw that same expression on her face when she smiled at anyone else. And Carly never felt the same flutter in her chest as she did when she felt him studying her.

"Boomer Bannerman," Carly whispered, leaning out her window on a moonlit night. "Star light, star bright, first star I've seen tonight, make Boomer Bannerman mine!"

It was March and trees were in full bud, their lacy leaves silhouetted against the streetlights. Boomer had started walking Carly home after rehearsals ended at nine, suggesting it wasn't safe for a girl to be walking the streets alone, though in truth, the only crime committed in Verity had been speeding—and that by teenagers or people passing through—or minor acts of vandalism, such as firecrackers lit in rural mail boxes in the middle of the night.

When he finally got around to kissing her, it was a nice lingering sweet kiss that melted Carly and left her yearning for more. She went to bed and watched the moonlight shine whitely into her bedroom and sat in bed in her sheer baby doll pajamas, her arms hugging her knees, and said aloud, ''Oh, Boomer.''

In the room across the hall, Francey was also aware of the moon. The radio was tuned so low she had to strain to hear it, and a song was playing from the days when she'd been Carly's age. She'd thrown off her nightgown and was dancing around the room with an invisible partner whose face she couldn't see, but she felt his hand on her back as they danced and she swore he pulled her so close she could feel her breasts straining against him, his legs against hers as they whirled around the room in the moonlight.

Chapter 2

Boomer was a natural athlete, swimming farther and faster than anyone in the whole county. He was fearless in football and tackled with no thought to being injured, yet before he graduated from high school he ended up in the hospital with a dislocated collarbone, a broken nose, and a broken leg and one arm. The collarbone was from trying to jump a horse over a fence that was four inches higher than the horse had ever tried before. The broken arm was from falling out of a peach tree trying to rescue Tiger, Homer Barron's orange-and-white cat. The leg was from riding Bob Donovan's motorcycle, and the nose was from a fistfight in the sixth grade.

His daddy taught him to drive when he was fifteen, and for his sixteenth birthday gave Boomer a Chevy Bel Air. He was the only boy who drove a new car to school.

Every girl died wanting to go for a drive in Boomer's car. Boomer and his friends, known as Boomer's Gang, made for most of Verity's excitement. The senator had given him the car with the understanding he wasn't to take a drink, "not even a sip of beer, mind you" before he graduated from high school, when he'd be eighteen years, one month, and three days old. "I hear you've had a drink and I'll take that car away from you and you'll never get another from me." Senator Bannerman waved a finger at Boomer, even though he knew he didn't have to. Boomer had promised and Boomer never, not ever, broke a promise.

Besides, he worshipped his daddy. Senator Bannerman had instilled his own strict ethical morality into his only son.

He told Boomer how nice it was to genuinely like the girl if you were going to go to bed with her. Earl Bannerman respected women and he wanted his son to, as well. He particularly respected his secretary up in Austin, who came down to Verity several times a year "to catch up on work." Boomer didn't pay much attention to her. She wasn't pretty, she wore glasses, and she was old. She must've been thirty-five when he first met her a decade ago.

Boomer's father taught him a man's word is his bond and that a promise could be made with a handshake. Boomer was prouder of his father than any other boy in Verity could be. His father had brought electricity to Verity before Boomer was born, back in the days when he'd first gone to the legislature when FDR and his public works program had worked wonders in rural America and for the unemployed.

Boomer rarely traded on his relationship to his father. Instead, he tried to live up to being the senator's son, proud to be a

Bannerman. But Boomer was bigger than life on his own, especially in a town like Verity.

Boys, though they envied Boomer, weren't jealous. They wanted to be with him, cruise around town on Saturday nights trying to pick up girls, snickering about tits and asses.

Carly Anderson didn't hang out in the town square on Saturday nights, so they couldn't comment on her as they passed in Boomer's flashy car, but they never talked about girls without Carly's name and anatomy entering their conversation.

The town's mothers had ambivalent feelings about Boomer. They wanted him to ask their daughters for a date because he was Senator Bannerman's son and because he was the captain of the football team and because he was the most popular boy in town. But they also trembled at the thought, for when he met them in church on Sundays or in the parking lot at the grocery store and offered to carry their groceries to their cars, the warm friendly way his eyes looked right into them and the curl of his dazzling smile and his powerful muscles as well as his grace told these mothers that their daughters would not be able to resist him.

Boomer's large brown eyes were widely spaced across the nose that had been broken when he was twelve. His mouth was generous, his lips full, usually curved in an easy smile. His soft voice was gravelly and his manner charmingly chivalrous.

Surprisingly, he hadn't dated many girls by the time he invited Carly to the senior prom. He'd had his first sexual experience when he was fourteen, with a girl from Mt. Barker who put out for any boy who'd take her to the movies and buy her a milk shake. Though he liked the sensation, Boomer had his doubts about a girl who'd do it for just anybody.

The summer between his junior and senior years, he spent in haystacks with the Yankee gal who came down from northern Michigan to visit her aunt, Mrs. Ferguson, who lived across the street from the Bannermans.

All of Verity was in a tizzy when Boomer and Carly began to be seen together, at the Hot Shoppe drinking cherry Cokes, at the drive-in every Saturday night, and in church together Sunday mornings.

Carly was as suspect to the iron ladies of Verity as her mother, whose short skirts and bulging blouses, they concluded had gotten her a job at the diner.

"You know what Boomer wants with that girl," they said.

And, though it wasn't his one goal, it *was* what Boomer wanted with Carly. It had gotten so she was all he thought of. He'd be studying, reading a page over and over, at his desk late at night and all he could see was Carly, her laughing eyes and her golden hair, the vein in her neck blue against the whiteness of her soft skin. He could smell her, so clean, like woods or meadows under summer sun. He remembered how it felt to put his arm around her at the drive-in, when she'd trustingly laid her head on his shoulder and rested her hand on his leg. He'd hoped she couldn't feel what was happening to him then.

In classes he'd look at her from across the room and watch her shapely leg swing back and forth, her toenails painted bright red to match her lipstick.

Senator Bannerman had taken one look at Carly, in church at Easter, and decided Carly was a phase Boomer had to go through. By the time Boomer graduated from college, he'd have all that out of his system and would choose a more appropriate girl, one who didn't look like she was going to spill out of her blouse any minute and who didn't laugh quite so loudly. In the meantime, he had to be tolerant of the situation. When he learned Boomer was taking the girl to the prom, he suggested that Boomer arrange for an orchid corsage.

But Boomer was smarter than that and asked Francey what color dress Carly would be wearing.

"Red," said Francey, and she told him that one white camellia on a red ribbon would be perfect. Boomer liked Francey, despite the accent showing she was north of the Mason Dixon line.

She took pictures of them when Boomer arrived to pick Carly up. Boomer thought he'd never seen anything quite like

Carly, with her curls piled on top of her head and a couple of wispy ends cascading over her right ear. Francey's golden hoops hung from her ears, but Carly wore no other adornment other than the giant white flower at her neck.

"Don't wait up, Mom," Carly said, and kissed her mother good night.

They danced together all night, every dance, the slow dreamy ones where they had eyes for no one else, when he held her tight and whispered in her ear, "You belong in my arms," to the fast-paced wild new dances where they shimmied and shook and laughed aloud with the joy of it all. Carly had never had such a wonderful night in her life.

When it was over and crêpe paper streamers were beginning to fall from the gym ceiling, Boomer said, "Come on over to my house."

Though the legislature was not in session, the senator was up in Austin respecting his secretary, though Boomer didn't even suspect that. He just knew no one was home.

Carly had never seen such a big house with so much dark furniture and so many ancestors' pictures on the walls. She'd never seen a kitchen with two ovens, and pots hanging from the ceiling by means of pulleys. She'd never seen a bathroom larger than her bedroom.

She'd never seen Boomer's bedroom, and it was here that he led her after kissing her in every room downstairs and on each step of the long stairway until Carly was so drunk with yearning she was dizzy. She decided she was in love.

When Boomer's hand finally fondled her breasts she was ready to tear her clothes off and cast caution to the winds, even though she was nervous, wondering just what she was supposed to do, and if she'd do it correctly.

What she did know was that she wanted to feel his kisses all over her body, have his hands touch her, lie next to him, and see what a man's body looked like.

She let her dress fall to the floor. All she wore underneath was a pair of white lacy bikinis.

"Christ," Boomer said in a worshipful tone, pulling her

close to him. He guessed she must be even more beautiful than Marilyn Monroe in her heyday.

He began to unbutton his shirt, throwing it on a chair, unzipping his trousers and letting them drop. He picked Carly up and carried her to his bed.

She moved under him, responding to his touches, moaning when he gently bit her breasts, his tongue flicking over them.

"Don't stop," she whispered, forgetting her fear until she felt his hardness between her legs.

"You've got the most beautiful body in the whole god-damned world," he whispered.

Carly laughed as gooseflesh trickled across her neck and inched its way down her arms.

Boomer, for all his lack of expertise, played her like a virtuoso tuning up his Stradivarius, his fingering coaxing her to a shattering crescendo.

He only hurt her for a minute but she was so caught up, moving in a frenzy, that the instant's pain didn't even slow her down.

"Oh, my God, Boomer," Carly cried as unexpected warm waves washed over her.

"Jesus H. Christ," he whispered into her neck.

CHAPTER 3

When graduation came, the end of May, Carly was valedictorian. The ruling matrons of Verity were surprised, but then brains weren't given too much credence in Verity, particularly a girl's brains. Intellects were looked upon with suspicion; nevertheless, it was a surprise to them that those curves had a functioning head on top of them. But since intellect wasn't a criteria for fitting into Verity's society—maybe not half a dozen people there read half a dozen books a year—Carly's accomplishment was allowed to pass unnoticed, except that she won the First National Bank award of one hundred dollars for being outstanding student.

Boomer had won a scholarship to the University of Texas up in Austin, but he'd be home all summer, working at his back hoe job where he earned more in a summer than Francey earned in a year, including tips.

Carly had taken typing in high school. All the other courses she'd excelled in would have gained her entrance to a college if she could have afforded it, but they wouldn't help her get a job in Verity.

However, she got one before she even tried. The day after graduation, the president of the bank phoned and suggested she come see him. She'd never even been in the bank, the only one in town. Since Blue always paid her in cash, Francey had no need of a bank.

There were two teller windows, a tall counter with pens and extra checks and deposit slips and the door to his office, marked WALTER B. DAVIS, PRESIDENT. Francey had said, "He's probably making a nice gesture since they gave you that award. Maybe he's going to show you how to open a bank account."

When Carly walked into his office, the big man stood up and reached a hand across his black walnut desk. She shook it, thinking it was like a friendly paw, and he waved her to a leather chair. He smiled at her reassuringly, the sun glinting off his gold wire-framed glasses.

"I was impressed with your speech yesterday," he said, cutting the end off a cigar and searching under a pile of papers for a match. "Did you write it yourself?"

"Yes, sir. Thank you, sir."

He was a stocky man, his blond hair thinning, a slight paunch threatening middle aged spread if he didn't start exercising. For a man who decided on who got loans and if a mortgage was to be foreclosed, Walt Davis kept a low profile, despite being past president of the Rotary Club.

"You going on to college?" When Carly shook her head,

he puffed on his cigar, filling the room with an odor that made Carly feel slightly ill. "Damn shame. What are your plans?"

"I'm going to look for a job." She had no way of knowing her smile and her directness dazzled him.

"Before you got the First National Bank prize I found out about your scholastic average. Damn shame to waste such fine intelligence." He puffed. "You want to work here? One of my tellers is leaving to get married."

Carly blinked.

"Hours are eight to five with an hour off for lunch, two weeks vacation a year, and sixty-five dollars a week," he continued. Then he smiled in what she thought was a very fatherly way. "You're Francey Anderson's girl, aren't you? The waitress at the diner?"

Carly nodded. She wanted to hug him but knew enough to remain in the deep leather chair, her legs straight against each other, her hands in her lap.

"Well?" he asked. "You want the job?"

"Oh, yes, sir. Yes, I surely do."

He laughed, a pleasant sound, and his eyes danced. "Guess you need a vacation after twelve years of school, so I won't have you come learn the ropes tomorrow. How about two weeks from today?" He rose and offered Carly a handshake.

Carly reached across the desk, taking his extended hand in both of hers. "Oh, yes, sir. Thank you."

"My name," he said, smiling as she kept his hand, "is Mr. Davis, not sir."

"Oh, yes, sir. I'll remember that."

Boomer laughed as his fingers undid her bra. "You in the bank?" Actually, from the time he'd pick her up from work until after they made love he seldom heard a word she said, so concentrated was he on exploring her lovely body, of trying a new position, of seeing how Carly would react to oral sex. For that matter, seeing if *he* liked it.

* * *

Millicent Pilgrim had been at the bank for thirty-six years. Her gray hair was wispy and never cut quite evenly. She stared out at the world from behind thick glasses that enlarged her hazel eyes. Carly thought she looked like an owl. She was unfailingly polite to every First National customer, inquiring as to the health of a sick infant, the state of a cousin's pregnancy or a sister-in-law's goiter. She knew everyone who had a bank account. However, all she heard was information, not gossip, for her information came only from across her marble teller's counter and not from idle everyday conversation. Once work was over, Miss Pilgrim went home. Once a week, Thursdays, she stopped at the grocery store, but outside of work no one ever saw Miss Pilgrim. On Sundays she didn't even cross the street for the Baptist Church service.

Miss Pilgrim had never even heard of the Anderson women, except that Carly had won the prestigious First National Bank award. Miss Pilgrim received her news from Walter Cronkite or David Brinkley and knew more about what was happening in the Middle East or Bangladesh or New York City, for that matter, than what occurred in Verity.

In thirty-six years at the bank she had never made a mistake, not even by one cent. It was only in the last twelve years that a second teller was needed, and seven tellers had come and gone. Miss Pilgrim patiently taught each one of them all she knew, was infinitely kind when she had to repeat something two or three times, and never frowned when they made mistakes.

After Carly had been at the bank six weeks, Mr. Davis came to his door and asked her to come into his office. She thought maybe he was going to bawl her out for waving to Boomer earlier calling out to him from inside the bank. But Mr. Davis closed the door behind her and said, "I see you took two years of Spanish in high school."

Surprised, Carly smiled and said, "Sí."

He laughed in that nice fatherly way of his.

"But I can't really speak it," she went on. "I'm pretty good at conjugating verbs but that's it. And I can't understand a word when a Mexican speaks fast.''

Mr. Davis nodded. ''Tell you what I'd like. I'll send away to Berlitz and buy some tapes. After the bank closes at three, Miss Pilgrim can work on the accounts, yours included, and you study Spanish for an hour every day. There are so many Mexicans around here, and Miss Pilgrim gets the willies about them. Someone who can speak their language will improve our image and our business, as well as be a big help to them.''

Carly gave him a huge smile. She could hardly believe he was already giving her responsibility.

''Your father's dead, isn't he?'' Mr. Davis said suddenly.

Bewildered at the turn of the conversation, Carly nodded.

''Must be a hard life for your mother.''

Was it? Carly thought her mother was brave and resourceful, and she never acted like her life was hard. ''She hums around the house,'' Carly said, and then she realized what a silly thing that was to say.

''She does, huh?'' Mr. Davis snipped off the end of a cigar and all Carly could think of was getting out of his office before he lit it.

She stood up and said, ''I like studying, Mr. Davis. I wouldn't mind learning Spanish at all.''

As she walked across the office to the door, Walt Davis watched her hips and thought she looked a lot like her mother, whom he didn't remember seeing before the graduation ceremonies.

The next evening, as she tossed oil on the salad, Francey said to Carly, ''Your boss came in for breakfast this morning. He's real nice. Told me you're doing a good job and maybe the smartest thing he's done this year was hire you.''

Carly felt herself blushing.

Walt Davis stood in the doorway of his office and it was all he could do not to laugh out loud. The bank looked like a junior high party. The women were lined up waiting for Miss

Pilgrim and every man was waiting in line for Carly. Even when Carly had no one in her line, when a woman—except the teachers at the high school—came in, she'd wait for Miss Pilgrim before getting helped immediately by Carly.

By the end of September he noticed that the Mexicans who came to the bank waited in Carly's line, too.

But Carly's heart was breaking. Boomer had left the last week in August for football training in Austin, even though there wasn't a chance of his playing varsity his freshman year. He'd vowed he'd be home to see her before Thanksgiving, and told her, teasingly, she'd better not take up with anyone while he was gone. As though she'd even think of it. No one could compare to Boomer, ever. Even though he warned her he wasn't much of a letter writer, she wrote to him every week.

She missed looking up at lunch time to see him standing by the bank's front door, grinning at her. She missed his kisses and the way he looked at her that melted her heart. She missed making love and the things his hands and his tongue did to her body. She missed the feel of him, the smell, the taste. She was lonelier than she thought anyone could be.

"Mom," Carly said one night after they'd watched *Bonanza*. "It's about time you teach me to drive."

Francey nodded, sipping the one beer she allowed herself every night. "Okay," she agreed. She looked at her watch. "It's still light after dinner. You go get yourself a permit on your lunch hour tomorrow and we'll begin right away."

Their car was a nine-year-old Ford, and Francey washed and vacuumed it every Saturday afternoon, because she knew she'd never be able to afford another car.

Carly had her license in six weeks—six weeks in which she wrote to Boomer every week and conversed in a very limited but enthusiastic way with the Mexicans who came in to cash paychecks. One of them even opened an account. Most of them, of course, were paid in cash, under the table, at wages no Americans would work for. The Mexican women cleaned houses, washed dishes, cooked meals, shopped, changed diapers, generally taking care of all those who could afford help in Verity. At those wages, most of Verity could afford such luxury.

The Mexican men mowed lawns and pitched hay and dug weeds and repaired tires. A few of them rode herd or worked in the feed and grain store, hauling sacks. Few had business to conduct in the bank. But word was getting around about the new girl who spoke a little Spanish and whose smile made a man feel like shouting "Olé!"

In those six weeks, Carly received only a postcard of the state capitol from Boomer, telling her he missed her but he was having a great time and "see you Thanksgiving." No mention of coming home for a weekend before then.

Carly cried herself to sleep. She just knew he was going to frat parties with beautiful girls who were cheerleaders and who wore trim skirts and elegant pearls and smiled coolly and didn't let Boomer do more than kiss their closed lips. They probably rode horses eastern style and went to dances in long white dresses and joined sororities.

Well, she'd show him at Thanksgiving. She wasn't going to let him make love to her after all that time with only a postcard to show for it.

She kept her resolution for precisely one hour and forty-three minutes after Boomer got home the night before Thanksgiving.

The first week of December, when Boomer was back in Austin, Francey Anderson was surprised again to see Walt Davis enter the diner at seven-thirty in the morning and stand, hat in hand, surveying the tables, most of which were already full. Aside from being in the Rotary Club, Mr. Davis had served on the school board—had been president for two of those years—and had been on the board of trustees of the Baptist Church before he quit going to church. He was a Democratic precinct chairman. He was forty-two years old, and his house and Bannerman's were the largest ones in town. The biggest room was his library, the most extensive one in the whole county. He read a lot. Though he now lived a rather solitary life, until he saw Francey Anderson at the high school graduation last June he hadn't realized he was lonely.

Walt had not eaten more than orange juice, toast, and coffee for breakfast since his late wife Peg had had to stop getting his meals when her multiple sclerosis got too bad, a dozen years ago. No one was more surprised than he when one brisk morning the first week of December, when the sky was the color of cornflowers, he didn't put his coffee on to perk before he shaved but walked over to the diner after he'd showered and dressed. He had spent an inordinate amount of time choosing his tie and had come to the conclusion he needed some new, brighter ones.

Walt Davis had not been to bed with a woman for close to twelve years and he'd never had another woman besides Peg. But Francey Anderson had started longings in him that he didn't recognize. All he knew was he felt restless.

As soon as Francey saw him standing in the doorway, she walked over and smiled at him. "Well, Mr. Davis, how nice to see you again. How about this table over by the window?" She didn't wait for an answer, but led the way, and he followed, wondering why he felt so light headed. And light hearted.

He sat, placing his Stetson on the chair next to him.

Francey felt a fluttering in the middle of her chest. "My daughter talks about you all the time. You sure have made a difference in her life."

"You have a girl about whom you can be mighty proud."

"I am." Francey was amazed by the man's warmth. "What can I get you? Coffee to begin with?"

He nodded. "And orange juice. Can't start the day without that."

"We've got blueberry pancakes that can't be beat," she offered, when she returned with his coffee. "You take it with cream, no sugar?"

He nodded.

"I remember from the other time you were here. That's how I take it, too."

It was all he could do not to reach out and touch her hand as she stood there, pencil poised over her pad.

He watched her as she greeted other customers, obviously regulars the way she joked with them, though there was a ladylike quality about her, he thought. She laughed with her customers and called them by their first names, and he noticed they all treated her with respect even though the looks they gave her behind her back were far from strictly business.

It seemed like two and a half years before she returned with the steaming pancakes, even though it wasn't ten minutes. He yearned to grab her by the arm and ask her to sit and talk with him. Talk about *anything* just to hear that husky soft voice of hers. To hear that laugh which reminded him of a rippling brook. Though the breakfast was only three dollars and twenty cents, he left a five-dollar tip, and then, all the way to the bank, wondered if that would insult her. He didn't mean for her to think he was being patronizing.

When his lunch hour approached he wanted nothing more than return to Blue's and dine there, but for all the years he'd been a widower, and for nine years before that, the woman who cleaned his house prepared his lunch, too, and often when he came home in the evening he'd find a ham in the refrigerator or a chicken and knew that Doria was trying to make sure he ate. He couldn't insult her now.

That night, Francey told Carly, "Mr. Davis came in for breakfast again today."

"He's probably lonely," Carly said. "He lives all alone."

"He left a big tip. He likes you a lot."

"I'm going to drive out to see Zelda Marie and the baby tomorrow afternoon," Carly said. "That is, if you don't need the car. Zelda Marie is awful lonely these days."

"Seems so many people are lonely," Francey commented.

Carly looked up at her mother, standing by the oven, waiting for the soufflé to rise.

"Are you, Mom?"

"What, lonely?" Francey paused. "I've carried loneliness around with me so long it's become a part of me. I don't even think about it anymore."

Next afternoon, when the sky was pewter and all the bare branches made the oak trees look like dancing skeletons, and a drizzle gummed up the dirt road leading to Zelda Marie's, Carly drove the four and a half miles out to visit her friend.

She tried to be enthusiastic about the red, blotched baby, Sally Mae, but it was a strain. Zelda Marie, who'd hated the baby during all her pregnancy, was now obsessed with it. She could talk or think of little else.

But Carly could tell by the haunted look in her eyes that even having a baby all your own didn't cure loneliness.

CHAPTER 4

To Zelda Marie, the high point of the week was Carly's visit. She felt downright depressed when Boomer was home for Christmas and Carly spent all her time with him. Except for Christmas Eve afternoon, when Carly and Boomer drove out to deliver presents, Zelda Marie had been alone, if you didn't count wandering up to the main house each morning and talking over coffee with her mother. Her daddy was so disappointed with her that she timed her visits for when he wasn't home. They'd both hoped a grandchild might soften him but, Sally Mae being a girl, he hadn't been moved at all.

"Momma, I'm not the first girl to do this." Zelda Marie opened her shirt, one of Joe Bob's, and began to nurse her baby.

"Somehow he thinks you did it to spite him."

They looked at each other and sighed.

"Do you think I'm thrilled Joe Bob hardly even talks to me. He doesn't get home till long after I've gone to bed. I love my baby, but I sure hate being married. I'm so lonely. I got no one to talk with, just have to wash dirty clothes each day. Once a week, Saturday mornings, I get the car to go do the grocery shopping. Otherwise I feel like a prisoner."

"Your daddy tells me not to coddle you, honey, or I would."

"I know, Momma. I know. How come men got the right to tell us what to do? I wish I hadn't listened to Daddy and had refused to get married."

Not for the first time, Zelda Marie told her mother what it was like for her at Joe Bob's parents' house when they went for Sunday dinners. "It's always the same. Fried chicken. Always. And they fuss over the baby, and Joe Bob and his daddy talk cars and drink beer and look at ball games on TV and it's just like I'm not there. I help wash the dishes and all and Mrs. Lovett is pretty nice to me, but Momma, I just hate my life so much."

Mrs. Spencer walked over and put her arms around her daughter, tears in her eyes.

That night Joe Bob came home at ten-thirty, three sheets to the wind. Zelda Marie was already in bed, though she wasn't asleep. The moonlight was spread over the land, making everything look ghostly white and awakening yearnings in Zelda Marie she couldn't explain.

She heard Joe Bob come in, crashing a lamp onto the floor. She lay there, listening to his drunken curses. The baby began to wail.

Zelda Marie jumped up and ran down the hall to Sally Mae's room. There, she sat, holding the baby, humming to calm her down, as Joe Bob shouted obscenities to the rooftops, yelling that Zelda Marie had trapped him and the goddamned baby'd made it worse for him and he was leaving this goddamn house, never to return.

"Oh, I wish," Zelda Marie whispered to her daughter.

Then there was silence as she tucked the baby back in her

crib and crept down the hall. Joe Bob stumbled out of the bathroom and followed her.

She crawled back into bed and ignored him. When he slipped in next to her, his hand went out and touched her breast. She lay there rigid. He had not done that since they were married. She could smell the alcohol on his breath and her flesh crawled. Yet the way his fingers rubbed her nipple back and forth warmed her whole being.

No one had paid any attention to her in well over a year, and she could have died from being ignored. So, when his tongue thrust through her lips, she opened her mouth to him and pretty soon she felt trembly all over, just with being touched.

"You gotta be good for something," he whispered as he moved on top of her. "You just gotta be good for something."

She wanted to show him she was, so she began moving under him, arching her back and grinding against him until he whispered, "Well, I'll be damned," his whiskey breath surrounding her.

It was the second time her husband had ever made love to her. The second time any man had entered her and she'd been married exactly one year, with a baby nearly five months old.

She liked what he'd done to her, though it was all over before her body could even warm up. Maybe she was proving to him that she *was* good for something.

While he was still on top of her, she heard him snoring.

He didn't start coming home any earlier nights, and he wasn't around so she didn't have to cook dinner for him, but he started touching her every night, and in the morning he even grinned at her before he left for work, after she'd cooked his breakfast of sausage, grits, and eggs with five pieces of toast and a cup of coffee.

On one of Carly's Saturday visits, Zelda Marie's eye was swollen. That whole left side of her face was black and blue and a sickly looking sort of chartreuse. Zelda Marie didn't explain, so Carly didn't ask, but she told her mother.

"Oh, God," Francey said. "He's mad at Zelda Marie for having the baby and imprisoning him. Men take their frustrations out on women by using violence."

Carly shook her head. "Oh, Mom, not all men do that. Beat their wives."

"Maybe not," Francey agreed, her eyes gazing off in the distance.

Francey was having a new experience. With wonder in her voice, she announced, "Mr. Davis has invited me to dinner Saturday night."

He took her to La Brasserie, one of Corpus Christi's nicest restaurants, on New Year's Eve. They had champagne cocktails and an expensive chardonnay with their dinner. He ordered stuffed guinea hen that was served in a bed of lettuce with wild rice and peas that were as sweet as sugar and a Caesar salad, which the waiter tossed at their table. And sinfully delicious black forest cake for dessert.

Walt said, "I don't want this evening to end," and ordered Irish coffee. Cointreau came later.

Francey was surprised. He didn't talk much about himself, the way men usually do. Of course everyone in Verity knew of his accomplishments. His life was an open book. He'd been born in the town where his granddaddy founded the bank. He'd been sent north to school, to Phillips Exeter and then to Dartmouth, which pretty much explained why he had no accent, neither southern nor New England.

His mother had been afraid Verity couldn't hold him after that, but he came home at twenty-one and had had no desire to leave since.

He'd married a girl from up North, though, whom he met on a winter weekend when she'd come over from Mt. Holyoke as his roommate's date. Mr. Davis fell in love with Peggy that weekend and had never loved another woman, despite the fact that she had developed multiple sclerosis when she was twenty-six and been in a wheelchair for the last eight years of her life.

Dining with Francey Anderson, Walt found himself laughing more than he'd laughed in a long time. Francey was more animated than any woman he'd ever known. Perhaps it was all the champagne and wine but more likely it was this beautiful woman sitting across from him, her dark eyes sparkling, her red mouth curved in a smile, her ebony hair floating around her head, rhinestone earrings glistening in her ears.

They had to be rhinestone, he thought, but someday he'd put diamonds there. He was astonished at his own thoughts.

"I haven't had this good a time since I can't remember when. I was afraid I wouldn't know what to say." Walt sipped his cointreau.

Francey's hand lay halfway across the table. He reached out and, as his eyes met hers, covered her hand with his. The way she looked at him made him warm all over. He was sorry now he hadn't taken her to a place that had a dance band. He wanted to take her in his arms and move to the slow rhythms of a stringed orchestra. He wanted to inhale the perfume she wore.

What he really wanted to do, he suddenly realized, was kiss those bright red lips.

But when he bid her good night he stood a foot away from her and simply said, "I did, too," when Francey told him she'd had a wonderful time.

And she had. It was the first time she could remember that she'd been treated as though she mattered. Walt made her feel witty and clever. He laughed at her jokes and asked her about growing up in New Jersey. She lied to him and painted a pretty picture, and told him she hated the humidity of Texas most of the year.

He asked why she stayed.

"I didn't want to uproot Carly her last year in school." And then she giggled. "She would never have won the First National Bank prize then."

"So why do you stay now?"

Francey had shrugged her shoulders. "Inertia, I guess."

Walt didn't know many people in Verity who would know

what the word inertia meant, even though many of them practiced it.

"Besides, I like my job. The people who come to breakfast at Blue's are the nicest people in town. I've got my regulars. It's the only place I've ever felt I belonged."

She liked the way he had put his hand over hers and looked straight into her eyes.

When she got into bed, she lay staring into the dark with a big smile on her face.

What a nice man Mr. Davis—Walt—had turned out to be.

CHAPTER 5

One Saturday after they had been dating for two months, Walt picked Francey up at seven in the morning. She gave him a wicker picnic basket packed with fried chicken, potato salad, and a Lane cake, something she hadn't baked in years. She included a thermos of lemonade, but Walt brought two bottles of wine in a trim insulated bag that kept them chilled. They headed for Padre Island, where they spent the day, she in shorts and he with his pants legs rolled up, walking, with an easy familiarity, along the beach, their feet in the warm water. They held hands all day.

Francey jumped over the waves and splashed Walt, fogging up his glasses. They laughed and splashed some more, then spread out a blanket on the powdery white sand and opened the picnic basket. After lunch, Francey, sitting cross-legged with mayonnaise still in a corner of her mouth, leaned over and kissed him.

"I was getting to be afraid you might never try," she explained.

He reached out and pulled her to him, looking into her eyes before bringing his mouth to hers, and she tasted both a sweetness and an urgency. "I've been trying to work up the courage," he said.

"I couldn't imagine," he said, filled with happiness, "that someone like you would want . . ."

Francey smiled. "That someone like me—a waitress in a two-bit diner—could want the most interesting person in town? Why, I bet half the single women, if not all, have been after you for years."

Walt shook his head. "If so, I haven't noticed. And there's not a woman in Verity who can hold a candle to you."

"You're Irish," she laughed, throwing her head back.

Walt ran a finger across her throat. "Not an ounce of me."

"Well, somewhere you've kissed the Blarney Stone."

All the way back from the island Francey sat quietly in the curve of Walt's arm, not talking, filled with contentment. In all her life she'd never known such a gentle man. "Not only that," she said aloud, "but you laugh a lot."

"Not only what?" he asked, his arm tightening around her.

When he left her at her door that evening, she said, "Don't you think it's time you come around for a home-cooked meal?"

Wednesday night when Carly left work, Walt Davis walked home with her. Francey had prepared ham Hawaiian-style with pineapple and a rice curry and glazed carrots and peach pie from peaches she'd canned last summer.

Carly still had trouble imagining her mother and Mr. Davis together. She was sure it was just companionship. Certainly at their age there couldn't be any physical attraction.

After Carly went to her room to read and to think of Boomer, Walt and Francey sat on the couch and for the first time in more years than he could remember, the president of the First

National Bank reached out and fondled a woman's breast. To his delight, she wasn't wearing a bra.

He heard a low moan and realized it was his. Francey breathed, "Oh, that feels so good."

When he went home that night he had an erotic dream about Francey. It was to be his last: The next time they were together it became a reality. The lovemaking surpassed any dream he might ever have had.

It didn't take long for him to reach a decision. Saturday morning, Walt drove into Corpus Christi and spent over an hour choosing a diamond ring that he hoped Francey would like.

That evening he dined with her at La Maison and told her he'd wait until she was through work. Then he walked her down the long street, led her to a bench, and sat beside her.

Gathering her in his arms, he asked her to marry him.

She looked at him for a long time, and then said, her voice low and flat, "I better tell you some things."

"Okay." Walt sat, his hands between his knees, gazing at her. He smiled, though there was a trace of fear in his eyes. "But don't tell me anything you don't want to. I don't have to hear a confessional of your life to want to marry you."

She sat down and took a deep breath. In a minute he could tell she wasn't seeing him. "I grew up in a little town in western Jersey with a mouse for a mother and a father who beat me at the tiniest excuse. I once got a C on my report card, in seventh-grade Science, and he took his strap and raised welts on me. He'd make me lie over a chair and then beat me until I'd scream. I'd swear I wasn't going to give him the satisfaction, and I'd grit my teeth and even bit my tongue once trying to hold the screams in, but he wouldn't let up until I cried.

"I didn't make my bed one morning because I was late for school, and he beat me until I bled. I refused to eat brussels sprouts, and I sat there all night and wouldn't eat them cold in the morning, so he got out his strap. I still wouldn't eat them. That time he made me lean over his work bench, and started to whip me. He stopped only when blood streaked through my panties.

"When I was in my teens," Francey told Walt, "and my mother said I could date, if I came home one minute after ten, even on Saturday nights, he got out his strap.

"He told me the Lord called on me to be punished when I disobeyed."

She was silent a minute, staring into space. "I hated him. And I began to hate my mother nearly as much, because never once did she tell him not to do it. Never did she say 'Stop,' never did she try to comfort me. The day I graduated from high school, with twenty-seven dollars that it had taken me four years to save, I packed a bag I found in the attic and, in the middle of the night, crept down the stairs and took off for California with Fred Anderson, my boyfriend. I've never even written to my parents in all these years, not once."

Walt's face reflected the intensity of the pain he was experiencing.

"Fred and I jumped off the bus in Las Vegas and got married and then caught the next one to Los Angeles. I was pregnant by the time we arrived. We took a two-room apartment and Fred found a job.

"He wouldn't let me go shopping alone, even for groceries. He had to be with me every minute. He told me every man who saw me would want me and he didn't want me in danger. Whenever I smiled at a man, a stranger, a clerk in the grocery story, he'd punch me when we got home. It was Daddy all over again.

"We had no social life. I never went anyplace. Didn't have anyone at all to talk to. He got to coming home later and later. I never knew when, but sometimes it was so late I'd tossed the dinner out, it was so cold. But he'd drag me out of bed, screaming at me, and I'd have to get his dinner all over again.

"I stopped getting meals until he arrived home, but then if he had to wait over twenty minutes he'd bend my arm back until I screamed. He broke it the week before Carly was born. I was in labor with my left arm in a cast.

"He hated the baby's crying, he was jealous of the attention I paid her. He treated me like a nothing, a nobody. He'd been 4F because of flat feet but in early 1945, right after Carly was born and a few months before the war ended, he was drafted. I never heard from him again.

"I didn't even try to find him, because for the first time in my whole life I began to breathe without someone telling me how to do it. Suddenly I could do what I wanted if I had a job and some money.

"The only pretty life I'd ever seen was in the movies, and everyone told me that's where I should be. Folks told me I could make it easy, with my looks, but it would have to be by way of the casting couch. Well, that way I got lots of small roles, some of them even had a line or two, because of a half-hour horizontal in an office. I had just enough money to keep Carly in diapers and applesauce."

Walt's face was white. "You must have hated it."

Francey shrugged. "I sort of pretended it didn't happen. I'd concentrate on something else, like the palm trees outside the window, or imagining it was Gary Cooper kissing me, and it would all be over before it had scarcely begun and I'd have a little role and enough to eat for the next few months.

"I did get one real break. The director of a movie that was going to star Hedy Lamarr and Clark Gable and Spencer Tracy really liked me, and offered me the juiciest role of my career, if career you can call it. Only trouble was I'd just found out I was pregnant again and had to turn the role down. I didn't even know who the father was."

Walt closed his eyes. Francey knew he couldn't take it. She wasn't who or what he'd thought she was.

"I got a job slinging hash in a two-bit restaurant and planned to work until right before the baby was due, then give it up for adoption. But I had a miscarriage, right at work. I worked nights because the girl in the apartment across the hall agreed to sleep in my place to watch Carly. I'd get home about four and fall asleep until Carly woke up and then I was with her all day. I also had calls once in a while for bit parts, but I never went back to the casting couch. In fact, I haven't been to bed with a man since then. Not till you. I worked in one restaurant or another all these years, hoping each day for a studio call, and I got just enough to keep me going, to give me hope. I got parts in maybe fifty movies over the years, but never enough to live on. And finally I got tired of the rat race, got tired of hoping, decided I wanted to get away from Hollywood and find a nice little town where Carly could fit in. But Verity's never accepted Carly. Never. Nor me. I can take it, but it's broken my heart for Carly. I should have left that first summer, after she hated school so much, but I kept hoping, thinking if we stayed people would get used to us, see what nice people we were. But when I go to tryouts for their plays at the Little Theater, I know I'm better than any of them, even my southern accent's more believable on the stage, but they wouldn't give me a part if their lives depended on it.

"And, if it weren't for Boomer and Zelda Marie, my poor little girl would have curled up like a carrot peel. I want you to know, Walt, I can never love anyone more than I love Carly. She's the center of my life. She's made everything worthwhile."

Walt stood and pulled her up with him, his arms encircling her. "More than ever, I want to marry you. I want to take care of you and erase the unhappiness of the past. I want to show you what love can be like and I want to shower you with everything you want. I want you in my life. In my every day. Forever. I will be proud to have you for my wife. I love you. You have already become the center of my days, of my thoughts, and now I want you to be the center of my life."

"I'd like you in my life, too, but I won't marry you." Francey's tone was adamant. "I'd like to go on seeing you and taking trips and," her eyes teased him, "going to bed with you. Despite having sworn I'd never do it again. I didn't know it could be so good."

"Don't say no firmly," Walt said. "I'm a patient man."

* * *

Weekends Walt and Francey took to driving up to Houston, or over to Fredricksburg. One weekend, they even drove down into Mexico, as far as Monterrey. When Walt invited couples to dinner in Verity, people were surprised. Walt was more relaxed than they remembered, laughed more, and that Francey certainly was amusing. She made his guests feel important.

That same spring, Senator Bannerman had been feeling poorly. When his doctor in Austin diagnosed cancer, the senator asked, "How long?"

The doctor shrugged. "Six to twelve months. And prepare yourself. It's going to be painful."

The senator straightened out his fiscal affairs and came home to Verity where, in his upstairs office, he put a pistol in his mouth, pulled the trigger and spattered his head all over those unread books that lined the wall.

Boomer arrived back in Verity that night, in the last semester of his senior year of college, a dazed young man just turned twenty-two.

Carly ran over to the house. One glance at Boomer turned her heart over. He sat on the leather sofa in the room where his father's blood still stained the carpet, his eyes red-rimmed, his head in his hands.

Carly put her arms around him and, with his face muffled against her breasts, he cried. Wept as though he would never stop.

Carly held his hand during the funeral and put an arm through his as the senator's casket was lowered into the ground. She threw a white rose into the gray hole.

After the ceremony, she started to go home with Boomer, but, his eyes filled with pain, he said, "I need to be alone, babe. I'll call you later."

Five days after the funeral, Boomer was waiting for Carly in the doorway of the First National at five o'clock. Her heart began to quicken and her pulse race, just like it always had when she'd seen him waiting there for her.

He jerked his head. "You free for dinner?"

For four years Carly had been free whenever Boomer wanted. He took her arm and led her to his car.

"I don't want to be around people," he said. "Let's get a pizza and some beer and go to my house."

He said hardly anything on the way home or while they ate. After finishing the last slice of pizza, he wiped his fingers on a napkin, sipped the last Bud from the can, and finally looked at her.

"I'm not coming back after graduation next month."

Just as plain as that.

"Oh, Boomer," Carly's heart sank. She reached out to put her hand in his. She couldn't bear the pain in his eyes. "Can I do something?"

He shook his head. "This place is going on the market tomorrow. Dad left a lot of debts."

Carly couldn't believe she'd heard him right. "For sale, you mean?"

Boomer nodded.

"It's your home. Where will you live?" A tear fell down her cheek.

He looked up and met her eyes at last. "Don't wait for me, Carly. I'm not coming back."

CHAPTER 6

In the year after Boomer said good bye to Carly, while the pain still lingered, Carly thought she was going crazy. She talked about it with Zelda Marie, who by now had another baby. Carly didn't ask her how come she got pregnant a second time if Joe Bob never really touched her.

Things were looking better for Zelda Marie. Her days were full, and she didn't talk much about Joe Bob. Her house was tidier, she picked flowers to put on the dinner table, and she didn't sit around watching TV all afternoon. When one of her father's Herefords died giving birth, Zelda Marie took the calf to raise.

"Seems all I do is nurse the world," she said, tucking Michael J. to her breast while she held a bottle in her free hand for an orphaned lamb.

Zelda Marie, who'd made sure she never asked her daddy for anything since she'd gotten married, did talk him into building her a little barn.

Joe Bob wasn't interested in any of it. He thought living in the country was for the birds; it wasn't where the excitement was. He spent most of his nights at the pool hall in town or drinking and dancing out at Barney's.

Occasionally he did bounce his son on his knee, though he didn't pay much attention to Sally Mae. Sunday nights he slicked up and he and Zelda Marie and the kids went over to the Spencers' for dinner.

For Christmas that year, her father gave Zelda Marie a bright red Ford pickup. You'd have thought it was a million dollars, so thrilled was she to have her own vehicle, and a pickup at that.

Zelda Marie was so tired of chicken fricassee at the Lovetts' she thought she'd scream. So, when the hot weather came at the end of April, she invited her parents and her in-laws, including Joe Bob's sister and her family, to a barbecue picnic under the spreading oak trees after church on Sunday. The kids ran around, the cousins chasing each other and playing with the lambs, and she had Joe Bob set up the croquet set the Spencers had never even used, and went out to Western Auto and bought a badminton set, which Joe Bob strung up.

The Spencers and the Lovetts went out of their way to be pleasant to each other, since they shared grandchildren in common, and Mr. Lovett admired the red truck and beat Mr. Spencer at badminton. Until the bad weather began again in November, the picnic became a Sunday tradition, and Zelda Marie loved it that both families were getting along and they were coming to her house, and that Joe Bob seemed to be taking pride and pleasure in Sundays, too.

He took so much pride in what she was doing that she became pregnant with child number three by September of that year.

Of course Joe Bob wasn't making any more money being a mechanic in his father's garage than he had when they got married, but Zelda Marie had plans of her own.

"Daddy," she said, walking with him to the barn through the crunchy grass on Christmas afternoon. "I thank you so for the pickup. It'll make a big difference to me."

"Thought you could haul hay," he muttered.

"You know what I'd like to do? I want you to go on giving me all the orphan calves you get."

He grinned. He'd softened considerably toward his older daughter in the last five years. "Seems to me like you got your hands full now. What with two babies, and another on the way." As long as he could remember, Zelda Marie had never asked him for anything. He didn't think much of his son-in-law, but his respect for his daughter grew all the time.

"I want those calves. And if you ever have a colt who's orphaned, I want it, too. I'm goin' to raise horses."

Her father put his hand over his mouth to hide his smile. "Where you got time to take care of them?"

"Let me try, Daddy, that's all I ask. I been thinking on it for a long time. I don't aim to live on a mechanic's salary forever."

No matter how busy she was, Zelda Marie always had time for Carly's weekly visits. Until late in her pregnancy, they went out riding, and talked the whole afternoon away. Once in a while Carly would stay for supper, but Joe Bob was so sullen she always felt uncomfortable. One night when he walked her out to her car, he managed to brush against her breasts. The look he gave her made her feel even sorrier for Zelda Marie.

Zelda Marie was feeling equally sorry for Carly, who had told her that afternoon of her need to get away from Verity. "I feel trapped," she told her friend. "I'm almost twenty-two years old and nothing's happening in my life."

"So, why don't you go?"

"I can't bear to hurt Walt. He depends on me. He's given me so many opportunities at the bank, and I do appreciate them, but the bank's not enough to make my life worthwhile. I'm not a Miss Pilgrim."

"Seems to me," Zelda Marie said, "it's time you look out for yourself."

"I think so, too."

But how to free herself and not hurt the man she thought of as her best friend. He couldn't have treated her better over the years if she'd been his own daughter.

She wanted a city, she knew that. Houston or Dallas. Corpus was too small, and she had pretty much decided she wanted to go someplace big.

She guessed her life would have to change. Take direction. She didn't know just how to get there, but the direction she wanted was up.

She decided to learn shorthand. Being a secretary would be an entrée to the business world. She didn't expect to be a secretary long, but she had no other talents that would help her get a job. Her Spanish might come in handy, she'd keep up with that. Quien sabé?

As a first step she began driving over to Corpus Christi every Saturday morning to take a shorthand course. At the end of six months she told her mother what Francey had known for a couple of years and was just waiting for Carly herself to discover: She was going to leave Verity.

"How're you going to tell Walt?" Francey asked, who had plans of her own to tell him about.

"I thought maybe you . . ."

"Uh uh," Francey reached out to touch Carly's hand. "You've got to. He'll survive. He'll just be disappointed."

"I love him, you know," Carly said. "I don't want to hurt him."

"Honey, sometimes you've got to do things for yourself. I've known you wouldn't stay here. You're destined for great things."

Carly kissed her mother's cheek. "Just slightly prejudiced, aren't you?"

"Just a bit more than slightly." Francey had to swallow to keep from crying. She knew Carly should leave Verity, but even the *thought* of it left a hollow space in her chest.

"I have to get on with my life. I have to find some excitement."

"I know," Francey said. And she did. "Maybe we should never have stopped here. But then, I wouldn't have found Walt."

"Why don't you marry him?" For ages Carly had been wanting to ask the question.

Francey shrugged and smiled. "I've been thinking on it. Don't rush me."

It had been four years. Every Christmas Walt proposed again, and then they went on with their lives.

Walt forced himself to hold back tears when Carly told him she wanted to move to Houston. He gave her a thousand dollars as a bonus for her years of service. Next to Francey, Walt loved Carly more than anyone else in the world.

CHAPTER 7

Walt and Francey drove Carly up to Houston. They spent the weekend searching for an apartment, and Walt insisted on paying the first month's rent. Both of them looked like they were going to cry when they said good-bye. "Now, you phone us every Sunday, hear?'' Walt said. "And any other time you need us or want us . . .''

"Or feel lonely,'' Francey added.

It was the right move. Carly and Houston had a love affair from the beginning. Wherever she went, men introduced themselves and asked her to dinner and to night clubs and to Saturday afternoons at the zoo or playing Frisbee in the park.

She had dates every weekend, young men who were on their way up, not nobodies like in Verity. She began to laugh again.

She finally tucked Boomer in a corner of her heart and turned the key. Although she didn't quite throw the key away, she did stop thinking about him all the time and tried not to compare every man she dated with her high school love. She had a life to live.

"You know what I'd like to do?'' Francey asked.

She and Walt were sitting on his patio, where an awning shaded them from the hot sun, drinking coffee after church, nibbling at the cinnamon rolls Francey baked every weekend. She was dripping wet, having just emerged from the pool Walt had built two years ago after Francey, one hot humid June morning, had commented, "What I wouldn't give for a pool."

"Get married?'' Walt asked hopefully.

Francey smiled at him and reached over to take his hand.

"I've saved some money,'' she went on.

"No wonder, continuing to live in that little house."

"I spend most of my waking hours when I'm not working— and a few sleeping ones—over here,'' she said. Her mind was not on marriage. "Aside from Blue's,'' where she continued to work every morning and lunchtime, "and that Dairy Maid, there's not a single decent restaurant in town. No place folks can get dressed up to go to and eat wonderful food."

Walt raised an eyebrow. He sensed, uncomfortably, where she was heading.

"How many people in Verity get dressed up to eat out?''

"How many get dressed up to go any place else but church?

I mean just a *nice* restaurant, something a little sophisticated, someplace that'll serve drinks, have a bar even, but not one that'll appeal to the guys who hang out at Blue's. I want a pretty place, something people in Verity will think is classy. And with food that'll knock their socks off.''

Walt tilted·his head. "You aiming to spend all your nights in a kitchen?''

"Hardly.'' Francey shook her head. "I'll train cooks. I'll be there to oversee every little detail, but I won't spend time over a hot stove. That's not how I want to earn money.''

"Blue'll never forgive you if you leave.''

"He will be disappointed, but he'll forgive me. Maybe I'll eat breakfast there and he can eat dinner at our place.''

"Ours? Oh, so that's it.'' Walt didn't like the idea. It would cut into the time he and Francey spent together. He fished for something that would put a dimmer on her restaurant project.

After a few moments, he had it.

"What'll you do if you get the lead in a play again?''

Ever since he'd bought the old abandoned Baptist Church and given it, refurbished, to the Little Theater Group, Francey had gotten the lead in any play for which she auditioned. And when Francey was in a play, the whole countryside came to see it. She might not have been good enough for Hollywood leads, but she was better than anyone in Verity had ever seen. She lit up the stage.

"Well, you don't *have* to join me,'' Francey said, "but then I'll have to borrow money from the bank. I thought maybe you'd like to be in business with me.''

"I'd like to be in anything with you, and you know it. But I'm forty-six years old, honey. Why do I want to go into a new business? I'm ready to slow down.''

"C'mon, Walt. You have more energy than any two people.''

"I don't need more money. I like weekends free for us to take trips.''

"We've been doing all that for years. I'm ready for something new. I have love.'' She smiled at him. "Now, I want success.''

"Oh." His eyes reflected amusement. "You want success on your *own*."

"Something like that," she admitted. "Though I thought you *might* like to be a partner."

"A silent one?"

She cocked her head. "I always listen to your ideas and advice."

He leaned over and took her head in his hands. "That you do, my darling. You're very good for my ego."

She laughed and stretched to kiss him. "Is it too early for a margarita?"

"You and Carly. All you had to do was get near the border and you adopted margaritas. It's over the yardarm, so I guess it's okay." He couldn't get it out of his mind. "Where are you thinking of having this restaurant?"

"I'm not sure," Francey said. "You know that pond down past the electric company?"

Walt nodded. "I think Cece Braithewaite owns that land."

"Well, it's not doing anything. And that pond always attracts ducks and geese. I even saw some swans there not too long ago. We could clear some land but leave that lovely grove of willows and build . . . well, I have some drawings I've been doodling with."

The tranquil life Walt had enjoyed with Francey was about to fly out the window.

The Willows was a success from the beginning, Francey spent six afternoons and evenings a week there; Walt dined there nightly.

Monday was the only night they had to themselves. But, contrary to Walt's expectations, he found himself enjoying the new venture. He received immense pleasure from watching Francey make a success of her business. Even though Verity knew it was half his, everyone referred to it as Francey's. No one ever said "the Willows."

She'd dragged Walt over half the state, or so it seemed to

him, choosing glassware and linen. The carpeting was a soft forest green and the walls a pale mauve, as was the table linen. The white bamboo chairs had seat covers the color of the carpeting, and fresh flowers adorned the tables, which all had a view overlooking the pond. Guests were given day-old bread to offer to the ducks and other waterfowl populated there.

Sundays, families were catered to, but Saturday nights Francey created a more romantic atmosphere, even hiring a trio from the high school orchestra which played songs from the forties and fifties.

Verity had never seen anything like it.

Before too many months, a few people were even driving down from Corpus and Kingsville and up from Brownsville to dine at the Willows.

When Carly finally came home to visit she told her mother it was as nice as any restaurant she'd dined in in Houston.

Carly had been in Houston only a week when she answered an ad that Rolf Realtors ran in the *Post*. Rolf's was the largest Texas realtor outside of Dallas. It had branches in Baytown, Galveston, and any number of Houston's rapidly burgeoning suburbs.

Carly and about eighty other girls answered the ad. They were given a typing and spelling test, a shorthand test, and even one in elementary math. Those who passed were called back. Of those, five were chosen for Mr. Rolf to interview personally.

Mr. Rolf took one look at Carly and decided it was a darn good thing he was as old as he was; he could just enjoy looking and get on with business. Aside from that, she had scored highest on all the tests and hadn't misspelled a single word.

Within a year of working for him she knew what he wanted before he even said it. "You got radar?" he'd ask in his thin voice, the blue veins standing out in his almost parchment-like skin.

She liked him. She didn't mind bringing him coffee in the morning and tea in the afternoon, and calling for doctors' appointments, and buying his daughters and granddaughters presents.

She liked both the work itself and the responsibility he gave her. At Rolf's instigation, she took a course in real estate appraising, even though her secretarial work did not call for knowledge in that area. She began to understand the terms and language and real estate laws better than many of Rolf's commissioned sales people. A couple of the men earned close to a million a year. Of course they were commercial, into big-time negotiations, but a few of the others, including even some women, earned hundreds of thousands.

"How come the women don't sell business property and industrial land?" Carly asked him at the end of a dictating session.

Mr. Rolf shook his head. "Carly, what businessmen are going to trust a woman? Except for me, not many men in Houston, maybe in the world, think women have brains. Lookit Congress. Lookit your CEOs. Now, me, my wife's smarter'n I am. I like that. Keeps me on my toes. But not many men do."

Carly remembered when she first began to date, Francey had told her, "Don't let the boy see how intelligent you are. Just smile and act interested in whatever he's interested in."

Yeah, like football and holes-in-one and old cars.

Carly enjoyed Mr. Rolf and liked her work, but she saw its limitations. She was getting on to twenty-three and she wanted to make her mark. This seemed like a good moment.

Raising her chin, she asked Mr. Rolf, "How about letting me try to sell something?"

"To whom?" he asked, gazing at her, his elbows on his desk, his fingers a temple under his chin. "Don't think I haven't thought about it, but you don't have the right contacts. How many people do you know who could afford the kinds of sales it takes to make big money?"

All the people Carly knew, outside of work, were singles who lived in apartments.

"Naw. You got to have contacts," he said, pulling on his mustache.

But Mr. Rolf didn't forget that conversation. In her second year as his secretary he called her into his office. Jay Thornberry, their number-one salesman, was ill and couldn't keep his appointment with the bank. "I should go," Mr. Rolf said. "It's a big deal, but I've got a hunch and seldom are those wrong. You have all the information for that deal about the land on which A & S Petroleum wants to erect an office building. You know all the details about it. Go over to Union Trust and talk to the VP. He's the son of the owner. Cole Coleridge. It's a sure thing, but we need his signature. Give you a bit of experience, just like you've been yearning for. Also you'll get to meet one of the rising stars of Houston. Be good for you." He studied her. "Okay, girl, go for it. And if the vibes are right, invite him to lunch. I'll pay for it."

Carly drew herself up. "I don't invite men to lunch."

Mr. Rolf laughed. "Well, Cole Coleridge is a hard ass. He won't invite *you.*"

Carly smiled. "He's a man, isn't he?"

"Find out and tell me." Rolf grinned. "And maybe you'll be on your way to meeting the right contacts. He's loaded for bear. Or at least his daddy is."

When Carly turned to leave, Rolf said, "He's not married, either."

She laughed. "What's that name again?"

"Cole Coleridge," he said.

PART II

1969–1970

CHAPTER 8

"I have someone I think you should meet." Cole Coleridge's voice sounded emphatic over the phone.

Alexandra Headland sat in the leather chair that exactly fit her back, a black-and-gold pencil poised in her right hand, doodling on the pad on her faceted-glass-topped desk. She drew leaves. Identical leaves that began to cover the page.

"Want to fill me in?"

"We're too conservative over here, but you . . . you take chances. He came to us for a loan, that's all I'll say. He's in my outer office."

She glanced at her appointment pad. "I'm booked all day. But how about five?"

"His name's Brad Bannerman. Let me know what you do about him. I'll be surprised if he doesn't interest you."

Alex put down her pencil and wondered why she always drew leaves when talking on the phone. "A big sum, I gather."

She could almost see the smile in Cole's eyes. The only time he seemed to smile was when it concerned money.

"I'll send him around five." A pause. "Don't forget our date at seven, though."

It was going to be a tight squeeze. She'd like time for a shower before dinner at seven. And time to choose the right outfit—not that she ever did anything *but*.

The press usually referred to her as "the glamorous madcap oil heiress." Any party at which Alex appeared was also attended by a photographer. *Time* magazine, in writing an article on the "new" Houston royalty, featured her photograph. Those who did not know her yearned for the glamour she represented. Those who did know her smiled knowingly. Their Alex.

She also had a brain as sharp as a razor. Not even once had Alex ever doubted herself.

Her parents were Coleridge's parents' best friends and had been ever since Kevin Coleridge had staked Amos Headland to his first gusher, before Alexandra was born, before either of the men was married. Kevin had had some anxious moments worrying about whether the wild young man knew what he was doing, but as it turned out, Amos Headland brought in oil well after oil well after oil well. By the time his only child, Alexandra, was born he was a millionaire many times over.

Cole was five months older than Alex, and they had been brought up together, along with Cole's younger brother, Bennett. In the early years, Ben was cute and she'd really liked him better. Maybe she still liked him better. When she and Cole were in seventh grade at St. John's, they took ballroom dancing at Miss Shibley's on Friday nights. Ben would nag her until she'd show him steps and practice with him, even though he was only ten.

When they all went to Europe one summer, sailing on *Queen Elizabeth II*, it was Ben she'd spent more time with. He laughed easily, she could always beat him at Monopoly, and he had such a sweet though never boring nature. Also, she suspected Ben was brighter than Cole. Cole had to work for his marks, which were excellent, but to Ben getting good marks was as easy as falling off a log.

Cole and Alex never really had a date, though Cole would call for her and take her home from parties and dances and barbecues. They danced well together.

They both came from the old-time moneyed conservative element of Houston where nobody was anybody without their approval, and the only criteria for acceptability was wealth. Not just a couple of million, either.

By the time they graduated from high school, it was an unspoken understanding that they were engaged to be engaged.

Cole was one of two young men from his school to go to Harvard, and Alex was the only girl from the state of Texas to attend Bryn Mawr. It was the alma mater of her mother— a Main Line Philadelphian who met Amos when she'd visited her aunt in Ardis, Oklahoma, one summer where he was wildcatting. With Alex's intellect, her SAT scores, and her perfect high school average there wasn't a university in the country that wouldn't have wanted Alex.

The first time Cole kissed her was the night before he left for Cambridge. He pulled Alex to him and said, "I'm going to miss you," his lips touching hers. Alex didn't feel anything.

She was not beautiful, not even pretty, yet people turned to stare when she entered a room. She had supreme self-confidence. She knew she was smarter than most people and she knew she had style, a style that came from always being able to buy the best of anything. She also knew she had a good body. Too thin, maybe, but elegant like the models who graced the covers of *Vogue*.

Over the years, at Christmas vacations and during summers, she and Cole graduated from that one thin-lipped, close-mouthed kiss, but not to anything that excited her. Cole never seemed to let himself go, his lips always having a rigidity to them, his passion repressed.

After Harvard, he went on to Stanford for an MBA; Alex received hers at the University of Pennsylvania.

She and Cole never wrote to each other. They never mentioned marriage, yet both they and their families took for granted they would marry. Since neither of them had become involved with anyone during their university years, when they returned to Houston—in the summer of 1967—with more degrees than most Texans ever amass their mothers thought a wedding was in store.

Instead, all they got around to doing was going to bed together. Cole didn't make love with gusto, but mechanically, almost as though he'd read a how-to book. Afterward they'd light cigarettes, though all Alex wanted to do was go home to her own bed and fall into a dreamless sleep. He wanted to talk of future plans. Not theirs, but the bank's. His father's bank. He, with his new MBA, wanted to streamline it, make changes. His father insisted they go slowly. Financial institutions couldn't rock boats.

Patience was not one of Cole's strong points.

His giant weakness was his lack of a sense of humor, though women were attracted by his aloofness and his family's reputation and great wealth. Together they spelled power. Cole never attempted anything if he wasn't sure of winning. He would practice and practice until he became an expert. He *always* won at tennis, at hand ball, at studies. He appeared as sure of himself as did Alex. He was the one person in their circle of friends with whom Alex could talk business.

She'd made it clear she wasn't ready for marriage and that was okay with Cole. So they made love Saturday nights.

To her parents' disappointment Alex had chosen not to live with them in their twenty-one room mansion in River Oaks but had opted for a luxury apartment in a building her father owned downtown—five rooms with a balcony looking out over a spectacular sixth-floor view. Her living room was spacious, and she knocked the wall out between the two bedrooms, so her bedroom, all white, became larger even than her parents' bedroom.

The kitchen was black and white. Black refrigerator, black stove, black wall oven, black shining countertop, white marble floor, and a stainless-steel sink.

The living room had flat white walls, with black leather and steel furniture. A vivid Alexander Calder mobile hung from the ceiling and an immense Jackson Pollack covered one whole wall. Alex loved her apartment, reveling in her privacy.

She never had sex with Cole there, because she didn't want him or anyone else to stay overnight. She liked being alone, to be with her thoughts, to look at the late show, to stand on her balcony with a glass of Bailey's Irish Cream in her hand, gazing out over Houston and knowing that she was on her way to being one of its power brokers, just like her father. She'd been in training for that role all her life, and would have no trouble achieving it if she were a man. But she knew that, despite her background and money, it would be an uphill struggle. She was willing to fight every inch of the way.

She had no idea that at five o'clock something for which she was completely unprepared would enter her life.

Her secretary buzzed. "Mr. Bannerman is here."

The door opened and the man filled the doorway.

Alex, sitting at her desk, hands folded in front of her, observed that he had not dressed up to impress her, though his boots, scuffed as they were, shone with a recent polishing. He wore jeans, not new ones, either. His shirt was striped blue and white and he wore a bolo. A studded silver-and-turquoise belt looped through his jeans. From the neck down he could have been John Wayne, though his face was not craggy, but angular, his hair darker, his eyes browner. He was about her age, she guessed. Tanned.

He strode across the room and stretched out his hand. Paw was more like it, she thought, as she met his handshake.

"I like women with firm handshakes" were his first words. She gathered this meant he approved of her. She tried to push down the feeling of irritation she experienced. After all, he was supposed to be seeking *her* approval.

"Sit down, Mr. Bannerman."

He filled the whole chair and immediately leaned forward, his dark brown eyes filled with an urgency. "Every banker in town has turned me down, I better warn you," he said. "I haven't even got past the lower echelons . . ."

Echelons? Alex revised her initial impression that he was a

hick. After all, at his age her father must have had grease under his fingernails. Without thinking, she looked at the man's big hands and noticed the long fingers and the very clean clipped nails.

". . . to see the people really in charge of such money."

"Exactly," Alex interrupted, "how much money are we talking about?"

"Half a million."

Alex leaned back in her chair and made a steeple of her hands, resting her chin on her fingers. She waited.

"I never saw such gray eyes," he said, smiling right into them. "Like the ocean on a cloudy day."

She felt uncomfortable. "Flattery gets you noplace here, Mr. Bannerman." Alex's voice dripped ice, but she felt a flutter across her chest.

Her criticism didn't seem to faze him at all. "Wasn't a compliment. Just a statement of fact." His smile was ingenuous.

"Half a million's a lot of money." It wasn't really, she thought, but it was a lot for a young man in his mid-twenties to want to borrow.

"That's just for starters," he laughed. "I want to build apartment houses. Houston's growing so fast there's already a demand for housing."

Alex knew that.

"Luxury apartments. For people who don't want the upkeep of a large home. For singles who've made it. For people who want a good address right in the city. For those who don't like suburbs. For those at River Oaks whose kids have grown up and find their huge houses too big for them."

Her parents would never dream of leaving their home for a smaller place.

"You have land in mind?"

Her eyes were on his the whole time he told her his ideas. When he'd finished she said, "Half a million isn't enough."

He grinned. "I said for starters."

"How do you expect to get that land?" she asked. "It must be worth millions in that location."

"I already own it," Boomer answered. "My father bought it before I was even born, when that part of town was country."

Alex sat up straighter.

"I aim to make more than I could by selling it outright."

"That'll be millions."

"Yes, ma'am!"

"So, the land is your collateral?" That wouldn't be much of a risk, then. It was easily worth more than he was asking for.

"Not on your life," he answered.

"Then what is?"

He smiled that big lopsided grin. "I am."

Alex phoned Cole and said she'd meet him at the restaurant. She had to rush to be on time.

The first thing Cole asked, after they sat down, was, "Well, what about that Bannerman?"

Alex ordered a whiskey sour and then turned to Cole. "Yes, you were right. He interests me."

Which was an understatement.

CHAPTER 9

Alex ran a check on Bannerman's background and studied the architect's drawings he had given her. He'd worked in construction ever since he graduated from the University of Texas. He'd been foreman of three big construction jobs in the last three years, and his references praised him, each and every one. But being a foreman didn't quite prepare one for being *the* boss, managing the finances, the personnel.

A dream she could understand, but one had to have expertise and experience as well as vision. He seemed to have the ability to get a big construction job done, not only ahead of time but below estimated costs.

One reference stated his father had been a long-time Texas legislator. Well, well. That was a surprise.

After dinner, as she and Cole had sat through the Don Shirley concert, she thought about Brad Bannerman. When Cole reached for her hand, she wondered what Brad's big hands would feel like intertwined with hers.

She was a betting woman, and she would bet he'd soon be a big factor in Houston. He was going to make money. She could feel it in her bones. And for anyone with enough money, there was a slot in Houston.

She waited three days to call him, letting him sweat it out. She smiled to herself. He was going to get his money from a woman. She wondered if that would make him squirm.

"Mr. Bannerman, how about this afternoon? Five again?" She might even suggest a drink. There wasn't anything on her calendar after three.

Each night she'd sat on her balcony overlooking her city, thinking of Brad Bannerman, of his brown eyes and wide shoulders, of his bigness. He'd emanated power as he walked across her office, yet had a naive boyish quality. She thought of his self-assurance, despite the fact every banker in Houston had turned him down. And of his smile.

She was angry, she didn't know whether at him or at herself. She'd been careful over the years to make sure no man made her lose control. Until this Bannerman strode into her office Monday afternoon, she'd not faced any temptations. Even Cole knew the only part of her he had was her body Saturday nights.

When Bannerman appeared on the dot of five, Alex had a check waiting for him. She didn't tell him that a hundred thousand of it was out of her personal account.

He glanced at it, folded it up and put it in his shirt pocket. "Want me to sign something?"

She slid a paper across the desk. He read it, signed, and flicked it back to her.

"Where do you get this kind of money?" he asked.

"I invest people's money for them. Five people are backing you on this."

"Do they know it?"

She shook her head, thinking if his hair were longer it would curl over his ears. "No. They don't ask. I always make profits for them. You're not just promising to pay back half a million, you know. I've bought into your business."

"Silent partners?"

She nodded. If you don't screw up, she didn't say.

"Did you go look at the property?"

"And studied the drawings. I may take risks that conventional bankers don't, but I'm thorough."

He sat down. "You're pretty young to have so much money at your disposal. Who trusts you with so much?"

Alex couldn't help smiling. "Mr. Bannerman, I was born with money at my disposal. And anyone who knows me and knows my daddy trusts me."

She slipped the paper he had signed in a folder and pushed it to the side of her desk.

"C'mon," he said. "Help me celebrate. I know a great restaurant I bet you've never been to. And call me Boomer."

Boomer?

She imagined she'd never been to any of the restaurants he frequented.

He gazed at her gray shantung pantsuit with the green shirt that looked like a man's but was silk and clung to her breasts.

"You don't even have to change. You're okay as you are."

She tried not to laugh out loud. "Isn't it a bit early?"

"Be dark by the time we get there." He grabbed her hand and began striding out of her office. Alex's secretary stared in disbelief.

As Alex did when she saw the big black Harley-Davidson parked beside her Corvette.

Two helmets hung on the sissy bar. Boomer handed one to her and donned one himself.

"You've got to be kidding!"

Boomer just grinned. "Ever been on one of these?" He

reached over to show her how to place the helmet, not waiting for an answer. He knew just by looking at her she'd never been on a motorcycle. He helped her on and, before he revved the engine, he twisted his head around and ordered, "Hold on tight."

She held on so tight her arm muscles ached when forty-five minutes later they pulled up at a restaurant along the wharf in Galveston.

"Best shrimp in the world," he said, helping her off the bike.

When she took off her helmet he laughed, and looking at herself in the restroom mirror she could see why. Her hair was plastered to her head and she hadn't put lipstick on since lunchtime. Well, no one down here would know her.

She didn't even know herself.

"I've ordered," he told her when she returned from the ladies' room.

She hated it when men presumed to order for her. How did they know what she liked?

"You kidnapped me without my purse," she said. "I don't even have a comb."

"You look fine," he interrupted.

"Or a cigarette."

Boomer signaled a waiter. "What kind you want?"

She got the idea he disapproved. "Pall Malls."

The waiter nodded and was back in a minute. She tore the cellophane off the package and waited for Boomer to ignite the match. Finally she reached for one and lit her own cigarette, inhaling deeply. When she exhaled he brushed the smoke away, his hand waving through the air.

Twinkling lights from boats glittered, reflecting on the water. Sky and sea were one. The open-air restaurant, surrounded by palms, surprised her. There was a lushness to it if not elegance. A proliferation of greenery, parrots in cages, the soft background music of Duke Ellington. Fresh hibiscus in a bowl on the crisp linen tablecloth. Not the fast food she'd envisioned.

"Best seafood on the Gulf Coast," Boomer said. "Maybe in the world." She liked his smile.

When she sipped the tall peach-colored drink the waiter brought, she sighed. "Ambrosia. What is it?"

Boomer shook his head. "I don't know, but they're famous for it."

"Why aren't you having one?" He'd ordered mineral water with a twist of lemon.

"Hey, I'm driving, remember?"

"How can I forget?"

He leaned across the table, putting a big hand over hers. "You liked it, right?"

She had to admit it. "I don't know when I've been so exhilarated."

He pulled away and leaned back in the white wicker chair. "Okay, tell me. Tell me about you. You know what? I've thought of little else since I walked into your office Monday."

"Little else than getting the loan or going ahead with the project?"

His eyes narrowed. "You. Little else but you. How'd you get where you are and why?"

It was the first time in her twenty-six years that a man had asked her anything about herself before spending hours talking about himself. Except Cole. He didn't have to tell her about himself or ask about her because they had known each other forever.

"My life's an open book. Anyone can tell you about me."

He studied her for a minute. "I want to hear your story from you."

She smiled. He made her feel good, or was it the peachy drink? "There's not as much to tell about the first twenty-six years as there will be about the next ten."

He laughed. She stubbed out her cigarette as the waiter brought the first course. The shrimp were the most succulent Alex had ever tasted. A smile crossed her face. "I underestimated you," she said.

"Most people do." But he said it easily. "Go on," he urged. "Start your story."

She glanced over at him, her fork poised in midair. When she'd finished, seven and a half minutes later, she realized with a shock that there really wasn't a lot to tell.

"Sounds like an obituary," Boomer said, his eyes serious.

The waiter brought the main course. Boomer watched as she tested the flounder. Alex rolled her eyes toward heaven and murmured, "Magnificent."

After a minute, she said, "I hadn't realized I was so dull." She hadn't. Dull was not a word that she had ever imagined being applied to her. It was the first time in her life she'd given an autobiography, and she was dismayed it could be accomplished in so few words.

Boomer, chewing on his fish, muttered, "Seems to me you have tunnel vision."

"Meaning?"

The tone of his voice did not imply criticism. "You wanna show Houston and maybe the world you're as good as any— and better than most—man. You want to make so much money that no one'll doubt your power."

Alex put down her fork and stared at him. She hardly knew him and he'd walked right behind her eyes to her inner core and stripped her naked. No one had ever done this to her. For twenty-six years she'd been the Golden Girl, the brightest student, the best tennis player, the best daughter, one of the richest . . .

Boomer leaned forward and, in a confidential whisper, said, "It's okay. I've got the same kinks."

Was she supposed to say, Oh, share them with me? And then it was her turn to hear his life story? Had he only asked about her as an entrée to his self absorption?

"Kinks?" was all she said. She thought she had far fewer than most people.

"What do you do for fun?"

So he wasn't talking about himself. "Fun?" Like it was a foreign word. "Many things." Her mind scrambled. "I play tennis. I go to a lot of parties. The club. I . . .'' Then she smiled and let herself relax. "Let's face it, Mr. Bannerman. I work. I'm never happier than when I'm working.''

"The name's Boomer.''

Alex didn't know if she could even say such a name. Boomer, for a grown man?

"I understand your work is your pleasure. I feel sorry for all those people who just have jobs. Yeah, I like work, too. I love work. It's fun. But you gotta do other things. You've got to throw yourself into other pleasures, too.''

"I'm never bored,'' Alex defended herself. Since when had she defended herself to anybody?

"A particular man in your life?''

She leaned back in her chair, resting her elbows on its arms, folding her hands. "Guess.''

Boomer scooped up the last of the rolls before answering, and when he looked across the table, meeting her eyes, there was nothing she could see there. No amusement, no flirting, just an unreadable, unidentifiable brown stare. "Not many men, you don't have time for that. You're old to be unmarried according to Texas. So, not too many of the men have waited around. If there is someone, I don't see you,'' he let his gaze travel to her lips, resting there, "being in love.''

He leaned back in his chair and his eyes roamed the room, eventually gazing out at the gulf, watching the boats' twinkling lights. "So far your ambition has triumphed over other pleasures.''

The waiter interrupted, bringing dessert. The crême brulée was delicious.

They didn't talk as they ate, but their eyes were locked. Then he smiled, that puppy dog smile that made him seem so boyish. "Ma'am, you're one lucky lady.''

She raised her eyebrows in question.

"I'm going to rectify all that and introduce you to some of the pleasures of life.''

She thought he meant he was going to try to sleep with her. But, after they'd walked along the sea wall, with the water softly lapping against it, and had ridden, by moonlight, back to Houston at eighty-five miles per hour, it was after midnight.

He didn't even try to kiss her good night. He helped her off the bike, watched her unlock her car door and slide in behind the wheel, saw that she was safe, and as soon as her engine purred, he took off, leaving the exhaust from his motorcycle buzzing in her ears.

When she arrived home, she took the elevator to the sixth floor, undressed and walked in her nightgown out onto her balcony, filled with a desire she'd never known. She could still feel the wind blowing through her hair and her arms around the solid frame in front of her.

Aloud, she told herself that whether or not his project succeeded, she had a feeling she'd never find a wiser investment for her hundred thousand of it.

CHAPTER 10

Carly wondered if she should drive home and change to a more subtle color. She had worn her expensive fire-engine red suit this morning. She didn't buy many clothes but the ones she bought she prided herself on. Maybe it wasn't in the category of a designer suit yet, and maybe never would be, on a secretary's salary, but she knew it was stylish. She liked wearing red. And whenever she wore it, people commented on how good she looked in it. She was to pick up Mr. Schneider, the treasurer of Toyland, on her way to Union Trust, the Coleridge bank.

She had never met Mr. Schneider but actually, it wasn't up to her to say anything much. The deal was already arranged. This was just to sign papers, shake hands. Schneider could have done it on his own, but since Rolf's had arranged for the loan, accompanying their client to the bank was a courtesy they extended, no matter how small or large the sale.

Maybe he was just trying to have her meet people who would be potential customers. He'd told her she was the best secretary he'd ever had; in fact, he said he didn't even know how he'd run the office without her, and gave her a raise to show he meant it. But he also sensed the restlessness in her. He told her she was destined to be more than a secretary. By now, she knew the business better than most of the salesmen did.

Mr. Rolf had a degree from not only UT but a master's from the University of Wisconsin, and though his parents weren't from Houston, they were longtime Texas rich. He'd started out with money. Well, she'd like to show Houston what could be done by a woman who started out with very little.

Mr. Schneider did not seem delighted to see her, although Mr. Rolf had warned him he was sending a woman representative. He clicked his teeth all the time she drove to Union Trust. He even subtly suggested she wait here in the car for him, but Carly glided ahead of him through the revolving glass doors.

Third floor, Mr. Rolf had told her, and she preceded Mr. Schneider, not waiting for him to hold the elevator door for her, smiling at him dazzlingly.

Coleridge's was just a regular office, furnished with understated taste. Coleridge stood as Carly and Schneider entered the room, no particular expression on his face. He raised his eyebrows at Carly, but stretched his hand out to Schneider. His gaze, however, returned immediately to Carly.

"I'm Carly Anderson," she said, "representing Rolf's. This is Mr. Schneider from Toyland."

Coleridge gestured to the two leather chairs opposite his at his desk. He sat after they did.

Carly studied him. She thought he was about six feet tall and he looked as though he exercised. His hair was black, parted on the left, and he either spent time under a sun lamp or played a lot of tennis. His eyes were expressionless, not friendly, not much of anything. He hadn't smiled in welcome. He was businesslike, almost as though he were doing them a favor. Well, of course he was, lending Toyland three hundred thousand dollars to buy the land and to erect a warehouse. Toyland was opening stores all over Texas and now planned to build corporate headquarters and a warehouse. Finding the right property in a location that didn't cost an arm and a leg and was still accessible to major highways had taken several months, and Jay Thornberry had spent those months putting the deal together.

When Mr. Coleridge slid papers across his desk, proffering a pen with which Mr. Schneider could sign them, his gaze fluttered to Carly, and their eyes met. She smiled at him. He gave a barely perceptible nod of his head but did not smile back. That's what the rich are like, she thought. He reminded her of the ladies of Verity. She wondered if the blood in his veins might really be blue.

When the papers were signed, and Coleridge handed copies to Schneider, he then held out his hand to Carly. She was surprised that his handshake was so firm. She thought he held her hand for just a fraction longer than was polite, but she couldn't be sure. His black eyelashes were the longest she'd ever seen, and his eyes were sapphire blue. Hard, like jewels.

Cole Coleridge played as hard as he worked in a town where men worked hard. In order to reach the heights in Houston in the 1960's, it was not enough just to be rich.

Some of the most recently wealthy men hired public relations firms to make sure their wives' new diamonds and Paris frocks made the papers and the invitation lists. The public relations women taught the nouveau riche ladies how to dress and how to play tennis, recommended interior decorators and which houses to buy. Many of these ladies' husbands had been ordinary men who worked in factories or farmed and whose back yards had gushed up oil wells that just wouldn't quit.

The successful p.r. women saw that their clients' names were put forth, and approved, at the only clubs worth joining and introduced them, sparingly, to the old guard, telling the newcomers what to say and what to wear. They couldn't tell them how to say it; with TV and the country's mobility, it was no longer a prerequisite to have a southern accent but, nevertheless, there were few Yankees. Houston was too humid, too flamboyant, too oil-oriented to attract New York money, and few northeastern aristocrats were likely to invade a town with all those southern accents and that attitude toward blacks, who most Houstonites still referred to as coloreds.

By 1968 the vast majority of maids and gardeners in Houston were Mexicans and Guatemalans, imported for a year at a time, though some of them were even second-generation immigrants.

Houstonites—Texans in general—considered the eastern establishment effete anyway, even if not many of them had ever heard the word.

Texans loved horses, John Wayne and Gary Cooper, chivalry, fast cars, steaks, football, making money, dancing, New York musicals, and wide-open spaces. They particularly loved watching Herefords and Santa Gertrudis cattle wander over those open spaces and oil wells rocking back and forth, pumping black gold. Maybe above all, they loved Texas.

Though ostensibly Democrats, Texans in general and Houstonians in particular were among the most conservative political animals on earth, while being fiscal risk takers par excellence.

Texas men used four-letter words, but never in mixed company and seldom even in front of their wives. Women, Texas women at least, were supposed to be treated as ladies, and ladies is what they were expected to be.

Cole could never understand why Alex had to be so unlike all the other women they knew. Yet she'd always been different—restless, searching, impatient, not letting him or any male open a car door for her, saying in that amused, brittle tone of hers, "I'm not helpless."

Cole wasn't in love with her, but he'd known since he was fifteen years old, maybe long before that, that Alex was going to be his wife.

Now, he found himself growing impatient. Nearly everyone he knew was married and several of them even divorced already.

Maybe if he bought a ring, that might be the first step toward a commitment. In the meantime . . .

As well as the next man, Cole appreciated a pretty woman. But usually a woman's looks did not send him for a loop. Until Carly Anderson burst into his office, in a red suit that couldn't hide her voluptuous body. With her swinging golden earrings flashing as the sunlight hit them, Cole felt as though a drum was pounding in his chest.

Her long tanned legs were bare and she did not wear high heels with pointed toes as all the other women he knew did. She wore red sandals and her toenails were painted a bright red, unlike her fingernails, which had no polish and were nicely rounded. Like the rest of her.

He finally moved his gaze upward, to the generous red lips, to a face that glowed golden. Her eyes, big and round, lined with thin black liner, were the color of robin's eggs. Her smile dazzled him, showing perfect white teeth against her painted lips.

Cole shook his head, having to try for the first time in his life to look businesslike. Even as a teenager, he'd *always* looked businesslike, even when he was playing. Even when he was in bed with a woman.

He sat down and folded his hands on his desk.

"Well," said Mr. Rolf, his white mustache quivering as it always did when he smiled, "so he didn't invite you to lunch. He's not known for that sort of thing. I just wondered how he could resist you. I couldn't if I were young and single."

After a minute he asked, "What about Schneider? He make a pass?"

Carly shook her head.

"Hell, I've got to find a way to get you into a crowd where you can find customers. Two hundred a week, while it may seem good to you right now . . ."

"It doesn't," Carly said.

He nodded. "I know. And I don't want to lose you. I'll see

what I can come up with." She didn't imagine much. All his salespeople were at least thirty-five, and most of them older than that. They'd been around Houston a long time and knew the right people. Carly only knew guys she met at parties or through her girlfriends. None of them could lead her to the kind of real estate clients to whom Rolf's catered.

But before Mr. Rolf really put his mind to the matter, the next morning he received a call from Cole Coleridge. "I've a friend from Harvard going to be moving here from Minneapolis, and I'm wondering if that Miss Anderson could show me some apartments that might be appropriate for him."

Old man Rolf laughed. "That's as transparent as can be," he told Carly. "He doesn't have a friend." He patted her on the head. "Go for it, Carly. Here's a chance to get your feet wet, but don't count on a sale. Here's his number. You're to call for an appointment."

She dialed Cole at the bank. "I'd be glad to show you some places if you can be more definite as to what kind of apartment your friend's interested in," she said.

"He's going to work with Marriner and Lowe," Cole said, naming a prestigious law firm that even Carly had heard of. "I would imagine he'd want an upscale place. I thought I might look at eight or ten and narrow it down for him. He'll be staying with me until he finds a place of his own."

"Sure," Mr. Rolf cackled when Carly repeated this to him. "Well, there's the Washington Tower," which wasn't a tower at all. "There really are more apartments to rent than to buy, but let's see what we have."

Carly made an appointment to meet Cole at four Friday afternoon.

"That's so he can invite you to dinner," said Mr. Rolf.

Carly hoped so. But while they were talking, the phone rang, and after a lengthy conversation, Mr. Rolf turned to Carly, a twinkle in his eyes and said, "That was my daughter's mother-in-law. I don't know how Dierdre will feel about it, but her in-laws are moving to Houston from Dallas and she wants me to show her houses. Here's your chance, my dear. It may be an out-of-town contact, but give it a whirl."

By Friday afternoon, Carly was flushed with the success of her first sale. It had been as easy as pie. Mr. Rolf selected the houses he thought the woman would like, and Carly met the plane, took Mrs. Yarnall to see four of them in the morning, lunched at Petruchio's because Mr. Rolf knew his son-in-law's mother liked Italian food, and showed her two more houses in the afternoon. She had three more lined up, but as soon as Mrs. Yarnall saw the sixth house of the day, she said, "I want that one."

A mortgage needn't even be negotiated. She'd pay cash.

At half of six percent, Carly figured, she'd make more on the one deal than she earned in a year.

After Mrs. Yarnall had been put on the plane back to Dallas, Mr. Rolf suggested, "To make this legal, I better send you to take a real estate course so you can get a license."

Cole tried to remember the twenty minutes Carly Anderson and Richard Schneider were in his office. He guessed they conducted and finalized their business. He recalled signing the paper and pushing it across the desk to Schneider, but later he couldn't remember what the man looked like. When Carly Anderson rose to leave, she reached out her gloved hand and gave him a smile that warmed him into his belly.

It was sheer pleasure watching her leave. He'd never spent hours unable to concentrate, remembering how Alex glided out of a room. Yet all day, at the damndest inconvenient times, he remembered how this girl's hips moved provocatively as she walked away from him; recalled the pinkness of her tongue as it darted out to run across her lower lip.

As he fell asleep that night he smiled at the recollection of those wispy tendrils of golden curls that escaped from the pulled-back hairdo, held in place with a gold clip.

Were there men in her life? A husband? Boyfriends? A lover? There must be. No woman who looked like that could walk down Houston's streets and not attract attention. By the time she appeared at four on Friday, he'd spent three days thinking about her.

After she'd shown him three apartments, Cole said, "Let's drop the pretense."

Carly looked at him. Mr. Rolf had been right. She could easily discern from the fleeting glances he'd given the apartments she'd shown him that he wasn't really interested.

"You have no friend."

"On the contrary, I do." He had insisted on doing the driving, and the traffic had pretty much disappeared for the weekend. Twilight was descending. "But he doesn't want to buy an apartment. He wants to rent one."

"We do that, too." She couldn't help smiling. She was feeling good. She'd dressed carefully for this afternoon. Not a suit, but a dress, a cornflower blue that matched her eyes and whose skirt swished when she walked.

She liked his hands, the way they cupped the wheel, his long slender fingers.

"I thought they might send over some two-bit salesman instead of one of your caliber. I don't imagine you even deal in rentals, do you?"

She laughed. "No, I don't." He had no idea. She reached out and put a hand on his arm. "Why, Mr. Coleridge, I do think you want to take me to dinner."

He glanced at her. "Are you free?"

"If I weren't, I'd make sure I would be."

"The Excelsior all right with you?"

She'd never been there.

"Mr. Coleridge, I think the Excelsior is just fine."

"Cole," he said. "My name's Cole."

As they drove along, she said, "You were the last thing I thought of before falling asleep last night."

His hand reached out to encase hers.

CHAPTER 11

It was a week before Alex heard from Boomer again. By Thursday her nerves were so fraught she picked up the phone three times to call him but hung up before she dialed each time.

She'd never, not ever, felt this way.

As usual, she had spent Saturday night with Cole. They'd had dinner at the club, where they'd lingered, dancing to the band that played the kind of music their parents had grown up with. Houston was still formal and Cole, she thought, in his dinner jacket looked like he belonged. She hadn't even cared what she wore and had tossed on the gray chiffon with slender silver straps. It molded to her breasts, with a skirt that clung to her knees and then flared out in a circle.

Instead of dulling her, the gray gown, a shade darker than her eyes, silvered her. The diamond teardrops in her ears, her only jewelry tonight, had been given to her by her parents. She sparkled even when she felt short-tempered and impatient, her mind restless.

"You look beautiful," Cole told her as he pulled her close to him on the dance floor. His leg moved with hers and she closed her eyes, seeing Boomer's brown eyes rather than the blue of Cole's. She heard Boomer's gravelly voice instead of Cole's well-modulated one.

She was bored with the conversation, hearing hardly a thing anybody said, not even bothering to nod her head or pretend to participate in the conversation.

"Something bothering you?" Cole asked.

Last night, she'd lain in bed, unable to sleep. Her thoughts kept turning to Boomer. God, what a name. Boomer. She wanted to feel his lips on hers, taste him, feel his hands on her body, his tongue.

"I have a headache," she said to Cole. "I think I'll go home."

"I'll get your coat and drive you."

"No," she protested. "I want to be alone."

Boomer quit a good job that paid better than average the day Alex handed him the check for half a million. In six years he'd gone through the money he'd gotten for the Verity house and there hadn't been much more. There had only been twenty-one thousand, three dollars, and twenty nine cents in his father's bank account.

He could have sold the Houston property, but he saw it as an avenue to the beginning of his dream.

He hadn't scraped and scrimped. He'd bought a Triumph TR4 sports car and the Harley-Davidson. He liked speeding along a highway, preferably far from cities, in the wide-open spaces—red hills and sagebrush as far as he could see. It gave him a sense of freedom. The bonds of earth seemed to be ground into the asphalt, and whatever was pressing onto his shoulders slipped into the wind behind him.

He'd hooked up with Dan Bertelson, a young architect he'd drawn as a handball partner on his lunch hour at the Y five months ago. Dan was chafing at the bit. Three years older than Boomer, Dan was in his fifth year working at Yarrow, Golden, and McLure. He felt imprisoned there. "None of our clients would approve," he'd been told over and over whenever he wanted to try anything different.

"I ought to get out of here," Dan smashed the ball against the wall, "go to San Francisco or Seattle, someplace where they're open to innovative ideas. Oh, shit," he muttered as Boomer won a point.

"You any good?" Boomer asked as they showered.

"I'm better than the forty thousand they pay me. Yeah, I'm good. I have what they lack."

"Which is?" Boomer let the cold water needle him.

"Vision."

So do I, Boomer thought and looked at Dan again. "How about dinner tonight?"

"Sure." Dan grinned. "Even if you did beat me."

"Charcoal Grill. Six o'clock. Meet you in the bar."

Their collaboration began with pencil sketches on the back of the Grill's paper place mats and continued until well after eleven. It continued night after night, and, Saturdays, around the pool of the apartment complex where Dan lived.

Dan also quit his job the day Boomer showed him Alex's check.

"You're giving up safe money," Boomer worried.

"You have, too. So, it doesn't work out? I go to California or maybe Seattle."

Dan didn't stick to drawings but began to learn the elements of building, eventually spending time with plumbers, plasterers, finishers, electricians. He found he enjoyed every part of it, every minute of it. He worked in his shirtsleeves and, in hot weather, no shirt at all. It was in this state of undress, sweating, sawdust salted over the blond hair on his chest, that he met Tessa Oldfield. It was a Saturday and the work crew had left at noon. Dan and Boomer never seemed to leave, at least not until after dark, but Boomer had taken the weekend off, planning to cycle up to Sam Houston National Forest.

Dan was sitting on a sawhorse drinking a 7-Up and wiping sweat from his forehead when he looked up and saw a woman no bigger than a girl in her early teens surveying the first roughed-in building. He stared at her as she studied it, narrowing her eyes as though trying to imagine what it would ultimately look like.

Then she noticed Dan and walked toward him. Cute, he thought, like an elf. Tight red curls cascaded to her shoulders and, as she approached, he saw her pale redhead's skin was sprinkled with freckles. She wore jeans and a faded man's blue shirt, about four sizes too large. He bet she wasn't even five two. When she got within shooting distance of him he was riveted by her eyes, not green, not blue, but a clear aquamarine, a color he'd never seen in eyes.

Hands clasped behind her back, she stood with feet apart. Gesturing with her chin jutting out, she asked, "What's this gonna be?"

"Apartments."

She didn't look at him again, but walked over to study the hole in the ground, not even cemented in yet.

"How many?" she called.

"One ten."

"Wow." She looked around at all the vast empty space, the scrub oak not yet cleared, the weeds and wildness.

"Big job."

He nodded, wondering if under that voluminous shirt she looked more like a woman.

She walked back and hoisted herself up to sit beside him on the sawhorse, her feet dangling in the air.

"You work here?"

He grinned. "Sort of."

Now she turned her full gaze on him. "Sort of?"

"I'm the architect."

She searched his face, looking into his eyes, and then stuck out her hand. "I'm Tessa Oldfield."

"Dan Bertelson."

"Got the plans with you?"

"Why? You going to sign up for the first one?"

She laughed. "Never can tell, I might. I'm an interior decorator. I'm always interested in buildings."

"Whatever you are, none of the South has rubbed off on your speech. Where are you from?"

She laughed. "Honey chile, I am a Yankee, from about as far north as you can get and still be a citizen. Rochester, New York, snow belt capital."

She might look like a teenage tomboy but she smelled like expensive perfume. He wanted to keep talking with her. "Been in Houston long?" He wondered how she ever brushed her hair with all those tight ringlets.

"A year this month. I came down to work for David Jones."

"David Jones?" The largest interior decorating firm in town that only handled houses worth a couple of million.

She nodded, and her ringlets tossed like springs.

Dan had to laugh. She had a self-assurance and something else he couldn't quite define that he found appealing. Despite her crisp northern way of talking, he felt a warmth unusual in professional women. An openness. He was used to women who flirted as a way of life, who acted . . . Well, that was it. Who acted.

"You want to have dinner tonight?" he asked suddenly.

She threw her head back and laughed. "You don't know it, but you had no choice about asking me that."

He raised his eyebrows.

"I've been willing it, ever since I sat down here. How shall I dress?" she asked, sliding off the sawhorse. "Up?"

"Up?"

"Dress up or casual?"

He'd like to see her in something that would reveal more of herself. "Up," he answered. "Where'll I call for you?"

She gave him her address and phone number. "Bring your blueprints and sketches, too," she said.

Boomer zoomed through the east Texas countryside, the windows down as hot air blew through the car. He hated air-conditioning. Alex's hair blew across her face in the breeze. Her dark glasses kept him from seeing what she was thinking.

He'd appeared in her office in the middle of the afternoon yesterday, in his work clothes, telling her secretary, "I just need a minute," then had burst into her office with no preamble. "You have anything on this weekend you can't break?" he asked.

"Yes," she said, her voice cool. She hadn't seen or heard from him in eight days.

"What?"

"None of your business. I've a date tomorrow night."

"Break it," he said. "Wear something casual and bring a bathing suit. I'll pick you up at seven." He waited but the trace of a minute to see if she was going to refuse and then, a grin on his face, said, "A.M., that is," and left without closing the door to her office.

Men didn't treat Alexandra Headland like that. She was furious at herself for allowing this man to control her emotions, and knew that she was loving it. Weak at the thought that whatever he might ask of her, she might do.

He didn't ask anything of her. They'd driven to a lake she hadn't even known existed. A few cottages were scattered along the shore and there was a little motel with cottages nestled in a cove. A ragtag grocery store advertised bait. Boomer pulled up, tires crunching the gravel.

"This is it?" she asked. A cheap motel. She'd never stayed in a motel in her life, and this man who'd swept her off her feet was taking her to a cheap motel for the weekend? Ice water seeped through her veins.

Boomer didn't notice. He bounded out of the Triumph, which she had to admit had surprised and impressed her, as had his driving. He seemed so—so in control.

Well, he wasn't going to control her in a two-bit motel. Who the hell did he think he was? No one, but no one, had ever done this to her.

"Come on," he said when he returned from the store and opened the trunk. From it he took a carton and, not waiting for her to get out of the car, strode around the side of the motel office, in the direction of the lake. "Bring your bathing suit," he called over his shoulder.

He hadn't even waited for her, hadn't offered to open her door for her, hadn't . . . For a minute, she thought of sitting right here, making him come back, let him know she couldn't be treated like this.

But when he didn't return, she got out of the car, pebbles slipping into her sandals as she followed where he'd led. He was down by the water's edge, beyond the cabins that overlooked the lake, fiddling with the engine on an old outboard.

He winked at her. ''Want to show you a special place,'' he said, ''but first let me run back and buy some ice from Orin.''

It was just a little paint-peeling motor boat. She stood looking at it with distaste until Boomer bounded back, grabbing her around the waist and lifting her into the boat, settling her on the wooden slat that served as a seat.

The motor chugged into life, and the boat took off.

Boomer looked at her, grinning. ''Relax. You're perfectly safe.'' They rounded a point and the lake spread out in front of them, larger by far than it had seemed from the motel. The sun sparkled on the water, warming Alex as spray splattered over her.

Suddenly Boomer cut the motor and the boat just floated, hardly even rocking. ''Isn't this about one of the prettiest sights you've ever seen?''

She had to admit it was, and he was as openly enthused as a young boy. It had been a long time since she'd known any man to wax so enthusiastic about anything but a football game. Except maybe Cole's younger brother, Ben. Ben used to get excited about everything. Well, he still did, but such oddball things. Greenpeace, anti-war demonstrations, saving whales.

Cole wasn't at all like his brother. But Boomer was.

He sat looking around for maybe twenty minutes, not even talking. At first she felt restless out here on a lake, not doing anything, but gradually the gentle rocking of the boat, the silence cut only by the cry of a mockingbird, the green gold of spring leaves against the cobalt sky touched her.

She sighed with pleasure. Boomer reached out to start the motor again and slowly headed toward a cove.

''Picnic area and a beach which I don't think anyone else even knows about. At least I never find remains of beer bottles or plastic.'' He really did sound like Ben. Boomer brought the boat to a halt, jumping overboard in his tennis shoes and rolled-up trousers. He beached the little boat, and before Alex knew what he was doing, he lifted her and carried her to the dry sandy beach. Then he waded back to get the ice and the carton which she now realized contained drinks and sandwiches.

"You a good swimmer?" he asked.

"Am I a good swimmer?" She laughed, her voice a challenge.

"Go hide behind a tree and change into your swimsuit." He nodded toward the woods that surrounded the lake. In a quick motion he unzipped his trousers and let them fall on to the sand, kicking them aside, standing there in wine-red bathing trunks, leaning over to search for a bottle opener and a Coke.

After they'd swum, after Boomer offered her the chicken sandwiches, hard-boiled eggs, and bananas (bananas, she thought? Bananas?) he'd brought, he stretched out on the narrow strip of beach, his head resting on his hands, staring out over the water.

"What is it you want?" he asked. "Above all, what do you want?"

Alex looked at him and sat up, hugging her knees. "What a strange question."

He didn't say anything for a minute, and then, "Well?"

"Heavens, I don't know. Above all? I don't know that I've even thought about it like that. Above all."

"You don't want what other women do. Marriage, family."

"Yes, I want those, too, but I want it all," she found herself whispering. "I want that, but I don't want that to be my limits. I want a family. I want that path to immortality, but I don't want it to be my only path." She stopped, amazed to hear herself.

He was looking at her, his brown eyes mesmerizing her with the intensity of his gaze.

"I want to show the world . . ."

"The world?"

She laughed self-consciously. "Well, Houston. My world. Maybe Texas even, that I can be on top."

"Wealth and power."

"I don't care about wealth."

He nodded. "That's because you've always had it. So you don't even know that without it you can't have power."

She nodded. "Okay, then. Wealth and power. But not just

as somebody's wife. Not like my mother who's influential because she's daddy's wife. And not like now, where I have a modicum of success mainly because I'm my daddy's daughter. But be somebody on my own. The richest, the most influential . . . My God?'' She shook her head as though to clear it. ''You didn't expect such an answer.''

''I don't know what I expected,'' he said, sitting up and reaching out to take her hand. ''I want those things, too. Everyone in Houston's going to know my name and respect it. I'm not going to have to sign any paper when I walk into a bank and get a million-dollar loan. The president will know my handshake's it. Next loan from you, you'll do it that way, too.''

''Next loan?''

He nodded, still holding on to her hand. ''This may not be my next project, but one of them. This lake. That's why I brought you out to see it. Close to nine hundred acres. Over two hundred fifty homesites. A restaurant. A golf course and country club. A marina. All within less than two hours of the city. Second homes so exclusive and so expensive they're going to be begging to get in. But I'm not ready. I have things to do in the city yet.''

''You've barely begun your first project,'' she said, liking the feel of his hand around hers.

''We're going to be partners on our way up.''

You, she thought, have a lot farther to go than I do.

''If I had the money, even for a down payment, I'd buy this place. It's going for three hundred an acre. Ten years from now, even undeveloped, it'll be a couple thousand, at least. Mark my word. Just look at it.''

He stood and pulled her up. ''No one else even knows about it. I wanted you to. And if you're smart and can round up the dough, you'll buy it now, so when it comes time for us to work on this together, it won't cost something that'll send all our profit down the drain.''

She was delighted to discover she'd misjudged him. The motel wasn't even part of his plans. Instead, they drove back to Houston through the sunny afternoon, talking and laughing.

Boomer braked suddenly, swerving across the gravel onto the parking lot of a roadhouse. "I forgot about this place. Sort of early, though, isn't it?" He glanced at his watch. "Just five-thirty. But they've got the best ribs around."

"I've never had ribs," Alex said.

He opened the door. "You must be joking. Lady, are you going to be glad you met me!"

As they slid into seats in the darkened restaurant, she told him, "I've never met anyone like you."

"I know."

After they ordered, he turned to her. "And I've never met a woman I could talk business with, someone I can share my visions with who understands." Then he grinned. "Pretty good we met up with each other. I must remember to thank that guy who sent me to you. I don't even remember his name."

"I'll thank him," she said. "I remember his name."

CHAPTER 12

Tessa could have been a boy from the neck down. Well, almost. Her legs were great, and the way she gestured was feminine, and those giant turquoise eyes, but she had next to no bosom. Dan noticed that immediately. She wore a full-skirted dress of emerald-green silky fabric. It had a scoop neck but wasn't cut low, probably because there was nothing to show. Her sleeves weren't anything but a couple of ruffles. Her shoes were dyed to match the dress and their heels were narrow and very high. Dan wondered how she even walked in them, but she did so most gracefully. Pearl earrings the size of oysters hung from her ears.

He opened the door for her, walked around and slid in behind the wheel.

"Nice car," Tessa said. "I've never been in a convertible. Rochester doesn't have convertible weather."

"Is that why you moved here, the weather?"

"Partly," she said. "The hotter the better. I love heat."

"Houston's weather is the pits. Too humid. And in winter it rains."

"Where are you from?"

He grinned at her. "St. Paul."

"Minnesota? Well, you must be here for the same reason I am."

It wasn't all they had in common. It seemed there wasn't anything of importance they didn't share, but it wasn't until dessert that Tessa said, "I'm thirty."

Dan raised an eyebrow. "You look eighteen, tops."

She smiled and nodded. "I know. Also, I've been married."

His chest felt tight.

". . . and when I divorced five years ago I went down to New York and enrolled at Pratt to study design and came from there to here."

When Dan didn't say anything, Tessa went on. "Someday before too long I'm going to leave David Jones and go out on my own, but right now I make seventy-five thousand a year."

Dan gulped. "You must be good."

"I'm the best."

He reached across the table and took her hand.

"I don't want any kids," she said, her voice husky.

He let go of her hand.

"Ever?"

"Ever. I lost one. It was stillborn. I'm never ever going through that kind of emotional pain again. I thought you should know."

He leaned back in his chair and looked at Tessa. Then he signaled the waiter. "A double Scotch," he said.

Elevator music played; Frank Sinatra sang "You'd be so nice to come home to . . ."

Neither of them said anything, Dan looking at Tessa, Tessa

looking around the room until the waiter brought his drink. They both studied it. Dan took a swallow.

"You're telling me one of two things and I don't know which."

She blinked her eyes; she had the longest lashes he'd ever seen.

"You're either warning me off, telling me to get out now when I can, or it's an open invitation but I'm to be careful."

She smiled, picking up her empty wineglass and twirling it in her fingers. "I hadn't realized it, but yes, I guess so."

He sipped his drink. "Well, which is it?"

When Tessa's eyes met his, he knew which it had to be.

"Shit," he said. "When I got up this morning I never even heard of you."

He finished his Scotch. "One trouble with your premise. You take for granted I can still get out if I want."

"No." She shook her head, the trace of a smile crossing her lips. "Not really. It was too late for me by the time I sat down on that sawhorse. I was walking along minding my own business on a beautiful Saturday noon, mentally making out my grocery list, and I looked up and saw this blond Adonis in front of a building that seemed like it was going to be shaped not quite like most others and I turned and walked in and it was already too late. When was it too late for you?"

He grinned. "When you told me you earn seventy-five thousand a year."

She kicked him under the table.

"Well," he said, after a pause where they just looked at each other. "We might as well go home."

"Yours or mine?" she asked, standing up, not even coming to his shoulder.

"My bed's not made."

"Mine is. Let's go unmake it. Besides, I want you to see how I decorate."

She walked ahead of him out of the restaurant.

His voice teasing, he asked, "Are you afraid I'll back out if I don't like it?"

"No," she shook her head. "You'll like it. You'll see how we're going to make millions together."

He slid in behind the wheel. "That's not exactly what I'm thinking of making tonight."

"You'll like that, too," she promised.

Alex was watching Boomer pull away from the curb. This morning she'd been upset thinking he had a cheap motel in mind for them, and now he'd left her after a day she'd enjoyed completely, barely kissing her good night.

He'd stood as she unlocked the door to the foyer of her apartment building, not telling him hers was the penthouse suite, and gathered her in his arms, bending to bring his mouth to hers, kissing her gently, his lips caressing hers.

It was on the tip of her tongue, along with the burning feeling he'd left there, to invite him up, but she'd never invited a man to her apartment, not alone. For parties, yes. For dinners with several people. But never just a man. Not even Cole. Not at night. Not alone.

Boomer didn't even suggest coming up.

Don't fall in love with him, she told herself. When she was with Boomer she didn't act the way she did with the others. He brought out a softness, a femininity she hadn't known she had. He liked, didn't seem to feel threatened by, her intelligence and power. It was as though they fed each other.

"Sweet Jesus," she said aloud.

Cole had gone to the club alone, but he was restless. He didn't stay for dinner. Had two drinks at the bar, table-hopped for half an hour, and left. He was only slightly irritated that Alex had canceled tonight. He hadn't been alone on a Saturday night for longer than he could remember, but he found he didn't feel lonely. Just restless.

Maybe he'd take in a movie, have a bite to eat afterward. But a soft warm breeze rustled the leaves, and the scent of verbena filled the air. Nothing like the Chanel No. 5 that Alex always wore. Always the same. No matter the occasion, Chanel No. 5. A lovely aroma, to be sure. But that first day she'd walked into his office, Carly had smelled of lily of the valley. Yesterday the odor of lilacs accompanied her. Last night he dreamt he walked through fields of flowers.

Carly wrapped a towel around her wet hair and studied her reflection in the bathroom mirror. She'd canceled her date for tonight, preferring to wash her hair and do her nails and roam around her apartment, thinking of Cole Coleridge.

She'd had a pleasant time with him last night. She liked the feeling that he'd wanted to see her enough that he'd tried subterfuge, thinking perhaps she wouldn't have wanted to go out with him. How many girls turned down Cole Coleridge?

Though he wasn't handsome, he was nice-looking in an aristocratic sort of way. When she'd first met him, she thought he looked as though ice water would flow in his veins, but he'd thawed considerably last night, and while he wasn't exactly charming, he magnetized her in some way. She was sure money and power were part of the draw.

She couldn't tell what was behind those blue eyes fringed by those thick black lashes. He hadn't tried to kiss her good night or even made mention of seeing her again, but she had a feeling she *would* see him. She was amazed how much she'd revealed of herself, how she'd told him she had never felt she belonged, that she had hated Verity.

She hadn't spent time talking about how she'd loved growing up in California, but she did tell him that she thought she and Houston were destined for big things together. He told her he'd decorated his apartment himself, which surprised her, and he was interested in the Impressionists, and someday would like to collect paintings. Maybe even have a collection so impressive he could will it to a museum.

They were both film buffs, though Carly saw more movies

than he did. He found it fascinating that she was so caught up in business and asked her if she'd made many big sales.

She did not tell him the truth. She just smiled what she hoped was a Mona Lisa smile and said, "Oh, one or two." She couldn't even have said *one* three days before.

It had been quite a week for Carly. She hoped there would be more of the same. More sales. More Cole Coleridge.

She did not worry when he did not phone all week. If he never called she would be okay, but it would be nice to think a man like that wanted to be with her again.

What she did concentrate on was real estate school, which she attended Tuesday and Thursday evenings.

"Make another sale," Mr. Rolf said, "and much as it'll kill me I'll find another secretary and let you spread your wings."

Carly didn't want to just spread her wings. She wanted to soar. She had the feeling that she was just taking off.

Moving to Houston was the smartest thing she'd ever done.

CHAPTER 13

"I like the way you only wear one earring and always in your left ear," Walt told Francey. "I like the bright colors you wear. I like the idea that every man who looks at you envies me."

"Oh, Walt! I didn't notice any of them making dates with me. Hell, no one in Verity ever even pinched my bottom."

He laughed and reached out to do so, leaving his hand there, caressing her buttocks. "You've brought a whole new dimension to my life." He leaned over to nibble her neck.

"You know that always gives me gooseflesh," she said, continuing to chop celery, though more slowly. It was Monday, the one night the Willows was closed, and Francey enjoyed getting dinner.

He moved so his body folded against her back. "Why don't

you marry me?'' If he'd said it once he'd said it a thousand times. ''Now that you've proved you're a success in this town, marry me.''

Francey laid down the knife on the cutting board, put her hand over his and whispered, ''You better be ready to finish what you're starting.'' She turned and began to unbutton his shirt.

He slid to the kitchen floor and pulled her down on top of him.

When she finally stood up and slipped back into her blouse, she asked, ''Would I have to give up the Willows and be just a housewife?''

Walt blinked in disbelief. ''Are we actually negotiating about marriage?''

Francey grinned as she sliced carrots with a vengeance. ''I'm getting tired of hopping out of bed in the middle of the nights to go home or to say good night to you. But I don't want to lose my independence.''

He grabbed her around the waist and gave the rebel yell. ''I don't want to put any restrictions on you at all. Just my name. My God, hon, are you serious?''

''About time for you to make an honest woman of me. I just don't want our relationship to change.''

''Let's call Carly,'' he said. ''I want her to know she's going to have a daddy at last.''

Carly cried all through the ceremony at the Baptist Church. Francey wore a pale lilac dress of soft silk and chiffon, and carried two dozen white orchids that were splotched with purple. She told Walt she didn't care if all of Verity thought it was overdone and in poor taste, but she was going to have a wedding Verity would talk of for a long time. Walt just nodded and grinned and shelled out the money.

The reception was at the Willows, even though barely half the people could fit in there. The weather cooperated, and the lawn was strewn with umbrella-covered tables, which accommodated all those attending the reception, which was just about everyone in Verity and the surrounding countryside. Zelda Marie and Joe Bob were there with both sets of parents.

The night before the wedding, Walt presented Francey with his wedding present. "I bought that land you've always liked, just north of town. That place with the little hill on it and that big oak tree on top. I thought you'd like for us to build a house on that knoll. You can see it for a couple miles. I figure no woman wants to live in another woman's house, and I've lived in this one long enough. We can spend the summer drawing up plans."

Francey flung her arms around him and kissed his ear. "Walt, you are just about the kindest man in the whole world."

"I'm a man in love," he said, holding her wrist, "and anything that makes you happy I want to be responsible for."

Carly spent her mother's wedding night thinking of Cole Coleridge. He'd called Friday afternoon to invite her to dinner Saturday, but she'd told him she was flying home to Verity. She'd be back Sunday afternoon. He said he might call her Sunday evening. Might.

She'd worried about herself a couple of years ago. Why couldn't she *feel* something deep down inside her like she had for Boomer? She'd so enjoyed making love with him, for a while she'd worried if perhaps she was a nympho, but now she'd wondered why she didn't just hop into bed with one of the guys who continuously begged her. Had desire died when Boomer left her? And then she found it awakened in the most unlikely place, and with the most unlikely person when the slim, elegant Cole Coleridge entered her life. Entered? He hadn't really become part of her life.

Yet.

When Carly drove out to Zelda Marie's the next day, she wondered how her friend could live like that. She and Joe Bob and their four kids in that little cottage! "Joe Bob doesn't earn enough for us to rent a house in town," Zelda Marie explained. "If Daddy didn't let us live here I don't know what we'd do."

"Has Joe Bob ever thought of quitting his father's garage? There's scads of work in the oil business."

Zelda Marie cocked her head and looked at Carly. "What, and work real hard? You must be foolin'."

Over rose hip tea which Carly had brought, knowing Zelda Marie probably didn't have anything that was a luxury, Carly told her, "I met a beautiful man."

"Beautiful? A man beautiful?" But Zelda Marie looked at Carly with eager eyes.

"Well, I don't think it's going any place, but I never met a man like him."

"Like what?"

"Rich. And he's nice-looking, not really handsome but sort of mysterious, aloof in some ways. Elegant looking. He moves sort of like I imagine a panther must move, with real grace. He dances like a dream. And he kisses nice. You know, so many men don't even know how to kiss."

No, Zelda Marie didn't know. Joe Bob was the only man she'd ever done anything at all with, and she didn't know how any other one did anything. Certainly Joe Bob didn't waste his time on kisses.

"Well, he kisses real nice. But I don't dare let myself care too much. I'm not in his class. He's not going to marry someone like me."

"What do you mean, *someone like* you? You're special, Carly. I bet you've had half a dozen proposals."

"It's true. But they've all been from guys I haven't cared a twig about. I didn't even want to sleep with them, much less spend the rest of my life with them."

"You been to bed with anybody since Boomer?"

Carly shook her head. "Nope. It's taken me years to stop comparing every guy I go out with to Boomer, and you know, he was just a teenager out for some sex and I was the hometown girl who gave it to him. I don't think Boomer really loved me. I think maybe at first he thought he did.''

"So what's the difference between thinking you're in love and actually being in love?''

Carly shrugged. ''I don't know. But whatever it was, the flame went out a lot sooner for him than me. All he wanted me for was a roll in the hay, and I got my heart all entangled with him. It's about time I close that drawer and keep it shut, and not do that to myself again. I'm having fun with Cole, and maybe I'll even sleep with him, but I'm not going to get caught up in any false expectations.''

"Marriage isn't the be all and end all,'' Zelda Marie said.

"I hope it is for Mom and Walt.''

"Your mom's some lady,'' Zelda Marie said, turning on the gas stove so she could prepare a bottle for her littlest one.

"I'm real proud of her. And someday she's going to be real proud of me.''

Zelda Marie smiled at Carly. ''Honey, your mother's been proud of you since the day you were born.''

Carly sighed. ''I guess. I wonder how our lives might have been different if my father hadn't been killed in the war.''

"Who knows . . . my daddy's turning out to be a real strong support. Didja see that menagerie out back?''

"Who could miss it?''

"All those little orphan lambs and calves are mine. Mine to nurse and to raise . . . to keep and sell. I'm waiting on a colt. That's what I want. I want to raise horses. Horses that'll win shows and make me a bundle of money, and famous, too.''

Sure, Carly thought. We all need dreams to keep us going.

"I wonder,'' Francey said, stretching, ''if I married you for your money.''

It was the morning of her first full day of being Frances Davis. The sliding-glass door was open and the soft Caribbean air billowed the curtains. Even from her prone position on the bed she could see the vibrant shades of the sea: aquamarine, turquoise, pale blue, dark purple.

Nothing covered them.

"I think I've bought my way into heaven, then," Walt murmured, opening one eye. They hadn't gotten to sleep before three.

Francey sighed with contentment. "If I'd known marriage would be this wonderful I'd have said yes years ago. I want champagne for breakfast," she murmured, biting him gently.

"My darling, you shall have anything you want for breakfast or for any other time of the day or night."

She ran her tongue up his belly, across his chest, until her mouth met his. "You are the sexiest man in the entire universe."

"Hey, it's you doing all the work," he grinned.

"Work? You call this work?"

He pulled her over on top of him. "Well, what would you call it."

"Sheer passion," she whispered as he stretched to take a nipple in his mouth.

"Oh, God," she said, as she began to move rhythmically back and forth.

"You're riding me to the moon," he gasped.

"And the sun and the stars and whatever else is up there called heaven," she managed to say before she was at a loss for words. Or thoughts. Or anything else but love.

CHAPTER 14

On Sunday morning, at nine-thirty, the ringing phone awakened Boomer. He glanced at the digital clock, its numbers staring at him. He never slept this late.

"Boomer, hope I didn't wake you." It was Dan.

"Hell, no," Boomer murmured, his eyes still fogged with sleep.

"Come on over for brunch. One hour."

Boomer's eyes focused. "Brunch?"

"Here's the address." Dan sounded as though he were reading from something. "It's not far from you." Dan began to give vague directions, and then a female voice cut in. "Got a pencil?" and gave very specific ones. "It's apartment 3D."

Boomer raised himself on an elbow. "And who are you?"

She laughed, a silvery sound reminding Boomer of a waterfall. "Tessa Oldfield."

Boomer nodded. "An hour."

"Or less is okay," she said.

Brunch? He hauled himself out of bed, showered, and slipped into tan chinos and a yellow short-sleeved shirt. Another Harley-Davidson day, he thought, looking out at the bright glare. He grabbed the paper on which he'd written Tessa's directions and took off. As he drove through the empty Sunday morning streets, he wondered why anyone would want to live anyplace but Texas. But then there was no humidity today, for a change, and the sky looked as if it were part of a Technicolor movie.

He parked in front of an upscale apartment complex, maybe not as ritzy as Alex's, but definitely in the high-rent category. He followed a path that pointed to the D Complex, walking on flagstone steps surrounded by colorful impatiens and petunias.

Dan answered his ring, more dressed up than usual, except that his jacket was over the back of a chair and his sleeves were rolled up. Boomer whistled, walking in, absorbing his surroundings.

"Something, huh?" Dan said, and Boomer could swear there was pride in his voice.

He turned to look from the room to Dan, a question in his eyes.

A woman who barely came up to his chest appeared in a doorway, wiping her hands on a white muslin apron. She looked about eighteen, he thought, with eyes that sparkled like the sea when it was shallow.

"I'm Tessa. I've been hearing about you ever since we woke up."

We woke up? Boomer glanced over Tessa's head at Dan, who wore a look of delighted amazement.

"Anything you don't like in an omelet?" she asked.

"Mushrooms."

She gestured with her head. "Come on out to the kitchen, men, and pour yourselves coffee. I like company while I cook."

Dan poured coffee from a sleekly modern coffee maker while Boomer surveyed the narrow room.

"Tessa's an interior decorator, in case you're wondering."

She whisked the omelet, shredding cheese onto it, onions, red and green peppers, crumbled bacon in the center. She slid it expertly, held the pan above the flame, and said, "Voilà."

Boomer didn't know what he was doing here, but it didn't matter.

"I don't have a formal dining room," Tessa said, handing a plate to each of the men, "but it's such a lovely day the patio seems right."

The table, Boomer observed, was set with expensive silver and crystal, colorful hand-embroidered place mats and napkins, all under a blue-and-white striped umbrella. Little rolls, sugar encrusted, were enclosed by a napkin. Fresh red and white carnations were in the center of the table.

Dan had never mentioned her, but then Dan didn't know that Boomer had taken Alex to the lake yesterday. Dan didn't even know about the lake. About Alex, all he knew was that somehow she was bankrolling them.

The omelet was sheer heaven. "You don't make it as a decorator," Boomer said, "you could always hire out as a cook."

Tessa's smile was delightful. Already Boomer thought Dan a lucky man and wondered aloud, "How long has this been going on?"

Dan and Tessa looked at each other, laughing. Dan glanced at his watch. "Almost exactly twenty-three hours and twenty minutes, give or take."

Before Boomer could comment, Dan continued, "Tessa's got some ideas that I want you to hear soon's we're finished eating."

None of them, however, seemed in a hurry to finish, lingering over cups of coffee.

Artfully arranged slices of melon, papaya, and grapes followed the omelet. And more cups of coffee. After the third cup, Boomer commented, "This may possibly be the best coffee in the world."

"I like you, too," Tessa said. Boomer wasn't used to such forthright women, but he guessed she'd zeroed in on part of what he meant.

"I want you to hear Tessa's ideas."

Boomer leaned back in the padded chair, surprised at its comfort. "I'm listening."

Tessa began, her eyes shining. "Dan and I've been looking at his plans for your apartments all morning . . ." She stopped to look at Dan and smiled. "Well, part of the morning. Do you know that what you're doing no one else around here's trying?"

Boomer nodded. "Of course we know that. That's the point."

"I can get you *at least* fifty thousand dollars more an apartment than whatever you'll ask if you're going to sell them. Or if you rent them, five hundred a month more. At a minimum." She sat back very erect, her hands folded on the table, looking for just a minute like a schoolgirl who'd just given the right answer and was waiting for the teacher's approval.

"Okay, I'll bite. How?"

"By decorating them. Do you know who Dorothy Draper is?"

When he didn't respond she went on. "She's my idol. She decorated the Greenbriar."

Which meant absolutely nothing to either of the men.

"It's just about the top resort in the whole country, in White Sulphur Springs, West Virginia. She decorated all the rooms, each one different. Each one exquisite. Now, my taste tends, to be more modern than hers.

"Of course, who knows, five years from now my taste may

have changed. And I adapt pretty gracefully. But if you let me decorate three—or, my God, I'd give my eyeteeth for five—model apartments, you'll get more money. Who knows, some may even buy the furniture, too. A package. But even if they're going to bring their own antiques or whatever, the whole look'll sell the apartments, rentals or otherwise. They'll look elegant, I promise you. They'll look," she closed her eyes, "distinctive. Tessa distinctive."

"Like this," Boomer gestured toward the living room.

"Oh, each one completely different, of course, but you get the general idea of what I can do." Then she asked, "What about landscaping?"

Boomer had an answer for that. "Once we're nearly done I thought I'd call in a landscape firm and turn it over to them."

"No." Tessa shook her head. "Let Dan and me do that. I know it doesn't sound like much, but he told me he took a landscape architecture course years ago, and I have definite tastes. And I'm original. Let's make the outdoors as exotic as the indoors. Let's get in all the newspapers. Let's get people lusting to live here."

"Lusting?" Boomer laughed. He noticed that under the table Tessa's bare foot was running up the inside of Dan's cuff. "So, what do you want me to do?"

Dan leaned forward. "Let's form a business. Tessa's not ready to quit her job with David Jones yet, but . . ."

". . . but if and when David hears I'm moonlighting he'll have my head on a platter."

"Hey," Boomer threw up his hands, "this is all pretty sudden. Twenty-four hours ago you didn't even know Tessa," he said to Dan.

"And one day you and I played handball and the next we were partners."

"Let me think on it," Boomer said. "It has its appeal but it'll take more money." He suspected it was already a fait accompli. He liked Tessa, and if Dan wasn't already in love with her he was on the way. Love? In one day?

When he returned to his apartment in the middle of the

afternoon, he took a beer out of the refrigerator, picked up the phone and carried it to the couch, where he stretched out and dialed Alex's number.

"Hi." His voice was soft, intimate.

"Well." He could tell she was smiling. "How nice."

"Am I interrupting anything?"

"Nothing that can't wait. I'm just getting ready to go over to my parents for the ritual Sunday night supper." She hadn't phoned Cole after all.

"How do I go about checking up on someone?"

"Credit rating, you mean?" Her first thought always concerned money.

"That and other things. I want to find out about a woman. Name's Tessa Oldfield."

A woman? Alex felt a plop in the middle of her stomach; was it her heart sinking?

After Boomer gave details on Tessa's background there was a moment's hesitation. "Is this business or personal?"

Did he detect a note of jealousy? He hoped so. "Business. I want to know how good she is at her job and what kind of person she is."

"I know someone who can find out. What's her name again?"

He repeated it, and then said. "I won't keep you. I guess I'd been hoping . . ."

"Then give me more notice," Alex said. "I promised my parents just a couple of hours ago."

Tuesday afternoon Alex appeared at the construction site, pulling up in her silver Jaguar, dressed in black silk pants and a black-and-white polka dot blouse that had a collar so big it became a ruffle. A mixture of elegant businesslike and totally feminine. Small pearl earrings were her only jewelry.

She picked her way through the workmen until she found Boomer, shirtless in the hot afternoon. He rubbed the back of his hand across his forehead to wipe the sweat away.

"You're supposed to sit behind a desk and let others do the heavy work," she said.

"I'm not like others."

"I know."

"You're a sight for sore eyes."

She smiled at him, still astonished to find herself flattered by the likes of Boomer Bannerman. "I have the information you wanted."

He took her arm and led her toward a grove of trees. "That was fast."

"This lady sounds too good to be true. A friend of yours?"

"If she's that good, she may become one. Did you run a check like this on me?"

"Of course." She wanted to kiss him, kiss the corners of his smile. Right here in front of the workmen.

She handed him two sheets of paper. He squinted as he read it.

"You're a quick reader. Do you do everything quickly?"

He didn't smile as he looked at her. "There are some things I take a great deal of time doing."

Gooseflesh ran down her spine as someone called out to him, and he said, "Just a minute. Don't go away."

When he returned he said, "How about dinner tomorrow night?"

"I'd like that." She'd had to come by. It had been three days since she'd seen him, and she spent half her time thinking of him. She knew it was silly. They came from different worlds.

"Pick you up at seven?"

She nodded and, picking her way through the debris, gingerly walked back to her car. He watched her go. She didn't look all that sexy from the rear, but he kept thinking of touching her, of really kissing her, of . . .

He called her at work the next day. "Don't dress up. Real informal."

Maybe he didn't even know how to dress up. Just because his father had been in the state legislature didn't mean he had class. Now, the U.S. Congress, that was different. Or the governor. She knew all of them. On the other hand, there was LBJ. Even when he was in the White House he wouldn't have known class if he'd fallen over it. Lady Bird was another story. How could she have stayed married to that man, and the way he'd treated her, in public, too?

When Boomer arrived, he wore the same outfit he'd worn Saturday. Freshly laundered, but the same. "You're taking me someplace I've never been before, I gather. You always do."

"Always?" He laughed. It was only the third time they'd been out together. "I've got some people I want you to meet. We want to pick your brains."

Alex felt a stab of disappointment. She'd struggled all her life to be accepted for her mind, and here was this man who, except for a brief good night kiss, accepted her on those terms. But she found herself wanting more.

"What are you laughing at?" he asked as they drove along.

"The irony of life," Alex answered. "Who are these people I'm meeting?"

"One is the lady who you said is too good to be true."

"Tessa Oldfield?" In a way she felt a sense of relief. He hadn't wanted a background check for personal reasons.

"The other's Dan . . ."

"Ah," she remembered. "Your architect."

He looked over at her. "Good memory."

"I have money invested in this, remember?"

"So, some of this is your money?"

Alex looked straight ahead. She hadn't wanted him to know.

"Dan quit his job, just like that. Works at the site, doing carpentry work . . ."

"You attract recklessness."

"Hey, you hardly know a thing about me."

But she knew how she felt. "I don't know if you're reckless," Alex said, "but you invite that in others."

He reached a hand across the stick shift, enfolding the hand in her lap. His eyes danced.

She continued to stare straight ahead. "It's not just me. I'm sure you have the same impact on others."

"Reckless, huh?" She could tell he liked that.

"And you've never been reckless in your life before. Right?"

"Not true. I take financial risks all the time. I thrive on risks."

He tightened his hold on her hand, driving expertly with just his left one.

"Scared?" he asked. "Not of the road. Of feeling reckless?"

Alex smiled. "It's the same sort of feeling the motorcycle ride gave me."

"I never get used to that," Boomer said, alternating glances between the street and Alex. "It's why I do it. Living on the edge. Hoping for safety, but . . ." He shrugged.

It was the first time she'd been with a man where she hadn't been in control. She wondered, if she tried, if she could be.

CHAPTER 15

"I think you should consider forming a corporation. Or a partnership," Alex said.

"What's the difference?" Tessa asked.

"Different tax advantages." Alex shrugged. "Any of you three have a lawyer?"

Tessa, Dan, and Boomer exchanged glances.

"You must," Boomer said.

"You don't need mine." She smiled. "He's too high powered and expensive for what you need. Forming a business partnership is relatively simple, but you need the nuances explained. I'll get someone for you."

Alex sat back in the chair. She envied these three. She'd been impressed with Tessa before even meeting her, but now she found herself also liking her. She was bright and enthusiastic, with an infectious joie de vivre. Alex suspected maybe here was a friend.

"You haven't known each other very long," she warned.

"Partnerships are like marriage. I've known some that have made the partners really unhappy."

"Are they hard to dissolve?" Boomer asked.

"Not with the assets you have now, but if you make money . . ."

"*If* we make money?" Tessa whooped. But then she added, "I don't want this to be known. I've got to keep my job until, well, one of us has to bring in some money."

"At least I won't have to pay rent anymore," Dan said.

There was a second's silence. If they'd been alone Boomer would have asked, Move in with her when you haven't known her a week?

But Dan went on. "We're going to form another partnership. We're getting married Saturday at noon."

Good Lord, thought Boomer.

Tessa giggled. "Exactly one week after we met." She turned to Alex. "I know we don't really know each other, but I don't have any real friends here yet. Would you—I mean, you don't have to, but I'd really appreciate you being my maid of honor." She reached out and touched Alex's hand, smiling into her eyes.

Alex had signed up to participate in the tennis tournament at the club. Suddenly, that didn't seem important even though she'd been practicing for it for months. "I'm flattered," she answered, wondering why she was. She couldn't understand herself lately. It wasn't just Boomer, it was spreading to other parts of her life. At least, parts to which he was connected.

It didn't take Cole long to realize he wanted Carly. Wanted her every night and every day. Yet, he told himself, she wasn't his kind of woman. She wouldn't fit into Houston society. His parents would be shocked. His friends, too.

Well, he didn't have to marry her. He could just have an affair with her. That's what he wanted, a hot, torrid affair.

Then he laughed at himself. Hot and torrid. Sure. He didn't even know how to be hot and torrid.

He'd always been afraid that the women he took to bed considered him tepid. Not wild and wonderful.

But Carly would be wild and wonderful. He dreamt of her. Asleep and awake.

When he'd pick her up, he tried not to look directly at her, not to let her see the hunger he knew was in his eyes. When they parted, he watched those long perfectly shaped legs, the way her derrière moved, he watched her blond hair, piled on top of her head sometimes, or curling along her shoulders.

He wondered what her apartment was like. And what did she think of him? Did she ever think of him when they were apart? Did she tell her friends about him?

Carly was the first woman who had ever made him question himself. And she did it just by being the most beautiful woman that Cole Coleridge had ever seen. He wondered if Carly was even aware of what she did to men.

The first week in February, his father barged into Cole's office. "We have a marvelous opportunity staring us in the face in Mexico," he said. "That hotel man, José Rosas y Riberas, has asked us to bankroll a new hotel complex he's building in Acapulco. After he's finished building that one, he wants to start another one north of there, too, in a town he's certain is *the* next Mexican resort area. I'd like getting a toehold in Mexico. Fly down this weekend to talk with him. Trouble is, his English is probably as limited as your Spanish is."

"And my Spanish is nil," Cole said. But the idea intrigued him. Entering the money market in Mexico, and with someone like Casas.

"When you get down there, hire an interpreter. No problem."

But that night, when Cole and Carly were having a late supper after attending an Alley Theater production, Cole told her about the approaching Mexican visit.

"I'll miss you," he told her. She was aware this was the most personal thing he'd said to her in their six weeks of dating.

He continued, "Hope I get by, all I know is sí and no habla español."

Carly smiled at him. "My Spanish is very good."

Cole looked at her, sitting back in his chair and gazing into her eyes. "Are you suggesting what I think you are?"

"I didn't know I was suggesting anything."

Cole put a hand on her arm. "Come with me, Carly. Separate rooms. Come be my interpreter."

The thought of her in a bathing suit nearly drove him wild.

Carly sat in the window seat, her legs crossed with little ropes that passed for sandals barely covering her graceful feet, with their brightly polished red toenails.

Cole thought of kissing those toes, one by one. That thought had surprised him because he'd always thought feet rather ugly and certainly had never thought of kissing a toe. As Carly turned the pages of the in-flight magazine, Cole thought of putting each of those toes into his mouth and sucking them. Of tickling the arch of her feet with his tongue.

He leaned his head back and closed his eyes. He thought he must be going nuts. Who the hell sucked anyone's toes?

"You all right?" He heard her voice and felt her hand on his arm, through the jacket of his suit.

"Sure, why?" His eyes flew open.

"You moaned."

Oh, God. "I don't know where my mind was."

She was smiling at him. "I think this is such fun. Acapulco!"

Acapulco in 1969 was still where dream vacations took place. Carly could hardly sleep the night before they took off. Cole offered her the window seat and laughed at her enthusiasm as she exclaimed at the rugged mountain ranges that carved themselves into the length of Mexico. Her elbow touched Cole's now and then. She liked the way he smelled, and she supposed that was the result of expensive after-shave. She wondered if he could smell the perfume she'd spent so much on? She'd also paid a scandalous amount of money for a nightgown and peignoir, not to mention a new bathing suit. Two evening gowns used up the last of her savings.

She wondered why she'd bought the nightgown. Cole wasn't likely to see it.

Cole, his eyes closed, reached over to hold her hand, imagining those breasts of hers uncovered, visualizing pressing his hand against her white belly, kissing that blue vein in her neck, gently biting her shoulder, flicking his tongue in her ear.

He had never been obsessed with a woman before. When he was at Harvard, and even more so at Stanford, he had had women, but of all the women he'd had, Alex was the only one he'd spent any time really thinking about. And most of that was spent wondering if she would ever lose her cool, if she really liked the things they had done together, if she ever thought of them as a couple when they made love. It seemed to him that she was experiencing pleasure in a vacuum, that it had nothing to do with him. Alex never surrendered herself to sex, but seemed to demand something from him. He was never sure whether or not he delivered.

Carly with her dewy lips and those round blue eyes, looked like she would actually enjoy sex.

He wondered if she had the same feelings for him, sometimes he thought she did. It was in the way she looked at him, and the way his hand felt when their fingers brushed together.

Now here he was, with Carly, flying away to the tropics. And he'd hold her in his arms because he knew he was going to dance with her. That wouldn't be going too far, and her body would move next to his, his arm would be around her, and she'd be so close he would feel her breath.

It turned out that Señor Rosas's English was impeccable. As was his eye for beautiful women. The second he laid eyes on Carly, he wanted her. She was so blond, so voluptuous, so seductive. At the same time there were those big round innocent-looking eyes and that uninhibited way of laughing. He suspected that Mr. Coleridge had brought her to seduce him, to assure himself of the deal. Yet, she did not flirt with him, or flaunt her considerable assets.

He knew she and Cole had separate rooms, for he had made the reservations.

He was sorry he had brought his wife. She was a beautiful woman whom he hoped Mr. Coleridge would find delightful. The rich American could see that Mexican women could be sophisticated and alluring, too. He was proud of his wife, considering her a business asset as well as the excellent mother of their three children.

Señora Rosas was delightful. She looked more like a *Vogue* cover model than the mother of three children, two of them teenagers.

The men agreed to get together again at six to talk business, but now it was siesta time. Carly was thankful, for she wondered how much longer she could stay awake after two margaritas at lunch.

"I'm going down to the beach," she told Cole on their way up in the elevator. "Under one of those umbrellas and let the surf lull me to sleep, as though I need anything to do that. No wonder Mexicans take siestas."

Cole knew if he joined her he wouldn't be in a frame of mind to discuss business in two hours. He'd take a short nap in his room and a cold shower before dressing to meet Señor Rosas. He'd put Carly out of his mind and out of his sight and concentrate on how far he thought the bank should go into this Mexican deal. It seemed sweet, right now. He'd phone his father with the details tomorrow, Tuesday. Wednesday Señor Rosas wanted to fly them in his private plane to a little fishing village, where he had visions of making the miles of sand beaches into Mexico's next big playground. Let the middle class go to Puerto Vallarta and Mazatlán, he envisioned a resort of such luxurious proportions as to stagger the imagination and attract the pocketbooks of the rich and famous.

He wasn't proposing to develop it for another couple of years, not until after this hotel deal.

Señor Rosas was from Monterrey, where his family had

made their fortunes in steel, and now he was turning his gaze toward other horizons. He probably could have built the hotel with his own money, but he wanted American capital, American connections that would attract Americans to his resort.

"It will be built with Mexican labor, as required by law, but I want American know-how. I want an American architect. I want the Americans who visit to have no complaints that it is lacking any luxuries to which they are accustomed, but I also want it to contain the charm of Mexico."

"If it's built with Mexican labor," Cole said, "the American builders will be driven crazy with the slowness and the lack of efficiency."

Señor Rosas sighed. "I know. I shall have to give that thought."

"An American foreman on the job site would help," Cole suggested.

"I shall work things out," Rosas said, more to himself than to Cole.

Cole was interested. He knew his father would be, too. Expanding into world markets.

Señor Rosas was suggesting that they might like to see some night life, see the swinging side of Acapulco. Would eight o'clock be a good time to meet in the lobby? His car would be waiting for them.

Carly looked absolutely stunning. Her hair was piled high, curls cascading down the left side of her head. The black chiffon dress molded against her from the waist up with thin slivers of rhinestone straps while the skirt fell in soft folds from her waist. She decided to wear red satin high-heeled slippers and in her hair, above the dangling earrings that matched the dress's straps, she wore a single gigantic red hibiscus flower she had picked in the garden.

The red accents would have jarred the senior Coleridges, of that Cole was sure, but he found her wonderfully alluring. He had known her shoulders would look like that. Ordinarily Cole would have been pleased to dance with someone of the exotic looks of Señora Rosas, a delightful, intelligent conversationalist, who talked more when not overshadowed by her husband, but he could not keep his eyes off Carly, dancing with Rosas across the room. The Mexican had asked Carly to dance before Cole had a chance even to sit down.

"Señorita Anderson seems to be having a good time," Señora Rosas said, observing Cole's glances. "This afternoon on the beach we conversed mostly in Spanish. Her accent is marvelous."

Cole wondered why he felt pride at that.

The music switched to a fast Latin beat and he had to apologize to the señora. "I'm afraid this isn't the kind of music I can dance to." They wound their way back to their table and sat down.

Carly and Señor Rosas kept up with the music, and Cole noted that Carly had already captured the gaze of every male and most women. Soon the couple was the center of attention and obviously enjoying it. Cole saw Señor Rosas whisper something to Carly, and with eyes sparkling she nodded her head. They danced over to the bandstand and Rosas said something to the bandleader. In a few minutes a tango began. The floor cleared, and Carly and Rosas took over, hamming it up for their audience. Where in the world had she learned to tango so expertly?

Señora Rosas was smiling, sipping her margarita, and enjoying the spectacle her husband was creating. "Aren't they fantastic?" she said. He could see no evidence of jealousy.

Why couldn't he enjoy himself, watching Carly be the center of attention, proud that she was with him? And he knew why. He wanted her. He desired her all to himself. He craved to hold her in his arms, feel her move against him, see her eyes laughing up at him. He'd wanted her, he knew, from the moment he'd first seen her standing in the doorway of his office.

Applause broke out from the other dancers as the music ended, and he saw Carly and Rosas threading their way through the tables. He stood as they returned and held out Carly's chair.

"Isn't this fun?" Carly said, breathless. "My, Señor Rosas, you sure know how to dance. I don't know when I've enjoyed myself so much." But, as she sat down she reached under the table for Cole's hand and squeezed it. He looked at her and her eyes met his. Her hand remained in his and her leg brushed his fleetingly.

The orchestra segued smoothly into a medley of American songs. "Your turn," she said to Cole.

He stood up and held out his hand, leading her onto the dance floor. She moved into his arms.

"We've never danced," she said, her voice a whisper. "I've lain awake nights wondering how it would feel to be in your arms."

He pulled her against him, so close he could feel the beating of her heart, the swell of her breast.

"And that may be just where you'll be for the next five days." He wondered why his voice sounded so unnatural. "In my arms."

"Promises, promises," she breathed into his ear.

CHAPTER 16

In Verity, Francey hummed happily.

Though the new house wasn't finished, she and Walt had moved in. It was a gracious, sprawling single-story home of ten rooms. One would think it was made of windows, for there was glass everyplace; you could look out over the countryside and see for miles, even see across town, over the treetops where the drooping willows and the pond of the Willows were visible.

Francey called the house her refuge. The kitchen was outfitted with more appliances than the restaurant, yet there was a homey atmosphere to it and they ate more often there than in the formal dining room. There was an office, too, and since

they decided they didn't want to be apart, even when they had
work to do at home, it was outfitted with two large oak desks,
on opposite sides of the room so that if they were both working
at the same time they wouldn't bother each other. It was here
that Francey kept her accounts and did her ordering mornings.
If Walt used his desk at all, he did it evenings when Francey
was at the restaurant. He had dinner there every evening, and
Francey always took time to have a leisurely dinner with him.
She changed the menu weekly so that he would never tire of
the food.

Their bedroom, Francey thought, could have fit hers and
Carly's bedrooms—and the living room—from the little house
where she'd lived. It was done up in Wedgwood blue and
cream, and Francey had been surprised that Walt had wanted
to be so involved with the decorating. She approved of his
taste. She told him he certainly improved hers. She thought the
whole place looked like it should be on the cover of *Better
Homes & Gardens*. She had never seen a house she loved more.

A princess in a fairytale, that's what she'd become.

One beautiful morning at breakfast, as she glanced out over
the backyard with its neat rows of marigolds, petunias, and
roses and a riotous border of variegated nasturtiums, she'd said,
"Wouldn't it be fun to have a greenhouse? We could start
seeds and have seedlings ready to transplant all year long. We
could grow our own herbs, too."

Neither Walt's mother nor his wife had ever used herbs.
Onions were as far as either of them had gotten around to, in
flavoring the regular routine of meat.

It was just a casual statement which she forgot two minutes
after she'd said it. Walt made no comment. But three and a
half weeks later, at two-thirty on a Monday afternoon, a truck
pulled up in front of the Davis house. "Where do you want
it?" the driver asked Francey.

It was prefabricated, in hundreds of pieces, and it took the
trucker and a helper until after dark to unload the parts for the

twelve-by-fifteen foot greenhouse, which included an automatic sprinkler system.

Francey could hardly believe it. She chuckled the whole time the men worked on unloading all that glass and metal.

When Walt drove up the long driveway and saw the truck, Francey was waiting for him and he could smell a cake baking in the oven. He just bet it was chocolate.

Francey greeted him with a kiss, which wasn't unusual, but she also threw her arms around him and said, her voice teary, "There isn't a person in the whole universe any sweeter'n you are."

"Funny," he grinned, "I thought it was the other way around."

"You silly man, I don't know a thing about starting seeds and transplanting."

"Well," he suggested, "let's go over to the library," which was on the second floor of the building that housed the electric company downstairs, "and find some catalogs to send for. We can drive over to that bookstore in Corpus and see what they have, too. You can figure all that out while we put it together."

"We? I don't know anything about that kind of stuff."

" 'Bout time you expand your horizons."

They had a wonderful time putting it all together weekends before Francey went off to the Willows at four. It became a passion they shared. In November and December they poured over catalogs: Park Seed, Burpees, White Flower Farm. Even Thompsons and Morgans all the way from England. Walt drew plans, and they sat around and discussed what would go where and decided they maybe should buy the lot in back of them so they could do all they wanted with all the seeds.

In the spring, after they'd mixed the earth just as the books told them to, and had laboriously planted each seedling to the right depth and labeled them, they sat on the back patio, drinking iced tea and staring beyond the pool at the greenhouse they'd constructed as if they could see and hear the seeds sprouting through the dark earth.

Walt always waited to go to bed until Francey got home

from the restaurant around ten, and when the evenings were warm they kicked off their shoes and, with Tony Bennett or Frank Sinatra on the phonograph in the living room, which they could hear through the open windows, they'd dance in the grass to the slow old sensual rhythms they had grown up listening to.

Since Carly always asked about Zelda Marie in her weekly letters, Francey decided she ought to drive out there one day and see for herself how the young woman was faring.

She hadn't been out to the Spencers since Zelda Marie's wedding reception nearly eight years ago. When Francey drove up the long tree-lined dirt drive past the big Spencer house and up the lane to the cottage where Zelda Marie lived, she was appalled at the sight that greeted her.

Zelda Marie's lawn looked as if it hadn't been mowed in a month of Sundays. Lambs cavorted around the side yard, and there were kittens and puppies every place. The porch was strewn with toys which looked like they were relics from the Salvation Army. A couple of Adirondack chairs and a wooden swing which hung from the ceiling all had peeling paint.

Zelda Marie must have heard her coming up the driveway, for she opened the screen door, which had three holes in it, and smiled. "How wonderful. I'd hug you but I've got my hands full." On one hip was her youngest, and holding her other hand was a baby scarcely able to walk. The house looked like a cyclone had swept through it.

Francey had the urge to roll up her sleeves, don an apron, and start scrubbing. In the kitchen, dishes were piled high.

Four other children, ages two to seven, ran around the house in bare feet, stumbling over toys and yelling at the top of their lungs, pretending to be Indians. They each wore paper crayon-colored feathers in bands around their heads. The dining-room table was loaded with cut-up paper and two dozen crayons and scissors.

"You can see what we've been doing," Zelda Marie said

to Francey, no hint of apology in her voice. "Can I get you a cup of coffee?"

Francey hesitated, but then decided she would fight her distaste over the condition of the kitchen and get Zelda Marie to sit down and talk. "That sounds nice," she said.

Zelda Marie poured Kool-Aid for the older children and shooed them outside, put the baby in the crib, and was left with only the nearly-two-year-old clutching her skirt. It seemed relatively quiet, with the children outside, and Francey began to breathe a little easier.

She and Zelda Marie, who handed a couple of cookies to the two-year-old, sat at the kitchen table, scratched and covered with the debris of the children's artistic endeavors.

"Carly says she doesn't hear from you, so I thought I'd give her a firsthand report."

Zelda Marie's face was drawn and tired. "You can tell her firsthand why I never seem to have time to write. All these kids. Sometimes I think it's time to get my tubes tied. I swear, all Joe Bob has to do is look at me and I get pregnant."

"So," Francey said, surprised at how good the coffee was, "why don't you?"

"Why don't I what?" Zelda Marie asked. "Have my tubes tied, you mean? I can't. Joe Bob would have a fit. He's Catholic."

"Are *you?*"

"No, but . . ."

"Seems to me that it's your body."

Zelda Marie thought about that. "Maybe, but Joe Bob'd be furious."

Francey cocked her head and looked at the young woman. "What about you? You like having these babies year after year?"

"Well, I do love 'em, but I think I've had about enough. But I can't, well, it sounds good, I'd sure like not to be pregnant all the time, and God knows, it's about more than I can do to handle them all. Joe Bob never does a thing. If I didn't work a big vegetable garden and we didn't have our own meat I don't know how we'd live. And he's not home most evenings, anyhow. Says the noise of the kids is too much for him.''

Francey stared at her, saying nothing.

Zelda Marie looked back at her. ''You're thinking why don't I hear what I'm saying, right? Listen, he'd leave me if I tied my tubes . . .''

Francey just kept staring at her.

Zelda Marie began to laugh. ''Mrs. Davis, I think it's just wonderful you came out here today and made me start thinking.'' She leaned over and kissed Francey's cheek.

''I don't even think it's a major operation anymore. I heard they do it with lasers. Don't even have to cut you open,'' Francey said.

''I'll think on it, honest I will.'' Zelda Marie glanced at her watch. ''Come on out to the barn with me. I've some lambs it's time to feed. You can help me.''

Francey discovered Zelda Marie was also training an orphan colt her father had turned over to her.

When Francey left, Zelda Marie said, ''Tell Carly I love her and I think of her and when she comes home, she's to come right out here and see me.''

They kissed each other good-bye. ''I don't know how you manage to look like you do,'' Zelda Marie said. ''My mother looks like a mother. You look like you should be in the movies. Mr. Davis sure is one lucky man.''

''I'm the one who's lucky,'' Francey answered.

''Nice to know someone enjoys marriage,'' Zelda Marie said.

Francey shook her head all the way back to town. She wondered where Zelda Marie got the stamina. Lambs and colts along with all those children? No wonder her house looked like it did.

CHAPTER 17

Carly smiled up at Cole as they danced, "I don't know when I've had more fun," she said.

He pulled her even closer. His voice was low, in her ear. "You look beautiful." But then she always did.

She moved her leg so that it met his. And though his hand against her back felt impersonal, the look in his eyes was not. She wondered if there was any sense of playfulness about him. Well, maybe she could awaken one. She had another few days.

She hadn't been to bed with a man since Boomer Bannerman, and something about this aloof, always gentlemanly man challenged her. She melded her body to his and felt his hand around hers tighten. She smiled to herself.

The Rosas took them to a different night club, and then another one. Though Cole did not drink heavily, having but one drink in each, by the time they reached the third bistro, it was after midnight and Cole had loosened up enough that Carly could talk him into trying the cha-cha.

"You're a wonderful dancer," she told him, the sharp beat of the dance filling her whole being.

"It's all those years at Miss Shibley's dance school," he laughed, feeling a new sense of freedom. Certainly he was going into business with Señor Rosas, and maybe he wouldn't even call his father. Just go ahead with it.

When he danced, he had a rhythm Carly would never have imagined from such a stiff man. He threw his head back and laughed as they cha-cha'd. And in the slow numbers his hand wasn't impersonal against her back anymore. He held her as though he possessed her, as though she were a part of him, pressing her so that she knew he could feel her breasts against his chest. Her cheek next to his, she blew gently into his ear.

He almost missed a step, pulling his head back to gaze into her eyes. "Why, Carly Anderson, I do believe you're teasing me."

She smiled. She swore she could feel his heart beating through his shirt, felt her own blood coursing through her veins.

When they returned to the table, Señor Rosas said, "My wife tells me it is far past her bedtime." It was after one, but Carly had seen their heads together. She suspected Señora Rosas had suggested to her husband that they leave Cole and Carly alone.

When he dropped them off at the hotel, Señor Rosas said that he would leave Cole on his own the next day, to speak with his father and to study the figures he had given them. He would pick them up at nine Wednesday morning to fly north to see the property he wanted to develop in the future.

As they stood under the porte cochere, Cole asked, "Want a nightcap?"

"Not really," Carly said. "But I'd like to walk a bit. The air is so soft. And I love listening to the ocean."

"Come, then," he said, taking her hand and leading her down the steps to the beach. She kicked her high heels off and left them by a plumeria tree and walked barefoot down the steps behind Cole. From a distance, music floated into the night air, scented with the blossoms of tropical flowers.

"I feel like I'm in a romantic movie," Carly said. "The whole day has been just marvelous. I can't imagine a more perfect day."

Cole stopped and turned, a step down from her and, still holding her hand, pulled her to him. His other hand came up and brushed her cheek, and he said, "I've been wanting to do this all night." His lips crushed hers.

Carly sighed. "I've been wanting you to do that all night, too." He kissed her again, before resuming their walk to the beach.

The ocean broke gently against the sand. The glittering stars seemed close enough to touch.

When Carly picked up her long skirt and waded into the warm water, Cole thought he had never seen anyone or anything lovelier.

"Do you know how lovely you are?" he asked aloud, wondering if he should take off his shoes and socks to join her in the water.

She turned to smile at him, her skirt bunched up in her arms. "I feel beautiful right now. I like the way you look at me."

He didn't say anything, but stood on the dry sand staring at her, wishing he could be as abandoned, as free as she seemed. He wanted her as he had never wanted another woman, as perhaps he had never wanted anything. Did he dare? Would she be offended? Was it too soon?

He didn't care. Only the moment mattered to him, and for the first time in his life, he entered into something without thinking of the consequences.

Carly waded out of the ocean and into his arms.

After they'd walked up the long stairway hand in hand and she'd picked up her shoes under the fragrant frangipani tree, they took the elevator up to their floor. Cole followed her into her room, leaning down to kiss her lightly. Carly immediately turned off the air-conditioning and walked over to the sliding-glass doors and slid them open, strolling out onto the balcony, turning to face Cole.

He took off his jacket and folded it neatly across a chair. Then he walked out to her, gathering her in his arms. He ran his hand through her hair, tilting her head back and kissing her neck. He found her mouth, opened it with his tongue, his arms enfolding her, pulling her to him.

Could she really feel his heart beating in synchronization with hers? The even beats were like tom-toms, hypnotic in rhythm.

She felt his tongue touching hers. His fingers caressed her face. Desire welled within her, painfully strong.

Unzipping her dress, he led her over to the bed and sat on

it, his hands easing the dress off her shoulders, letting it fall to the floor. She slid out of her panties and kicked them onto the floor. As Cole gazed at her, he moaned.

She ran her hands down his wrists, up his arms, as his kisses became more insistent.

Then he picked her up and laid her on the bed, moving on top of her, looking down at her with eyes glazed with passion. He took her hand in his and kissed each of her fingers slowly, then kissed the pulse in her neck.

Arching her body beneath him, she cried out and threw her arms around him, pulling him in to her, raising herself to meet him.

They united easily, their rhythm frenzied, their passion unleashed.

Shudders shook Carly. The intensity was unexpected. She never wanted it to stop. She wanted the motion, the rhythm, the undulating togetherness to continue forever as the gentle insistent waves of warmth rolled over her, peaking and crashing until she was unconscious of everything except unbelievable exploding pleasure.

She heard Cole cry out as he buried his face in her neck.

On the day that Carly made love with Cole, and two days after Alex and Boomer made love for the first time, Zelda Marie decided she had taken it one too many times.

Joe Bob learned that his wife had had her tubes tied. It didn't take him two seconds to bring the whole length of his arm whizzing through the air. He hit Zelda Marie so hard on the side of her head that she fell to the floor. For a minute she made no sound, but sat blinking, breathing heavily.

"You goddamned bitch. You'll rot in hell for doing that to me." His voice was a fierce whisper.

Zelda Marie hoisted herself up, and stood, legs apart, her hands on her hips. Joe Bob raised his hand again, but before he could swing it Zelda Marie pulled her right arm back and, with adrenaline surging through her, pushed it right into his face, managing to land squarely between his left eye and his nose. They both heard a bone-crunching sound.

Joe Bob let out a wail.

Zelda Marie just looked at him. "You hit me one more time and that's the end of your life," she said, her voice on a cold, even keel. "You don't like what I do, you can move out. This is my parents' house, and if you don't like the way I live my life, you don't have to share it. And from now on, that's just what I'm going to do. Live my life. I'm not going to take care of the kids and do all the farm chores and cook dinner for you and wait to see if you're coming home to dinner, and then wait to be hit or not depending on your mood. You can walk out, and good riddance, that's fine with me. You don't support me anyhow. You don't like the rules, that's fine with me. Get your clothes out of the closet, and go somewhere else. I don't need you around here. You don't do nothing anyhow."

She didn't know whether he'd heard one word she said. "Shit, Zelda Marie," he said through his tears, "you done broke my nose."

She walked over so that she stood but inches from his face and looked up at him. "You ever hit me again, you ever raise one finger to hit me or the kids again, and that's not all about you's going to be broken."

He scrunched his face up in pain.

"You hear me?"

He nodded.

She turned away from him and he couldn't see the smile that covered her face. "You better take the truck and go see Doc Clarke."

Late the next afternoon, she looked out the window to see her father walking along the dirt drive from his house. He was leading his favorite horse, who was swollen with pregnancy.

"I think Cleo's going to foal within the next day," he said. "I've gotta go to a meeting in town, so thought I'd put her in your barn where you can look in on her till I get home." His eyes twinkled. He knew it was like giving Zelda Marie a present.

At seven-thirty Zelda Marie glanced in the barn and forgot

all about her children or anything else. She phoned her mother and, within ten minutes, Mrs. Spencer was running down the lane.

Zelda Marie never got around to putting her children to bed. She spent the evening in the barn with the belabored Cleo and Michael J., who was six. Zelda Marie thought he was old enough to experience birth. She invited Sally Mae, also, but her daughter said, "Ugh."

Cleo made loud gasping noises and writhed in pain. "She shouldn't be doing that," Zelda Marie told her son. "I'm going to have to go in after the foal."

"Go in?" Mike gulped.

"Yup," Zelda Marie answered, walking down the barn to the sink, where she started scrubbing her hands and right arm up to the elbow. "She needs help."

Cleo lay still, her eyes filled with fear as well as pain, hardly moving. Zelda Marie slipped her arm up inside the horse, who tried to lift her head, whinnying. Then it gave a gasp, which Zelda Marie thought meant she was dying. The mare lay motionless, her breathing ragged. Zelda Marie looked at Mike and wondered if he was going to be sick.

"Damn foal's stuck." She twisted her arm and made some moaning sounds herself, hoping she understood what she thought she felt inside the mare. One of the colt's legs was forward and the other was tucked underneath. Slowly she tried to pull the legs forward and then, with a look of relief on her face, pulled two little hooves out of Cleo, while Mike looked on wide-eyed. Zelda Marie had seen lots of calves and colts born, but she'd never had to turn one around, never had to go inside one before, except a goat once, when she was a teenager.

"Here," she said to her son, "get a towel and wipe off this little beauty while I get the afterbirth."

As Mike dried off the foal, it tried to stand on its wobbly legs. Cleo raised her head. "Just a couple of more minutes, girl," Zelda Marie said, soothingly.

"It's beautiful," Mike said.

It was. A beautiful black little filly whose eyes reminded

Zelda Marie of a Disney animal. "It's the most beautiful horse in the world," Mike said.

"Then we'll name it after the most beautiful person I know," Zelda Marie said. "Carly. This is my Carly."

"Yours?" said her father's voice from the barn door, but a big grin covered his face. "Well, well."

Cleo made a neighing sound and thrust herself up, looking around, wild-eyed until she spotted her newborn. She made some sort of sound that beckoned the wobbly-legged filly to her. The baby immediately began suckling its mother.

"How does it know to do that?" Mike asked.

Zelda Marie shrugged.

"Must've been easy," Mr. Spencer said. "She couldn't have been in labor long."

"You shoulda seen Ma," Mike said. "She stuck her arm up the horse's rear end and pulled it out."

Zelda Marie and her daddy stayed out in the barn until nearly two, to assure themselves the colt was nursing. Mike was sound asleep against a bale of hay.

After Mrs. Spencer got her grandchildren tucked into bed she spent hours, until midnight, cleaning the house. When her husband came in to urge her to come out to the barn and see the new colt, she admired it and acted as though it could have been her sixth grandchild. She looked around the barn and wished Zelda Marie could keep the house as neat as she kept the barn. But she knew there were only twenty-four hours in a day. Maybe she herself wouldn't have cared so much how her house looked if her husband hadn't cared about her. She knew Zelda Marie was living in an emotional vacuum.

Zelda Marie loved her kids, though, that was obvious. She just didn't care about what they wore or how the house looked. She got satisfaction from things other than cleaning her house or cooking meals. Remnants of lunch were strewn across the kitchen table when Mrs. Spencer arrived. A can of cold beans, a package of baloney, half drunk glasses of milk and orange juice. It broke Mrs. Spencer's heart. No happy person would leave her house like that, she thought.

Never once did she criticize Zelda Marie or even look as though she thought her daughter was anything but wonderful. Someone had to give her support. And certainly the children seemed happy and well adjusted. They laughed a lot and played together and, their table manners were even quite decent.

But they were hellions. Affectionate ones, however. They always greeted their grandparents with cries of joy and hugs, if not kisses from the boys.

The Spencers stayed overnight in Zelda Marie's bedroom while Zelda Marie dropped onto the couch. Mrs. Spencer thought Zelda Marie was going to have to add on to the house if each kid was to have a bedroom of his own as they grew up. She didn't know how she was going to do that. That useless son-in-law hardly brought home pocket money. Zelda Marie would have been better off not marrying him and just having the baby and waited until she found someone worthwhile. Mrs. Spencer wondered if her husband realized that, too.

She was glad he'd gotten over being angry at his daughter, acting like she'd done it to spite him. Now, Zelda Marie was what made his life worthwhile. The two of them spent hours poring over pedigree charts, breeding cattle and horses that Zelda Marie was convinced were going to win prizes.

As for Zelda Marie, she was growing her own food, slaughtering her own beef and pork, and was living in her parents' house rent free. She sewed all the kids' clothes. The cattle and horses cost her next to nothing, except for grain. She grew all the straw and hay she needed and had enough left over to sell.

She thought she better remember to phone Mrs. Davis and thank her. If she hadn't come out that day and suggested getting her tubes tied, maybe she'd have gone on having babies every year. Maybe she'd never have had the nerve to sock Joe Bob. Maybe she'd never feel this newfound sense of freedom. From now on her life wasn't going to revolve around Joe Bob and whether or not he was home and what he wanted her to do. If he was going to stay, and he did want to do things in bed with her at night, she was damn well going to tell him he had to learn to please her, instead of just rolling off her and going to sleep after he'd had his fun.

And if the Lovetts continued to come out to the ranch every Sunday, the other women could jolly well help her so she didn't have to prepare all the food, and the men could take care of the kids for an hour or two, show them how to play quoits or something. Any damn thing.

She knew her life was going to be different from now on. She was going to see to it.

Since she was up until well after two in the morning with the new foal, Mrs. Spencer had packed Mikey and Sally Mae's lunches and seen them off on the school bus. Zelda Marie was dragging around too tired to even see straight, but she felt good.

CHAPTER 18

Alex called Tessa and suggested lunch, something they had begun to do weekly. This time she had something particular on her mind.

"What do you think of my apartment?" Alex asked.

"In what way?"

"Boomer thinks it's stark."

Tessa laughed. "That it is, but it becomes you. What are you thinking?"

Alex shrugged her shoulders. "I used to love it. I used to think it was the most wonderful retreat in the universe. It was. But now . . ."

Tessa smiled and reached across the table to touch Alex's hand. "Love does that, you know."

"Love?" Alex looked puzzled. "I don't know that it's love."

"Well, then, what is it?" Tessa took a healthy bite of her club sandwich.

"I'm not sure. Not like anything else I've experienced, I

know that. I never know what to expect. A motorcycle ride a hundred miles away for dinner. Building sand castles on Padre Island. Camping at Big Bend. Learning to water ski. God, things I've never done, and I find I enjoy them all. I'm having a wonderful time, but love? I don't know."

"How is he in bed?" Tessa asked.

Alex was shocked. Sex was not something she'd ever talked about. She felt herself blushing.

"Well, until last Thursday we'd never . . ."

Tessa let out a loud laugh. "Are you serious? My heavens, wait until I tell Dan. We took for granted . . . He and I went to bed the first night we met."

"And got married a week later."

Tessa nodded. "Best decision I ever made. You should be so lucky," she told Alex. "And maybe you can be. It's wonderful to be in business together. By the way, I'm going to tell David I'm quitting. Big step, huh?"

"Well, I don't know what it's like to worry about money . . ."

"Lucky you," murmured Tessa, signaling the waitress and ordering coffee. She wanted to stay awake and alert this afternoon.

"You want a job?" Alex asked. "Do something to my apartment."

"I'll do it, but not for money," Tessa said. "I can't take money from friends. Besides, if you like it as it is, we just have to decide what to add."

Alex sipped her mineral water.

"Take my advice about something?"

Alex looked across the table and smiled. "Maybe."

"Don't redecorate completely. Don't do it just because you hope it'll please him. Do it for yourself. If you want to soften the 'starkness' fine, but keep the part that *you* really like, that makes *you* comfortable and happy."

Alex nodded her head, absorbing Tessa's advice.

"Well, you didn't answer. Is he good in bed?"

Alex felt herself reddening again. "Very."

"So what's not to love? You guys are terrific together. What was it someone said about Fred Astaire and Ginger Rogers? He gave her elegance and she gave him sex appeal. With you two it's the other way around. Has he told you he loves you?''

Alex shook her head. ''No, and I don't want him to. I'm not ready to be that serious. I'm having a wonderful time, and want it to go on just like it is.''

''Ha ha,'' said Tessa. ''Nothing goes on just as it is.''

''I *am* confused, when I let myself think about it. But most of the time I just flow with it. I get such energy from the relationship. I'm doing things in business I might not have dared to try three months ago. I lie in bed at nights and think of the future projects we talk about on Sunday nights. I'm having fun.'' Alex laughed. ''I'm not sure I've ever had fun in my life before, not the kind Boomer and you and Dan bring into my life.''

Tessa cocked her head. ''Well, dear friend, I suspect it's that big four-letter word. I took for granted you each knew it, too. Certainly Dan and I do.'' Tessa glanced at her watch and stood up. ''I have to get back to work. It's taking all the gumption I can muster to be able to tell David I'm quitting today. He'll have a fit when he discovers I'm going to be competing with him.''

Alex reached out a hand. ''Are you happy, Tessa?''

''Happy?'' Tessa's voice cracked. ''I live in constant fear that something absolutely terrible is going to happen because no one deserves to be as happy as Dan and I are. I'd think the gods would be jealous. I am so happy, every damn minute of my life, that I pinch myself.''

''But you and Dan come from the same kind of background, don't you?''

''You mean middle class? I suppose so, but Dan was far more middle than I. His parents could afford to send him to college. And, of course, he never had a husband who beat him to a bloody pulp a dozen times a year.''

''Oh, God,'' Alex exclaimed. ''I didn't know that.''

''Beat me up so badly I lost the child I was carrying.'' Tears formed in Tessa's eyes. ''We may have had the same kind of background in some ways, Alex, but we haven't had the same life experiences. Marriage takes work. It doesn't just turn out magically, you know. It's a challenge, and Dan and I both thrive on challenges.''

Maybe she'd felt the same way, Alex thought. The afternoon she met Boomer she'd known something important had happened, for she couldn't put him out of her mind. But she hadn't let herself think *love*. He wouldn't fit in with her life, with her parents. She tried to envision Boomer opening presents with her mother and father on Christmas Day, and just knew it wouldn't work out.

''We don't even like the same music,'' she told Tessa. ''When Boomer and I are at my place I play symphonies and operas. At your place Sundays we listen to John Denver, or Peter, Paul and Mary or Mama Cass.''

Tessa studied her friend, then said, ''In relationships, compromises are necessary.''

''You're not seeing Cole?'' Mrs. Headland asked.

Alex didn't answer but her eyes met her mother's.

''Do we not see you Sunday evenings any more because of a man?'' her mother pursued.

''More like a group of us,'' Alex hedged around the truth of Boomer.

''Cole's not in it?''

''No, Mother, he's not.'' Her voice indicated she wanted to put an end to the discussion, but her mother ignored it.

''Well, why don't you bring your group some Saturday?''

Alex hadn't thought of that. Boomer and Dan and Tessa seemed so removed from that life. ''Maybe I will.''

Test the waters. Tessa could handle any situation, but Boomer and Dan? Boomer probably didn't even own a dinner jacket.

Later, Alex phoned Boomer. ''I'd like to have a little dinner party Saturday evening. You, Tessa, Dan. At my parents' club. Thought it would be a change of pace.''

When Boomer got to work, Dan said, ''Tessa thinks you

might not know you should wear a dinner jacket Saturday night.''

''I don't have one,'' Boomer said, bending over a drawing board.

''Rent one.''

Boomer nodded and looked around his living room. His mind was on other matters. ''You know, if Tessa's quitting her job, this place is just too crowded for the three of us to work. It's about time we have an office.''

''Where are we going to get money for that?''

''That first tier of apartments is nearly finished. Let's take over that one in the downstairs front.''

''That whole bunch of rooms for an office when we could be getting rent for it?''

''Hey, we've got to look affluent. Impressive offices will send out good vibes. Tell Tessa to decorate it. The way it's laid out we can each have an office, a conference room, and a reception area. I suppose we'll need a receptionist.''

Dan raised his eyebrows. ''Where do you expect to get money to pay someone?''

Boomer gathered up the blueprints in a roll, tucked them under his arm, and headed for the door. ''Now, if we had an office out there already, it'd be far easier. Ask Tessa to get to work on it. She has the company credit card. Tell her not to stint.''

Dan wondered how the company credit card bill was going to be paid.

CHAPTER 19

Carly laughed as she splashed in the ocean. The blue sky, the waving palms, and the warm water delighted her.

She knew Cole was watching her from the blanket on the

sand, and she played for his audience. She raised her hands in the air, stretching, and plunged into the next wave. She was reveling in her power. Cole could hardly keep his hands off her.

When they sat around a table with the Rosas, Carly would take her sandals off and wiggle her bare toes under Cole's pants leg and try not to laugh as he struggled to concentrate on Señor Rosas's conversation.

"You bewitch me," he told her.

They were north of Acapulco in a little village whose name Carly couldn't even pronounce, where Señor Rosas wanted to build what he called "a total resort." Untouched by progress, it was still a sleepy town with mangrove swamps and miles and miles of white sand beach where the aquamarine ocean broke softly, with no undertow as there was along so much of the Pacific coastline here. Palm trees fringed the wide expanse of beach, and this afternoon, while the Rosas had their siesta, there was no one in sight. Cole had told her last night that the bank was going to help finance the Acapulco Hotel and, once partnership was established with Rosas, they'd probably be interested in this stretch of beach, too. The plans sounded fabulous to Carly.

"Where does the bank get its money?" Carly asked.

"Oil."

Millions and billions of gallons of oil. Natural gas, too. There were banks on nearly every street corner of Houston.

Carly could tell Cole hadn't had much sexual experience. Or, if he had, his skill was limited. She might not have had much variety in men, but those four years with Boomer had given Carly a sense of adventure where sex was concerned. She had been surprised at Cole's lack of expertise. But now, he seemed to be cutting loose.

She hadn't had to teach Cole much, just sort of led the way, and he responded in ways that thrilled her. She had forgotten just how wonderful good sex could make her feel. Touching and being touched. Being kissed and held and stroked. Being looked at as though she were the most desirable woman in the world.

She wondered, as she splashed in the water, how much money and power really had to do with her attraction to him. And if what she was offering was enough to make him want more.

She turned and looked back at the shore and saw him waving at her.

She genuinely found him attractive—the first man since Boomer to have captured her imagination.

It had been a waste of money buying that expensive night-gown, though; she hadn't even had it out of the drawer. Cole had suggested they change their plans and, instead of flying back to Houston Friday, return on the Sunday evening plane. It would be fun, he'd said, to have a couple of days just to themselves, without the Rosas.

"Sounds good to me," she said, leaning over to kiss his ear. Cole said if they stayed for the weekend, maybe he could get them the penthouse suite.

She could take more days of lying on the beach, and she could lie out on the roof garden where no one could see her and get tan all over. Wasn't it Marilyn Monroe who'd said she felt blond all over? It would be exciting to lie naked on the roof garden and make love with Cole with the sun beating down on them. Fun to make love in a hot tub, in steamy swirling water.

She liked it that after they made love he didn't just roll over and go to sleep, or smoke a cigarette. He talked with her. He wanted to know what growing up in Verity was like, and he asked her questions about her mother and Walt. He heard about Zelda Marie, and acted interested in everything she said about her friend. There wasn't a thing Carly said that didn't interest him.

She dove under a wave, wondering what was going to happen when they left paradiso.

As she emerged from the sea, throwing her head back and brushing a hand through her hair, she looked at Cole. Did she really want to *marry* him? Just because he was the second man she'd gone to bed with? Well, why not? She was twenty-five. Walt was beginning to worry she was going to be an old maid. Carly laughed. She knew that was not what fate had in store for her. Yet, until now she hadn't even thought of marriage to anyone but Boomer.

Patience, she told herself. Let it build up.

The next evening, after they'd moved to the penthouse suite, they dined in the hotel dining room. The Rosas had left before noon, so Cole and Carly had had the afternoon to themselves. They had spent that time on the beach. For dinner Carly dressed in a turquoise gauzy dress she'd bought in a shop in town. She pinned a yellow hibiscus behind her left ear.

They danced between the dinner course and dessert. Carly rested her head on Cole's shoulder. His hand on her back held her close to him. She brushed her knee between his legs in a quick motion, unnoticed by others, and felt his body tremble.

When the set was over they returned to the table. Carly refused dessert, but Cole ordered flan. They both wanted coffee.

"I have a wonderful idea," Carly said.

Leaning back in his chair, his mouth curled in a smile, he said, "A Jacuzzi?"

"My sentiments exactly." She reached across the table to touch his hand. "Are you a mind reader?"

"I think," he was obviously amused, his blue eyes twinkling, "that it has more to do with body language."

CHAPTER 20

The day after Mr. Rolf said, "Interview for a new secretary and let me see your final candidates, you're getting to be too busy in sales," Carly answered the phone to hear someone ask for her.

The caller said, "This is Tad Jones." Which meant nothing to her. "My wife saw a For Sale sign on a house she's had a yen for for years. Hope it's still available. We'd like to look at it ASAP."

Carly found the card file on it; one and a half million dollars.

"Let me phone and see if today's convenient, and I'll call you right back."

How did he get her name?

She walked into Mr. Rolf's office and told him about the call. "Tad Jones?" He grinned. "He could buy ten of them and it wouldn't bother his pocketbook a bit. He owns Jones Aviation. They're the biggest airplane manufacturers in Houston. They don't build the big commercial ones, just made-to-order private planes. He inherited the business from his father. His father's not even my age, but he handed the business over to Tad, and he and his wife moved to the Virgin Islands. Bought an island all their own."

"Ah," Carly said thoughtfully. "That means they'll sell the house they live in now."

"Go for it, girl." Rolf grinned.

"Wonder why he asked for me. How could he ever have heard of my name?"

"You're beginning to move in the right circles, I'd guess. And oh . . ." He reached into his top desk drawer. "I forgot. Your realtor's license arrived while you were gone."

Carly tilted her head and smiled.

"Let's see," Rolf extended his hand, reaching for the card that Carly held. "Ah, Myrtle Goodrich's house. She died last month. Guess her kids want to get rid of it. None of them lives here anymore. I'm surprised it wasn't sold before going on the market. Except it's probably not worth a million and a half. Bet you can get it for one and a quarter."

Carly quickly calculated. Her portion would be thirty-seven thousand five hundred dollars.

She made an appointment for noon, then called Tad Jones.

When she returned to Rolf's office he was finishing up a call. "Yes, she'll be there in half an hour." He hung up, wrote something on a slip of yellow paper, handed it to Carly and grinned. "This is the store where my wife always shops. My daughters, too. I just phoned and told them you'd be there momentarily. I want you to buy a suit that looks like you earn a million."

"Why?" Carly looked down at her coral suit. She had paid over a hundred dollars for it and thought it reeked of success.

"Just do it. Pay me back from your commission check. Or better yet, if you make this sale, it's on me. The suit, I mean."

When Carly appeared, five minutes early, to wait for the Tad Joneses, she wore a black-and-white thin-striped worsted suit with a tailored white silk blouse that cost several weeks' salary. She had argued with the sales clerk over small pearl earrings, and she had won. The black onyx earrings were larger than the clerk suggested and almost as expensive as the blouse. Black patent-leather high-heeled shoes matched the purse. Carly thought she looked as though she herself was ready to buy the house.

Tad Jones arrived alone in a dark-green Porsche. "Liza will be here in a minute." He gazed at Carly with appreciation. He was medium height and dressed in gray flannel slacks and a blue blazer, with a wine-red tie.

"How'd you get my name?" she asked as they waited outside the wrought-iron gates.

"Cole Coleridge. He said you were the best salesperson in town. Honest, too."

Carly smiled. So these were the kinds of people he hung out with when he wasn't with her.

Liza Jones came barreling around a corner, tearing full speed ahead so that her brakes screeched as her silver Caddy came to an abrupt halt behind her husband's car.

"Of course I've seen this place any number of times," she said after introductions were over. "I don't even know why

I'm looking. When I visited as a girl, I said that someday it would be mine.''

A butler showed them around the house, which had seventeen rooms and six baths. The furnishings were old, the Persian rugs in impeccable condition, the furniture dark and Victorian. The Joneses spent two hours. Liza took a lot of notes. ''Our sofas would be perfect in here,'' she said to her husband.

There was a six-car garage, floodlit tennis courts, a pool not quite Olympic size, a cabana down by the poolside. The garden was a blaze of perfectly trimmed flowers. Beyond the tennis court was a greenhouse for starting seedlings. For having year-round cut flowers.

''A steal at one and a half, don't you think?'' she asked Tad.

''Hon, if you want it, what does the price matter?''

''I think we could dicker and get it lower. At least we could start lower,'' Carly said.

''Let's not take a chance,'' Liza said. ''I want to know today that it's mine.''

Tad pulled out a checkbook and, leaning against the pool table, wrote out a check for one million five hundred thousand dollars.

Carly's first two sales were the two easiest things she'd done in her life, and they brought her over sixty thousand dollars. She could get rich doing this, she realized. Already, she had more money than she had ever dreamed of.

''Would you like me to come look at your house and give an estimate?''

''Would you?'' Liza asked, smiling up at Carly. ''That'd be splendid of you. How about five-thirty? Have a drink with us then and take your time.''

Carly pinched herself.

CHAPTER 21

"Is this a test?" Boomer asked, as they pulled up the long curving driveway of the club. It was the most exclusive one in Houston, its membership severely restricted. No new members had been accepted in the last four years.

"Test for what?"

"See what your kind of people think of me?"

She laughed, but of course it was. "I've never cared what anyone else thinks of what I do."

He let the matter drop. "My father would have liked you," he said.

She had taken for granted that the family of anyone she dated would not only have approved of her but been flattered their son was dating a Headland girl, so it surprised her to feel pleasure at Boomer's words.

From the backseat, Tessa said, "Dan and I have been thinking that we ought to have a big blowout, a real whopper of a party to announce the grand opening of the apartments. An open house before the open house."

Boomer nodded. "Fine by me."

Tessa tapped Alex on the shoulder. "You know everyone worth knowing, don't you?"

Alex nodded. After all, a hundred thousand of her own money was invested in this project. "I'll take care of it," she told Tessa, thinking she'd get Sally Burgess to arrange for a big bash. No one could plan a more elegant party than Sally. By the time Sally got through, people would be fighting for an invitation.

"Won't it cost a fortune, though?" Dan asked. "Booze for dozens of people?"

"Don't worry. I'll take care of it," Alex said. None of them knew how much had come out of her own pocket already. She didn't resent a bit of it. Whatever money she was spending, she'd never gotten as much out of life as she had these past months, including a good woman friend, something she'd never had before. A group who was in business together and also had fun together. Fun. That's what she was having.

And sex. A world-class lover. Boomer was all sorts of wonderful things in bed. Tender yet powerful. Creative and inventive. Uninhibited, and helping her to become more so each time they went to bed together. She felt fulfilled, in love with life, no longer waiting and working for the future, but enjoying the present. More than projects, she was involved with people, and for the first time in her life they were more important to her than her work, her goals. And none of the three of them were like the people she'd known all her life.

"Where shall I park?" Boomer asked Alex.

"Just leave the keys in it. Miguel will take care of it."

Boomer had just been introduced to valet parking.

Alex tried to remember when she had last felt so nervous. Lending money didn't do this to her. Taking tests in school had never fazed her. Not even the first time she had ever slept with a boy.

So, why was she nervous? Why did she peek to see if there was lint on Boomer's jacket, if his shoes shone? What did it matter if the Saturday-night crowd stared, wondering who Alex's guests were? So what if they collectively decided her guests didn't pass muster? They'd be courteous anyway. That was a given. Any guests of members were welcome, and Amos Headland had been one of the club's first members, invited in at Mr. Coleridge's invitation, and Mr. Coleridge was one of the founders of the club.

Alex put her hand through Boomer's arm, leading her friends through the foyer, nodding to the manager and walking regally down the stairs to the dining room.

Most of the tables were already filled. Alex had made a reservation and told her mother they were coming, but made no suggestion that her parents join them.

The orchestra that always performed on Friday and Saturday nights was playing "I had a dream, dear, it was of you . . ." Alex saw her parents on the dance floor, saw her mother whisper to her father, saw them both look at the man holding Alex's hand. She threw back her head, her tawny hair fanning out, and she smiled at Boomer. The maître'd led them to her table.

A waiter appeared immediately. Alex ordered her favorite daiquiri, Boomer a Scotch and water, Tessa asked for a whiskey sour, and Dan mineral water with a twist of lime.

"This is beautiful, Alex," Tessa said, glancing around the room. "Couldn't do better myself," she smiled.

Todd Cooper materialized at Alex's elbow. He'd been at St. John's with her and she'd known him forever. In fact, if she remembered correctly, he was the first boy to kiss her. She must have been thirteen or fourteen. But they'd never really dated. He was one of the few from their class who was still single.

"Alex, haven't seen you in weeks." And then, surprise evident in her eyes, he said, "Why, Boomer Bannerman! What are you doing in Houston?"

Boomer smiled widely. Hadn't this guy been in Sigma Chi?

"Haven't seen you since our senior year." He turned to Alex. "Of course you know he was our star football player."

Alex had not known. "Todd, meet Dan and Tessa Bertelson."

Todd smiled at them, holding out his hand.

"Moving to Houston or just visiting?" he asked Boomer.

"I live here," Boomer said, remembering he'd never much liked Cooper, the little he'd known of him.

Just then Alex's parents sauntered over to the table. Mr. Headland was a stocky man with gray curly hair, bushy eyebrows, and bright blue eyes. One would never guess that he'd worked in the oilfields as a young man, but it was easily believable that he was president and majority owner of the Headland Gas & Oil Company, and known in Texas as bringing in the Kidder 7, one of the largest oil wells ever to be drilled.

Boomer and Dan stood up. Boomer guessed immediately

who these people were; Mrs. Headland and Alex looked alike, the eyes of mother and daughter identical. Mr. Headland leaned over and kissed the top of his daughter's head.

"Mother, Daddy," Alex said, "this is Brad Bannerman." Her father stretched out his hand and gave Boomer a firm handshake.

Mrs. Headland's mouth curved in a smile, but her eyes were like Alex's, seldom changing expression. "Mr. Bannerman," she murmured. Her glance took in everything visible about him.

Alex introduced Tessa and Dan. Her hand floated out to hold her father's.

"What business are you in, Mr. Bannerman?" asked Amos Headland. The first question he asked any man.

"I'm in construction, sir," Boomer answered.

"Oh, here in Houston?"

"Yes." Boomer volunteered no more. If Alex wanted, she could fill him in.

"Come over and talk with us after you've eaten."

Alex let go of her father's hand.

"Save a dance for me," her father said, as they left.

Todd Cooper stood on the edge of the circle, watching. "Save one for me, too, Alex," he said, as he walked away.

Todd Cooper hadn't asked Alex for a dance since high school.

The waiter took their orders as the music began again. Alex reached out for Boomer's hand and stood up. "Dance?"

She knew every eye in the room would be on them. Might as well get it over with. Tessa and Dan stood, too, and followed them to the dance floor.

Boomer took Alex in his arms. "So, you grew up with all this, huh?"

She smiled up at him. "Going to hold it against me?"

"Among other things."

"Is that a promise?"

He laughed. "You're a Texas princess, aren't you?"

"And someday, I'm going to be the Queen," she said.

He pulled her closer. "That's going to be quite a ride," he said.

She almost whispered, Want to come along? But didn't. Couldn't yet.

He was holding her so close that their legs moved as one entity. She wondered if he could feel her breathing, feel the heat of her body.

"You *look* like a princess," Boomer said. "That dress matches your eyes. But you know that, of course."

"Of course," she said, wondering what people were thinking, seeing how close she and Boomer were dancing.

She saw the first course being served at their table and, taking Boomer's hand, led him back to the table. She waved across the room at her parents.

Tessa and Dan returned to the table. "Someday," Tessa said, her eyes aglow, "we're going to belong here."

Alex picked up her fork and began to eat the prawns. She didn't want to tell Tessa there wasn't a chance of that, not at all. And she suddenly realized it didn't make a difference. In some way, these three friends were setting her free.

Boomer's knee met hers under the table. "Does this sort of stuff matter to you?"

She hesitated only a minute. "It used to."

Toward the end of the evening, Alex felt hands on her shoulders and turned to see Ben Coleridge smiling down at her.

"Ben." She stood and threw her arms around him. "I've been hearing terrible things about you. Are they true?"

He grinned at her and she could smell the alcohol on his breath. Alex had always been glad Ben was younger, for if she'd been in his class at school, if she'd been five or six years younger than she was, she'd have lost her heart to him.

Boomer was standing now, beside Ben, and Alex introduced them. "Boomer, this is the man I lost my heart to when he was about seven and I was twelve, Bennett Coleridge. What are you doing? I didn't know you were home."

"Just got back from the Grand Tour. England, France, Italy, Greece. Ah, the Greek islands, Santorini . . . I thought of you when I was there."

"I'll bet you did!" Alex laughed. "While you were seducing all those beautiful dark-haired women on those topless beaches."

"Dad wants me to go in business, any business, and me with no head for business at all."

"Come see me tomorrow," Alex suggested. "Let's have lunch and we'll talk business."

"And much else, I hope." He grinned, his boyish smile.

Ben, faint glints of red shining in his blond hair, was an inch or two shorter than his brother, with broad shoulders and a narrow waist. His sea-green eyes twinkled and looked haunted at the same time. Alex thought of all the men she had ever known, Ben was the best looking. He had a charm that Cole lacked. Ben could charm everyone. It was a quality he'd been born with. His father, who disapproved of him, and his mother, who wrung her hands in frustration over him, couldn't resist him, especially when he smiled.

Later, when Alex tried to recall exactly what her parents had said to Boomer and he to them, when she wanted desperately to remember the look in her father's eyes as he asked Boomer about his construction business and how they looked at her when she and Boomer left their table after twenty minutes of conversation, all she could really remember was how sad Ben's eyes looked behind his bright smile.

She had wondered for years if it was because of his left hand that hung limp at his side, the one that had splintered when he was twelve years old when he had shot himself in the hand so that he'd never have to fire a gun at a bird again. He had done it to punish his father for insisting that he kill pigeons, but he had suffered the consequences of his actions ever since.

He had never been able to participate in sports again. Alex always wondered if that useless hand was the reason for the look in Ben's eyes.

CHAPTER 22

Cole Coleridge could hardly believe himself. He had never cared what a woman thought. Well, that wasn't quite true. He'd tried to discover the inner Alex for at least eleven years now, but he guessed he'd given up, feeling he would never know her better than he did now.

He understood now, too, that Alex would never lie in his arms and sigh with contentment, the way Carly did. Alex would never give him little teasing kisses across his belly, she would never be all soft curves and responsive yearning. She would never look up at him and laugh, her lips dewy, her eyes shining, as though he was the most exciting person in the whole world.

Alex would never run barefoot in the ocean, would never lie naked in the sun with him. She would never, not ever, say, glee in her voice and teasing in her eyes, "Let's fuck." When Carly said it, a word he'd never heard a woman say out loud, she said it in such an innocent way that he wasn't offended. In fact, it excited him. Everything Carly did excited him.

Yet, he sensed it wasn't just their lovemaking, it wasn't just being naked with Carly. Something deep within him was awakening. Mental as well as physical. He couldn't stand being away from Carly though he had forced himself to for two nights, futilely practicing self-discipline. He wondered what she was doing. At least a dozen times before he made the actual phone call, he picked up the phone.

Perhaps she was out with another man. Maybe she was just washing out her underwear. Was she missing him? He found himself pacing around his apartment.

He looked at the place with new eyes. What would Carly think of it? Would she like it? He had furnished it himself.

Aubusson carpet, in rich burgundy and navy, sleek Danish modern furniture. Clio mobile, Chinese porcelain vases.

He walked into his bedroom. More navy and burgundies, and wine-red sheets. Was it too masculine? Alex had never commented on his apartment. He had taken care and pleasure in choosing everything for it, gradually accumulating the little touches that made a home. He knew that once he married, he would have little to say about how his home would be decorated. That was a woman's province.

But now he wondered if Carly would like the apartment, and he laughed at himself.

He had not asked Carly if there was another man, other men, in her life. At least she didn't go to bed with any of them. He remembered how he felt last week when she'd leaned across the table, her voice a whisper so that the other couples in the restaurant couldn't hear her. "Do you know, I hadn't slept with a man in nearly five years until you?"

He'd dropped his menu, incredulous. "You've got to be kidding."

She shook her head. "I'm not. I just thought you should know you're pretty powerful, to be the first man in all those years to break down my defenses."

And now here she was, standing on his threshold.

He watched her as she surveyed his living room, wondering why he was so eager for her approval. He did not have to wait long.

"Oh, Cole," she whispered, "this is beautiful. You must've had a good decorator." She knew that rich people always used decorators.

"I did it myself." He felt enormous pride. Ridiculous. He'd never waited for anyone's reaction to what he liked and wanted.

Carly turned to face him. He reached out to gather her in his arms, his mouth crushing hers with insistence and yearning. "Oh, Carly," he breathed into her ear.

Later, as they lay naked in his bed, the burgundy sheets entwined around their legs, Cole said, "I don't want you to go

home. I want you to be here next to me when I wake up. I
want to make love before we go to work.''

"I sure can't go to work in that dress," Carly giggled.

And Cole knew he couldn't be seen taking her home at the
crack of dawn.

"I know. I was just wishing aloud." She lay in the crook
of his arm as though it was where she belonged.

They didn't talk for a long time, but then he asked, "Either
you've read a lot about sex or you had a hell of a relationship
with this guy you knew in high school.''

"Maybe it's just instinct," she said, trying to remember what
she and Boomer had done. It was so long ago. "But Cole, what
I did when I was a teenager has nothing to do with us. You
make me feel better than I knew a person could feel." She
kissed his cheek, feathering her fingers across his chest, across
the hair on his belly. "I love your body," she smiled.

He leaned over and kissed her right nipple.

"God almighty," she said, "when you do that I think I could
start all over.''

"Let's." His voice was muffled.

I'm falling in love, Cole thought. Goddamn.

CHAPTER 23

Francey phoned to ask Carly if there was any chance she could
come home that weekend.

Every couple of months, she'd take an early-evening flight
on a Friday and spend the weekend with her mother and Walt.
Walt always paid. He told her he'd pay for her to fly home
every weekend if she wanted.

Carly thought of the symphony, for which Cole had tickets.

It would be her first time. She'd bought a new dress only yesterday.

"Well, I'll tell you," Francey went on. "I think Zelda Marie could stand seeing you. I went out there and, my heavens, she has her hands full with five kids and that no-count husband of hers does nothing to help, fools around down at Barneys most nights, playing pool and drinking, and I suspect sweet-talking, too." Francey might never lose her Yankee accent, but she had picked up some Southern expressions. "She could stand a friend," Francey added. "She didn't go into details with me, but I think she would with you."

"I'm going out Friday night, but I could get the six-forty Saturday morning flight and be there a bit after eight."

Francey's relief was evident. "That'll be wonderful. Walt'll meet the plane and I'll have breakfast ready. Wait until you see all our flowers."

Carly laughed. "I can't even imagine you two as gardeners."

"Wait until you taste it all."

"No okra, Mom."

Francey hated the slimy stuff, but Carly knew Walt loved gumbo.

Cole wondered what was wrong with him. He'd been proud to be seen with Carly in Acapulco, but he was embarrassed to be seen with her at the symphony in the Coleridge box. She wore a fire engine-red dress with sequins, and her blond hair was piled elaborately on her head. Glittery earrings hung from her ears. The outfit must have been expensive, but it was more appropriate for Hollywood than Houston.

His parents hadn't arrived by the time the music began. He hoped for a minute that they'd changed their minds and weren't coming.

The music was heavenly to him—Rachmaninoff, Stravinsky—but Carly leaned over to ask, "Don't they play anything that has a melody?"

A melody? The world's greatest music and she wanted a

melody. She did turn to him and smiled when she recognized a piece. "Ah, 'Stairway to the Stars,' " she said.

She leaned over again and whispered, "I knew you were important, but I didn't know you were *this* important. People are staring at us."

"They're looking at you," he whispered back.

"At me?"

Because you're not what's ever been in the Coleridge box before. "Because you're so beautiful."

At intermission he didn't suggest that they go down to the bar, but he stood and stretched just as his parents came in.

"Sorry, dinner lasted longer than . . ." Cole's mother stopped in mid-sentence.

It didn't take Carly a minute to realize Mrs. Coleridge was looking at her just as the ladies in Verity always had. She knew in that second that her dress was wrong and her earrings were in poor taste and her hair should have been pulled back so that the curls didn't escape.

For a minute she wanted to sink into the floor, but then she stretched her hand out and offered it to Mrs. Coleridge. "Nice to meet you," she said.

Mrs. Coleridge shook Carly's hand limply. Mr. Coleridge coughed as though clearing his throat and, when Cole introduced them, said simply, "Miss Anderson."

Mrs. Coleridge was not the doyenne of Houston society for nothing and smiled graciously, casting her white mink stole on the seat behind her. "Tell me, is it up to par?" she asked, referring to the orchestra.

An usher entered at that moment with four glasses, lemons, and Perrier water.

"Are you enjoying the music tonight?" Cole's mother asked.

Carly scrunched her mouth up and said, "Well, I always think it's a good thing to expand my horizons. I guess liking music without a beat is an acquired taste, like olives."

Mrs. Coleridge's smile was tight-lipped.

"And where did you go to college, Miss Anderson?"

Carly only laughed. Cole's mother was trying to put her

down. She'd be damned if she'd try to impress them. If Cole couldn't take it, that was his problem. Still, Carly thought, she'd better learn to dress properly.

When the concert ended, Mrs. Coleridge waved to someone in another box and, turning to Cole said, "We're meeting the Morrisons."

Carly noted the stubborn set of Cole's jaw. She was suddenly tired. It had been a busy day at work, and she had had to rush through supper in order to be on time for the symphony. She wanted to go to bed. Alone. And read a book and wake up in the morning and not have to do anything at all. Not even think. Certainly not rush to the airport to get to boring old Verity.

But Cole had other plans. "I've ordered a supper sent in," he said, smiling as though this would be a lovely surprise. Carly wished she had an aspirin with her. "A nice romantic midnight supper."

"Music to dance to also?"

"Music to dance to. And whatever else you wish."

As they walked out into the night air, men stopped to shake Cole's hand and women kissed him lightly on the cheek, murmuring greetings. He introduced Carly to so many people she couldn't remember anyone's name.

As he drove to his apartment, Cole put on a soft music station on the radio. He held her hand the whole way there.

At eleven a caterer arrived with roast pheasant, wild rice and peas, tiny hot rolls, and chocolate cheesecake. Carly had to laugh out loud. The table was set with fine linen and silver, and a bowl of white roses. Cole turned off the lights and lit the candles.

"This is indeed romantic," Carly said. "I didn't know you could be like this."

Cole drew her into his arms, "I never *was* like this. You do something to me."

Carly began to hum a Cole Porter song, and Cole nibbled her ear. She was feeling much better.

"I hate the thought of your going home tonight," Cole said.

"Stay here and I'll drive you to the airport tomorrow at the crack of dawn."

"I don't have a toothbrush," she said. "And I need my overnight bag for the weekend home."

"I want," he said as he tasted the pheasant, "I want to nibble every part of you tonight, too. I've been fantasizing about you ever since Tuesday," which was the last time they'd been together. "I can't seem to get enough of you. I think of you more than I think of business. I lie in bed at night and think of your body and . . ." He reached over and squeezed her hand. "I know what was happening to you tonight."

She cocked her head to the side. "What do you mean?"

"My parents. It was like being back in Verity again, wasn't it?"

She stared at him, amazed that he would have caught that. She stood up and walked the few steps to him and put her arms around him. "Cole, you are quite the nicest person in the world."

"Nicer than Walt?"

She smiled. "No one's nicer than Walt. But you're right up there."

He put his hands on either side of her face and leaned over to kiss her, unpinning her upswept hair.

"Get a move on, Carly, or I'll ravish you right here in the dining room."

She laughed and stood up, reaching in back of her to unzip her dress, letting it fall to the floor. All she wore beneath was a pair of bright red panties.

"Oh, Christ," Cole murmured.

It was after one-thirty before they got up from the rug, took the cheesecake out of the refrigerator, brewed coffee, and sat on the floor, cross-legged and naked, talking long into the night. It was still dark when Cole drove her to her apartment to get her suitcase and then to the airport.

He stayed until the plane took off, until it was a speck in

the sky, until he could see it no longer. As he watched Carly disappear, an emptiness welled within him like no emptiness he had ever known before.

CHAPTER 24

"Any man at all in your life?" Walt asked.

"I don't know for sure." Carly's smile was like a Cheshire cat's. "I mean, yes, there is, and I'm having fun, but I really don't want to talk about it yet."

Walt and Francey exchanged glances. Maybe at last Carly would let herself get involved. Maybe someday she would even get married.

On Saturday afternoon, Carly drove out to the ranch to see Zelda Marie. She'd phoned, and they agreed on four o'clock. Zelda Marie said Joe Bob wouldn't be around till real late, seeing as it was Saturday. But you never could tell with him.

Carly told Francey she didn't know when she'd get home. It would depend on Joe Bob. She wasn't going to stay if he was around. Francey nodded, saying she'd wait as late as eight for dinner.

"I should certainly be home by then," Carly said as she backed Walt's Cadillac out of the driveway. The motor sounded like a huge cat purring.

Which got her to thinking about Cole. She thought women worried too much about the future, where their relationship was going, and didn't let themselves enjoy the present. And she was enjoying the present more than she had anytime since Boomer had been the center of her life. She was more alive than she'd been in over five years.

She turned off the blacktop and drove along the dirt road,

remembering how many happy weekends she'd spent out here, Zelda Marie teaching her how to ride, swimming in the creek up beyond the woods in back of the house. She might hate the town of Verity, but here, just four miles outside of town, it was mighty pretty, with the big mossy oaks and all those Herefords and Santa Gertrudis dotting the countryside. She wondered why Zelda Marie didn't go bonkers, though, living out here in the country with nothing to do.

What different paths their lives had taken.

Carly shook her head as she approached the house, flanked by two- and three-wheel bikes. Toys were scattered every which way, and a couple of puppies romped at the base of the big oak that shaded the front porch.

There was no sign of any of the children. As Carly opened the car door, she shivered. An eerie silence filled the air.

The house could stand a coat of paint. A couple of boards were cracked on the front porch, a piece of the railing broken. The place looked depressing, downright run-down. Poor Zelda Marie. All because once she . . .

Carly heard what she thought was crying. She knew better than to knock at the front door. No one ever used the front door. She wondered if its hinges even worked. In the summer the door was open to let in any breath of air that might rustle through, but even then no one entered or left via that entrance.

She walked around back and heard a whimpering sound. She began to run toward the open kitchen door, its screen riddled with jagged holes. As her feet hit the step, she heard Zelda Marie's voice screaming, "Don't you dare touch him!"

Carly dove into the doorway to see Zelda Marie cowering in the corner of the kitchen by the big wood stove, her arm raised in front of her, her mouth bloody and one tooth missing, her left eye swollen and almost closed. Joe Bob stood over her, pummeling her as though she were a punching bag. Standing in the doorway to the dining room, was one of the children, crying a muffled, "Stop, Daddy, stop!"

Joe Bob had obviously been at him, too, for his left arm hung sickeningly askew.

Joe Bob turned from Zelda Marie and reached out to grab his son, but the little boy backed away just as Joe Bob's arm hit the side of his head enough to knock him down.

"You bastard!" Zelda Marie's voice shot through the air. When Joe Bob began to kick her in the stomach, Carly saw the cast-iron frying pan on the stove and grabbed it. Without thinking, she raised it high in the air and brought it down on Joe Bob's head.

He folded up on the scuffed linoleum, didn't even seem to fall. Just suddenly he was there on the floor. He didn't moan. He didn't make a sound.

The little boy stopped crying, staring at his father. Zelda Marie sat up a little straighter, looking in surprise at Carly. Carly held on to the frying pan.

There wasn't a sound.

Then Zelda Marie crawled the few feet to Joe Bob and put her ear to his chest and then to his nose.

"I don't hear anything," she whispered through swollen lips.

"I hope he's dead" came from the young boy.

"He is," said his mother, her voice stronger.

"Oh, my God," breathed Carly. She sat down hard on the slatted wooden chair, still clutching the cast-iron pan.

For a moment Carly thought Zelda Marie was going to burst into tears. Instead she began to laugh, hysterically, unable to stop.

Carly stared at her in disbelief, and then, unable to help herself, she began to laugh, too, laughing so hard she had to hold her sides.

The little boy began to laugh, too.

None of them could stop. Not for almost five minutes.

CHAPTER 25

Zelda Marie was the first one to come out of it. She calmly walked over to the phone and dialed the police, hardly able to talk through her swollen and cracked lips. She grasped her stomach, obviously in pain.

"You saved us, Carly," she said, her voice ragged and indistinct. "He never hit Little Joe before." She turned to the little boy. "You okay, honey?"

He stood, his eyes wide and his arm swinging at his side, his elbow sticking out in front. Zelda Marie tried to gather him in her arms, but he wriggled away from her, pain evident in his eyes. He began to sob.

Carly turned to her friend. "We've got to get him to a doctor."

"We've got to talk to the police first," Zelda Marie said.

Carly was suddenly terrified they would put her in jail. She picked up the phone and dialed Francey's number. Walt would help.

"Mom, put Walt on, please," she said when Francey answered.

Walt was on the other phone in a second. When Carly asked him to get right out to the Spencers', he didn't even ask why.

"You saved our lives," Zelda Marie said again. "They're not going to blame you." But the tone of her voice wasn't convincing.

Carly knew it'd make the papers. One other thing for Verity to judge her by. Would the people at the bank hear about it? Would Cole? Certainly, her killing a man would put an end to their relationship.

Zelda Marie limped over to Carly and put her arms around

her friend, beginning now to cry, too. She and Little Joe made whimpering sounds.

The oldest boy, Mike, came careening into the room but soon stopped cold. He stared at the blood on his mother. Zelda Marie turned and said to the boy, "Go keep your brother and sisters out of here. We're okay, but Daddy's dead."

Mike's eyes rounded and his jaw hung open.

"It was an accident," Zelda Marie said. "Daddy hurt himself."

Little Joe stared at his mother, his thumb going into his mouth. "I killed him."

Mike looked at his brother skeptically.

"I did, too. With that frying pan." The kid couldn't be more than five, Carly thought.

"Mikey," Zelda Marie was shaking her head, "just see the other kids don't come around. We'll talk about this later, okay?"

In the distance a siren wailed. When Michael J. just stood there, Zelda Marie raised her voice, "You hear me, Son?"

Mike looked at his little brother and said, "I wish I'd done it," before turning to go.

Neither of the women said anything as they waited, hearing the siren grow increasingly louder.

The car with flashing lights drew up beside the house. Zelda Marie turned to Little Joe and whispered, "I don't want you to say a thing, you hear?"

The little boy shook his head, sucking his thumb.

The sheriff rapped on the open door and stepped in, not waiting for an invitation. He surveyed the scene, glancing at Little Joe and Zelda Marie. Without saying anything, he walked over and knelt beside Joe Bob, laying his fingers against his throat. After a few seconds, he said, "He's dead."

Anyone could see that.

Sheriff Redford stood up and turned to Zelda Marie. "Looks like we better get you two to the hospital."

Looking at Little Joe's arm swinging so crazily was enough

to make you sick, Carly thought. And blood had begun to stain Zelda Marie's skirt.

"You look like your face could stand a few stitches, too, Zelda Marie." The sheriff had known her as long as she'd been alive. "I'll call for an ambulance."

"Sheriff," Carly said, wanting to get this over with.

For the first time the sheriff turned to really look at her. "Oh, you're Walt's stepgal, aren't you? You a witness to this?" Without waiting for an answer, he turned back to Zelda Marie. "There won't be no trouble, honey," he said. "He's been asking for this for years. Even his poppa won't be surprised, I bet. There won't be no trouble, not as long as I'm here."

He turned back to Carly, "You swear, don't you, she did this to protect herself and that young 'un of hers? We probably won't even need a statement, but just in case, you did witness it, didn't you?"

"Sheriff," Carly tried again, but this time Zelda Marie interrupted.

"Yeah, she witnessed it. I hit him just as she was coming in the door. He was twisting little Joe's arm, and when his back was turned I heaved that fry pan as hard as I could. I'm glad I did."

Carly's mouth fell open.

"Zelda Marie," said the sheriff, "you're not the only one who'll be happy this happened. We on the force can rest a little easier now, too. Not get called out to Barney's ever' weekend to break up the fights he always started. You got yourself a lemon there, gal. Lookit, let's get an ambulance out here and get you two tended to. I got a even better idea. Keep your mouths shut and we'll just say he fell down the steps. Coupla broken boards out there testament to that fact. No sense makin' waves where none have to be." He turned to Little Joe and knelt in front of him. "You probably don't even know what I mean, do you?"

"I killed my dad," Little Joe said.

"Wishful thinkin'," said the sheriff. "Lotsa people will want to take credit. But none're goin' to. He fell back down those steps out back, drunk as a coot and hit his head on a board. No inquest, no autopsy, no nothing. Just a little paragraph in the *Clarion*. Okay, ever'body?''

Redford turned to Carly. ''That okay by you? You keep silent 'bout this forever?'' Carly thought she ought to right the situation, but somehow she knew he wouldn't listen. Didn't matter to him who killed Joe Bob.

Just then they heard steps on the porch and looked up to see Walt standing in the doorway. ''My God,'' he said in a hollow voice, checking to see if Carly was all right.

''Afternoon, Walt.'' The sheriff nodded. ''You got here just in time to save me calling an ambulance. You wanna take these two to the hospital? They both look like maybe Doc Clarke can take care of them in his clinic. If not, he'll send you over to Corpus. You don't mind, do you?''

''Of course not,'' Walt said, picking Little Joe up in his arms, being careful not to touch the swinging arm that looked like it had been pasted on backward. He turned to Carly. ''You stay with the other children,'' he told her.

Oh, God, thought Carly, stay with the children whose father she'd just killed? She was beginning to tremble.

Zelda Marie picked up the phone and dialed. ''Momma,'' she said, ''we just had an accident and Mr. Davis is here and he's going to take Little Joe and me into the hospital. No no. We're okay, I don't want you to meet me there. I need you to come and take care of the kids. We may even have to stay at the hospital overnight.''

She waited a minute. ''No, that's not it. Joe Bob's dead. No, Momma, don't cry. It's okay. It's all okay. Carly'll stay until you get here, but wait until I get back to tell you what happened. Okay? Momma, stop it. It's all okay. Yeah, right away.''

The sheriff nodded his approval. ''I'll get a couple of the boys out here to move the body. You want it taken to Muellers?''

Zelda Marie nodded. ''I guess.''

The sheriff walked over and put an arm around her. ''Honey, I'll wait until your mother gets here and explain what happened. You don't have to do it all. I'll tell her not to worry. Not a person beyond this room, not even the guys who're gonna pick him up or even your momma, unless you tell her, will know it wasn't an accident. Don't you dare let yourself feel bad, honey. You been puttin' up with too much for too many years now.''

Zelda Marie began to cry again.

Walt raised his eyebrows and glanced at Carly. He was still holding Little Joe.

Carly thought maybe she was going to be sick.

"I'm not cryin' about Joe Bob,'' Zelda Marie explained. "I'm crying 'cause I hurt like hell.'' The stain of red had spread all over the back of her skirt.

"Come on,'' Walt said, walking swiftly out the door. He was back in a minute and picked up Zelda Marie and carried her out, too.

"Fine man, your stepdad,'' said the sheriff, turning to call his office and request Verity's two policemen sent out. "Tell them to bring a body bag,'' he told the girl on the phone.

Carly was wondering if she would suffer guilt the rest of her life. She'd killed a man. But, on the other hand, she'd saved Zelda Marie and her son.

She went into the bathroom and threw up.

By the time Carly reached home it was dark. She knew she'd have to tell Walt and her mother the truth. Would they ever forgive her?

The moment she walked up the steps, Francey opened the door, the light shining behind her, her arms outstretched. "Baby,'' she said, folding Carly in her arms. She'd been crying.

Walt stood in back of her. "Zelda Marie told me,'' he explained. "She thought you'd need some consoling. But no one else is going to know, Carly. No one. Ever.''

"Oh, baby,'' Francey cried. "How awful for you. And for Zelda Marie. To think what she's been going through all these years.''

"Remind me never to turn Dick Redford down if he wants a loan," Walt said.

"You don't think I'm awful?" Carly asked, weak with relief.

"Honey, you did the world a favor, and certainly you did one for your best friend and her family."

"But I killed a man," Carly said to Walt as Francey pulled her into the house.

"There are worse things," he said.

"Men who kill in war are heroes," Francey said. "You're a heroine, at least in our eyes."

"Oh, Mom," Carly said, "no one in this world has better parents."

They walked into the kitchen, where Walt had margaritas waiting. "Got home just in time to whip these up for you."

The smell of pot roast permeated the house. Carly knew she couldn't eat a thing.

"Talking of us being such wonderful parents," a smile glinted in Walt's eye. "We were wanting to broach it to you over this weekend, anyhow. You might think you're a little old for this, but I'd like to officially adopt you."

Tears sprang into Carly's eyes.

"I want to be your father," Walt said, and his eyes were moist, too. "I want the two most wonderful women in the world to belong to me."

Carly burst into tears.

CHAPTER 26

When her plane landed back in Houston, Carly was surprised to find Cole waiting for her. For just a second she considered walking right past him. She really didn't want to face anyone right now, least of all Cole.

"Well," he said as they headed to the parking lot. "Did you solve your friend's problem?"

Oh, God, did I ever, Carly thought. Instead, she nodded and said, "I think so."

"You look like you were up all night," Cole commented.

"I was, pretty near," she said. She figured he'd take off quicker than a jackrabbit if she told him what had really happened. It didn't make her feel warmly toward him. "All I want to do now is have a hot bath and sleep."

He frowned slightly, and grabbed her hand. "You're too tired for me . . . ?"

"Yes," she said. "I am. I know that's why you met me tonight, but I'm exhausted." She didn't want to be with anyone. She needed some space, some time to herself to absorb all that had happened over the nightmarish weekend.

She'd seen Zelda Marie at the hospital just before she'd left.

Carly had tried to tell her how sorry she was but Zelda Marie held up her hand. "Carly, you did me and the kids a favor."

"Did he have any insurance?"

Zelda Marie shook her head. "Heck, no. But we'll be fine. He never was much help. Daddy's been pretty much supportin' us ever since we got married. And you know what he told me this morning? He was wrong. He should never have made me marry Joe Bob. I never thought my daddy would say that."

"I'm willing to tell the sheriff the truth, you know."

"Shucks, he just took one look at Little Joe and me and figured I'd done it and with good reason, too. Look at me. My eyes are swollen shut nearly as bad as my lips are cracked open. Besides, no one's going to think I killed him, only the sheriff. And how about Little Joe? Only five years old and he was going to take the blame so no one would hurt me. Don't that take the cake?"

Carly had to admit it did.

"What I'm worried about," Zelda Marie said from the hospital bed, "is you. I know you well enough to know even if you think you did me a favor, even if you think you saved Little

Joe and me, you're going to feel awful you killed someone. That's what I'm worried about. Your conscience.''

"My conscience is fine," Carly lied.

"And so's our friendship. More solid than ever." Zelda Marie reached out to put her hand over Carly's.

Zelda Marie tried to laugh but her mouth wouldn't move that much. "Look, I'm in pain right now, but as soon as I get through with physical pain the other kind of pain in my life isn't going to be there anymore. I love you, Carly, more than ever. Best thing you ever did for me was to come down this weekend.''

Carly kissed her friend and let herself out of the hospital room, walking down the hall and out into the bright sunlight. She inhaled deeply, thinking how blue the sky was. She had the distinct feeling that although Joe Bob would never see the sky again, Zelda Marie might really begin to live. She must tell herself from now on that she had not killed a man so much as saved a friend.

Nevertheless, the emotions of the weekend had taken their toll, and she didn't want to talk with Cole. But, in the car, he held her hand tightly as he drove, glancing over at her, his eyes warm. Now that they were alone, his face was more open.

"I didn't know that I could miss someone so much in just two days.''

When she didn't respond, he asked, "Did you have a good time?''

Carly searched for an answer. "I probably gained two pounds. My mother cooked all my favorite foods, and you know what?''

"What?''

"Walt wants to adopt me." There was wonder in her voice. "Hmm, I wonder if he'll want me to change my name to Carly Davis." Carly was looking straight ahead, but she wasn't seeing the street or the trees. "I wouldn't mind at all.''

"You really love him, don't you?''

Carly, still staring at nothing, answered, "I love Walt Davis as much as I love anyone in the world.''

"Lucky man." Cole's voice was so soft she turned to look at him. "You have a picture of them?" Cole could imagine what they looked like. Grant Wood type people.

Carly fished in her purse for the photo they'd had taken shortly after their wedding. When he stopped for a red light, Cole reached out for it. "Wow," he said. "She's so beautiful."

"She's the prettiest woman I know."

He whistled. "Pretty isn't the right word. She's gorgeous. She's . . . she looks just like you except she has dark hair."

By the time they pulled up in front of her apartment, Carly was feeling better than she had when he'd met her. "You can come up and bring the bag. I could call out for a pizza, if you want," she said.

In all his twenty-six years, Cole had never called out for a pizza. But he did want to see Carly's apartment.

He followed her to the elevator. Her apartment was on the third floor. She unlocked the door, and he followed her in, setting her bag down. While it certainly wasn't elegant, he liked it. For such a small place, it did not seem claustrophobic to him, but cozy. The walls were white, as were probably all the walls in the building, as were about seventy percent of all apartments in the whole country. A soft dark-green carpet set off the pastel-flowered couch and chair.

Carly walked over to the sliding-glass windows and opened them. "Let's air this place out," she said.

Against one wall was an old-fashioned roll-top desk with papers cluttering it. On the other side of the room was a TV and stereo. Lining one entire wall was a built-in bookcase, loaded with books, many of them best-selling paperbacks. He turned to look at Carly, who was hanging up her jacket and saying, "I hope you don't mind if I take a bath. Here's the number for the pizza. I want pineapple, bacon, cheese, onions, and green peppers on mine. Okay? In the kitchen," she pointed to the door, opposite the one to her bedroom, "is some stuff for making drinks. I think there's some gin and maybe tequila and Cointreau, since I'm partial to margaritas. There's beer in the fridge but probably not much else except orange juice and Coke. I'll make some coffee after I have a bath.''

Cole looked at the card in his hand. What did you do when you ordered a pizza? How big a one, or should he order two? Should he go pick it up or would they deliver? He suddenly thought he might be the only person in America who had never ordered a pizza.

He picked up the phone and dialed. The kid promised the pizza would be there in forty minutes.

Cole walked into the kitchen, a standard apartment issue that Carly had definitely made her own, with blue-and-white curtains, a blue tea kettle, and cupboards she had painted Wedgwood blue. A row of cookbooks was lined up neatly on top of the refrigerator.

He found the gin, a stray lemon, and the tonic and mixed himself a drink. Walking back into the living room, glass in hand, he studied the records beside the stereo. What he'd call smoochy music—some old Nat King Coles, Jefferson Airplane, John Denver, Peter, Paul and Mary. He flipped a record out of its holder and placed it on the turntable.

Walking out on the tiny balcony, he stared into the darkness. The third-floor apartment wasn't high enough to look out over the city lights, but there was a pleasant view of trees and a pool. The music soaked into him, and he felt strangely comfortable, at peace. He was allowing himself to relax with the sexiest woman in the universe—his universe, anyhow—the most beautiful and the sweetest.

He wanted suddenly to meet Walt and Francey, see what Carly's family was like. If Walt was the president of a bank, even in tiny Verity, he had to have some class. Hadn't Carly told him the grandfather founded the bank, so no doubt the Davises had been Verity's leading citizens for decades. At least three generations. And Walt Davis had married Carly's gorgeous mother, and he wanted to adopt Carly. Tell the world she was his daughter.

When Cole heard Carly come out of the bedroom, he turned to face her; she looked different to him. It wasn't the peach-flowered kimono, and he'd seen her hair dripping wet down in Acapulco, but she looked different and he couldn't explain how. It was as though now he was looking beyond that beautiful satin skin, looking beyond those robin's-egg blue eyes into something he had not let himself see.

They looked at each other for a minute, without talking, and then Carly went to the kitchen and got a beer. She returned and went out to stand on the balcony with him, leaning against the wrought-iron railing.

She took a deep breath and a swig of beer, drinking straight from the bottle.

"Did you tell your mother about us?" Cole asked.

Carly shook her head. And then she smiled. "Well, I might have said there was some man, but I didn't name names. You think I tell her about every man I go to bed with?"

Cole grinned. "Every man? Me and that high school boy?"

He reached and pulled her to him. Their lips met, and his tongue parted hers. Her arms wound around his neck, and her kimono slipped to the floor.

"Show me your bedroom," he murmured.

"Later," she said, untying his tie. "Right now I can't wait that long."

But just as they sank to the floor, the doorbell rang.

Carly reached for her robe, tying the belt as she walked to the door. She found her purse on the chair where she'd tossed it, opened the door and took the pizza.

While Cole climbed into his trousers laughing, Carly mixed herself a drink, then opened the pizza carton and cut the pizza into eight slices. She set the table with silverware and blue-and-apricot straw place mats, poured water, and put coffee on to perk.

She walked back out to the balcony and leaned against the railing, looking out over the trees. She turned to look at Cole.

"I killed a man yesterday," she said, studying him as she told him.

He only stared at her.

She walked back into the kitchen and sat down, putting a piece of pizza on her plate. Cole still stood on the balcony.

"Going to join me or run?"

Cole slowly came into the kitchen, pulled a chair out and sank into it, staring at her the whole time.

"Tell me about it."

Holding the pizza with her fingers, Carly bit into it.

Cole didn't say anything; nor did he reach out for any pizza. He stared at her. Watching her eat three slices, he finally asked, "Are we talking a car accident?"

"We're talking murder. Violent murder," she answered, wiping her fingers on a paper napkin.

There were at least two minutes of silence, which seemed to last an hour. "Why?" he finally asked. "How?"

"With a frying pan." She began to relate the whole story and was surprised to find at the end that she was crying and shivering uncontrollably.

Cole sat rigid. He wanted to hold her forever and tell her it was all right. He wanted to show her that the gruesome story she'd just told didn't matter to him, but nothing came out of his throat. No words, no sound of any kind. He wanted to reach out and touch her, but he simply couldn't move.

"Thank God it won't be in the paper" was what he said. His parents need never know anything about it. "You don't have to tell anyone else, Carly. Your secret's safe with me."

"If I didn't think it was, I wouldn't have told you. I thought you ought to know." She was feeling better now, better than she had since "it" had happened.

"Where's your bathroom?" he asked.

"Through the bedroom."

Her bedroom was rather like he imagined it would be, all frills and ruffles and pink and white. He had planned to stay overnight, but all he wanted to do now was get the hell out of here. Get out in fresh air. Walk around. Go home and think about this.

When he returned to the kitchen, he said, "I think you need

time to be alone." Could she have made love twenty-four hours after killing a man with a frying pan?

"I'll be okay," she said, noticing his coolness. "I need to keep busy."

Though he did not move to touch her, standing in the doorway, he said, "Thank you for telling me, Carly."

"I wanted you to know."

He nodded and, without saying anything else, opened the door to the hallway and disappeared.

Carly noted he had not said good night.

She went to bed and slept for thirteen hours straight.

CHAPTER 27

"You and Cole," Ben asked, "aren't a thing anymore?"

Alex shrugged and sipped her Cointreau. "I don't know that we ever were."

"Oh, come on," objected Ben. "You've been a thing since you were kids."

She smiled at him and changed the topic. "Do you even know what you want to do?"

"Sure. I'd like to climb the Himalayas, sail the southern seas, write poetry . . . In lieu of that . . ."

"Wait. Why not climb the Himalayas or sail the southern seas? You're young. Why not do it before settling down?"

Ben sighed. "I wish I could answer that. No guts. I've always been gutless. I wanted to major in English, but no, it had to be economics. I don't understand economics, I don't care about math or logic or money . . . If I hadn't been gutless, I'd still have the use of this hand." His left hand lay flat and lifeless on the table.

"Don't be silly," Alex said. She knew he was self-conscious about his hand, even after all these years.

Ben held up his good hand. "Enough, Alex. I don't want to talk about it." He changed the subject. "Is there a man in your life, Alex? Mother says you and Cole haven't been seeing each other for months."

She hesitated before answering. "Sort of."

"Who? No one I know, I gather?"

She shook her head. "The man you met at the club. Brad Bannerman."

How could she tell Ben Coleridge there was a man in her life named Boomer? "Look, we came here to talk about you."

"I don't know what the hell to do. I don't want to go back to school if I have to major in something to do with business. It bores me to hell and gone."

"Doesn't *anything* attract you?"

"Sure. But nothing that makes the kind of money a Coleridge is expected to earn. I'd like to go work on a little country weekly."

"A newspaper?" Ben was so impractical. But then, Alex supposed, that was another one of his charms.

"Yeah. I'd like to live in a small town and get to know everyone and put out a newspaper. I've been thinking of trying to find one that needs a reporter, though most of them barely make enough for the owner to need anyone else to work for him. Someplace like Nacogdoches or Aransas Pass or Big Spring."

"You really do want the boonies, don't you?"

"I want someplace where people don't try to impress each other, where people really get to know each other, where life is basic rather than all this fake hoopla we're caught up with."

"Fake?"

He nodded. "The Coleridges and the Headlands don't live in the real world, Alex. You must recognize that. But I've noticed something. You laugh more'n you used to. You sort of bubble from inside. It's this guy, isn't it? He makes you laugh."

She changed the subject. "So, what's the worst that could

happen if you could go find a small-town newspaper to work for?"

"Dad would have a shit fit. He thinks unless your nose is to the grindstone at least sixteen hours a day you're not paying your passage in this world."

Alex shared much the same view. "What about your mother?"

"You know her. If I marry a girl who hasn't been to college, and to a good college at that, or I marry someone who doesn't know how to dress elegantly, Mother will cringe. She wouldn't mind at all if the girl's not from Texas as long as she has a pedigree. A Boston accent wouldn't be bad to bring to the family. She doesn't care what kind of work I do as long as it's something that will reflect well on the family, and she can put her arm around me and introduce me as her 'darling baby' and do it with pride in her voice. With her, appearances are everything."

"I like your mother."

"And you are exactly what she wants in a daughter-in-law. If you and Cole aren't getting it on, maybe you and I should start. That would please her."

"You're too young for me."

"Do you think when I'm fifty and you're fifty-five that it'll really matter?"

"Do you ever think of getting married?"

"Shit," Ben said, "I don't believe in monogamy. And I don't believe in dishonesty. So why enter something when you know from the beginning it's not going to be what you promise to bring to it? No. I don't envision getting married. For God's sake, I'm just twenty-two. What about you?"

"I think of it now and then, but I'm not ready. I don't want children to interfere. I don't want to be tied down either."

"Or monogamous?"

She thought about that. "If I get married I expect to be faithful and I expect the same from my husband. If one's not willing to make those commitments, why bother with marriage?"

"You may be older but you're not necessarily wiser. I think you're naive, my dear Alex."

Alex had never thought of herself as naive, not since the day she was born. It was Ben who was the innocent, the dreamer.

"Are you going to be in town for a while?"

Ben shrugged. "I guess until I find out what the next step is."

"Call me at the office and we'll have lunch again next week, okay? I've got to run now."

She stood up and bent down to kiss Ben's forehead. "The bill's been paid."

She turned and sailed out of the restaurant.

When Boomer phoned her at ten that night, she asked, "What are chances of driving up to Nacogdoches this weekend?"

"Any particular reason?"

"Yes. Anyhow, I'd like to go look it over and I'd like it even better if you were along for the ride."

"Sure," he said. "You want to take the cycle?"

She always enjoyed the thrill of the wind in her face, of hugging Boomer for hours on end. A couple of weeks ago, dragging Tessa with her, Alex had even self-consciously bought a set of leathers to wear when cycling. She refrained from buying the same colors as Boomer's, thinking that would be just too cute.

She wondered how he'd react if she asked how he felt about beginning to call him Brad, instead of Boomer. It was about time to test bringing him home for dinner. She knew that. Perhaps wondering how her parents would react to Boomer was what kept her from letting her heart free.

She pretty much knew what their reaction would be if she told them she was serious about this roughneck who looked and dressed like an oil rigger, who wore work boots and open-necked sometimes unironed shirts to work, whose pants and jackets seldom matched, and who went without a tie whenever possible. Come to think of it, she'd never seen Boomer in a suit, except for that rented tux. Well, she'd have to rectify that. Talk him into a shopping spree. Certainly buy him a decent-looking pair of shoes, too.

It wasn't that he didn't have taste. God, those apartments that were nearly ready, they were gorgeous. He, Tessa, and Dan together were a real class act when it came to design and construction. Alex liked the touches Tessa was adding to her own apartment, softening it yet leaving her own preference of black and white and steel. Boomer no longer thought it looked so stark.

Tessa's taste was going to appeal to the elegant of Houston, Alex suspected. And Dan's designs had the cleanest lines, simple yet with an aura of luxuriousness. The three of them were going to make money from the up and coming, who when they got there would still remember to call on Tessa and Dan and Boomer for their homes and even perhaps their office buildings. So, why did Alex think Houston society, as she knew it, would look down on them. She guessed a second step, having taken them all to the club as the first, would be to invite her mother and Tessa to lunch together. See how her mother reacted to her new best friend, the only best friend she'd ever had.

Alex picked up the phone and dialed Tessa. "Would it be asking too much of you to have lunch with my mother next week?"

Tessa replied, sounding slightly harried, "Alex, I would love that. I need a surrogate mother down here once in a while."

Alex cocked an eyebrow. Sometimes her mother intimidated even her. She'd overpower Tessa. Though Alex knew her mother loved her, Mrs. Headland was not what anyone in the world would call maternal. Her father might think of her as a perfect wife. They probably had a satisfactory marriage, one of the few she knew of. Well, maybe the Coleridges did too, though Alex often wondered how Aunt Maude could stand that stiff-necked tight-assed husband.

Funny, she'd never thought in those words or even thought of Mr. Coleridge in those terms. It was Boomer's influence. She saw the whole world in a different light now.

CHAPTER 28

"Now that you can see light at the end of the tunnel," Alex said, referring to the near completion of the first unit of the apartments Boomer and Dan had been building, "do you have any ideas for the future?"

"A hundred," Boomer answered, a burrito poised in his hands. It was Sunday night and they were at Dan and Tessa's. "But none we've talked much about."

"Well," Alex smiled, "I think I may have an offer that will appeal to you."

The three of them looked at her expectantly.

"I needn't tell you Houston is becoming *the* boom town. I, for one, think within the next twenty years it's going to become one of the largest cities in the U.S., and certainly the most exciting one. Anyhow I have a client who owns a chunk of the most expensive downtown real estate and he wants to erect an office building that'll really make the country understand that Houston counts. He's willing to invest millions."

"Millions?"

"*And* millions, on the building alone. I told him about you three."

They sat looking at Alex. She smiled smugly, and picked up her burrito. Tessa made the best Mexican food. She told them she had learned how to up north in Rochester. Alex was the only one eating. The other three stared at her.

"An office building?" Tessa asked. "I know this is self-centered and selfish, but where's a role for me in this?"

Alex's smile remained. "I think I can talk my client into insisting that everyone who wants to lease office space use you as a consultant, even if they have their own decorators. I also think, with only a little persuasion, most people will be thrilled to have you decorate. Businessmen have so little taste that way.

"As for you, Dan, aside from designing the exterior—and my client would like it very modern with a lot of glass—you'd design each of the offices as they're leased and we know the needs of the clients."

Only the purring of Tessa's cat could be heard.

Then Boomer picked up the burrito he'd laid down on his plate and began nibbling on it. "We don't need to borrow anything on this, right? We're not financially responsible? We get paid to do it?"

Tessa put her hand on his arm. "Now, Boomer, let's listen to all this before you start acting like you can't stand to be employed by someone else."

"You'll make close to a million net profit, you three, if it works out the way I think it will. And it'll lead to other opportunities. I've been working on a plan for this the last few weeks, and my client appears willing to go along with everything I throw at him."

"Who's your mysterious client?" Boomer asked.

"J. Wellington Rockford."

Boomer let out a whistle and Dan raised an eyebrow.

"Oh, goody!" Tessa said. "A dream come true! Well, guys, what do you say?"

Boomer turned to Alex. "Wanna fill us in on the details?"

Three hours later, by eleven, they'd agreed Alex should arrange a meeting for the three of them with Rockford.

J. Wellington Rockford was a Texas legend. A self-made billionaire, he dabbled in oil, in Longhorns, in gas, in construction, in television. He had owned the first FM station in Dallas, and now owned two of the largest TV stations in the state. He was a patron of the arts, a self-taught guitarist, and owned the largest truck manufacturing plant in Texas, reaping millions in government contracts.

He had married at nineteen, but his wife died in childbirth

two years later. He'd never remarried. His passion was his business, and he was always hatching new schemes. Now he wanted to build the tallest and grandest office building in Houston. One that would make it into the pages of *Life* magazine.

He was a quiet, soft-spoken man, and if you didn't recognize his name you'd never know he wielded all that power. Alex called him Uncle Jay, for J. Wellington. She had known him since she was a child, and he had told her even then, "Set your eyes on the stars and don't let the fact you're a woman lessen your vision."

He'd followed her progress with keen delight. And if she could put together a package for building this dream of his, he was more than willing to toss it in her lap.

He took one look at Boomer Bannerman and decided he was the right man for his girl. He took one look at Alex and figured she already knew that.

"Give me a time frame" was all he asked.

Dan said he'd get to work on drawings right away and they'd toss over ideas. Boomer said he still had to finish the apartments, but they agreed if Dan could start with drawings and the three of them begin bouncing ideas off each other, then maybe the entire project could be complete in two years.

Rockford nodded. Didn't seem impossible to him. And it didn't seem impossible to Boomer, either, after Rockford told how much he was willing to invest in the project. They could employ a lot of men for that.

"Well," Boomer said as he drove Alex to her apartment after the dinner meeting was over. "Seems like my lucky day was the day I met you."

"Are you going to come up?" she asked. It was wonderful being in business with a lover. The two intertwined.

Boomer leaned over and smiled at her, his lips touching hers. "Was that an invitation?"

"Oh, hurry up," she said, as she unlocked the door to the building, "or I'll seduce you right here in the foyer."

"That might be fun. Novel, anyhow." He grinned, following her to the elevator.

The minute they entered her apartment, Alex began to unbutton her taupe silk blouse, unzipping her skirt and letting it fall to the floor.

Boomer laughed out loud. "Alex, one of the things I love about you is your lack of coyness."

He looked at her bare breasts. She could excite him like no one ever could. No one since Carly Anderson, so many years ago. He gathered her in his arms and lifted her off the floor. She raised her arms high in the air, soft moans escaping her. Boomer nibbled her belly. She trembled.

"Put me down," she said, her voice a whisper.

When he did, she took his hand and led him to the couch and unbuckled his belt.

She lay down, grabbing his hand and pulling him on top of her. He lay on top of her, kissing her until she said, "I can't wait," and he entered her with a thrust that sent shivers cascading across her flesh. She arched her back, her hands going around him to cup his buttocks and pulled him into her until they were one. The sweat of their bodies mingled as Alex cried out, over and over again, until finally she shouted, "Now!"

Later, when Alex placed the Baileys on the coffee table, Boomer said, "Marry me, Alex."

There was a moment's silence and then she laughed, a sound that tinkled like silver across the room. "Don't be silly," she said, handing him a glass.

"Why? Do any two people get along better? We have the greatest sex in the world. We're in business together. I'm going to make a bundle out of this deal you've dreamed up, and maybe I can't support you now in the style to which you're accustomed, but with two of us working . . . I'm not a man to be intimidated by a wife who earns more than I do. On the other hand, if you should want to stop, within two years I'm sure I'll be at a place where I can do pretty well by you.

"Besides, Alex, I'm crazy about you. That must have been

obvious from the first minute I walked into your office. If you don't know it, you're blind.''

He knelt on one bended knee and, grabbing her left hand, in a melodramatic voice said, ''Alex, I'm madly, totally in love with you. Say you'll be my wife.''

Alex drew her hand back and snapped, ''For heaven's sake, Boomer, stop acting like an idiot. Don't ruin something so beautiful.''

He jerked his head and stood up. ''Don't ruin it? For God's sake, don't you want to have kids before you're too old to play with them?''

It wasn't that she didn't want to have children, but she didn't want to have them yet.

''Come on.'' Boomer reached out to take her in his arms and pulled her close to him. ''Let's get married. I hate leaving here each night and going home to my lonely bed. I want to wake up next to you, kiss you awake, I want to sleep every night naked next to your nakedness. I want to wake up at three A.M. and screw the daylights out of you. Come on. We can take the biggest apartment in our complex, the one with three bedrooms. We can show how stylishly people can live over there. Be our own best advertisement. Tessa and Dan can stand up with us . . .''

''Boomer!'' Alex's voice was sharp.

''Okay,'' he went on. ''So we have a formal wedding, so big it'll knock the socks off everybody, and your father can give you away and you can wear white with a train six yards long . . .''

''Boomer!'' she repeated.

''I love you. When two people love each other, they get married and start families and share their lives.''

''I'm not even sure I love you.'' Her voice sounded like a little girl's.

Boomer sat down. He looked at her with blank, uncomprehending eyes.

Silence hung between them.

She walked out onto the balcony. The night sky was inky;

the stars looked like they were hung there. She thought she might be able to pull one to her.

He followed her and grabbed her shoulders, turning her around to face him. "What the hell does that mean? You don't know!"

She sighed. "Oh, Boomer, we agree about the things we have in common. We've never even talked about all the other things."

"What other things? What the hell else matters?"

The way you dress. Your not knowing which is the salad fork and which the dessert fork. The way people looked at you at the club. The way my mother raised her eyebrows when she saw me with you. Your not liking Mozart. But she didn't say any of those things.

"Can't we just go on like this?" she did say. "We're having a wonderful time. We probably spend more time together than most married couples. Can't you leave it at that?"

"No," he said. "I can't. I want us to come home to each other. I want what Tessa and Dan have."

She wrenched herself away from his grasp and walked into the living room. "Don't press it," she said. "Boomer, I'm enjoying this as much as you are. Do you need a piece of paper to make sure I don't leave?"

He thought about that. "I guess it would make me feel more secure."

Her face twisted, and for a moment he thought she was going to cry. "Boomer," she said, her voice breaking, "I've never felt this way about any other man. About anyone at all. But even if I *were* sure I loved you . . . marriage?"

"You haven't even *thought* about it?"

They stood facing each other, Alex with her arms crossed, Boomer standing with his legs wide apart, in the stance of a fighter.

Then he walked over to the couch where he'd tossed his jacket, picked it up and, without putting it on, opened the door, took a backward glance and exited, slamming it hard.

CHAPTER 29

Carly had trouble sleeping all week. She'd drop off easily because she walked around exhausted all the time, but by one o'clock she was wide awake and couldn't get back to sleep until four or five and was in a deep sleep when the alarm jolted her awake.

She had nightmares. And always in her hand was a frying pan, which with each passing night grew larger and heavier. Joe Bob stared at her, with wide, frightened bloodshot eyes, screaming silently. She was unable to hear his voice but his mouth formed "No!" over and over again.

He reached out from the grave to grab her, always missing her ankle by inches. She would awaken with her pillow damp and sweat covering her body.

Cole hadn't phoned her all week. It was over, and she knew it.

She guessed she'd always known it wouldn't last. And she had to admit if he'd told her he'd killed a man, she'd have to take time out to think if she wanted to be mixed up with a murderer. That's what she was, wasn't she? If you killed someone you were a murderer, weren't you?

He'd said he wanted to meet Francey and Walt, but now he probably never would.

Was he missing her, or had he been able to cut her right out of his mind? Did he no longer desire her, or was he fighting those yearnings? He obviously wasn't going to see her this weekend. It was nearly five now, Friday afternoon. She should stop pinning her hopes on the idea that he would phone her, that he would take her in his arms and say it didn't matter that she killed a man.

"Damn," she said.

Loud and clear he'd said a silent good-bye, hadn't he?

She told herself she couldn't blame him. She'd known from the beginning in spite of his power and money, he was not strong. He'd never have had the courage to take her into his life, full-time, anyhow.

She left the office and walked down the street, studying her reflection in the glass of the storefronts as she passed them. Men's glances told her she was good-looking. Cole had told her she was the most beautiful woman in the world.

She passed Eddie's, one of the downtown places that began to be crowded about this hour five nights a week. She'd go have a drink. Sit at the bar, even, and look around. Listen to the jazz. She'd never even been in Eddie's. Maybe tonight was the night she should try. Who knew what might be waiting for her there? She'd have a margarita and sit on a stool and look around the room and see if a new Prince Charming was waiting for her.

She was on her second margarita, enjoying the music and shaking her head no to the numerous offers to buy her a drink, when she nearly fell off the bar stool.

Walking into the bar, silhouetted against the still bright light from outside, was a figure she would have recognized anyplace. The angry expression on his face was not one she'd ever seen on him before, but over four years could change anyone.

He stood in the smoke-filled bar, his eyes beginning a survey, but before they got too far they stopped, seeing her. He stood stock-still as though he didn't believe his eyes, then his face wreathed into a smile, and he snaked his way through the crowd toward her.

"Carly Anderson. Well, I'll be damned."

The man on the stool next to Carly slid off and Boomer sat down, gathering Carly in a bear hug. "Little Carly Anderson, you sure grew up into something," he said admiringly.

"You look pretty successful yourself," she said, wishing he'd go on holding her like this. She hoped she wouldn't burst into tears.

"Scotch and branch water," he told the bartender, letting

go of her, a smile creasing his face. "It's been a long time."
He looked her over and said, "Too long."

"Boomer Bannerman," she said, her voice filled with
wonder.

By midnight Carly wondered what she'd ever seen in Cole.
She hadn't felt this sense of exhilaration since she'd last seen
Boomer.

He made her laugh, and he asked her all about the people
they knew in Verity. The only one he'd ever kept in touch with
was his Aunt Addie.

He told her of his best friends, Dan and Tessa, and of their
big project, due to open the first tier of apartments in another
two weeks. They were going to have a big splash, inviting
newspaper and TV reporters and offering free champagne and
tours. He wasn't nervous. He knew they'd create a stir and
would be successful. He thought three apartments were already
rented, and he was going to take one himself. Maybe one of
the large three-bedroom ones. Ought to be some perks to being
boss. She listened more than she talked, but Boomer told her
he wanted to hear all about what she'd been doing for the last
four years.

It seemed as if she'd been talking for hours, when at eight,
he glanced at his watch and declared, "I'm starved. Let's get
out of here and go find a nice Mexican restaurant. You still
like Tex Mex?"

She nodded, pleased he remembered.

They walked a block in the twilight evening to his car.
"Wow!" Carly whistled.

"You were always the only girl I knew who could whistle."
He grinned, unlocking the door and helping her in.

They drove three miles before he pulled into the parking lot
of an adobe-type building that had a big cactus lit by neon over
the door. "Doesn't look like much," he admitted, stretching
his long legs out of the car, "but the food's great."

It wasn't someplace he would ever have brought Alex, he realized.

The food was worthy of his praise. After dinner, they sat drinking endless cups of coffee so that they'd have a reason to stay. At eleven, though, the waitress said, ''Sorry, guys, but we're closing.''

Boomer glanced at Carly. ''I don't want to leave you when I've just found you again.''

Carly laughed. ''Oh, Boomer, you make me feel like a schoolgirl.'' They stood up. ''We can go to my place, if you want. I'm not ready to call it quits for the evening, either.''

''The evening?'' he asked, opening the door of the restaurant. ''It's going to be longer than that, Carly.'' He took her hand. ''Your place it is.''

The minute he closed the door behind him, he gathered her in his arms. ''Seems like old times,'' he said, kissing her.

Carly closed her eyes and felt herself surrendering to feelings she had tried to bury years ago. Boomer. Boomer was back.

She could feel the heat from his body. He held her so close that nothing was between them, except their clothes. And she could tell even those wouldn't be a barrier much longer.

Later, much later, after they'd made love, once quickly and a second time in a slow, sensuous lingering way, Boomer asked, ''How did I ever leave you behind in Verity?''

''I've wondered that for years.''

He laughed. ''I'll bet.''

''It's true, Boomer. I've never loved any other man but you.''

He turned on his side and leaned on his elbow, looking down at her. ''There haven't been any other men in your life?''

''I didn't say that. I just said I've never been in love except for you.''

He exhaled and stared at her, then he sat up on the edge of the bed and asked if she had any milk in the fridge.

She nodded.

He padded naked through the living room and came back with a tall glass of cold milk.

"Do you believe in fate?" he asked, sitting back down on the bed, leaning against the headboard. The glass of milk in one hand, he reached out to grasp hers in the other.

"I hadn't thought much about it."

He smiled. "Carly, you are the softest thing in the world to touch. And you make a guy feel, God, I don't know how to explain it. You make me feel like the most important thing in the world to you is making love with me. You always did that."

"When you're kissing me, when you're touching me I think if I died right then, I'll have died happy. I never thought to see you again, Boomer. I feel like any minute I'm going to wake up and it's all a dream."

Despite herself, she found her eyes closing. She was tired. She could hardly keep her eyes open, but she didn't want to miss a minute of Boomer. He went on talking and she tried, very hard, to listen, but his voice kept getting fainter and fainter.

The next thing she knew sunlight streamed through the curtains. Carly felt cocooned, lying in Boomer's arms. Remaining in the same position where she'd fallen asleep, she looked over at Boomer, not moving her head so that she wouldn't wake him. She stared at him for a long time. His beard was stubbly. His lashes fluttered slightly as he slept. She heard his even, deep breathing. Involuntarily, she raised her hand and traced imaginary lines lightly across his chest. When he stirred momentarily, she stopped. She rested her hand on his chest, refraining from caressing him further.

She lay there for half an hour, content and fulfilled, feeling an emotion so deep that she couldn't explain it to herself.

"I hear you looking at me." Boomer's voice was hoarse.

"I *am* looking at you," Carly murmured. "You look beautiful."

He opened one eye and raised his eyebrow. His mouth curled

into a smile. He stretched to kiss her. Then he opened both eyes, putting his other arm around her and drawing her to him.

At breakfast, they lingered over coffee. Carly's toes toyed with his under the table. Her eyes brimmed with happiness.

Boomer poured himself more coffee and leaned back in his chair, stretching out his legs. He gazed at Carly.

"It feels like my life's just been on hold ever since I last saw you," she said to him. "I think I've just been putting in time waiting to meet you again."

CHAPTER 30

So, Carly had killed a man. Well, Cole decided, that showed how brave she was. What he should have done when she told him was gather her in his arms and kiss her cheeks and her hair and say, "Everything's going to be all right and I'm going to take care of you and you never have to worry about a thing."

Instead, he'd imagined how his parents would react if the truth leaked into the newspapers. How his parents would react, no matter what she did or didn't do, at his marrying Carly.

Well, he thought, they'd buy a home in River Oaks and move into it as soon as they came back from their honeymoon. Where could he take her that would delight her? White Sulphur Springs? New Orleans? Europe? No, he couldn't get away for that long right now, Europe would have to wait. He laughed. He knew where she'd probably get the greatest kick—Disneyland. *He* wouldn't be caught dead at Disneyland, but he imagined Carly would love it. She'd have a ball.

He shook his head, wondering how he could possibly think of marrying a girl who would love Disneyland. But he was going to. She'd bring sun and light to him every day. She'd make him laugh, and pretty soon ordering pizza might be second nature, and perhaps one day, maybe after they had children, they would go to Disneyland. With Carly, he might even enjoy it.

He'd have his mother teach her how to be a charming hostess, how to dress. He knew how grateful she'd be. She'd never have to work again and he'd see that she had everything she wanted. She'd think she was the luckiest girl alive. When, really, he'd be the luckiest man.

"Look," Boomer said, smiling down at Carly with a tenderness she remembered well, "I have to do some things with Tessa and Dan, but I'll call you when I'm finished, okay?"

Carly nodded. That sounded just lovely.

After he left, she walked back to her bedroom and saw the unmade bed. She sat down on it and pulled close the pillow that still bore the imprint of Boomer's head, hugging it.

The phone rang.

"Carly." It was Cole's voice. "I'd like to drive down to Verity today," he said. "I want to meet your mother and Walt."

Carly sat up straight. The pillow dropped to the floor. "You want to what?"

"It only takes about four or five hours, doesn't it? How soon can you be ready?"

Carly wondered how long he must have been thinking about this. He so seldom did things spontaneously. "I don't know, Cole. I mean . . ."

"Come on," he urged. "It's a beautiful day. Maybe we can even stay overnight, if they've room."

"They have plenty of room. But, Cole . . ."

"Call, if you think they need advance warning. Tell them we expect to dine with them. I'd like to see the Willows."

"Cole, I was just there last weekend . . ."

The memory of Joe Bob, of Zelda Marie's swollen face, floated before her. "I don't think I want to go back so soon." Or ever.

"Carly, we have to move forward."

"We?"

"Look, I'm ashamed of the way I've acted, or not acted, all week. Please . . ."

He'd never asked anything of her before. He'd never said please.

But Boomer . . . he was going to call. Well, she'd phone him and tell him tomorrow . . . she couldn't say no to Cole's "please" even if he had abandoned her when she really needed him.

"Sure, Cole. Give me half an hour. I'll phone Mom and tell her to expect us."

And, it *was* a beautiful day.

"We'll stop for lunch on the way. It's spring, Carly, it's spring."

What in the world had happened to him? Carly had to laugh.

She hung up and flipped through the phone book, not able to find a Bradley Bannerman. What had he said the name of his company was? It was initials. Okay, his friends' names were Tessa and Dan. Tessa and Dan what?

She sighed. Well, if she didn't answer the phone today, he'd call tomorrow. She knew he'd do that, especially after last night. Last night. Nothing, nobody could compare to Boomer . . . She shook her head and stood up, walking over to her closet, deciding to wear the pale-blue-and-white seersucker pants suit. She probably wouldn't need the jacket, it was so warm, so she'd wear her new white ruffled blouse. White sandals.

She walked back to the phone and dialed Verity.

When Carly opened her door, Cole gathered her in his arms and kissed her with an urgency and need she'd never felt in him before. "Come on," he said, grabbing her hand. "This was a day made by the gods."

In another month Texas would be taken over by a relentless humidity that wouldn't let up until November, when rain would prevail, but today it *was* gorgeous.

* * *

Cole sped out of town, south on route 59, before he began to talk. Their windows were open and the warm air blew Carly's hair. It felt good.

"I had a bad week," he started. "What about you?"

"I've had better."

"I certainly didn't behave like much of a man," he admitted. "Maybe it served as a catalyst, though. I've done a lot of soul-searching."

"You must have come up on the top side," Carly smiled. She imagined Cole was going to expect her to sleep with him tonight. She didn't think she could sleep with two different men on two successive nights. That somehow seemed immoral.

"Accept my apology," he said, reaching out for her hand. "I'm not proud of how I've acted. Carly, if you killed a man, no matter under what circumstances—"

"I hardly think . . ."

He held up a hand to shush her. "Let me finish. You acted admirably, with no thought of yourself. What you did was an act of love." He sounded pleased with himself, as though he had come to an heroic conclusion.

"I still don't know how I feel about it," Carly began.

"I understand that. And of all the weeks in your life when you might have needed a shoulder to lean on, someone to hold you, I screwed up." He pulled into a restaurant that looked like a log cabin, and cut the engine. "But I'm here now, bowed and ashamed. And, Carly, I do want you to lean on me. I do want to hold you. What I want, darling, is to marry you and take care of you forever."

Carly's mouth dropped open.

Cole grinned. "We're on our way to Verity not only to meet your mother and Walt, but to ask them for your hand."

Carly stared at him.

"Old-fashioned, aren't I?" Cole hadn't stopped smiling. He opened his door and slid from his seat, stretching as he stood up. He walked around the car and opened her door. Carly sat immobile.

"Come on, I'm starving. Even a hamburger and french fries will taste good." He leaned over and brushed his lips against hers. An older couple, looking out the restaurant window, smiled at them. "Christ, a week without you is like living in exile." He walked ahead of her, leading the way up the path. Carly followed him, stumbling on the first step.

The waitress seated them and handed them menus, Carly felt herself trembling inside.

"You order for me," she said. "I'm going to the ladies' room."

"The beginning of forever," he grinned. "I'll order for you from here on."

When Carly entered the darkened restroom she peered at herself in the mirror. She expected to see her confusion reflected there. Good Lord, Cole asking her to marry him? Taking for granted that's what she wanted, too?

A week ago, six days ago, there'd have been no hesitation at all. She'd have thought herself the luckiest woman in the universe. Mrs. Cole Coleridge. Carly Coleridge. It had a nice ring to it, she had to admit. How come she'd never tried that name on before, even in her fantasies.

All the way to Corpus Christi, Carly slept. Cole woke her at the outskirts of town and asked her to direct him.

It was a bit over an hour southwest. Carly felt a tightening in her chest, remembering what had happened to her last weekend. When they passed through town Carly saw the house where she and Francey had lived when she was in school here. For a minute she thought of pointing it out to Cole, but then decided not to bother. He slowed down as they drove down the main street, laughing as he commented, "Looks like the movies' version of small-town America. God, look at all the chicanos. Are you sure we haven't driven south of the border?"

"Some of these people's ancestors were here before Texas

was part of the U.S.," Carly said. "When it was still part of Mexico. That's just a little over a hundred years ago, you know."

"Hey, I didn't mean to get your dander up," Cole said, looking at her in surprise.

"Turn right here," Carly pointed.

They drove north about a mile and a half when Carly said, "Now, left," as they passed through the wide-open wrought-iron gates and down the palmetto-lined dirt drive. At the end was the rambling ranch house Walt had built for Francey. Climbing roses spilled over the front porch railing, which seemed to go on for an acre. Carly thought Cole couldn't help but be impressed, but he made no comment.

At the sound of the approaching car, Walt came down the three steps that led from the verandah and stood waiting to greet his visitors. Carly's heart always warmed at the sight of Walt. His waist that was tending to flab when she first knew him eight years ago was lean and hard, although now his blond hair and mustache were flecked with gray, in some ways he looked younger than the day she'd gone to work for him. The sun glinted off his gold-rimmed glasses, and he leaned over to open the door for Carly, gathering her in his arms. "Didn't expect to see my girl two weeks in a row," he said, but she could tell he was studying her to see if he could detect how she *really* was. He turned his gaze to Cole, holding his hand out as Cole walked around in front of the car.

"Carly's told me a lot about you, sir." Cole shook Walt's hand.

"You're at an advantage," the older man said. "I don't even know your name."

"Cole Coleridge."

Walt raised an eyebrow, glanced at Carly and then back at Cole. "Of Union Trust? That Coleridge?"

Cole nodded. "That Coleridge."

"Well, at least we have something in common," Walt said.

Carly was wondering what Walt thought of Cole. She didn't think to wonder what Cole thought of Walt.

Francey appeared in the wide doorway of the house and opened the screen door.

Cole did not move up the stairs with Walt and Carly but stood staring at Francey. Carly and her mother hugged each other and then Carly turned to introduce Cole, who still stood at the bottom of the steps. He saw her look and hurried to join the group.

"Mom, this is Cole Coleridge. Cole, my mother."

Francey's smile dazzled Cole. She held on to his outstretched hand with both of hers, gazing up into his eyes. "We haven't met a friend of Carly's since she moved to Houston," Francey said. "I'm pleased to meet you, Cole."

He made no move to draw back his hand until she let go of it and moved back into the house, into the large living room. "Do you want to wash up after your drive, or are you ready for a drink?" The skirt of Francey's yellow-flowered dress billowed as she walked. "I know Carly said we could dine at the Willows, but I love to cook and thought it would be much more intimate if we ate here. We can talk more easily." She went over to the armoire, opened it, and flicked a switch. Soft music from the early fifties filled the air.

"What would you like to drink?" Walt asked, "Carly and Francey have a penchant for margaritas. What about you, Cole?"

"Gin and tonic," Cole answered, surveying the room. "This is a lovely house, Mrs. Davis."

Francey was looking at Carly. "Will you gentlemen excuse us a minute?" she asked, taking Carly by the arm and moving out into the hall, toward the kitchen.

"My goodness," she whispered to Carly in the kitchen, "he's elegant. Is he here to look us over?"

Carly shook her head. "Mom, on our way down here, he asked me to marry him."

A delighted look flew into Francey's eyes until she looked at Carly. "You don't sound thrilled."

"Oh, Mom, if he'd asked me last week I'd have said yes in a minute. But, oh I don't know."

Francey put an arm around her. "Don't do anything unless you're sure of it."

"He's rich, Mom. Richer than anyone we've ever known."

"That should be only a slight consideration. Come on, let's see how we all get along."

The women returned to the living room where Cole and Walt were already deep into a banking discussion.

The conversation flowed more easily than Carly would have imagined, and Cole was more ingratiating than she'd ever known him to be. She studied him, wondering if there had ever been a time, even once in his life, when he hadn't been sure of himself.

She got through the cocktail hour in a fog. She thought of Boomer. She looked at Cole.

Was it even a matter of making a choice? Boomer had just come back into her life for a night. That didn't mean it would lead to anything permanent. It hadn't before with Boomer. She was almost twenty-five years old. Would any offer ever equal Cole's?

Marry Cole? Be Mrs. Cole Coleridge? She wouldn't even have to struggle to belong. Not like Francey, who had had to work at it even after she met Walt. She wouldn't have to work another day in her life if she didn't want to. She could stay in bed late, in satin sheets with a maid who brought her breakfast, just like she'd seen so often in the movies. She'd play tennis at the club. And they'd dine with friends . . . He must have a multitude of them, having been raised in Houston, but he'd never introduced her to even one of them. She'd have an unlimited charge card and could buy anything she wanted, decorate her house just as she'd like.

Francey announced dinner.

It was her famous Virginia ham with homemade applesauce, sweet potatoes, and carmelized carrots, with cole slaw on the side. She turned the overhead lights down low and let the flickering candles dance shadows on the walls. An enormous bouquet of flowers was the centerpiece. Grown in the greenhouse, Carly guessed.

Cole cleared his throat as he raised his wineglass. He smiled at Carly. "We have come," he said, "to ask for Carly's hand in marriage."

The silence was powerful. It forced Carly to meet Cole's eyes. Then Walt said, "I don't think it's up to us. Whatever Carly wants is fine with us."

Cole was grinning.

"Well," he asked, "do you want to set the date?"

"It's hot in June" was all Carly could think of to say.

"April's a lovely month," Francey said.

"That's just next month," said Carly.

"I don't know if I can wait that long." Cole downed his wine. "April it is. Name the date, Carly."

Carly thought a minute. "Any day is fine with me."

"The thirtieth is a Saturday," Cole said, glancing at his wallet calendar.

"That will give us six weeks," Francey said. "Plenty of time."

"The thirtieth it is, then," Carly said.

She pushed Boomer out of her mind.

CHAPTER 31

Alex paced the floor like a caged animal. She had walked back and forth across her carpet at least three dozen times.

Thursday night, when Boomer left, she'd been angry at him. Why did he have to ruin the best thing she'd ever known?

Friday night she slept fitfully. By morning her sheets were so entangled they looked as though an army had marched across them. Saturday night she slept not at all. By Sunday evening she looked a wreck. Her eyes were bloodshot, and though she had napped briefly on the couch in the early afternoon, her nerve ends were so raw she thought she might throw up. She'd existed for two and a half days on coffee and little else. A piece of toast Saturday. Sunday morning she'd gone out for a walk and paced the streets of Houston for over three hours. In the afternoon she searched her refrigerator for something to nibble on and could find nothing that appealed to her. No wonder her stomach was queasy.

In the midst of one of her more forceful swings around her living room she made her decision. "I'll do it," she cried aloud. "I don't give a damn."

Her parents would come around. They weren't going to disown her. They might be cool at first, but once Boomer began to make money, once she got pregnant and bore a Headland grandchild, they'd give in. Once Boomer made his first million. Once they saw he really was quite lovable and thoughtful. Once she smoothed his rough edges.

Two and a half, nearly three days of realizing Boomer wasn't a part of her life was more than she could stand. He'd forced her to face herself, compelled her to ask herself questions she'd been afraid to ask. *Did* she love Boomer Bannerman?

How could she love a man with a name like that? A man who . . . Oh, did it matter how or why? There was no rhyme or reason to love. And she had to admit to herself she was in love with Boomer. Madly in love. No man had ever meant as much to her as he did. No one had ever excited her as he did. No one brought more joy to her life than he did. He made her feel wonderful all the time.

She laughed. She wanted to bring Boomer breakfast in bed, to stand in the shower and have them soap each other and make love while the shower pummeled needles of water onto them. She shivered with ecstasy at the thought.

She wanted to sit around every Sunday night the rest of her life with Boomer and Tessa and Dan and laugh or go to the movies and have late suppers. Boomer had taught her what fun it was to behave spontaneously.

She laughed. She could just see it all. Walking down the aisle, her white train yards long. Hearing the whispers as she placed her hand through her father's arm, carrying a spray of white orchids with pale lavender centers. "Well, Alex never does anything you expect. Marrying someone named Boomer Bannerman!"

Her mother might shiver with distaste and her father might feel heartbroken, but she'd hold her head high. After all, she was Alexandra Headland and she could do anything she wanted and get away with it.

She went to the phone and started to dial his number. No. She'd rather surprise him. She glanced in the mirror and decided she'd better refresh her makeup. Brush her hair. Perhaps put it up in a chignon. Look glamorous. Put on that smoky dress she and her mother and Tessa had chosen last week. Dress to the nines. Telling a man you accept his proposal was not to be done casually.

She felt exquisite joy. She would spend a lifetime with Boomer. It didn't even matter that her parents might disapprove. They had never disapproved of anything she had done in her whole life. It was about time she kicked up her heels and created a bit of a scandal.

As she peered in the bathroom mirror and applied eye shadow, she smiled at the thought of Boomer's reaction. He would be so thrilled. And wouldn't this make the business even more exciting? Maybe she'd formally become a partner. After all, she was the one who dreamed up the business deal with Uncle Jay. The four of them together. Wouldn't it be wonderful.

The gardens were a lush tropical delight. The Olympic-size pool meandered under a bridge that divided the pool, one half surrounded by a rock garden where a stream constantly recycled itself, the sound of running water soothing. One rule Boomer insisted on, no children under sixteen were allowed in the apartments or the pool. This should appeal to the young up-and-comings as well as to retirees. No loud noises, no shouting.

Bougainvillea, hibiscus, oleander, plumbago flowered under the towering palms that Tessa and Dan had brought in. Alex thought it more a botanical garden than an apartment complex's garden. It was a place of tranquility and beauty. A cabaña for changing clothes and for lounging was hidden in the tall shrubbery, and a bar was at one end of the shallower pool. One could swim up and order drinks or saunter up from the chaises.

No piped music, Tessa said, for everyone had different tastes and someone was sure to dislike whatever was playing. A sauna and exercise room were behind the cabaña. They had hired an instructor, who would give individual lessons and, if there was call for it, group instruction. Dan, as usual, was worried that they'd gone overboard. Alex reassured him that the backers didn't even expect to break into the black for two years, so he should relax.

Tessa had furnished seven of the apartments, in styles so different that each had a distinct individuality.

Thanks to Sally Burgess's clout, it seemed that half of Houston—the half that mattered—turned out for the inaugural party. The Sherwood would be open to the general public tomorrow.

Two hundred thousand of Amos Headland's dollars were invested in the project of the man Alex had been afraid to tell him she loved. She had a hundred thousand of her own in it. There were three other silent partners, all of whom were at the soiree this evening, looking the place over but only casually, having enough faith in Alex that they weren't worried. Also, of course, having enough money that if they lost a bit on this it wouldn't break them.

Tessa, Dan, Boomer, and Alex were there by five. Sally had told them to leave everything to her and all they had to do was charm people. Dan didn't dare ask Alex how much this had cost.

Suddenly, from the crowd of people, Boomer saw Carly on the arm of some aristocratic-type guy who looked like he wouldn't know red blood if he punctured himself.

Alex reached out her hand to take the man's arm and kissed his cheek. "Cole, how nice of you to come."

Boomer watched as this Cole introduced Alex to Carly. He thought Alex looked like a glamorous mannequin compared to

Carly. Every hair in place, everything she wore an understated elegance. Her voice so modulated, her conversation so formal.

He had tried not to think of Carly. Ridiculous that one night with Carly could so change his feelings for Alex.

He kept telling himself Alex would be the perfect partner. Involved in his business. Interested. Supportive, emotionally and financially. No one could look at Alex and not realize Boomer had to be somebody to have her as his wife.

Even her parents had been more welcoming than he'd been prepared for.

But each time he'd made love to Alex, since that night with Carly, something had been missing. Boomer was pretty sure what was missing was Carly herself. But he'd also come to the conclusion she was a bitch.

She hadn't told him she was in love with someone else. When they'd seen each other across that crowded bar, he'd thought she felt the same electricity that coursed through him. She certainly was passionate when they went to bed together. And all that crap: "There's really been no one since you, Boomer."

And the wild way she made love. Her soft moans. That voluptuous ripe body. All curves, not like Alex's angles.

Cut it out, he told himself, still smarting from the way he'd been treated by Carly. He'd tried all that Saturday afternoon and evening to get hold of her, even driving back to her apartment and Scotch-taping his phone number on her door.

All Sunday morning he'd tried. Finally, at five that afternoon she'd answered, and when he suggested dinner, she said, "I'm so sorry. I'm getting married, Boomer, in six weeks."

Nothing about Friday night.

And now . . . he glanced around at the hundreds of people who'd shown up for the opening. He told himself he was exactly where he'd wanted to be. Engaged to Alex. A June wedding planned. "The wedding of the summer," Mrs. Headland announced, "if not the year."

Forgetting they'd met briefly or that Cole was the one who sent him to Alex, Boomer shook hands with Cole and tried to keep his eyes from meeting Carly's. She was smiling and chatting with Alex. He heard her laugh and his spine tingled.

Alex turned toward Boomer, and Carly smiled dazzlingly at him. "Darling, do you remember Cole?" Alex said, "Cole, this is the man you sent me, Brad Bannerman." She scolded herself. It was still tough to introduce him as Boomer. She wanted to kick herself.

But Boomer said to Carly, "I didn't expect to see you here tonight." So, Carly was also going to marry into Houston society. Some coincidence.

After Cole and Carly had moved on, Boomer, his eyes unreadable, said, "Quite a turnout, isn't it? I really hadn't expected anything like this."

"I told you it would be."

Boomer's eyes followed Carly and, when Cole left her for a minute, he sauntered over to her. "You look radiant," he said, so low that no one else could hear.

"Wish me happiness," she said. "Want that for me. And I want to tell you, I ... had fun with you. I had a wonderful time with you."

He couldn't say anything; his throat was locked.

They sauntered over to where Alex was telling Cole about how sure she was BB&O was going to become big. She told Cole their next job was tackling J. Wellington Rockford's block in the center of the city. They were going to erect the tallest skyscraper Houston had ever seen.

"Maybe I'll have a project for you, too," Cole said to Boomer, and wondered what the hell he was doing. "We're going to build a hotel in Acapulco and we want an American firm to be in charge of it.

"Come see me, Bannerman," Cole pursued. "Alex has my phone number. You do still have it, don't you?"

"Of course." She squeezed his hand.

Alex turned to study Boomer as he watched Carly disappear into the crowds. "You know her?"

"We went to high school together."

"Fancy meeting a person from Verity here," Alex mused.

Funny that Cole was dating someone from Boomer's little hick hometown. Though the woman was truly gorgeous, she was a bit flamboyant. Certainly Cole couldn't be serious about her. "Is she nice?"

"Yeah," Boomer answered, reaching for a drink as a waiter passed by. "I used to know her pretty well. We went to the senior prom together."

"Isn't that amazing. I went to mine with the man with her."

"What's he like?" Boomer wondered.

"I've known him since we were kids. In fact, I dated him rather steadily until I met you."

Boomer's eyes twinkled. "So, you dropped him for me?"

Alex put an arm through his. "You might say that." Though he hadn't called her for months. "What's that girl like?"

"Carly's bright and smart. She was our class valedictorian."

"How long since you've seen her?"

Two weeks, one day, and nearly eight hours. "Years," Boomer answered.

CHAPTER 32

Carly had been warmed by the Coleridges' acceptance of her. Neither of Cole's parents could be described as affectionate, but Mrs. Coleridge proffered her cheek and, in turn, kissed the air beside Carly's left cheek. They asked her amazingly few questions about herself, so Carly surmised that Cole had already filled them in on her background.

The first thing Cole and she must do, Mrs. Coleridge said, was choose an engagement ring. So, by the time Cole and Carly appeared at BB&O's party, Carly was sporting a diamond which was, she said, "as big as the Ritz." It weighed down her left hand, but she constantly held it up to admire it.

Cole had laughed when they were in the jewelry store and she'd pointed at the ring. "You really want one that big?"

But he'd purchased it gladly, choosing the matching wedding ring, studded with diamonds also.

When Mrs. Coleridge rolled her eyes, Carly gathered that she thought it was a bit gaudy. She didn't care. She'd like to drive down to Verity and walk along the streets wearing it. Most of the girls in Verity who'd married right out of high school didn't even *have* an engagement ring, of any size.

Mrs. Coleridge then asked how Carly and her parents would feel about having the wedding in Houston.

Carly didn't even want anyone from Verity to be there, except Zelda Marie.

So, the mothers conferred by phone, and Mrs. Coleridge invited Walt and Francey to come up the following weekend. "Of course, you'll stay with us, and we can make plans."

The plans included inviting over four hundred of the Coleridges' friends and acquaintances.

"We'll be happy to pay for the reception," Mr. Coleridge told Walt.

Walt gave Cole's father a level gaze and announced, "I can handle it nicely, thank you. I've never given a daughter away before."

"Well, I'd like to have the reception at the club, and they won't let you pay. Besides, we have no daughters to give away. We'd consider it an honor," Mrs. Coleridge announced. Carly figured if it was done her way, she wouldn't be embarrassed by any hicks from Verity.

Francey glanced over at Carly, who sat on the white sofa saying nothing. Carly nodded imperceptibly. She was going to have the biggest, most expensive wedding anyone from Verity had ever had.

Cole was willing to let the women take over completely, and didn't even participate in the plans. "Anything you want is fine with me." Carly thought he really meant that anything his mother approved of was okay.

"We'll have to coordinate our dresses, too," Mrs. Coleridge

told Francey. "Stay until Monday and we can shop for our gowns and choose the bridesmaids' gowns. Six weeks is such short notice."

Carly insisted that Zelda Marie be her only attendant. Mrs. Coleridge thought there should be six bridesmaids, but Carly said she didn't even know six women. Cole said it was fine if Carly only wanted one attendant, and he'd have his brother, Ben, as best man. Fellows he'd gone to school with could serve as ushers; he'd been in so many of their weddings, that was only right.

Carly held up her hand to study the diamond on her ring finger, watching the sun glint off it. This would impress even the Queen of England, she thought.

When they were alone, Francey said, "If you don't like all Cole's mother's ideas, all you have to do is say so, you know."

"Mom, I figure she knows what to do more than we do. It doesn't bother me at all to let her run the show."

"So long's you don't care. I mean, we both know neither one of us has a thing to do with this wedding." She glanced around the guest room where she and Walt were staying. "Do you love him?" Francey took her stockings off and stood barefoot, readying herself for a shower.

"Of course, Mom. What a question."

"Here's another. Have you slept with him?"

Carly laughed. "Going to talk to me about the birds and the bees?"

"No." Francey shook her head and drew her dress above her head, tossing it on the bed. "Just want to make sure that part's good. If it's not good now it won't be later."

So, she's telling me she went to bed with Walt before they got married. Carly wondered if everyone had trouble imagining their parents making love.

"I went to bed with him before I thought I was in love with him. Maybe that helped."

Francey nodded. "Okay, honey. Just wanted to make sure. If you hadn't I was going to tell you to."

* * *

Mrs. Coleridge went with Carly to choose her silver pattern and the china and to register at the stores where Houstonites registered for such things. Mrs. Coleridge was sure several of her friends would want to give Carly showers.

Carly hardly devoted every day to preparing for the wedding and choosing patterns and colors. She sold real estate. "You'll stop working, of course," Cole had told her. "Why wait until the wedding? Give yourself time to do everything."

But Carly was having more fun selling real estate than choosing bathroom colors. Mrs. Coleridge chose everything for her, or told her what she should choose. In real estate, she was in charge. Besides, they hadn't even talked about where they'd live, so she didn't even know what color any bathroom would be. She guessed she'd move into Cole's apartment, because it was larger and far more attractive than hers.

So, she was stupefied one night when two things occurred.

While they sat in the Coleridge library, having drinks before dinner, Mrs. Coleridge said, "I'm having such fun. I can't tell you, Carly. I thought all this would be denied me because I didn't have a daughter. Thank you, my dear, for making it possible."

Just then, Adonis entered the room. Carly thought the sun had suddenly come out and she looked at the ceiling to see if there were a skylight she hadn't noticed.

The young man's blond hair fell in a lock over his forehead, his tanned skin showed time spent outdoors. He was the same height as Cole, a tad under six feet, but whereas Cole was dark, the young man was fair. His eyes were blue, as were Cole's, but they were darker. His lips were not narrow like Cole's, but sensuous . . . My God, Carly thought. She was engaged to be married and she was thinking some other man's lips were made for kissing. She found herself blushing. He was dressed in an open-necked shirt a shade lighter than his eyes. His white pants were slightly rumpled, and he looked as though he'd just come from a tennis court. His shirtsleeves were rolled back nearly to his elbows and soft blond hair covered his arms. He moved with an easy grace except that his left arm didn't move as he walked.

He stood in the doorway surveying the scene until his eyes rested on Carly. He stared at her with such an intensity that Carly felt herself being undressed. He stood there while the others continued to talk until Mrs. Coleridge looked up and saw him. When she said, "Ah, Bennett," he came into the room and leaned down to kiss his mother's cheek.

Cole stood up and went over to shake hands, and their father nodded from the easy chair in which he always sat.

"I have come to meet my new sister," said the young man, turning to give her a smile that did not touch his eyes and was not nearly as personal a look as the one he'd given her from the doorway.

Cole, draping an arm around his brother's shoulder, introduced him to Carly. "My brother, Ben."

All she'd heard of him was that he was the black sheep of the family. Five years younger than Cole, he'd dropped out of at least three universities. Or was it *kicked* out of?

Cole had told her that it was always Ben who could charm everyone. Ben who coasted along without really studying, Ben who thought up the high-jinks his group participated in. Ben who was the one girls circled around.

Yet, despite his considerable charm, he seemed to carry a chip on his shoulder, never totally enjoying anything, never really wanting anything. Not giving a damn about work, or about money. Sometimes, Cole thought, not even about women. He tended to be sarcastic, Cole had told her yet Carly immediately sensed in Ben a sensitivity for which Cole had not prepared her.

His left arm hung lifelessly at his side. Cole had not mentioned that to her. She noticed again that it did not move as he walked across the room to her, his right hand outstretched. She reached up to shake it and, while still holding her hand, he sat down beside her and said in a low voice that seemed to exclude everyone else in the room, "No one told me how beautiful you are."

Carly laughed self-consciously.

"I don't even remember your name," Ben said.

"Carly. Carly Anderson."

"How did my brother get so lucky?"

"You don't even know me," Carly said.

"You're right. Underneath that gorgeous exterior you may be a complete bitch."

"Bennett!" His mother sounded horrified.

"You'll have to get used to Ben," Cole said, half smiling. "Don't pay any attention to him."

Ben pulled his left arm onto his lap. His fingers looked normal, but they did not move.

Carly heard Mr. Coleridge sigh. Ben had obviously embarrassed him more than this one time.

To change the topic, Mrs. Coleridge said to her husband, "Why not tell them now, dear. Then we can drive over there after dinner."

Cole's father cleared his throat—a prologue to an announcement of major proportions. "We'd like to help you young people get off to a flying start, one that will reflect Cole's position with Union Trust. This week the Hawthorne house came up for sale. Your mother and I've bought it for you as a wedding present."

Carly's mind raced, trying to think what she knew of the Hawthorne place. My God, it couldn't be the immense one whose picture had come through Multiple Listing this week . . . She tried to remember the photo.

"Why, Dad. Mother." Carly could tell from his voice that Cole was overwhelmed. He looked at Carly.

"I'm afraid I'm in the dark," she said. She felt a stab of disappointment. Someone else choosing a house for her.

In a flash, Ben, who was still holding her hand, turned to his parents and said, "Don't you think you should have given the bride a choice?"

Had her feelings flowed through her fingers to his that he latched on so quickly to how she felt?

Mrs. Coleridge's posture became even more erect. A fleeting look of confusion was reflected in her eyes.

Cole gave Ben a dirty look and walked over to his mother. "Of course Carly will love it. I've always admired that house."

"It's large enough until children arrive," Mrs. Coleridge said.

"I'm most grateful," Carly said, forcing a lilt to her voice. "That's a wonderful, generous present."

Mrs. Coleridge smiled at her and then looked at Ben in much the same manner Cole just had. "After dinner, we can all drive over and look at the house. Of course, with that old-fashioned furniture in it, it may not tickle your fancy . . ."

Tickle her fancy? Carly tried not to laugh.

"But then we can have such fun decorating it."

We? *We* can decorate it?

Ben put a hand on her shoulder. She did not turn to look at him, but she felt he was giving her courage. He was aware of how she felt.

"Tessa Oldfield is the new decorator everyone's talking about."

Tessa? She's Boomer's partner, Carly thought. The one who decorated those apartments we saw last week. Well, she'd thought they were beautiful.

All five of them drove over to the Hawthorne house after dinner. Carly felt a thrill when she saw the house. There was a circular driveway leading up to the brick Tudor which she guessed must have been built in the twenties. The house was guarded by two towering oak trees. In the back there was a swimming pool. "Beyond that," Cole said, "there's enough room for a tennis court."

The house was in immaculate condition, as Carly imagined every house in River Oaks must be. The wooden paneling was dark. Carly thought she'd talk the decorator into painting it a light color. She'd buy a copy of *Better Homes & Gardens* and maybe *Architectural Digest* tomorrow and begin studying.

Ben whispered in her ear after the tour was completed, "Well, can you live with this?"

"Easily." Carly smiled at him. "You just have to realize I'm a girl from a small town and all this is new to me. I'm easily impressed."

"Don't let any of it throw you," he said, as they walked behind the others. "You're going to be able to get away with anything, just being a Coleridge."

"Is that how it is with you?" she asked. "You can flunk out of schools and get into all manner of scrapes and not have to earn a living and it's okay because you're a Coleridge?"

"Ouch," he said. "I had the feeling we were going to be friends."

"Would I speak to you like that if I didn't feel the same way?" Ben was the first Coleridge with whom she felt completely comfortable.

"Carly, my dear," he said, as Cole turned to wait for them, "I have the distinct feeling you and I are going to keep each other honest."

CHAPTER 33

Her hands immersed in dishwater, Zelda Marie glanced out the window to see her mother's car pull up in the grass behind the house. The dirt driveway ended abruptly beside the house, but most visitors just kept on coming over the unmown grass.

She watched her mother get out of the car, then turn to say something to the man sitting in the front seat. Mrs. Spencer, dressed in the kind of cotton waistless dress that she'd worn as long as Zelda Marie could remember, opened the back door of the car, and a Mexican woman emerged. She wore a clean, pressed but faded blue dress and huaraches. Her shining black hair was pulled back and held in place by a rubber band.

Self-consciously, the woman looked up at the little house as she followed Mrs. Spencer across the lawn and up the two porch steps. She stood in the doorway as Mrs. Spencer swept into the kitchen. Zelda Marie dried her hands on her apron.

"Happy Birthday, darling." Zelda Marie's mother kissed her cheek and hugged her.

"Thanks, Momma." She glanced at the Mexican woman.

"This here's Aofrasia." Mrs. Spencer gestured for the woman to enter the kitchen, but she continued to stand in the doorway, her hands clasped together.

"She's your birthday present, sweetie," Mrs. Spencer said. "Someone to take care of the house."

Even the poorest people in Verity had daily maids. But Joe Bob had never earned enough and, besides, Zelda Marie couldn't drive into town every day to pick up a maid.

"You have too much to do," Mrs. Spencer said. "You can't keep house and take care of all those kids and your horses and calves, to say nothing of the chickens and lambs, and work nights over at the Willows."

"Momma, is this another of your wetbacks?" For as long as Zelda Marie could remember, her mother had fed myriads of illegal Mexicans who had traversed hundreds of miles through the Mexican desert to what they hoped was the land of opportunity.

"They're entitled to opportunity as much as anyone. Not one white woman I know will do what the Mexicans will. Just be grateful. I thought Aofrasia and her husband, Carlos, could live here. I've lived out here away from civilization for over thirty years, and I've been ready to move into town for a long time now. Last night your daddy and I bought that little white house at the corner of Post Oak and Magnolia, kitty corner to the high school. He can drive the four miles out here each day without hurtin'. So, you come live up at the big house."

"Momma, you didn't!" She'd heard her mother yearning to move into town since she'd been twelve years old, she guessed.

Mrs. Spencer nodded. "Aofrasia cooks, too, and Carlos will mow the lawn and do the gardening and anything else needs doin' around here. Daddy and I'll pay them for the first year as your birthday present."

Zelda Marie laughed. "Momma, you're just ashamed of this place."

Mrs. Spencer nodded. "I don't want any grandkids of mine growing up like white trash, it's true. And I don't want our yard to look a shambles. But also, Zelda Marie, even your daddy is proud of the way you done here. And now you're all alone with them kids, honey, I don't know anyone works harder'n you. Ao and Carlos will be a big help. They'll take care of everything. During the day, before you go to work at five, all's you'll have to do is take care of the horses and do what you want and you won't be worn to a frazzle. You're as skinny as a ghost."

Mrs. Spencer turned to the Mexican woman and told her in pidgin Spanish that Zelda Marie would leave all furniture and all the china and silver and kitchen equipment. This very day she and Carlos could help move Zelda Marie and her kids up to the big house, and tonight she and her husband could sleep here.

"Momma, you're not going to move into your new house tonight, are you?"

"You better believe it," her mother answered. "If all's that's there is a bed, I'm going to move in. And I'm going over to Corpus tomorrow and buy new furniture, every stick of it. New dishes and new towels and new everything. I told your pa we never had time for a honeymoon or a trip of any kind, so he could make it up to me by doing this. And he's willing."

"I'll be damned," Zelda Marie said, flinging the dish towel on the counter. "Well, Momma, let's go clean out the closets. Maybe we can have this all done by the time the kids come home."

"Each of them can have their own room."

"Momma, you do beat all. I think it's just the nicest present you could give me."

Aofrasia was staring around the room, clucking her teeth.

"C'mon." Mrs. Spencer grabbed Zelda Marie's elbow. "Let's start packing, and Aofrasia can clean up the kitchen. Let her spend the day doing that, and Carlos can help us with the moving. I'll take 'em to the market after she's finished to buy what groceries she wants. I'll come out each Wednesday and take her shopping, so you better make out a list." She was beaming. "I was afraid I was going to have to fight you on this."

"Fight, Momma, when you know I hate housework!"

"You're going to have to show her how to work the washer and dryer and teach Carlos how to operate that riding mower."

"How'm I going to do that when I don't know Spanish?"

"You can learn Spanish just like they learn English. You've lived in Verity all your life. You must know some."

She walked back outside, over to her car, and opened the back door, gesturing to the man within. Out stepped a good-looking Mexican Zelda Marie guessed to be in his late twenties, a little older than his wife.

Zelda Marie lowered her voice and whispered, "D'you think it'll be safe to leave the kids alone with these . . . these strangers? You know, alone with everything?"

"Oh, come on," Mrs. Spencer said impatiently. "Pretty soon you're going to leave your own life in her hands as well as your children's."

PART III

1974–1975

CHAPTER 34

Mrs. Coleridge hinted about children at least a dozen times a year. Not that she really cared about having little children around, Carly knew, but she loved the idea of the family going on. The step to immortality. Carly didn't care about immortality. She wanted children. She lay in bed nights thinking of cuddling a baby, nuzzling its soft fuzzy head, kissing its sweet-smelling skin, bathing it.

She'd finally consulted Dr. Beckwith, who, upon testing her, declared there wasn't a reason in the world she shouldn't conceive. He suggested Cole come in to have his sperm count tested. So far, Cole hadn't done it.

So, Carly immersed herself in selling homes, which irritated Cole to hell and gone. He couldn't understand why she wasn't happy to do what the wives of his friends did. Tennis at the club. Lunch there, too, or meeting a friend in some chic restaurant. Bridge afternoons.

She'd done that the first year she'd been Carly Coleridge and found herself bored silly. The conversations seemed so vacuous. Who was sleeping with whom, the latest diet fads, who had not been invited to someone's party. Which of the middle-aged women had had a face-lift. Who was going to Europe or Fiji that year. She tried to care. She really tried very hard, because these Houston women, these friends of the Coleridges', these women whose husbands made club membership possible, had accepted her. Society in Houston wasn't based on background but on money, and the Coleridges had money. Most of these women, too, were new to megabucks. They were not about to look down on another newcomer, especially the daughter-in-law of the president of Union Trust.

For the first time in her life, Carly felt accepted. Not, of course, because of who she was, but because of the man she was married to and who her in-laws were. She guessed that was the only way women were accepted anyhow. Not for themselves. And, she was surprised to discover that what she thought she'd wanted all her life wasn't enough.

So, much to Cole's exasperation, she went back to work for Mr. Rolf, and within two years was earning half a million a year, herself. Not only selling houses but making business deals. She was one of only three women in Houston who catered to the commercial real estate trade. Then, seven months ago, Mr. Rolf told her, "I want to retire. Move to Hawaii. You want to buy the company? I'll make you a deal. There's no one else I can think of who'll carry it on the way I want it to go."

Carly talked it over with Cole, who was adamantly opposed to the idea. "Jesus, Carly, we don't need the money."

"That's not the only reason I work. I love the idea of owning my own business. Besides, all *you* think of is money."

Cole stared at her. "That's different. I'm a banker. A man."

"I'm bored not doing anything," she explained not for the first time. "And I can earn twice as much if I own the company."

"Well, I'm not willing to put up that kind of money. Get pregnant and stay home and be a mother."

"I might stay home if I had kids to take care of," Carly pointed out. "God knows we try."

Cole walked over to her and put his arms around her. "That's over half the fun, don't you think?"

She nodded, her mind on Mr. Rolf's offer.

"All I have to put down now is a hundred thousand and pay him annually for five years."

"Carly, it really doesn't look good to have my wife in business."

She jerked her head to look at him. "Doesn't look good to whom? Who do you have to impress? Half of Houston tries to impress the Coleridges and Union Trust. Besides, if you admire any one woman it's Alex. She runs her own business even though she has a child. She probably earns more than the two of us together."

Cole winced.

"I want you to be here for me when I come home. I—"

"When am I not around when you want me to be? And I'm the one who suggests we go on trips together, but you're always too busy."

Not too busy to spend Saturdays golfing.

"Cole, I don't enjoy just waiting around for you until you have free time. My idea of life is not biding my time until you're free for me."

He raised both hands as though giving up an argument. She picked up the phone and dialed Walt, asking him if she could borrow a hundred thousand dollars. She said she'd draw up a contract to pay him back within four years at ten percent interest.

Walt laughed. "Why should I charge you more than anyone else? Besides, I think it sounds like a great idea."

She'd bought Rolf's, with the proviso she keep the same name for the next five years at least. She had no trouble accepting that.

Ever since Cole had contracted with BB&O, nearly five years ago, to build the Acapulco hotel for Señor Rosas, and then gone on to erect the one in that darling little village, she and Cole had dined weekly with Boomer and Alex and Dan and Tessa.

Alex always looked impeccable, not a hair out of place. Carly wished she could have that kind of cool elegance. She and Alex had never become intimate, as she and Tessa had.

Like Tessa and Alex were, too. Once in a great while, the three women had lunch together.

Cole and Carly disagreed on so many things that it was sometimes difficult to find something to talk about without getting into an argument. They had agreed not to discuss politics. Cole got angry when Carly didn't agree with him. Carly couldn't understand how anyone, much less her husband, could believe the things Cole did. He thought the United Nations was subversive. He believed Negroes, and Mexicans, too, had inferior intellectual abilities. He thought any sort of government aid, even to the indigent poor or to unwed mothers, was immoral. He did not believe in abortion, yet was in favor of capital punishment. Carly espoused hardly any of the same causes and beliefs as Cole did. She and others in her financial status could always get an abortion, even if it meant flying to Sweden. Carly had prayed that the right to choose become legal.

She debated whether she should call Tessa and see if she was free for lunch. She didn't see nearly as much of her as she had before Tessa got so busy. Once she'd decorated Carly and Cole's new house in River Oaks, she was on her way. Everyone who came into the young Coleridges' house asked who had decorated it, until Tessa had more business than she could handle. She decided to leave BB&O and open her own business, but Dan and Boomer prevailed, telling her she was free to take on individual jobs. Not every project they participated in had to involve all three partners. BB&O was their dream come alive. She couldn't leave them, the two men argued. So, while Boomer and Dan were involved only in large projects, Tessa took on decorating not only offices and the lobbies of the buildings BB&O built, but house after house after house.

For each house, she felt she had to take time to know the owners, understand their psyches and social lives as well as whatever image they wanted to project. So, Carly suspected that Tessa wouldn't have time to go out to lunch with her. She'd be too busy, discussing colors with a client.

Dan was now commanding ten percent of the cost of any

building he designed, which sometimes amounted to over two million dollars. Many of the iridescent modern glass buildings that jutted into the sky to create Houston's modernistic skyline were Dan's designs—executed by Boomer, for even more money.

Carly was interested in buying some land west of Houston, where there were farms. She'd rather put money into land than a fur coat, any day.

Before Carly had a chance to dial Tessa, Alex phoned her, asking if they could meet. It would be the first time Carly and Alex had lunched alone together.

As soon as they'd ordered—a Caesar salad for each—Alex began to speak. "I heard you talking the other night about wanting to buy land west of River Oaks ... Do you have something specific in mind aside from the tickle at the back of your neck that Houston's going to move in that direction?"

Should Carly share her vision? Why not. If things worked out as she envisioned, she'd want BB&O to be involved, and though Alex wasn't technically a partner in that outfit, she was married to its leader. And Alex had access to millions of investors' dollars.

"Have you heard of shopping malls?"

Alex shook her head.

"Up in Rochester, New York, they've put a roof over downtown, so that people don't have to brave the elements to go from store to store. I have a gut feeling it's the coming thing."

"New York and Texas have different weather. We don't have snow and—"

"No, we have humidity instead. And wanting to faint with the heat of summer."

"A roof over downtown?" Alex couldn't quite envision it. "So why not the same here if that's what you're thinking?"

"Because I think downtown is going to be all offices. The suburbs are exploding and women don't want to go all the way downtown, to those crowds and that traffic, to do their shopping. If what I read about has any validity, I think stores are going to mass together in what they're calling malls, with roofs to protect them from the weather. That section west of town would have perfect access.''

The two women talked until late in the afternoon, and when they parted, Alex said, ''I'm extremely interested. Maybe I'll fly up to Rochester and look it over. I'm *very* interested, Carly.''

''Well, I'm just thinking of accumulating land right now. I'd like this kept under wraps.''

Alex smiled. For the first time in their four years of knowing each other, Carly felt a strong sense of rapport.

''If you need money or want a partner, let me know. I think I could raise money for such a commercial project if it seems viable to me. And, if you want a partner in purchasing land, look to me, please, not other investors.''

As Carly drove back to the office, she realized that maybe she was developing a friend. There were so few women with whom she had much in common.

CHAPTER 35

Carly's secretary's voice jiggled through the intercom a few minutes before five. ''Mr. Coleridge is on line two.''

Cole? He seldom called her at work. But it was Ben's voice asking, ''Carly, you free for lunch tomorrow?''

''I'll make myself free if it means seeing you.''

His voice indicated pleasure. ''That it does. I'll be in Houston about noon. How about lunch at one. That okay?'' He didn't wait for an answer. ''I need some business advice. I'll pick you up at your office.''

Carly couldn't help a smile flashing across her eyes. ''You want my advice about business?''

A hesitation. ''Make it the Shamrock. I'll take a room there.''

"Ben, if you're staying overnight, come stay with us. We haven't seen you since Christmas."

"No, I prefer a hotel. I don't even know that I'll stay overnight, but I want a room there anyhow."

He had other people to see, business to conduct. Maybe even an interview. Shortly after Carly and Cole were married nearly five years ago, he had moved to the little town of Nacogdoches, and the editorials he wrote for the weekly were sometimes printed in the *Post*. Homespun philosophy on a global scale. None of them had had any idea Ben had this in him. She knew the *Post* had approached him about carrying some of his articles on their editorial page. A syndicated column, even if it was just one other newspaper. She felt a sense of pride in her brother-in-law. He'd found his niche working for that weekly, that was for sure. His father continued to think Ben was wasting his time, for he certainly wasn't on his way to becoming rich, but the whole family was relieved he'd kept a stable job for four years. He had surprised them all by flowering in the small town.

Carly wondered if there was a woman in Ben's life. She assumed that there must be women, but was there a particular one?

The only time the family got together was at Christmas, when Ben drove down Christmas Eve for two nights, staying with his parents, dressing as Santa Claus the night before Christmas and distributing presents, making a big scene of eating the cookies Mrs. Coleridge always left out for St. Nicholas. She always made a point of saying grandchildren should be leaving the plate of sweets for Santa ... but so far there were no grandchildren. For as long as the Coleridges and the Headlands had been friends they dined together on Christmas Day, and that meant sharing Christmas with Boomer and Alex and their eighteen-month-old son, David. Francey and Walt drove up to Houston and all the families had shared Christmas.

Carly spent the afternoon wondering how it might work out

to be partners in a land deal with Alex. It would certainly mean being able to buy a big swatch of that land out there.

At noon the following day Ben phoned her at the office. "We on for lunch?"

"Of course. Don't even have an appointment all afternoon, so I can devote myself to you and whatever it is you want."

There was a long silence. Then Ben said, "Whatever I want?"

Carly laughed. "You make it sound more exciting than I imagine it is."

Another silence. "It can be as exciting as you want."

Carly felt a shiver pass through her. "You always have the knack of making me feel totally irresistible, Ben. You're good for my ego."

"Well, then let's not rush lunch. A nice long luxurious one where I can feast my eyes on you."

"And vice versa."

She glanced in the mirror before she left. Her white silk suit was accented with a pale pearl-gray chiffon ruffled blouse peeking out of the jacket. Her very high-heeled gray suede shoes almost exactly matched. The only spot of bright color were small sapphire earrings, which matched her large bright blue purse.

Ben's first words were, "You make all other women pale in comparison."

She offered her cheek for him to kiss. His lips lightly brushed it.

Ben wore his hair longer than any of the men she knew. She quite liked it. He was dressed in a casual sports jacket, with an open-necked shirt. No tie. He was movie-star handsome, his dark-blond hair parted on the left and a lock falling over his forehead. His face was tanned, and his eyes bluer than any outside of Paul Newman's. But no matter how those eyes sparkled, there was always a hint of rebellion about Ben.

When they were seated in the dark, paneled dining room in

a restaurant that specialized in steaks and looked like an English pub, and sat sipping Brandy Alexanders, Ben reached across the table to take her hand.

"I want to pick your brain."

Carly cocked an eyebrow. They'd never had to make superficial conversation.

"Flattery will get you everywhere."

"I'm thinking of buying a weekly down in Aransas Pass. That's near your neck of the woods, isn't it? The owner of the Nacogdoches paper works damn hard, and he makes enough to live decently. Not luxuriously. I can afford to buy it from my grandfather's trust, but I don't know if I have any business sense. Just because I write good editorials and don't die of boredom attending a school board meeting doesn't mean I have the sense to run a paper. It would please Dad, I'm sure, even if it is small potatoes to him, but I don't want to be in business for the reason he does. To me, it would mean freedom to write what I want."

Carly tried to look very businesslike. She sat back in her chair, as though thinking about it. "How much?"

He told her.

"Why are you asking me? I sell real estate."

"Well, I trust you and you seem to know more than anyone else I know about such things. You can even tell me if it would be too much to pay."

Slowly she finished her drink. "I think it's a fair price, though we ought to look at the books to be sure. I'll drive down there, though the one you should talk with is Alex. She's a whiz about business."

"Alex is like Dad and Cole. Unless you can make a bundle they don't think it's worth considering. People don't get rich running country newspapers."

"If they did, you probably wouldn't want to do it."

Ben grinned. Carly thought he looked like an ingenuous little boy. She wondered if women fell all over him.

"I don't care about getting rich. I've been rich all my life. There's got to be more to life than money."

''Easy to say when you have it.''

The waiter brought Carly's lamb chops and a rare T-bone for Ben.

They ate in silence for a few minutes, and then he asked, ''Well, does it sound interesting?''

Carly reached across the table to brush her fingers against the back of his hand. ''Ben, you should know after all this time that anything you want interests me.''

He gave her a strange look.

''What about you?''

''Me?'' Carly concentrated on her food for a minute. ''I don't know. I'm making big money.''

''Bully for you. Since that's what Cole worships, I imagine he's proud of you.''

Carly was puzzled by the conversation. ''You need some money?'' she asked.

He shook his head. ''The only problem I never have in life is money.''

They ordered coffee and were silent waiting for it. Carly glanced around the room. Ben looked at her.

''Well, what about you? Why don't you seem happier?''

Her eyes met his. ''Is it so obvious?''

He sat, not saying anything, their eyes locked until she looked away.

''I'm ashamed of myself. I have everything any woman could want. More than I ever allowed myself to dream of, yet . . .''

''Is it you and Cole?''

She shrugged. ''I don't know what it is. Nothing I can put a finger on. Maybe it's . . . Well, I'd like children. Your mother acts like she thinks if I were a real woman we'd have three by now and she nags all the time because I enjoy working. Again, if I were a *real* woman I'd be content to do nothing and then maybe God would reward me with a Coleridge baby.''

The waiter brought mint ice cream, and they ate it in silence. When he brought coffee, Ben said, his voice low, ''I'll give Mother a Coleridge grandchild.''

Carly looked at him and, through parched lips, asked, "Are you suggesting what I think you are?"

"I'm offering to give you and my brother a child and my parents a Coleridge grandchild."

Carly stared at him.

She couldn't swallow, much less answer. After fully a minute, she reached for her water glass and gulped greedily.

Gooseflesh swept down her back. She found her voice. "What a ridiculous idea."

"And not terribly ethical, either." Why did his eyes suddenly look so pained?

She blinked and swallowed the water. The ice cubes rattled against her teeth. She took a deep breath. "You're far more immoral than I ever suspected. You're suggesting committing adultery with your brother's wife."

He nodded. "I'm suggesting giving my parents a grandchild."

"You could get married and do it morally."

"I haven't met anyone I want to marry."

She continued to stare at him.

"And how would I react at seeing my child brought up by Cole? How would I handle not admitting that my child is mine? How would I feel when I look at your son, or daughter, and know that what is mine can never be acknowledged?"

Her breath was coming in ragged bursts. "You've thought about this. You're really serious?"

"I have never been more serious in my life."

"Well, how would you feel about those questions you just posed?"

"I don't know."

"How do you think I'd feel about myself? About committing adultery?"

"It's done every day."

"But not by you and me."

He shrugged. "I think you desperately want a child. Mother told me you'd consulted a doctor and there's no reason on your part . . . and besides, you and I have wondered what it would be like to make love with each other since the day we met. If I hadn't thought it would have created havoc in the family, I'd never have let Cole have you once I met you. Carly, if you and I had made love years ago you'd never have married Cole."

She just stared at him. The lamb chops weren't sitting too well in her stomach.

CHAPTER 36

"My cousin, he talks with horses."

Zelda Marie glanced over her shoulder and observed Carlos standing in the open doorway to the horse stall, pitchfork stuck in a bale of hay at his feet.

"What's that supposed to mean?" she asked, massaging the ankle of the mare who'd been favoring her left leg.

"I see you," the Mexican continued. "You pretty good breaking a horse, but I see the look on your face when you can go no further. You need someone who can make your horses famous."

"A jockey, you mean?" She didn't think Carlos understood. She was into showing, not racing.

When Carlos looked perplexed, Zelda Marie rephrased her question. "A boy to ride the horse?"

Carlos shook his head. "No, señora. Someone who tells a horse how to move. And my cousin, Rafael, he talks with horses."

"To horses."

"No, señora." Carlos's liquid black eyes smiled. "Con. With. If Rafael can not do it, it can not be done with a horse," Carlos went on.

Zelda Marie hefted herself to her feet, wiped her hands on her jeans, patted the horse on its flank and walked out of the stall. Carlos slid the door shut behind her.

"And how do I find this Rafael?"

In his mellifluous voice, Carlos murmured, "You can't. You must let him find you."

Zelda Marie turned to look at him. He had taken to doing everything outdoors that needed doing, and sometimes carpentry inside. He could fix a leaking faucet and a water pump, could set to rights any machine that needed mending. He loved the riding lawn mower and feeding the horses. He even milked the solitary cow, Dulcinea, from whose milk Aofrasia made butter. "And how does that happen?" Zelda Marie asked.

Carlos's voice took on a pitiful sound. "It takes money, señora."

Of course. "How much?"

"Hmm," Carlos appeared to give the matter great consideration. "It costs four hundred dollars for a coyote."

"A coyote?" Zelda Marie laughed.

"Sí, señora. That is what a coyote charges to get one safely across the border."

Zelda Marie nodded. Another illegal wetback. "How does a coyote do that?"

Carlos shrugged as though the world's mysteries escaped him. "And then, of course, my cousin must either walk hundreds of miles across the Mexican desert or take a bus to the place of the coyote . . . somewhere on the other side of the Rio Bravo."

More money. "How much for a bus?"

"Twenty-eight dollars, señora. The coyote will meet him and get him across the river. Then Rafael will find us."

"How," she asked, smiling, "will he ever find us?"

"We did."

So, her mother's reputation spread far down into Mexico. The woman who will feed us. The woman who will let us sleep in her barn on our way north. The woman who will pay a doctor to look at sick babies. The woman who is a saint. Zelda Marie realized how little she'd known of her mother.

"And if I pay twenty-eight dollars for a bus and four hundred for a coyote, what if your cousin doesn't want to come?"

"He will come, señora. That I promise."

"When?" She wondered if she was nuts. What was she doing, sight unseen, offering a place to live and work to a Mexican wetback? She was already supporting Carlos and Aofrasia and their baby, but she was earning good money now that she was managing the Willows for Carly's mother.

Would Rafael bring a wife and baby and, if so, where would they all fit.

Well, as things were now, she didn't stand a chance in hell of entering any of her beautiful horses in shows that really mattered. Just one good season could put her horses on the map.

Her foals were selling well. Not enough to buy luxuries but enough to take care of expenses and then some. Of course Daddy's signing over the ranch to her was a boon. He just kept the south eighty acres where Humble Oil had drilled and now filled their own tanks with black gold. That had made it possible for Mr. Spencer to sit on his front porch in town and rock all day.

He had given over the rest of the ranch to his daughter, which meant no rent to pay. For that Zelda Marie was eternally grateful, but it would mean another mouth to feed with Rafael. Or mouths.

Poor Ao. Every night she cooked dinner and cleaned up the kitchen and then walked down the lane, little Josefa on her hip. In the house where she and Carlos lived she then cooked dinner for her little family. She'd do her own dishes, put the baby to bed, and then maybe clean her own house.

Zelda Marie thought perhaps she'd suggest that Carlos come up to the house evenings, and he and Ao could eat at the same time she and the kids did. Cut down on Aofrasia's work. That big butcher table in the kitchen could feed an army. Why hadn't she thought of it before? Women should stick together, and if she could find a way to lessen Aofrasia's drudgery, so much the better.

The phone in the barn rang, and Zelda Marie walked over to answer it.

4 BESTSELLING HISTORICAL ROMANCES BY YOUR FAVORITE AUTHORS CAN BE YOURS, FREE!

Kensington Choice brings you historical romances by your favorite bestselling authors including Janelle Taylor, Shannon Drake, Rosanne Bittner, Jo Beverley, and Georgina Gentry, just to name a few! Each book is filled with passion, adventure and the excitement of bygone times!

To introduce you to this great club which is part of Zebra Home Subscription Service, we'd like to send you your first 4 bestselling historical romances, absolutely free! And once you get these 4 free books to savor at home, we'll rush you the next 4 brand-new books at the lowest prices available, as soon as they are published.

The way the club works is that after your initial FREE shipment, you will get our 4 newest bestselling historical romances delivered to your

doorstep each month at the preferred subscriber's rate of only $4.20 per book, a savings of up to $8.16 per month (since these titles sell in bookstores for $4.99-$6.99)! All books are sent on a 10-day free examination basis and there is no minimum number of books to buy. (A postage and handling charge of $1.50 is added to each

shipment.) Plus as a regular subscriber, you'll receive our FREE monthly newsletter, *Zebra/Pinnacle Romance News*, which features author profiles, subscriber benefits, book previews and more!

So start today by returning the FREE BOOK CERTIFICATE provided. We'll send you 4 FREE BOOKS with no further obligation: A FREE gift offering you hours of reading pleasure with no obligation...how can you lose?

*We have 4 FREE BOOKS for you
as your introduction to
KENSINGTON CHOICE!
To get your FREE BOOKS, worth
up to $24.96, mail the card below.*

FREE BOOK CERTIFICATE

Yes! Please send me 4 Kensington Choice (the best of Zebra and Pinnacle Books) Historical Romances without cost or obligation (worth up to $24.96). As a Kensington Choice subscriber, I will then receive 4 brand-new romances to preview each month for 10 days FREE. I can return any books I decide not to keep and owe nothing. The publisher's prices for Kensington Choice romances range from $4.99-$6.99, but as a preferred subscriber I will get these books for only $4.20 per book or $16.80 for all four titles. There is no minimum number of books to buy and I may cancel my subscription at any time. A $1.50 postage and handling charge is added to each shipment. No matter what I decide to do, my first 4 books are mine to keep, absolutely FREE!

KC1197

Name _____

Address _____ Apt. _____

City _____ State _____ Zip _____

Telephone (___) _____

Signature _____

(If under 18, parent or guardian must sign)

Subscription subject to acceptance. Terms and prices subject to change.

"Miz Lovett, this is Joel Miller." The nice young man from Humble. When he'd talked to her just recently, it was the first time since Joe Bob died that she'd felt a flutter feather across her chest. Five years. "I was wondering if you'd let me take you to dinner this weekend?"

She glanced down at her jeans, at her dirty fingernails, cut short and square, and was glad there wasn't a mirror around. She couldn't remember the last time anyone had invited her out to dinner. Maybe since she'd been married. Not in a decade, she guessed. She suspected he was just being nice to try to get her to sign away her mineral rights, allow Humble to drill on her land. But, nevertheless, it felt sorta nice to be invited out.

"I think I'd like that fine, but it'll have to be Sunday." That was her day off.

"How about I pick you up about six. There's a restaurant opened up right on the gulf between Verity and Corpus that's supposed to be really neat."

Meaning dress up. Oh, God, she thought, she hadn't a thing to wear. She wondered if Wilma Jean could fit her in for a shampoo and set? She hadn't had one of those since she'd been married, either. In fact, come to think of it she hadn't done one social thing since she made out with Joe Bob in the backseat of his daddy's car over a dozen years ago. She'd been cut off from anything social for so long she might not remember how to act. Of course that wasn't counting the Willows, but that was work.

She'd have to buy a dress. She hadn't worn a dress in ages. Certainly none she ever owned would fit her now. She weighed in at nearly one thirty, and that was far too heavy at her five four. Well, she couldn't lose fifteen pounds in four days, so she'd have to work around that. And she'd have to tell Aofrasia to stop with all those fried foods. And all that midmorning pan dulce.

She hung up the phone and then dialed her mother. "Momma, will you make an appointment with Wilma Jean for me. And will you babysit Sunday night?" Ao took care of the kids when Zelda Marie worked, but Zelda Marie thought her maid should have one night a week free. Especially Sundays, which they spent with other Mexicans.

She could almost see her mother's smile. "Why, honey, you goin' out someplace?"

"Mr. Miller, that young man's been out to the ranch several times," four to be exact, "has invited me to dinner, and Momma, I haven't a thing to wear."

"You come on into town tomorrow morning, and we'll see what Miss Margaret May has in your size, and if we don't find anything we like, I'll make you something. The Mercantile has some pretty fabrics."

Momma to the rescue, as always.

Come Sunday night, Zelda Marie thought she looked prettier than she had since high school. She studied her reflection in the mirror, pleased with the slimming black dress Miss Margaret May told her looked as if it had been made for her. Mrs. Spencer agreed. She had sworn she'd have nothing to do again with a man, ever. And lookit her. The first one that showed any interest, the first one whose eyes smiled at her, she got all tittery.

She knew perfectly well Joel Miller wasn't interested in her as a woman. What kind of man would be interested in a twenty-nine-year-old woman with five kids? Well, she knew who. Someone who wanted something from her. She suspected this one wasn't after her body, like Joe Bob had been. She felt thick-waisted and dumpy after so many babies and too many years of not caring how she looked. So, she knew he was just trying to sweet-talk her in order to get oil leases.

Zelda Marie thought the thousands that Humble was willing to pay just for exploration would be a big help. She could do a lot with that. Buy a van, for one thing, to cart around all the kids to all the places they wanted to go to in town. Maybe she should teach Carlos to drive. Bet he wouldn't mind carting them around if he could drive the car. She fancied that idea.

She liked Carlos as much as she did Aofrasia. He did everything she asked of him and then some. The first spring he and

Ao had been here he'd asked Zelda Marie to take him to the nursery, where he told her to buy seedlings. By May the yard was a riot of flowers. He planted them around his and Ao's little house, too, and in front of the barn doors. In the house, Aofrasia artistically arranged the flowers her husband had grown.

Sunday mornings one beat up old pickup truck or another came barreling down the lane to pick up Ao and Carlos and their baby to take them to church. They didn't return until after dark. Every few months a slew of dusty trucks came moseying down the lane and the crowds of Mexicans set up card tables and pulled out baskets of food and laughed and used a hand-cranked Victrola to make music.

Zelda Marie would sit on her porch and listen to the laughter and the singing in the distance. She imagined them taking off their shoes and dancing in the tall grass to the Mexican music they played. She was filled with longings on those Sunday afternoons when the other Mexicans came out to the ranch. She longed to be part of that happy group. She longed to be with them, wanted to listen to their guitars and their songs and eat their food that smelled so wonderful all the way up to her house.

Sunday evening she heard the sound of a car coming up the dirt road and glanced out the window to see swirls of dust trailing after it. Not the pickup Mr. Miller usually drove out to the ranch but a sleek black Oldsmobile. She stood behind the curtain of her bedroom and watched him emerge from the car, straightening his jacket. Even from here she could tell it was an expensive suit, not like the ones she saw in Verity. Of course, in Verity not that many men wore suits, except Mr. Davis at the bank and a couple of others to church, not that she'd been to church since she'd been married, either.

Joel Miller stood, hat in hand, at the front door, the one that no one ever used, all spruced up. She'd only seen him in a plaid shirt with a bandana tied around his neck, and snakeskin boots. His eyes took her in from head to toe and he whistled. "Well, well, you do look good enough to eat."

Shivers trickled across Zelda Marie, and if Joel Miller had been standing behind her he'd have seen the gooseflesh, because the dress had no back to it at all.

CHAPTER 37

Zelda Marie knew that half a dozen kisses had affected her mentality. She was ready to let Humble drill wherever they wanted. So she invited Joel Miller to dinner. Mrs. Spencer had taught Aofrasia how to fix a pot roast and mashed potatoes and gravy. Ao stuck her nose up at such bland food, but she cooked it as though born in Kansas. And Joel loved pot roast.

After the main course, Zelda Marie asked, "Okay, give me the best and worst scenarios."

Joel looked at her. "The worst first. Your land is riddled with pumps, gas, and/or oil spurting in streams from the earth, creating an ugly-looking skyline. Pumps rocking back and forth, back and forth endlessly, into infinity."

"Where do the cattle go?"

"You won't need cattle, except if you like to look at them."

Zelda Marie sat back in her chair and studied her fingernails. "You're making what you hope will be the best sound like our worst. So, what's the best?"

"Hundreds of thousands of dollars. Maybe millions."

Zelda Marie's eyes sparkled.

"Millions?"

"You asked for the best. In all truth, I think it'll be somewhere between those two. I don't think we'll have to drill that many holes. We're only allowed so many per acre, you know. We're not allowed to deface the land."

"What do you call oil rigs rocking back and forth if that's not defacing the land?"

"Yeah, well, environmentalists and idealists try to defeat us by talking philosophy, but ideals don't buy things. Don't run cars, or heat homes, or make plastics and polyester."

"Why *my* land?"

"Geological studies indicate there's oil right below. Your father's well, over on that patch of land he kept, is along the same fault as what's right under us this minute."

Zelda Marie thought aloud. "I think it sounds pretty nice." Then she asked, "So what if nothing's there and you've put down all those holes?"

"We pull out, and you have a hundred thousand or more for your inconveniences."

"I'd sure like that," Zelda Marie said. "I'd like to fix this place up a little and enter some horse shows and do some more breeding. I'd love to get famous in the horse world and be able to afford to go to shows in Colorado and California."

"Is being important important to you?"

Zelda Marie thought about that. "Having my horses sought after has been my dream since I was twelve years old. I guess having a famous stable that's known throughout the horse world is a dream I've had forever. Well, you go ahead and draw up contracts and we'll have cousin Andy look them over." Andy was the family's only lawyer, and he was down in Brownsville. He did the family's business for expenses only.

Zelda Marie knew Joel Miller would move on to other pastures, that he'd stop seeing her once he'd gotten what he wanted, those signed contracts. But right now his brown eyes winked at her, and she knew he'd kiss her good night and she'd feel like Jell-o inside.

It was three weeks later Zelda Marie rocked back and forth on the wooden swing of the front porch. Michael J. and Sally Mae had stayed in town with their grandparents so they could attend some school function. The other children were out back playing ball and chasing the cats. Their happy laughter echoed in the distance.

It was the first time she'd sat down all day. Her busy life and telling Aofrasia to cut out so much fried foods was helping. She'd lost over twelve pounds in the last three months, and she liked the way she looked. So, apparently, did Joel Miller, who, to her surprise, still invited her out once a week. She could tell he liked feeling her body against his when they danced, and he crushed her to him when he kissed her good night, but he never got fresh with her or tried to do anything she'd have to say no to. He was a gentleman, and sometimes she wished he weren't. Not that he excited any passion in her, but she did think about him during the day, wondering if he'd call her or if there were other women in his life, and what he really felt about her. She also wondered if she thought about him because he was the only man paying attention to her.

The big machines were moving onto the land already, but out of sight way out back, not too far from where her daddy's well was. Men in steel hats and heavy boots drove out in jeeps and four-wheel drives and trucks every day. Truckloads of pipes.

It seemed peculiar to have so much noise and machinery pass down the lane when for so many years it had been quiet enough to hear the birds sing. Joel had told her that once all the machinery got out in the field she wouldn't even know anyone was around. She wouldn't hear the drilling, and it would all be like it was before the machines came to move the earth.

It didn't bother Zelda Marie. Her mind was occupied with the possibility of getting the stallion she'd been lusting after, and the hundred thousand it would take to buy him.

Her reverie was broken by the sight of a man walking leisurely down the lane, carrying a cardboard suitcase in one hand and a guitar in the other. The sun dappling through the leaves of the trees shadowed him at one moment and made him stand out in sharp relief the next. He wore white cotton pants, tied at the waist with a piece of clothesline, and his open-necked shirt was a pale blue. Huaraches covered his feet, and he wore no socks. A smashed-down straw hat was cocked at a rakish angle.

The Mexican walked deliberately, as though he had a definite destination, and even from a distance she could see his thick mustache, dark against his olive skin. It was the cousin of Carlos. What was his name? Curling on the swing, she watched him move with a grace that was leonine.

She could tell when he caught sight of her, for he started to cut across the lawn, not slowing his pace.

She didn't move until he was about ten paces from the porch and then she stood up and looked down into the blackest eyes she had ever seen. She swore he gave a little bow even though he did not move. "Es la casa donde es Carlos?" he asked.

"Sí." She nodded. "Está su primo?"

The man's eyes lit up and he smiled, showing teeth so white they dazzled even though he stood in the shade. "Ah, habla español?"

"Not mucho, I'm afraid," Zelda Marie answered. "Como se llama?"

"Me llamo Rafael."

Ah, yes, she remembered, and wondered how many miles he had walked today. At this hour of the evening he probably had not eaten.

She crossed the porch and walked down the steps. "Come," she said, walking ahead of him. "I will take you to the house of Carlos and Aofrasia."

"Gracias, señora."

He did not walk behind her as she half expected him to, but beside her. "I know un poco English," he said.

"And," she smiled at him, "I know un poco español."

They smiled at each other, unable to converse further.

The air was soft and birds twittered in the trees. In the distance a cow lowed. The hay field had just been mown, and Zelda Marie thought there wasn't a much prettier smell.

Two of her dogs came loping from Carlos's house. She knew Aofrasia must have fed them scraps from the table. They set about barking, and Carlos came to the door to shout at them until he saw Zelda Marie and Rafael walking down the dusty lane.

Carlos shouted over his shoulder to Ao and bounded out of the door, the screen slamming behind him, running toward Rafael, his arms stretched wide and welcoming.

Aofrasia, her apron around her waist and Josefa in her arms, appeared in the doorway. When she saw Rafael a smile spread across her face, and Zelda Marie thought she detected a tear rolling down her cheek.

Rafael knelt and reached for Josefa, cradling her in his arms. His black eyes glistened as he looked around. "Que bonita," he said, and Zelda Marie couldn't tell whether he thought the baby or the scenery was pretty.

There was enough room in the little house for Rafael, since he did not bring a wife and child. But perhaps he would send for them. Or send his money home to them.

Josefa tugged on his great mustache and they all laughed.

Zelda Marie thought she would like to see him dance when the Mexicans next came out to Carlos's and Ao's. She imagined the Mexican girls would flirt with him, that they would hang golden hoops in their ears and pray that he would dance with them.

He stood up and turned to face her. He reached out his hand. She stretched hers, too, but he did not shake it. Instead, he drew it to his lips and kissed it, saying, in a voice that sounded like honey looked, "Un mil gracias, señora."

Her hand was still in his, and it fleetingly passed through her mind that servants should not kiss the hands of mistresses. But then she laughed. After all, he was not a servant. He was a man who talked with horses.

The Mexicans smiled at her laughter.

All the while she walked back up the lane to her house she studied her hand, marveling at the way it glowed golden as the bars of light from the sinking sun shone on it. Feeling the soft hairs of his mustache as they'd brushed it. Soft and not bristly at all.

When the phone rang at nine, she knew it was Joel, but she

didn't answer it. She sat on the wooden swing on the porch, sipping iced tea and fanning herself. She couldn't force herself to summon the energy to rise from the swing. Instead, she watched the fireflies dance and leaned her chin on her hand, the hand that Rafael had caressed with his mustache and touched with his lips.

Chapter 38

Breakfast was the one time of day Cole and Carly seemed to connect. On Monday morning he told her, "I'm flying down to Mexico to look over Señor Rosas's new venture."

"When?"

"Tomorrow."

She buttered her toast and spread marmalade lightly over it. "For how long?"

"Just until Friday. I'll be back for the weekend."

"You won't be here for the Johnsons' dinner party Wednesday?"

He shook his head. "That's right."

"You could have told me Friday, so I'd have let her know."

"What difference does it make?"

"Boomer's down there, isn't he?"

"Yup. I want to see how he's coming along. The project should be nearly finished." BB&O had come through ahead of schedule, even in Mexico, and with quality that was impressive. Dan designed the hotels to look straight out of fairy tales, which is what Rosas wanted. Not at all what Dan had done to the Houston skyline.

The maid brought in the coddled eggs. Carly tried to take time for a healthy breakfast but didn't always succeed. The breakfast room overlooked the backyard with its manicured lawn and profusion of flowers, all white this year. The tennis court and pool were away to the right and only the edge of the pool could be seen. Manuel was already vacuuming it.

"Do you want Rosario to pack a suitcase for you?"

"No, I'll do it tonight. I don't need to take much."

"Is the bank a full partner in this Mexican hotel deal?" She was usually interested in Cole's business dealings, but now she was thinking of something else and didn't even hear Cole's answer.

"I'll give you a Coleridge grandchild."

It had hung just above her forehead, out of sight, since she'd lunched with Ben three weeks ago.

She wondered why she even continued to think about it.

They finished breakfast and Cole rose, leaning over to brush his lips along her cheek. "What're chances of our dining alone tonight and getting to bed early? My plane takes off at dawn."

"That would be nice," she said absently, her mind still on his brother.

They dined early and he went to bed. To sleep.

Carly wandered around the downstairs, restless.

In the morning, she offered to drive Cole to the airport but he said, "I'm only going to be gone three nights. I'll park the car there."

She arrived early at work, an hour and a half before her secretary would be in. She sat there and tapped her long fingernails on the desktop. She made coffee and drank three cups. She took the elevator to the lobby and walked around ten blocks of downtown Houston. The air was brisk and clear. The early-morning sun was reflected in the tall buildings, whose glassed walls were dark green, bright blue. Dan's ideas, Boomer's construction, many of them. Houston's skyline wasn't like any other city's.

At nine-fifteen she was back in her office, dialing Ben at his home. Home? She didn't know whether it was a house or an apartment. No response. She tried the newspaper, and he answered.

"What a pleasant way to start the day," he said when he recognized her voice.

"I thought," Carly said, finding she had difficulty breathing, "I might drive down and spend tomorrow looking over the books, if you still want me to."

"I've been hoping you'd call. I'm here on a month's trial. See how I feel about it. Learn what I can. Tomorrow would be great. Plan to get here at noon and we'll have lunch first. I won't brown bag it as I usually do."

Ben brown-bagging lunch?

"I'll give you a Coleridge grandchild," he had said. She thought of herself as a moral person. She couldn't possibly commit adultery.

The pencil she was holding snapped in two.

Since it was nearly a five hour drive to Aransas Pass, which wasn't much more than half an hour from Corpus, down on the coast, Carly set the alarm for five-thirty, and was on the road by six-thirty. She'd spent an inordinate amount of time deciding what to wear, having tried on numerous outfits the night before and discarding them, leaving them piled high on her chaise for the maid to put away. She remembered Ben didn't like women to wear black.

She finally chose a red suit, which seemed appropriate somehow. She studied herself carefully in the mirror as she applied lipstick and perfume behind her ears. She stuck the perfume in her bag. She told herself she would not take a suitcase. She was not going to stay overnight in Aransas Pass. She was going to study the books, look over the town, and drive over and spend the night in Verity, where she kept a toothbrush and nightgown. She'd stay through tomorrow so she could not only surprise Francey and Walt but see Zelda Marie, too.

She'd taken to wearing her hair in a French twist, which was easy to care for, even if it did take extra time in the morning. With a bit of spray it stayed in place all day. Yet no matter how hard she tried, there were always a few tendrils that escaped and curled over her ears. Alex seldom had a hair out of place, and Carly envied the smooth look she never had quite achieved herself. She guessed she could wear the dangly kind of earrings she liked today, instead of the small earrings she wore to work. Her sheer white blouse accentuated the vivid suit, and her shoes and purse were black patent leather. She pirouetted in front of the mirror, aware but not quite understanding the vague discontent she felt.

Look at her. Her own successful business, married to a wealthy, handsome banker with an Ivy League background and a razor-sharp mind. Many of the young married women in their group openly flirted with Cole. And anyone who'd ever been to their home certainly envied her that beautiful place. They didn't know it bothered her that Mother Coleridge had not only chosen it, but she and Tessa had decorated it. That was before Carly and Tessa had become close.

At dawn she stopped at a roadside stand and bought a plastic cup of steaming black coffee and hoped she wouldn't spill it on her suit. She turned the radio to its highest volume and sang along with John Denver as she sped south through the flat Gulf country.

She drove so fast, enjoying the feeling of power that speed gave her, that she arrived at Ben's office twenty minutes before noon.

The few wooden desks in the office were battered, and only two typewriters were evident. One desk near the back was obviously a secretary's. Or the bookkeeper's. Someone stood behind a counter, but it wasn't a receptionist. Just someone working there. He glanced at Carly, his eyes taking in someone more cosmopolitan than he was used to seeing.

"Help you?" he asked, a southern drawl evident in his voice.

"Mr. Coleridge is expecting me," Carly said.

The man nodded toward an open door in the back. "You can wait in the office."

Before she reached it, she heard Ben's voice call her name.

She turned around to see him, breathless, his tie awry and the top button of his shirt undone, a grin on his face.

He raced toward her, grabbed her arm and led her back out

of the office, calling over his shoulder, "This here's my sister-in-law, guys." There was only the one guy.

Ben had a little dark-blue Dodge Dart to which he led her.

"Isn't this a little early for lunch?" Carly asked, when he'd opened the door for her.

"Not around here. Not in a place where they eat supper at five-thirty. We go to bed pretty early around here, too." Ben started the car, easing away from the curb. "Thought we'd go to a good Italian place. You do like Italian food as I recall."

She nodded, not believing a really good Italian restaurant existed down here in this little coastal town. But she was wrong.

Carly said she didn't want a glass of wine. "If I drink before five I get sleepy, and I don't want to waste the afternoon napping. Mineral water, with a twist of lemon, please."

"The spaghetti here is about the best I've ever eaten."

She followed his advice and found he was right.

"I've found what I want to spend my life doing, Carly."

"Newspaper, you mean? Well, pretty soon you'll be ready for a big city, I imagine."

"Not on your life," Ben said. "I love little towns. I think I already am in love with this particular one. I like nobody's knowing or caring that I'm Kevin Coleridge's son or Cole Coleridge's brother. They never even heard of my family. They're far more conservative politically than I am, but then who in Texas isn't? Now that LBJ isn't President any longer, I see it as my mission to jog their consciences."

"I'm proud a couple of papers have picked up my editorials. I'm going to show the world that a little weekly newspaper in a little south Texas town can be important. They'll be proud of me, Carly. I'll know over half the town, I bet, on a first name basis within weeks."

She looked across the table at him. Her chest felt tight in a way she couldn't understand. "You'll get married and have a family and be an upstanding pillar of the community."

"I'd like that," he said. "But I haven't yet met anyone who even compares with you."

"You're so full of blarney. No wonder all the women fall for you."

He didn't deny that.

"Are you thinking of modernizing that office?" Carly felt a sudden need to change the subject.

"No, of course, I'm not. I'll hire a reporter, maybe two. Or maybe one full-time and one a part-time. We already have two, including me. Three people work in the printing department. I'm thinking of expanding that. Print things for people. Invitations. Newsletters. Whatever people want printed or copied. Letter-heads for stationery. That sort of thing."

Carly laid down her fork. "That *was* delicious." And then, "You don't care about making money at all, do you?"

An earnest look crossed Ben's face. "But I do. When you see my apartment you'll realize I like nice things. But I don't care about it in the same way you and Cole do or my parents or all the kids I grew up with. It's not an end in itself. I'd like to earn enough to support a family, live in a nice house, take vacations in Yellowstone. I'd like to do a different national park each year . . ."

Carly couldn't help laughing. "Ben Coleridge, All American boy."

"I even like Wheaties."

By three-thirty she'd finished looking over the books and thought the price the owner was asking eminently fair.

"Let's go someplace and talk this over," Carly suggested to Ben when she was finished.

"I have just the place," Ben said. "Mine. Follow me in your car."

His was one of about twenty in an apartment complex, shaded by towering trees, hedges lining the walks. It was middle class and attractive, but not a place where Carly could any longer imagine herself living.

Ben's apartment was impressive, however. The walls were covered with Impressionist paintings. Copies, no doubt, but still she liked them. The overstuffed, very modern sofa and two chairs were dark gray-and-white plaid, with red pillows tossed on them.

"Why, Ben," she said honestly, "it's charming."

"Want a drink?"

Did she dare?

He must have read her mind, for he put his hands on her shoulders and faced her. "Look, Carly, I'm not going to do anything to you you don't want done. I'm probably going to try to talk you into something, but only if you want it, too."

His hands on her shoulders seemed to burn her right through her suit.

"I guess I'll have that drink, then. How about a—"

"I'll surprise you," he said with a grin.

He certainly did that.

CHAPTER 39

Carly sped along the road toward Verity. She glanced at the car clock, stepping on the accelerator. She should have left Aransas Pass before noon. She should have left Ben after breakfast.

What she really should have done was not come.

He had stroked her, touched her, bit her gently. Her brother-in-law had done things to her, had touched not only her body but other parts of her—until she began to cry. Ben hadn't even asked why she was sobbing. He just held her in his arms, cradling her, kissing her hair and her eyelids, murmuring soft unintelligible sounds. They had lain inextricably wound around each other's bodies, their legs twisted, their arms enfolding the other, though his left arm lay on the bed, not moving at all. It wasn't until nearly dawn that they had fallen asleep. When they awoke she was horrified to see that it was nearly ten. She saw that Ben had taken his phone off the hook.

He would not let her leave until they had made love again.

"Will you regret this night if you don't conceive?" he asked.

She shook her head and smiled at him as he lay, still naked, on the bed.

He was leaning against their plumped-up pillows. He reached out to grab her with his right hand. "Will you come back?"

"You could come to me next time," she said. "It's only when one doesn't want to get pregnant that it takes the first time, I imagine." She reached over to kiss him. "I would like to have your child. To think I was carrying a part of you around within me."

"Oh, Christ," he said, his voice low.

She stood up, straightening her skirt. "Look at you, Bennett Coleridge. You may be just about the most glorious-looking man in the entire universe."

"Even with this dead hand?"

"Stop it! I hate when you talk like that." She started to button her blouse, then turned to look out the window. "I wonder . . ."

When she hesitated Ben prodded her. "Yes?"

"I wonder what we've set in motion. Something terrible or something wondrous."

"Will you divorce Cole and marry me?" His eyes took on an intensity, a hard brightness like sapphires.

"Of course not," she said, knowing that even if it weren't scandalous, she would never marry Ben. "But I don't know that I ever had a more astonishing night than last night. You sure do know how to show a girl a good time."

Ben laughed.

That's what she still heard as she sped toward Verity. Ben's laughter.

Had she started something awful? Even if last night never happened again, hadn't she done something for which she could never forgive herself? She'd made love with her husband's brother, in the hope of having a child. But also partly, she thought, because she was missing something in life. Passion. Ben had certainly awakened that in her. She could tell he had made love often. No one could be that expert without practice. And oh, how he could kiss. He had been self-conscious about his left arm, but everything else more than compensated. She had not expected anything like last night. But then she told herself she was lying. Last night was just what she'd fantasized about. Just what she thought might happen. Only more so.

Nothing had touched her like Ben did—not since Boomer, a decade ago. When she was so young.

She stepped on the brakes and slowed down as she came to a small town, divided by the highway. She waited for the light to change.

What if she did conceive? Would she feel guilt her whole life when she looked at her child? What about Ben? He had wondered about the ramifications. Could he stand it?

What if Cole ever found out? But did she care what Cole thought?

There was more traffic on the road now, and she began to slow down to the speed limit.

Yes, she guessed she did. She liked Cole even if, after the first couple of years, there seemed no more excitement left in their marriage. All he ever thought about was business. Nevertheless, she and Cole did have fun discussing his plans. They enjoyed deciding which stocks to invest in, though Cole was better at that than she was.

His way of expressing love was through what he gave her, and it was usually something ostentatious. She smiled, recalling his Christmas present. A mink coat. Ridiculous, in Texas, yet in her circle as necessary as a swimming pool and tennis court.

She glanced at the speedometer. She'd passed through Kingsville and would soon be in Verity.

Whether she'd regret it or not, it was too late to do anything about it. She was guilty. Guilty as sin. Sinful.

Now, how was she going to go about living with that fact?

Well, she rationalized, if Cole had only been willing to find out about his sperm count.

Well, damn, she thought as she pulled into Francey and Walt's driveway. Whether I have done something I'll regret, I want to do it again. And probably again. And again.

She was glad Cole was in Mexico and she was in Verity. She didn't want to face him tonight.

Cole looked out the plane's window at the high jagged mountains that creased Mexico. He sighed.

He appreciated the responsibility his father allowed him, but yearned to make the really big decisions. That would be a long time coming. His father was just in his fifties.

Whenever he came up with a new idea, Cole tossed it around with his father before they presented it to the board. Only once had Mr. Coleridge nixed an idea of his, and in retrospect Cole realized it was a good thing, though he had felt miffed at the time.

Certainly this partnership with Rosas showed all signs of success. It would be several years before they saw any money from the investment, but if the three-year-old hotel in Acapulco was any indication of their mutual success, Cole could rest on his laurels. This new resort, north of Acapulco, had only been a dream of Rosas when Cole and Carly went down there five years ago. God, could it be that long?

It looked like something straight out of a Disney fairytale. He'd listened to Rosas and no one else and come up with a fantasy that thrilled the Mexican. There were no other hotels there so far, except the nearly finished one a couple of miles south of a slumbering fishing village. Just miles and miles of uninhabited white sand, where the breakers were the only sound. Would luxury make up for the lack of excitement? Rosas assured them the resort would supply its own excitement. No one visiting there would have any urge to be anyplace else. People would return year after year after year, perhaps several times a year.

Let's hope so, Cole said aloud to himself.

He had grown to like Rosas, even if sometimes the Mexican

way of doing business drove him bonkers. It was Boomer and his construction foreman, though, who bore the brunt of the different work ethic. Boomer griped constantly, but good-naturedly. He liked Rosas, too.

Bannerman had brought the Mexican foreman to Houston for three months before any construction got under way and introduced him to BB&O's methods, trying to stress that time was of the essence and there would be a definite deadline to be met.

Since the Acapulco hotel had been brought in on time, Cole refused to let himself get uptight about this next project. BB&O was gaining the reputation of being as reliable as it was innovative. The innovation was Dan's; the reliability Bannerman's.

Cole shook his head. Bannerman. Sometimes he liked him. When it was strictly business, he couldn't ask for someone more accommodating, more conscientious than Bannerman. One could do business on a handshake with him and not feel nervous about it. More casual than Cole, that was for sure. All of BB&O was that way, despite their elegant-looking offices. Rolled-up sleeves, loosened collars. Except for Tessa. Now there was one classy lady. Cole liked Tessa. It was Dan who left him feeling short. Damn Yankee in his philosophy, like his egghead professors at Harvard and Stanford in his political philosophy. He thought all people should be treated equally, were created equal, even blacks and spics. Well, that had nothing to do with business, anyhow, Cole thought. That only came to light at those times when they socialized, which he and Carly and Dan and Tessa and Bannerman and Alex did frequently. Of them all, he only felt completely at ease with Alex.

He could understand why Tessa and Carly hit it off. Two stylish-looking women, who not only turned heads when they walked into restaurants but were clever and witty, and serious about business.

He knew he and Carly were a handsome couple. Their social calendar had become so full that they'd finally agreed to accept no more than three invitations a week. Carly claimed she couldn't keep up with so many nights out and work, too.

But, somehow, Carly no longer made him feel like King of the Castle, though when he thought of coming home and of his wife, what he really wanted to do was screw her silly. Even after four years, the thought of making love with Carly could drive him nuts.

From the plane, he saw Houston's skyscrapers loom into view. The Fasten Seat Belt sign had been on for over five minutes. His city.

As the plane began its descent, he thought about what he wanted. To be one of Houston's power brokers. Even Ben was making a name for himself, and none of them thought he'd ever be anything but trouble. When he went to the boonies they'd all felt relief, but for Christ's sake, he was making a name for himself, and it had nothing to do with Kevin Coleridge or Union Trust. With anything but himself. And, Ben, he was almost four years younger. He'd always been off center. Making a name for himself like that, yet living in a little one-bedroom apartment. Not that Cole had ever been to either Nacogdoches or Aransas Pass to visit Ben, but his mother had told him. She drove to see him about once a month. She liked the drive, she said. She couldn't understand why Ben chose to live off the beaten path, but the family had breathed a sigh of relief when they thought Ben had settled down.

Cole wanted *his* name to be known. He didn't want to be known as the Vice President. As Kevin's son. As the Coleridge kid who had it made.

He was still thinking these thoughts when he entered his office at four-thirty. The sun's rays sparkled like dust through the windows, casting golden bars across his desk.

"Get Mrs. Coleridge on the phone," he told his secretary. The way he felt right now they'd make love before dinner. He couldn't wait.

"Mrs. Coleridge is out of town until tomorrow," his secretary told him.

"Out of town?"

"Yes, sir, she's visiting her parents."

He felt like a balloon whose air has just fizzled out of it. Shit.

CHAPTER 40

Carly had driven fast, with open windows that blew her hair so that she was windblown and slightly disheveled when she returned to her office. She had enjoyed her whirlwind visit in Verity, dining at the Willows last night so she could see Zelda Marie, who insisted Carly come out to the ranch for breakfast. She had things to tell her.

Francey was delighted with the job Zelda Marie was doing at the restaurant. "I think she has a boyfriend, but I'm not sure. I'd hate to think of her getting married and quitting, though I'd sure be happy for her. She's what makes it possible for me to take it easy."

"We're going to St. Thomas for three weeks," Walt told Carly. "First time I've been able to talk your mother into a vacation since she opened the Willows." The restaurant was known as "Francey's place." Francey liked that. And her one-earring had become her trademark.

When Carly had left their place at seven-thirty this morning to have breakfast with Zelda Marie, Walt walked her out to the car. "Sure is purty," he said, nodding at her sleek car.

Carly kissed his cheek and slid in behind the steering wheel. Walt leaned through the open window and asked, "You happy?"

Carly keyed the engine. "Of course. After all, I made a sale that netted me over a third of a million dollars ten days ago."

"That's not what I'm talking about and you know it. What's money got to do with happiness?"

"You've always had it," Carly said, "but every time I make that kinda money I'm as proud as a peacock."

"And with good reason," Walt nodded, "but I'm asking about the other part of your life."

"Sure, I'm happy," Carly said. "Why wouldn't I be?"

"Scout's honor?" he asked, pulling his head out of the window.

Carly threw him a kiss.

All the time she drove north to Houston she didn't let herself think about Tuesday night in Aransas Pass. She thought of trying to sell BB&O on building a shopping mall on the land maybe she and Alex would buy together. If the two women bought all the land around the area that Carly envisioned as one of the new malls, when other businesses located out here, around the mall, she'd be able to sell them that land, too. She thought Zelda Marie might just possibly have black gold gushing into her bank account, but she saw stacks of dollar bills, as high as Jack's beanstalk, coming to her for her vision of the future.

Funny how she'd gone along all these years seeing Alex several times a month but not feeling any warmth. Actually, Alex had intimidated her, what with her social background, her two college degrees, her innate sense of style and that cold regal attitude. She knew she was better looking than Alex, but that didn't stop her sense of insecurity.

Well, now suddenly because of lunch last week she felt a kinship with Alex. Could sense the possibility of friendship.

She thought about what she would wear Saturday night to the Wilmers' anniversary party. She thought of everything she could so that she wouldn't remember what she and Ben did together Tuesday night. So that she wouldn't remember his lips on hers, their bodies locked together. So that she couldn't hear his laughter or feel his breath in her ear.

She called home as soon as she returned to her office, telling the cook she'd like pork chops for dinner.

She called the hairdresser's and managed to get an appointment at five. Thursday was slow there. Then she'd shower and have martinis ready when Cole got home. He'd be tired flying back from Acapulco today.

She called his office to find out what time his plane got in and was surprised he was there.

"Got in yesterday," he said. "Sorry you weren't home. Missed you."

"I hope we can have dinner alone tonight," she said. "I'm tired."

"Yes, I've nothing planned," he said. "It'll be nice to have an evening together for a change."

But Carly was sound asleep by nine-thirty and Cole spent the evening watching an old movie on TV before he went to bed.

She and Cole were having breakfast when Alex phoned her.

"I've just come back from Rochester," she said, "and hope we can get together today. You free?"

"How about lunch?" Carly asked, feeling a flush of pleasure.

"No, I want to make it earlier. I can't wait to see you. How about eleven, and then we can spend a couple of hours talking before lunch."

Carly had a sense Alex wanted to drive around looking at land. In other words, they might be about to go into business together.

"Of course," she said to Alex, when they meandered the blacktop roads off the beaten path, "it means taking a chance. What if we can't interest anyone into taking the risk of building a shopping mall."

"The way I'd do that is get a couple of the big department stores to anchor it. Like Dillards and Foleys and Sears and Neiman's . . ."

"Oh, Neiman Marcus won't come down here from Dallas, will they? And to a mall?"

Alex shrugged. "We'll see."

"And when we have a couple of them lined up, others will fall in line. Have it eighty percent occupied before it opens."

"We need a couple of upscale hotels. When rich Mexicans fly up here to shop, they'll stay at these hotels and shop in the mall. One-stop convenience."

Carly pulled over to the edge of the road and cut the engine. "See that pretty house." It was a white clapboard, freshly painted, with a couple of towering mesquite trees shading it. Behind it was a silo and a barn nearly as pretty as the house. "That man runs three hundred Jerseys. He's going to be the most expensive to buy out."

"How many millions are you thinking of spending on land?" One thing about Alex. Like Carly, she never thought small.

"I'm not sure. I have nearly two hundred acres so far. It's not just the mall I'm thinking of. I see a long-term investment. I want to be able to wait it out, so that when office buildings, when little stores that can't afford a mall's rent want to be where the action is, we'll be able to sell land all along a strip on either side of the highway. Besides, within ten or fifteen years I envision subdivisions north and south and west of here."

"You really think so?" Alex asked, but her voice indicated she didn't need an answer. She studied Carly with coolly appraising eyes. "You know, I think I underestimated you."

Carly turned a bright smile on her. "I always thought you did, too."

They laughed together.

"I shall not be guilty of that again," Alex assured her. "What we're talking about here is buying up the land and owning it, leasing it out, right?"

Carly nodded. "Cole thinks I'm out of my mind, though you watch. Someday Union Trust'll have a branch out on this side of town. And then he'll be sorry he didn't buy it at today's prices. But I don't want to share this with a lot of others. I want to be my own boss. Develop this land the way I see it. Over a period of twenty years make millions off it. I mean, millions."

"I'm ready to be a partner if you want."

"How does Boomer feel about it?"

"I haven't even told him. I said I was going to New York

on business, and unless business includes a design and a building he doesn't even ask. I gather you want to talk Dan into designing this mall and BB&O to develop it?"

"Bingo." Carly smiled again and started the engine. She nodded her head toward the pretty white house. "You want to make Eldridge an offer on this land?" She gestured at the countryside dotted with brown-and-white cows. "How high are you willing to go?"

"I leave that up to you. You're the real estate expert."

Over lunch, they decided they'd better put something in writing, but they wanted it as loose as possible. They talked about how they felt about working together and what their responsibilities were going to be. They decided not even to approach BB&O until they had bought up at least six hundred acres. Tomorrow Carly would approach the Eldridges.

"They paid seventeen thousand for their one hundred three acres in the forties," Carly said. "I'd like to start by offering them two hundred thousand. They won't want to sell, but the idea of that much money will get them to thinking. I'm willing to go to half a million."

"My," Alex said. "That is a lot."

"Does it make you nervous?"

Alex's eyes flashed with fun. "Carly, nothing about money scares me. The more risky, the more fun. And I'm sold on this idea. And, after all, this is a sideline for each of us."

"Alex, we're going to do just fine together. Does this surprise you as much as it does me?"

"I have to admit," Alex said after ordering coffee, "I wasn't prepared for someone who looked like you to have brains."

"I've never understood what looks are supposed to have to do with gray matter. But sometimes it helps me. People can't believe I know what I'm doing."

"Did Cole know?"

Carly cocked her head. "I don't think so. I was on my way to becoming successful when I met him, but he didn't expect me to come so far. He'd much rather I stayed home and played the whole wife role. But that bores me so. Maybe it wouldn't if we had children.''

"Well, I have a child and I love him to pieces," Alex said, "but it's not enough. I try to be home by midafternoon and spend a lot of time with David, but I'm just not cut out to change diapers . . .''

Carly laughed. "I can't even imagine you changing diapers.''

"Don't you underestimate *me* this time. I've changed plenty. So has Boomer.''

Carly wondered if they had a good sex life. If Alex appreciated Boomer's sexuality as much as she had. Alex looked as though she would never let a hair get out of place, as though passion was an unknown word to her. Carly wondered if Boomer was able to break through his wife's barriers and awaken in her what he used to awaken in Carly.

"Isn't life funny," she said aloud.

Alex knew Carly didn't expect an answer, but she gave one anyway. "It certainly *is* surprising.''

"Why do you think neither of us is willing to be traditional women?" She didn't expect an answer, either.

Carly wondered whether she and Alex were lucky or unfortunate.

CHAPTER 41

Boomer whistled as he tried to tie his tie. He gazed into the mirror, watching his wife's reflection in the mirror on the opposite side of the room. She was expertly outlining her eyes, leaning close to the mirror to make sure she drew a smooth line.

He guessed he was luckier than anyone he'd ever known.

Happier than he could imagine one man being. And no small part of it was due to Carly.

Once in a while he hated himself, feeling ungrateful. Not always, but sometimes when he was with Carly, when they sat together, their heads over a drawing board, or lunched together, usually with Dan and sometimes Alex, he felt longings for her. Couldn't concentrate on whatever business they were discussing because of her closeness. Because of the smell of her. Because her elbow brushed against his arm. Or her fingers touched his.

Saturday nights at the club when he danced with her, he tried not to think of Carly as a woman. She had become his friend, his business partner in some deals she'd cooked up. And this last one she'd just presented him with really took the cake.

Tessa had been in on the presentation in the board room at BB&O. Even though she'd have little to do with the project, she was still a VP of the company, and she whooped when she'd heard Alex and Carly's plans. "To think two women came up with this idea and have bought all that land!" she'd marveled.

"And kept it under their pretty hats," Dan marveled, "without even giving us a clue what they've been up to for months. I didn't know women could keep secrets that long."

Tessa kicked him under the table. "Chauvinist pig."

Dan grinned at her.

Boomer hadn't said anything. He had sat wondering how his wife, whom he thought he knew so well, had been buying up land and cooking up this mall idea for so long without sharing any of it with him. What else about her didn't he know?

Together Carly and Alex had bought over seven hundred acres on the outer fringes of Houston, land that could still be considered countryside. They'd apparently paid prime money for it, offering the farmers more than they could ever have dreamed of earning from that land with their milk cows and their truck gardens. Alex with her investment business and

Carly through her real estate enterprise had presented BB&O with an idea larger than any they'd yet participated in.

The two women wanted BB&O to start drawing up plans that they could present to future lessees. They didn't want to sell any of the land outright. They wanted lessees to sign long-term contracts, to agree that only BB&O would design their buildings, their tall hotels, their department stores, their little shops, their escalators and the central areas, the underground parking, and even the public rest rooms. Alex said she'd set up a management company which would manage the vast enterprise once it was ready, which probably wouldn't be for two years, at the least. Already Foleys and Dillards, Texas's two largest department stores, were interested.

Macy's was going to send someone to examine the project when Alex had a plan to show them. Maybe I. Magnin's. Gucci showed interest, as did Sophie's of Rodeo Drive. And yes, there was a glimmer of interest from Neiman Marcus up in Dallas.

After two days of intensive discussion, Dan, Tessa, and Boomer decided they'd participate.

Boomer was proud they were in a position, after just four years, of being able to take the chance. How fortunate he was to have met Cole Coleridge. How fortunate he was that his wife and his ex-girlfriend had ties to Cole and that Coleridge threw the Mexican venture into their laps.

He could, as he'd promised Alex when he first met her, borrow a million on a handshake and the lender knew his word was as good as gold. Maybe, he thought as he damned his inability to tie a bow tie, it was not only because of his sudden success but because he had married Houston's golden girl. And that was all right with him, too. He was proud of Alex. Together they made a damned attractive couple, and he liked the feeling.

He swore under his breath and turned to walk across the room. He stood behind Alex, gazing at their reflection in the mirror above her dressing table and said, "Tie my tie?"

She laughed. Not once in their marriage had he ever succeeded in making a bow tie look presentable. "Just a sec."

He leaned down to kiss her bare shoulder. She had the damnd-est fine shoulders in the world, he was sure of that.

"In the mood to be a mother again?"

"Is that an invitation?" she asked, her eyes filled with laughter. "Because if it is you're just a fraction too late. My makeup is in place and I'm not going to spend an hour doing it over."

"Time enough when we get home," Boomer murmured, his hand lightly touching her well-coiffed hair.

She gently pushed it away. She'd spent two hours at Mr. Kenneth's this afternoon and not even making love with Boomer was going to jeopardize her looks tonight.

"I meant that as a literal question. Don't you think it'd be nice for David to have a brother or sister?"

"I'm in the midst of so much fascinating work. I don't really want to take the time . . ."

He did not let that deter him. "You hardly took time off for David. We have a live-in nanny and housekeeper. A cook. Seems to me all you have to do is go to the hospital and have it. I can't do that."

Alex was still madly in love with Boomer, despite what she considered his shortcomings. He often embarrassed her with his brashness and lack of savoir-faire.

Alex hated the thought of losing her figure again, of looking so bloated, of waddling those last three months of pregnancy. Of vomiting that second and third month. It wasn't only a matter of giving up time to give actual birth, but she was afraid she'd be ill the second and third months if it was like her first pregnancy. She wouldn't feel well enough to give her all to the big project.

"Couldn't we wait until we have tenants lined up for this mall project?" she asked.

"We won't even have the first stages of it built a year from now," Boomer said, watching her reflection in the mirror again. "You could have the baby and be back to work by then."

Alex knew she'd do anything for Boomer. Even a second pregnancy.

"David'll be at least three if we're successful tonight," he said. "Time flies."

I'm thirty, Alex thought. Maybe time did fly. And perhaps it would be good to have a second child. She'd been so lonely growing up as an only child. Boomer was an only child, too. And a little girl might be nice. She'd found such enjoyment with her women friends these last few years, with Tessa and now Carly.

She'd asked Boomer a few times what Carly had been like in school, and he'd always answered, "The really brainy one of our class. Maybe of the whole school. I didn't get to know her until nearly graduation."

He did tell Alex that Carly's stepfather was Verity's banker. That's all he'd ever had to say, so Alex took for granted they'd not known each other well, even if they'd gone to the senior prom together. Well, Boomer had probably dated many girls. He and Carly never reminisced about high school, so apparently they didn't have mutual friends or memories, but they laughed a lot together now. Alex guessed she and Carly had more in common than Carly and Boomer did. Alex also had more in common with Cole than any of their little group did. Funny that she and Cole had ended up in the same tight little group. Of all her Houstonian friends and acquaintances only Cole was in her group and that was because of Carly, not because of him. Because of herself, too, since she'd gotten Cole and BB&O together.

She'd been brought up in a man's world and was still amazed to discover that in that world it was two other women with whom she shared success. And it was Carly who was bringing this big project to BB&O. Alex appreciated that. But Cole always seemed the outsider when the three couples were together.

Wasn't that funny. Cole Coleridge an outsider. In every other place in Houston he was part of the core. He was on the board at the club now, and because he was a Coleridge he was welcomed everywhere.

Well, Boomer was pretty much, too. Because he'd married

her, but also because of BB&O's meteoric success. There was nothing Houston loved more than success. *Big* success. Success that was changing Houston's skyline and now was going to provide it with a totally new concept. She felt in her bones that Carly was right. This was going to be the way to shop in the future. But Alex also felt a pang of sadness. If Carly was right, downtowns would disappear. City centers would attract business but not shoppers. The big old department stores would leave. There would be empty store fronts and the vitality of cities would be lost.

Well, the world was changing, and even if it saddened her that a life she loved might be on its way out, she was going to be part of the future, help shape it. She and Boomer and Carly and Tessa and Dan.

Where did that leave Cole? she wondered. She speculated briefly if Carly enjoyed sex with Cole. It was a good thing Carly had never made love with Boomer, because there was no comparison between the two men.

Within a month Alex was pregnant with their second child and vomiting every morning. She told herself it was a small price to pay to please her husband.

CHAPTER 42

It had taken Carly and Alex three months to buy seven hundred acres, but they had come in at nearly a million less than Carly had been prepared to spend. Farmers who had inherited their land or paid up to twenty thousand for it fifteen to twenty years ago walked away with hundreds of thousands of dollars. The seven hundred acres were not all contiguous but over four hundred of it was. And that was enough space for a mall.

"Why did we take this on?" Dan moaned. "We're up to our eyeballs with work already."

BB&O was not only finishing Señor Rosas's second Mexican hotel, but a committee from a proposed retirement home in Scottsdale, Arizona, had approached them, paying for Dan and Boomer to fly to Phoenix and spend two days talking with them. Again, Dan had to be talked into it. "Isn't Houston big enough for us?" he asked.

Boomer had dreams, if not of rivaling Bechtel's, the largest construction corporation in the world, at least of becoming one of those to be reckoned with on the North American continent.

"Hell," Dan said, "we already have more than we'll ever be able to spend."

"Don't be too sure," Tessa teased her husband. "The world is filled with things I haven't bought yet."

"Yet."

"Add touches that will add quality of life to the residents, such as my decorating the place, such as including a pool and a nine-hole golf course or at least a driving range, and frivolous things such as fountains ..."

"Don't you know how scarce water is in that part of the world?" Alex asked. She usually sat in on these brainstorming sessions, and when Boomer and his partners seemed to get carried away, she played devil's advocate.

"I'm just suggesting road blocks, and if they don't like them, you have an out. If they do like them, you have a chance of making news all over with the newest in luxury retirement living."

BB&O didn't touch anything that didn't reek of money. They wouldn't even consider jobs where the client pinched pennies. Instead of turning customers away, this attracted them like flies. As Dan said, they had more than they could handle.

BB&O was also building a ski resort in Vermont, skyscrapers in Minnesota and Caracas, and now Carly and Alex had them ready to take on a Houston shopping mall.

Boomer did not want to subcontract any of it. He wanted it

all to be built by BB&O craftsmen, by men whom he personally supervised. He wanted to control the quality.

Alex told Carly, "I don't know why I try to talk him into even more. He spends more time in the air than he does at home." She was three months pregnant with what they knew would be a girl. They'd already named her Diane.

"At least nothing interferes with weekends," Alex said.

Alex and Boomer argued a lot about Boomer's clothes. He finally stood his ground and told her he would wear exactly what he wanted and he'd appreciate their not discussing it each time they went out. He wore western outfits. He sported a white Stetson all the time, even when he dressed in a dinner jacket. If he didn't wear five-hundred-dollar boots, he wore sandals around the house and at the pool. He didn't own one regular pair of shoes.

Boomer couldn't have been more surprised about Alex's partnership with Carly. The major loves of his life were friends. It amazed him that they had anything in common. Of course, Alex did not know about his and Carly's love affair so many years ago. He hadn't asked Alex whom she'd slept with, and certainly wasn't going to volunteer that information about himself.

It astonished him that Carly was making such a name for herself in the business world, selling real estate, though he'd heard someone say that if you were hard-working and uneducated, the easiest way to get rich in Texas was to sell land. Particularly in the seventies when prices were going up up up.

He had to admit it was fun talking business with Alex and Carly. He didn't think there were too many men who respected women's brains, but he was almost as proud of Carly as he was of Alex.

He wondered why Carly and Cole didn't have children. Maybe Carly was afraid to lose that sensational figure of hers. Every head turned when Carly entered a room. And when she and Cole attended parties or when they came to the club Saturday nights, Carly was the center of attention. Cole seemed to relish the way other men admired Carly.

But everyone knew Carly was a one-man woman.

She'd flirt but in a harmless, ingenuous way. Boomer liked the way she flirted. The way Carly's body melded itself to his when he danced with her, no wonder she never sat out a dance. He could feel her breasts against his chest, imagined he could feel more when their legs moved in unison to a slow fox trot. He smiled to himself. He was sure he was the only other man in Houston, probably in the universe, aside from Cole who knew what it was like in bed with Carly.

He realized he'd only half forgiven her for running away from him that weekend. Not for the first time he wondered how different his life would be now if he'd married Carly instead of Alex.

"What happens if I become pregnant?" Carly asked Ben as they lay next to each other, bars of sunlight filtering through the hotel curtains, dancing designs over their naked bodies.

"What do you mean what happens?" Ben held her hand and kissed each of her fingers. "That was the initial reason for all this, wasn't it?"

"The initial reason, yes."

Without answering her question, Ben asked one of his own. "Do you ever feel guilty, going from me to Cole?"

He did not see the pain that flickered across Carly's eyes. "All the time. I feel immoral, unfaithful, and ashamed."

Ben turned to face her, amazement on his face. "Then why the hell have we gone on like this for the last five months? You never told me you felt that way."

She pulled him to her and kissed him hard. "Because I didn't want to give this up."

"If it's any comfort, I feel like a swine, cheating on my brother with his wife."

She heard him sigh, and then said, "You haven't answered my question."

He didn't respond for a minute. Then, "You mean if or when you become pregnant do we stop these weekly meetings?"

"Mmm."

"Well, our sole purpose for getting together was to get you pregnant with a Coleridge grandchild, wasn't it?"

It had been.

"Would it mean good-bye, is that what you're asking?"

Suddenly, Ben leaned upon his good elbow and stared in Carly's eyes. "You're telling me you're pregnant, aren't you?"

"I'm not sure. I have an appointment with Dr. Beckwith on Monday. But my period's way overdue and I'm feeling a little squiggly mornings."

"Oh, Jesus," Ben said, gathering her to him. He held her close.

He thought a sob escaped Carly, but when he drew his head back to look at her he couldn't read her feelings in her eyes. "So, I guess we've succeeded, haven't we?" He sat up, his legs dangling over the side of the bed. Without looking at her, he asked, "How do you feel about it?"

"I wonder," her voice was but a whisper, "how you're going to react to seeing Cole bring up your child."

Ben stood up and walked over to the window, gazing down at the city. "I never thought it would be easy, even when I suggested it five months ago."

Carly stood up. "I love what happens when we're together. There's no tension between us. I didn't expect it. I didn't know you'd make me feel so alive. Not just when we make love, but when we talk at lunch, not hurrying in order to get to bed, but letting the conversation go on and on so our time together lasts."

Ben turned to look at her. "Ah, Carly, my beautiful sister-in-law." He walked across the room and put his right arm around her waist, pulling her close. "Have we just made love for the last time?"

"For the last time?"

Ben nodded.

Carly was afraid she was going to cry. "Kiss me," she said.

Ben felt himself come to life again as his lips met hers. "If we're going to have a last time," he said, "let's know it's the last and give it our all." He pulled her down on the bed again.

An hour later, when they stood silently dressing, Ben said, "I don't know what I'm going to do without Tuesday to look forward to. Without carrying the scent of you home with me Tuesday nights, without your kisses, your . . ."

For a minute Carly thought tears glistened in his eyes.

"Oh, God," he said, and his voice sounded strangled as he pressed her to him.

Ben did stop coming to Houston weekly when Carly assured him she was pregnant, though he called occasionally to ask how the pregnancy was progressing. He kept his calls brief and to the point.

Cole was overjoyed, as were the older Coleridges and Francey and Walt. Carly didn't know how she felt. She missed Ben.

When she was six months pregnant and beginning to waddle, her mother-in-law phoned to say that Ben was coming up for dinner Thursday evening, and was even going to stay overnight with them. He scarcely ever did that. "He said he's bringing a guest and suggested we all have dinner together."

Carly hadn't seen Ben in five months. She wondered how she'd look to him, fat and waddling around. Carrying his child within her. She wondered if guilt would show on their faces, in the way they looked at each other.

But Ben hugged her cordially, told her that pregnancy agreed with her, acted as a brother-in-law should act, and introduced her to Liz Andrews, his new advertising VP who was now also his accountant and in charge of the financial side of the paper.

His eyes lingered on Liz.

Carly felt as though a knife had sliced her heart in half. She hadn't realized she'd cared so much, though she'd thought of Ben daily. And every time the baby wiggled, she had wanted Ben to be able to put his hand on her belly and feel their child coming to life.

She disliked Liz Andrews. Ben was hers, this baby was his, and she somehow had not imagined him with another woman.

Cole hadn't been making love to her ever since she'd lost her figure. When she'd made overtures to him, he'd turned aside and said, "After the baby comes, hon."

Maybe this was one of the penances she'd be forced to pay for what she'd done to him. What she and Ben had done to themselves.

But, she kept telling herself over and over, I am bringing a Coleridge child into the world. She hoped it would be a boy who would keep the Coleridge name going so that what she and Ben had done would not be in vain and so that her guilt would have some purpose.

CHAPTER 43

Rafael did indeed talk with horses.

Zelda Marie liked to stand in the barn, down in the dark end where she was in shadow, and listen to him. The Spanish she learned this way was the stuff of songs, for Mexicans did not talk to each other the way Rafael talked to the horses. It was the language of love.

When it came to breaking a horse, Rafael did not have a horse buck and try to throw him off. Zelda Marie thought it looked more as though the horse considered Rafael its sweetheart.

She spent many hours learning his way of dealing with horses, watching and listening. She studied him carefully. He must be in his early thirties, she guessed. Did he have a wife and children in Mexico and did he send part of his earnings to them?

He began to teach her, not only how he trained horses, but

the Spanish language. She wanted him to teach her, too, how to carry happiness around within herself, as he seemed to.

He was unfailingly polite to her children, who began to follow him as though he were the Pied Piper. He never seemed too busy to teach them games or songs, accompanied by his guitar. Carlos attended to all the mechanical things on the ranch and Rafael took care of the animals.

Aofrasia sang in the kitchen, and the Mexicans sat around the big kitchen table at night and ate as Zelda Marie and her children were served in the dining room. Zelda Marie knew her children wanted what she herself yearned for . . . to be part of the group.

As soon as dinner was finished, the children raced out to the barn, where Rafael was already waiting for them, ready to teach them a new song, making them beg to feed the horses, giving them riding lessons. He told Zelda Marie she would need a riding ring if she wanted to train show horses.

She drove into town and hired Bob Deckett to come build her an indoor ring. Deckett told her it would be three months before he had free time.

But within three months the riding ring she would build would be a showcase, for oil was struck, and Humble Oil began paying Zelda Marie twenty-five thousand dollars a month. Each and every month.

Within two years it was even more, and Zelda Marie decided to build herself a mansion. "Something so gorgeous and so big and so luxurious it'll seem obscene."

She decided she'd go up to Houston and visit Carly and get her ideas on designing a super-duper house, one that'd make all of Brooks County eat its heart out. Something so exquisite that people would drive up the lane just to ooh and ah.

Already the new barn and riding ring were unlike anything anyone in Verity had ever seen. When people came from New York and Lexington and Dallas and maybe even Hollywood to buy her horses they'd know they weren't dealing with any small-time operator. She thought that new foal was going to take her to the moon, or at least make the Arabian world aware of her. Rafael indicated his real passion was cutting. He knew enough English to tell her that. She was no slouch in that area, either. So, they trained together mornings after the children left for school. It was lunchtime before Zelda Marie was even aware of the passage of time. Aofrasia called them and brought out a picnic lunch and she and Rafael ate with the Mexican couple on the long picnic bench under the mesquite trees.

Zelda Marie had never been happier.

In Houston, Carly had a new home, too, one she had chosen all by herself. There she welcomed Zelda Marie. Zelda Marie was impressed with the house, which was about the size of a small hotel. It was surrounded with others of equal size but varying architecture. Cole's and Carly's house was long, low, and gracious, looking comfortable and lived in as well as elegant.

"Tell me all that's happening in that jerkwater town," Carly said, slowly sitting on a chaise out in the backyard.

When Zelda Marie told Carly of her plans to build herself a mansion, Carly said, "Buy some more land, too."

"Why?"

"Can't own too much land," Carly said. "How much do you own now?"

"More than I need. About twelve hundred acres," which she knew was nothing by Brooks County standards. Not enough to make a living on if she were raising cattle or peanuts or soy beans or watermelons, the typical crops down in that part of the world. But she didn't need to raise anything now. She could concentrate on horses.

Carly reiterated. "Buy land."

Zelda Marie told Carly she'd think about it. Right now she was more interested in a house.

"While you're here, let's talk to Dan. He ordinarily doesn't take the time for just one house, but maybe as a special favor to me . . ."

Carly looked beautiful even if bulging with pregnancy.

"Are you happy?" Carly asked her friend.

It was something Zelda Marie seldom thought about. "I've been happy ever since Joe Bob died."

"You look better than you've ever looked."

"I'm going to look even better. I'm going to buy clothes and clothes and clothes, even though I don't have anyplace to wear them."

"Don't you *do* anything? Go out any place?"

Zelda Marie shook her head. "I did for a while, but then Joel proposed to me and that ended it."

Carly looked inquisitive as she sipped mango tea. They were sitting on the patio overlooking the vast expanse of lawn and pool, trees as thick as a forest abutting the edge of their property.

"We'd been seeing each other a couple of months," Zelda Marie explained, "but I never could figure whether he wanted me for me or whether he thought I was going to come into a bundle. And, besides, he never lit any fire in me."

"Did you sleep with him?" Carly asked.

"I'm not that stupid. Even though I had to get my tubes tied, I'm smart enough to know that when a woman goes to bed with a man, she gets her emotions screwed up, and men don't always. I know that too well."

"Have you thought about what happens if you fall in love and want to get married and the man wants to have a child?"

Zelda Marie laughed. "Not likely. I've been pregnant enough, thanks. Besides, any man wanting to take on me and my kids is not after just me, but my money. It's a burden, you know," but she smiled as she said it. "I'm into horses more than men. I think this new trainer I got some months ago is my ticket to success. I want a stable that's known around the country. With Rafael, I think I stand a good chance."

"Rafael?"

Zelda Marie nodded.

"What does he know about showing horses?"

Zelda Marie smiled. "I can't answer that. But I can tell you if he doesn't know it about horses it's not worth knowing. He's the most fantastic person with horses I ever saw.'' Without realizing she was saying it, she added, ''And kids.''

Carly studied her friend, noting the difference in her tone of voice but said only, ''Look at us. Who'd have thought we'd be like this ten years ago?''

''Even five.''

Carly's new maid, Beatriz, appeared in the doorway to the drawing room, announcing a telephone call.

Carly pulled herself out of the chaise. ''I won't be a minute.''

Zelda Marie looked around. Carly had a house that was more beautiful than any Zelda Marie had ever seen. She was into real estate deals involving millions of dollars. And she was just thirty.

Zelda Marie wondered what she had to show for the same amount of time on the planet. If she built a new house it wouldn't be on account of anything she'd done. It was because there was all that oil under her land. And it wouldn't even be her land if her father hadn't given it to her. She guessed she really hadn't done much but bear kids.

''That was Tessa on the phone,'' Carly announced. ''We're going to have lunch with her and Alex. Alex is pregnant, too. About time my three best friends met each other.''

But Zelda Marie's presence inhibited conversation. It was the first time Carly realized that her childhood friend simply did not fit in with the crowd she ran around with in Houston.

Zelda Marie's grammar was not always correct. Her grasp of the kind of talk that stimulated the three Houston friends was beyond Zelda Marie's scope of comprehension. She said a couple of things, and Tessa and Alex looked at her with raised eyebrows, so she just kept quiet. They laughed at things that were alien to her. They discussed in great detail new developments at a shopping mall, which Carly had told her a little about. Carly seemed obsessed with it. Zelda Marie did not for an instant realize she was lunching with the three most dynamic businesswomen in Houston. All she knew was that she did not feel comfortable.

Maybe that's how Carly used to feel in Verity. She'd never

been able to understand Carly's feelings, for Zelda Marie had always belonged. She'd been born in Verity as had both her parents and her father's father and his father before him. She knew just about every native Texan who lived in Verity. And had known them forever. She never had had to pretend with anyone. Everybody knew who she was or at least who her daddy was.

But up here, she felt she didn't belong. She was from one of Verity's oldest families, ones who'd had ranches there before there was even much of a town, and the only relationship in her life she'd ever questioned was that with her husband. Now, suddenly, at lunch she had the distinct feeling that whoever she was didn't matter.

She didn't like the feeling.

She didn't even wait to buy all those fancy clothes she'd dreamed of, nor did she wait to talk with Dan about designing a house for her. She took off the next day, and all the time she sped southward, she visualized a tanned face with a black mustache and liquid dark eyes that magnetized her.

She wondered if he felt alienated in a strange country. To her, Houston was a strange country. Stranger in a strange land. Was that how Rafael felt? Would that mean that he'd leave Verity as she had left Houston? Would he return to Mexico when she needed him so much?

Or would some black-eyed daughter of a Mexican whose family had been in Texas longer than Americans had been lure him and draw him into her family? That would keep him here.

Not for the first time, she wondered if, when he made love, he used the same words as he did to the horses.

CHAPTER 44

Boomer's secretary stuck her head in the door. "Mrs. Coleridge is on line two."

Boomer picked up the phone. Another new idea, no doubt, even though she was ready to deliver any day. "Carly?"

Carly's voice sounded frazzled. "Oh, Boomer, I can't reach Cole."

"Hey, you've been to Mexico enough to know phones can be out for days. Weeks. They're supposedly installing phones in the hotel right now, but with Telemex you never can tell . . . I tried last night with no luck. Can I help?"

"Well, I thought he should know. My water broke and I'm going to call a cab and get to the hospital. I've tried and tried to get Alex, and Tessa, too. No one's around. It's two weeks early, but—"

Boomer interrupted. "Don't call a cab. I'll be right there. It won't take me twenty minutes, Carly. Can you hold on?"

Carly met him at the door and threw her arms around him. She pointed to her small suitcase. Boomer opened the car door and Carly lumbered onto the seat. "I can't fasten the seat belt," she said. "It won't fit around me."

Boomer drove like a madman, expertly zigging and zagging in and out of traffic.

"I called the doctor," Carly said, "and he should be there. Boomer, you're an absolute sweetheart." Carly bit her tongue, trying not to cry out at the pain, hoping they'd get to the hospital in time. She certainly didn't want to make a mess in Boomer's Mercedes.

He pulled up at the emergency entrance, his adrenaline flowing. A wheelchair slid up to the car door, and an orderly opened the door and reached in to help Carly, then whisked her up a short ramp and through the automatic sliding doors.

Boomer parked the car and stood for a minute, taking a deep breath. He walked through the lobby to the elevators. When he reached the fifth floor, he told the nurse on duty he was looking for Mrs. Coleridge.

"She's being prepped and will be taken into the delivery room any minute, Mr. Coleridge," she told him. "But the fathers' waiting room is through that door. There's coffee and a sandwich machine, and we'll let you know as soon as the baby arrives."

Mr. Coleridge. He let it pass. Maybe they wouldn't let him wait otherwise.

He walked into the waiting room. No one else was there. He sat down and picked up a magazine that featured the photo of a football player on the cover. He didn't see a word as he flipped the pages.

It seemed like a month, but it was scarcely an hour later when a nurse came in. "Mr. Coleridge, you have a son. Eight pounds, three ounces, and the doctor says he's just beautiful. You can see him in about ten minutes."

"And Mrs. Coleridge?" Boomer asked. "She's all right?"

"Right as rain. No complications at all. Easy as pie, the doctor said. In a few minutes you can see her, too, but she'll be pretty groggy."

He'd have to get word to Cole. Call Señor Rosas in Monterrey and make it his responsibility. He hoped Cole would find a way to phone Carly, and that he'd get the first plane out of there.

The doctor walked into the waiting room, a smile on his face until he looked around. "You're not the husband, are you."

"I'm an old friend. Mr. Coleridge is out of the country. I brought her in."

"Hmpf. Well, follow me."

Carly's hair was bedraggled, her complexion pale. She reached out to grasp Boomer's hand, albeit weakly.

"Did you see him?"

Boomer shook his head and smiled down at her. "Not yet," he answered, "but I will."

"Will you call the Coleridges?" she asked. "Mrs. Coleridge will have a fit that she wasn't here."

Boomer, having met Maude Coleridge, understood.

"And call my mother." Carly rattled off Francey's phone number. "Tell her I'll call her tonight, when I'm thinking more clearly. And see if you can get Cole, too?"

Then she was asleep.

A nurse trotted in. "Would you like to see your son now?" she asked Boomer. "You can look through the glass down the hall on the right. He's in the middle front. Looks just like a chipmunk."

Boomer leaned over and kissed Carly's forehead. Then he straightened and looked around. No one was in sight. He bent over and kissed her on the lips.

As he walked down the hallway he paused in front of the nursery, and there, wrapped in a pale-blue receiving blanket, his eyes vacant and his skin blotched red and white, was Carly's son. Boomer laughed and couldn't understand why he felt so extraordinarily good about it.

He whistled as he drove home from the hospital.

Every afternoon Boomer came to the hospital to see her and the still-unnamed baby.

The Mexican phone system was among the least reliable in the world. In that little town near the new resort, Carly imagined, there weren't fifteen phones altogether. When she and Cole had been there over five years ago, they were beyond the reach of phones. They'd thought it quite romantic at the time.

But she didn't now. She found herself getting angry at Cole, though she knew it really was not his fault. After all, the baby hadn't been expected for another two weeks. Maybe she'd miscalculated.

Funny how Boomer had turned into such a good friend.

But it was Ben Carly spent much time thinking of. Mrs. Coleridge had told Carly that she'd called Ben.

The nurse interrupted her reverie, bringing the baby in for his feeding. It was the third day, the day her milk had come in, making her chest feel like a ton of weight had descended upon her.

She reached for her newborn. His skin had lost its blotchiness, his forehead had rounded out, and his big eyes blinked beneath the longest eyelashes she'd ever seen on a baby. Wisps of hair haloed his head. She thought he was the most beautiful baby in the world. She gathered him to her breast, wondering why any woman who had enough milk would opt not to nurse her own child. She sighed with contentment as he began to suckle.

Looking at her baby, Carly decided from now on she could do much of her work at home. She didn't want to give up working, just as the mall was getting to the exciting part, but she could turn the library, which they seldom used, into a home office. She looked at this baby of hers, this creature who had grown in her body, and knew she wanted to be with him. She had reliable sales personnel and a trusted assistant who could run the office and with whom she'd be in daily touch.

She smiled as the baby stopped nursing and took a deep breath of what she could only imagine was fulfillment, its little fingers wrapped around one of hers. She leaned over and kissed the down on his head. She snuggled the baby to her as he began to breathe regularly. She could tell he had fallen asleep. She glanced around the room, which was filled with flowers. The hospital said they'd run out of vases. Carly hadn't realized she knew so many people who would know so quickly that she was in the hospital.

Cole wouldn't forgive himself for not being here, Carly was sure, but it was Ben's absence that made her feel rejected. Not a phone call. No rushing up from Aransas Pass. She must be careful not to show her irritation. Not even to feel it.

Every day Boomer and Tessa and Alex stopped in, separately. In fact, she had more visitors than she wanted. Sometimes, afternoons she just wanted to nap. But she barely closed her eyes when someone appeared, usually with flowers or a gift for the baby in hand.

Carly had turned down offers of rides home from the hospital staff, opting to accept Mrs. Coleridge's, knowing what pleasure that would give her mother-in-law. When Mrs. Coleridge appeared at eleven on the day of discharge, when the baby was four days old, Ben was with her.

He carried a bouquet of violets and there was a smile on his face, but Carly noted that his eyes were as blank as though nobody was there.

He held out his little bouquet and said, "Something for the mother."

The mother of my baby is what Carly knew he didn't say.

Just then the nurse brought her son to her. She was followed by an orderly with a wheelchair. "I don't know why they think I can't walk," Carly said. "I've been all over the hospital."

"No you haven't," the nurse said, "you've been standing in front of that window staring at your baby."

Carly laughed. "He is beautiful, isn't he?" She said to the nurse, "Let my brother-in-law hold him."

The nurse raised her eyebrows, as though in doubt, but held his son out to Ben. He reached out with his good hand and stroked the wrinkled little face, then gazed deeply into his son's eyes. The nurse held the baby up, and Ben kissed its forehead. "I didn't know babies were so soft," he whispered.

"What's his name?" Ben asked.

Carly shook her head. "When Cole left we hadn't decided on anything for sure. I thought I'd better wait until he gets back."

"Oh, yes," Mrs. Coleridge said as though she'd forgotten the whole thing, "he phoned from Guadalajara just as I left the house and said he'd be home in three hours. Mr. Rosas had just gotten hold of him this morning. He sounded so upset he wasn't here."

"I'm sure," Carly said, her eyes on Ben.

The nurse placed the baby in Carly's arms, along with Ben's nosegay. As the orderly wheeled her down the hall to the elevator, she felt Ben's hand on her shoulder. They went down the hospital corridor connected to each other—mother, father, son. Carly felt tears gather in her eyes, and looked up at Ben, who was looking straight ahead, his face as full of animation as a cigar store Indian.

"That baby," Mrs. Coleridge said to Ben, "looks just like you did when you were born. Both the spitting image of Grandfather Wheaton."

PART IV

1979–1981

CHAPTER 45

The light was too steady to be a firefly, but it danced through the dark of night. Sitting on the porch swing, Zelda Marie stared at it, mesmerized. The moon had not yet risen, and she could barely make out the outlines of the trees.

The pinprick of light came down the lane, from the direction of the house where Aofrasia and Carlos lived. And Rafael.

And then she knew. Felt it in her bones. Felt it by the way her skin tingled. Felt it by the dryness at the back of her throat.

He came out of the darkness, in his white clothes, like a ghost. She could not see his face.

"Good evening, señora," his soft voice murmured.

He did not ask but sat down on the steps, his cigarette in his left hand. He did not say anything for a long time. They sat in silence, the only sound the crickets and the hinges of the swing.

Finally he ground the cigarette out under his heel and threw it into the night.

"I see you," Rafael said, "sitting out here every night."

He did?

"And I think you are lonely."

"I am surrounded by people all day," she said.

Now she could see his outline clearly and she saw him shake his head. "But at night you carry loneliness within you."

She did not answer him.

After what seemed like a long time, he asked, "Do you miss your husband?"

Zelda Marie laughed sharply. "No." She could not see the expression on his face. "I hated him."

And then he was talking about himself. She had not imagined him lonely, living with Aofrasia and Carlos and their children. "Do you think often of your wife?"

She heard him sigh. "I almost forget what she looked like. It has been three years since she died."

"Did you love her a lot?"

"What is love?" he asked. "I married her when I was twenty. My mother chose her for me. She was very pretty."

Zelda Marie didn't know what to say.

The swing squeaked. Rafael lit another cigarette.

After a long time, he said, "I think Carlos or I should make a screen for your window. It is not always safe to sleep with an open window."

"I've slept with an open window all my life," Zelda Marie said.

"But anyone can climb in there," Rafael said.

"I am not afraid."

"Perhaps you should be, señora."

She wanted to get up and walk over to him, to take his hand and sit down next to him, to turn her face to his and stare into his eyes. But she feared he'd pull back, disappear into the night, and perhaps not even be here in the morning.

Beads of perspiration glistened on her forehead. "My, it's hot tonight."

"It is hot every night," Rafael said, "at this time of year. It is hotter than where I come from in Mexico. It makes the blood boil."

Zelda Marie swore there wasn't a sound at all. Even her swing was still.

Then she asked, "Do you think of Mexico?"

"Sometimes," he answered. After a minute, he added, "But I do not wish to return there. I am happy here."

"I am happy you're here, too," Zelda Marie said. She wanted to tell him she found him invaluable. What she said was, "Without you, my dreams would have no chance of coming true."

Five minutes of silence must have passed before Rafael stood up. "Good night, señora. Perhaps you had better keep your window closed and turn the air-conditioning on. After all, there are illegal aliens crossing this part of the country at night."

"I am not afraid of illegal aliens," she said, her voice husky. "I am not afraid of an open window or what may come through it."

Her hand fluttered into the air and brushed against her breast, which felt hot under her yellow gauze blouse.

She watched as he walked back down the path until the outline of his white clothes disappeared. She found herself breathing hard. She was not positive she had understood their conversation, yet there was no other way to interpret it.

Was he right—she was lonely?

Or had she wanted him from the first day she saw him?

They had seldom said a personal word to each other. Their conversation centered around horses and her children. Yet she spent her nights unable to sleep until long after midnight, thinking of him. Remembering his words that day, the way his hands touched the head of a mare, the words he whispered to the horses, the way a pulse beat at his temple. The way he laughed with her children, tossing quoits with them out behind the barn. Showing them how to tie halters of fine leather. Teaching them to jump barrels and now, with Mike, starting to show him how to cut. She thought maybe they were ready to enter some of the big-time shows. It was time to let Rafael show off, feel pride, have some fun.

She'd ask him tomorrow if that would interest him. She knew the answer, but it would give her such gratification to see pleasure reflected on his face, in his eyes, and to know that she was partly responsible.

She lay awake for an hour, her arms pillowed under her head, staring out the window at the gently waving leaves of the trees, at the curtains billowing gently in the soft warm breeze.

What she saw first was a shadow, and then a leg thrown over the windowsill, a body thrusting into her room, and she thought, what if it's not Rafael?

But he stood, silhouetted against the window. He stood that way until his eyes became accustomed to the darkness and he saw the bed, saw her dark form against the white sheets, and she saw him unbutton his shirt, slip out of his trousers and come toward the bed. He reached out for her, and when he felt her nakedness she heard him gasp. Gathering her in his arms, he pulled her to him, his lips finding hers, and she felt the softness of his thick mustache. She liked the smell of him, like horses and the barn. The feel of his skin against hers, his lips upon hers, soft and urgent, unlike any kiss Joe Bob or Joel Miller had ever given her. The sweetness of his tongue engulfed her, and she heard a moan from deep within him.

His hand touched her breast and feathered down her belly as he nibbled her neck. He did not hurry. He coaxed from her feelings she had only dreamt of, he touched her in places that Joe Bob had not hinted were even there. He was tender yet wild, with a passion such as Zelda Marie had never experienced.

She dug her nails into him, bit him, ground her belly against his, cried out in the night.

He did not leave until nearly dawn. They never exchanged a word.

She fell into a deep dreamless sleep and when she awoke three hours later she was sure she had dreamed it.

Certainly such a thing could not have happened. Rafael would never have come to her bed.

But there was the indentation of a head—his head—on the pillow next to her, and on the windowsill there was a little purple wildflower, the kind that grew in the woods.

CHAPTER 46

Rafael did not look at her when she entered the barn in the morning. She stood in the shadows as he fed the horses, stood at the barn door watching him exercise them. She watched as he rode Dancer, jumping one bar higher than he had last week. She heard the low murmur of his voice, talking to the horses.

All he said to her, was "Good morning, señora."

She waited for Rafael to appear the next night, but he didn't. He didn't walk down the lane or climb through her window.

She wanted to ask him why not, but he hardly talked to her. Even about the horses.

She wondered if he had another woman, a Mexican woman. She would look at him on the back of a horse and she wanted to tear her blouse off and lie down in the hay and have him make wild love to her, have him kiss her breasts, run his tongue over them, bite them. She wanted to see him naked in the sunlight, wanted her pale body against his golden one. She wanted his mustache to tickle her thighs, and his tongue to meld against hers. She wanted to be one with him.

Three nights later he came through the window again.

He hurt her this time, not deliberately, but he took her with such passion, such fire that she was sore the next day. At breakfast, by her place in the dining room was a single red rose.

She began to be aware of her body in a sense she never had before. She began to wear full skirts that showed off her spectacular legs, and frilly, tight fitting, low-cut cotton blouses. She bought golden hoops that dangled from her ears.

She couldn't find any Chanel No. 5 in Corpus Christi so she

bought My Sin. When she wasn't out in the barn, she wore thin-strapped sandals and began to paint her toenails.

"Must be a new man in your life," her mother remarked. "Whatever happened to that Joel Miller?"

"He hasn't been around for years."

It was a good thing Aofrasia cleaned and cooked and washed, for Zelda Marie was a woman possessed, and no one and nothing else mattered.

One Sunday, four months after Rafael had first climbed through her window, when the beat-up pickups and the ten-year-old cars began to drive down the lane, throwing motes into the dusty air, Zelda Marie controlled herself as long as she could. She waited until the middle of the afternoon when she knew they would be eating their savory food. Music was playing on a scratchy phonograph and she could hardly stand it, wondering if Rafael was sitting next to a young dark-haired girl, whose leg might rub next to his, or if he were dancing in the grass with a girl who thought she belonged to him.

She wondered, as she was drawn like a magnet to the little house down the dirt lane, if the Mexicans would be embarrassed to see her. If Carlos and Aofrasia and Rafael would feel uncomfortable in front of their friends. She imagined the silence that would greet her arrival, the doña, the señora who was not one of them. The gringo who paid them.

But when she rounded the bend by the big oak tree and came in sight of the little house that had been her home for all those Joe Bob years, no one was dancing. About two dozen Mexicans were standing around, the women preparing food. The long table was already laden with mounds of tortillas, bowls of steaming rice, of freshly made salsa, of onions and radishes and grated cheese, and of guacamole. The smell of barbecued chicken filled the air. Zelda Marie felt ravenously hungry.

The first one to notice her was Aofrasia. The woman wiped her hands on her apron and came toward her. Rafael looked up to see Zelda Marie standing by the tree. He stopped, standing as though frozen, staring at her across all the people.

Aofrasia smiled warmly. "Señora, welcome."

"You all sounded like you're having such fun . . ."

Ao put an arm around her and pulled her toward the group. "Come, eat with us. There is plenty of food."

Zelda Marie tried to wrest her eyes away from Rafael's, to say something gracious.

The relief she felt was immense. He had been talking with three other men; there were no young women surrounding him.

"Señora." He was by her side. For the first time in days, his eyes met hers. She saw in the liquid black a tenderness that had never before been directed toward her by a man. It was all right that she had come.

"I hope you don't mind," she said.

Ao answered. "We are honored, señora."

Rafael did not sit next to her, but across the table from her, and she tried not to let herself look at him, but the heat they generated was felt by everyone at the table. Two wrinkled women with gray hair nodded, not even trying to hide their smiles. No one could escape the way Rafael and Zelda Marie didn't look at each other.

She tried to concentrate on the women's talk. They spoke a mixture of English and Spanish, unself-consciously including her in their conversation, and though she understood no more than half of it, she did not feel awkward. They displayed delight when she tried to use some of her limited Spanish vocabulary. They talked of children and of recipes and of movies. They talked of a woman who had just died after a long illness and of the poor husband who was left to take care of two children, one a year and a half old and the other but three.

They talked of an old woman, so old no one remembered when she was born, but she had been born here in Texas, although she never learned English, who had outlived her family and had no one to care for her. They promised each other that they would look in on her and take her food during the week.

They talked of a woman who had died in childbirth because the baby came upside down and the doctor, knowing he would not be paid, refused to come. Nor would he admit her to his little clinic.

The only happy thing Zelda Marie heard about was that one of the women had a niece, the daughter of her brother, who had been voted the most popular girl in the high school—among the Mexicans. In the yearbook, Zelda Marie remembered, there were two of everything: One white; one Mexican. Most popular boy, most popular girl, most popular couple. Brightest. Most chance of success. Two of everything. One Mexican, one American. It had always puzzled her. As her mother said, Mexicans were Americans, too. North Americans, even.

It seemed to Zelda Marie, looking around, that Mexicans were so good-looking. But that poor little cross-eyed boy . . . perhaps she could do something to help him. An eye doctor, maybe, in Corpus.

They sat around in the twilight, laughing and singing, and she hummed along with them, not knowing the songs but feeling content and happy, forgetting that her children would wonder where she was and would fix themselves peanut butter and jelly sandwiches for supper and watch TV, or run around the yard, gathering fireflies into jars. Though she guessed Mike would be too old for that. Maybe they all were. Sally Mae was thirteen now. And here *she* was, not so young anymore—thirty-one, and possessed of a passion she hadn't even known existed.

CHAPTER 47

"Dad offered me a new job," Cole said.

"He's retiring?"

Cole shook his head. "That's not it. I mean, he's not sixty yet."

Carly knew his father's was the job Cole dreamed of. He'd been vice president of Union Trust since he'd returned from graduate school and that's what he'd been for the past thirteen years, with no hope of anything more until Mr. Coleridge either retired or died.

"Up in Destin there's a Savings and Loan he'd like to buy. And, if he does, he'd make me president."

"Destin?" Carly's voice cracked. Destin might be larger than Verity, but not by much. The town had grown so that the ranches and farms that surrounded it had a place to shop and bank. She'd never even been there, but it was a whistle stop and she knew it. She felt a chill along her spine.

Cole answered her unasked question. "We'd move the headquarters to Houston. God knows, I wouldn't live there, even if that's where my grandparents came from. It looks like Congress is going to allow S & Ls to make real estate loans anyplace. Until now they've only been able to make loans on property located in their market area. But if this new law goes into effect it'll allow a cash flow from cash-rich to cash-poor areas and increase loan opportunities."

"Oh?"

"Yeah. Dad's interested not only because it looks like deregulation is coming, but because he was born up there. He's sentimental about the place. A friend of his who's on the board of the thrift up there called him. They need an infusion of money. They're on the skids."

"Then why buy something that's going down the drain?"

"Because new deregulations are going to change the whole Savings and Loan business."

"What's the difference between a Savings and Loan and a regular bank?"

Cole loved his role as teacher. "Thrifts—that's what S & Ls are called—came into being because banks like ours don't lend money for mortgages. Savings and Loans make home ownership possible for the middle class. Neighborhood thrifts lend money to people in their little towns. Now they pay three percent for deposits and lend money to home buyers at six. We can double our money."

"I read," Carly said, "inflation is running at thirteen percent.

I wouldn't think investors would want to put their money in a bank that only pays three percent."

"There's going to be deregulation, I told you." Cole sounded as though he were talking to a slightly retarded child. "Something called a money market fund has come into being. It's uninsured, but it pays high interest rates. That means investors can place any amount of money in such a fund any time, earn rates that are higher than inflation or at last equal to it, and withdraw their money anytime they want."

"Wow," Carly said.

"Dad and I think money will flow like crazy from the S & Ls all over the country and into money market funds. But they're high risk. The only thing that'll save S & Ls is if Congress increases the FSLIC's insurance coverage *and* insures those deposits. Insuring up to a hundred thousand dollars would make investing one's money in an S & L very attractive. We could pick a couple up for a song now, and when deregulation comes through, as it's bound to when Reagan becomes President . . ."

"What makes you think he's going to win?" The thought horrified Carly. It might mean more money and lower taxes for people like her and Cole, but for the majority she saw only lower incomes. Fewer jobs. Of course, when she said this to a Coleridge, or any of her other friends, they looked at her as though she had a screw loose. Only Ben agreed, both of them harboring the hope that Carter would be reelected.

Cole went on. "Savings and Loans will be allowed to offer money market funds and a wide variety of other kinds of accounts, which will have no withdrawal penalties or interest rate regulation.

"They, or perhaps I should say we," Cole grinned, "can invest maybe up to half our assets in nonresidential real estate lending."

"Commercial lending is much riskier," Carly said.

"Yeah, but the potential returns are much higher."

"Your Savings and Loans could then be susceptible to huge losses."

Cole shook his head as though waving away everything Carly said. "They'll be insured by the government, don't you see? It's so safe it's not even a risk."

"What happens when the government has to pay for any losses?"

"Means we—the thrifts—don't have to. Safe as can be."

And what about the taxpayers? Carly didn't ask. What about people's tax dollars?

"As a practical matter, Congress just can't let the Savings and Loan industry founder. If they collapse, the whole country's financial stability will be at risk. Also, when deregulation sets in—as Reagan's advisors will make sure it does—they're going to have to change the law that requires an S & L to have four hundred stockholders with none owning more than twenty-five percent. The ideal will make it possible for one person to own a thrift."

"One owner? One person deciding who gets loans at what interest rate? Come on, Cole, that'll lead to corruption."

Cole leveled his gaze at his wife. "Carly, it is so obvious you know nothing about banking."

Carly shook her head. Cole had been saying that for the nine years of their marriage. Sometimes she believed him. But then she'd talk with Walt in Verity, and he told her she had an unusual grasp on understanding finances and the banking world. She knew for sure that she understood the real estate world, and that certainly dealt with large sums of money.

"Someone wanting to capitalize his own bank can put up land or other assets. But where will the actual cash come from?"

Cole sighed and put down his fork. "I don't know why I bother to tell you these things. You just don't understand."

Carly bridled. "Because I ask so many questions?"

Cole always did this to her. Started to talk business with her and when she asked questions, silenced her with, "You just don't understand." He never did continue long enough so that she *could* understand. She almost always ended up asking Walt the questions, and he would explain, and she *did* understand.

At these times, she got the feeling Cole did not think she

was a very good wife. Well, most of the time she did not think he was a very good father.

Cole had never picked Matt up when he was a crying baby and refused to change his diapers. He became irritated when the baby spit up on him. But now that Matt was nearly five, Cole laid out his plans for Matt: After twelve years at St. John's, he would go on to Harvard. He wouldn't have to get his MBA at Stanford, though Cole would like that. He'd follow in his father's footsteps by becoming a banker or, if he preferred, a lawyer. He would stay in Houston.

"What if he doesn't want to go to Harvard?" Carly asked so many times. "Everyone we know except you has gone to the university in Austin. It's where you go if you want to be anyone in Texas."

Cole gave her a cool, level gaze. "You can go any place if you're a Coleridge. You've discovered that."

"Don't you think Matt should have something to say about his life?"

"Of course. Just as I did. After all, if my parents had had their way I'd be married to Alex."

"Maybe you'd have been happier," Carly murmured.

Cole made no response.

Those evenings when they didn't entertain or have dinner out, Cole plumped himself in front of the TV after dinner, replying in monosyllables to Carly's comments. She'd give up and go to bed and read. She'd be in that twilight stage between sleep and waking when he'd come to bed shortly after the late evening news and reach out for her, touching her breast, rubbing against her curled back.

He couldn't understand why she wasn't interested.

"Talk to me, for heaven's sake," she'd tell him. "You come home and ignore me and then expect me to want to make love."

He'd turn his back to her and she could hear him sigh. He seemed to sigh a lot lately.

Once in a while she'd force herself awake and just lie there while Cole entered her, hardly kissing her. His sighs, after that, were ones of contentment rather than of frustration, and he was invariably pleasant to her at breakfast the morning after.

Even with Matt and her work, an emptiness was growing inside her.

"I could get away this weekend," Francey said as she and Walt were dining at the Willows, which they did anywhere from four to six nights a week. The restaurant was closed Mondays, and Francey took one other evening a week off, never the same one. She wanted the staff to keep on their toes.

"You want to go someplace?" Walt asked. They hardly ever got away. The idea appealed to him. Some nice slow-paced place where they could laze in a pool, lie in the sun, make love in the afternoon.

"Austin," Francey answered immediately.

"Austin? You mean drive up there?"

"Zelda Marie's entering a show up there. I thought she could use some hometown reinforcements."

"A horse show?" That wasn't exactly what Walt had in mind.

"I'm a friend. I'd like to go. She confides in me. I bet Zelda Marie tells me more about what's happening inside her than Carly does. Carly doesn't want me to know when she's unhappy or if she does something she thinks I won't approve of. But I made enough stupid choices. Who am I to tell someone else how to live?"

Walt grinned. "If you hadn't made those choices we might not be sitting here together tonight."

Francey reached over and put a hand over his. "Whatever I may have done to make me unhappy before I met you was worth every bit of it if it's meant arriving at this point with you."

Francey finished her salad, laid down her fork, and leaned back in her chair. "Well?"

"Well?"

"Austin. You want to go to the horse races this weekend?"

"If you want, I will."

"Thanks, Walt. I know it's not your cup of tea. Well, let's find the most expensive luxurious hotel up there . . ."

"In Austin?"

"And maybe we can find one that has a spa in the room . . ."

"In Austin?" he repeated.

"We could drive up Thursday afternoon and come back Sunday."

Walt didn't seem to resent anything that Francey wanted to do. When he compared his life now to the days before he met Francey when all he did was listen to the opera and ball games and fish a little, he thought maybe he had been dead in those days.

"I'll tell Zelda Marie we'll take her to dinner Saturday night. She'll either need a shoulder to cry on or will want to celebrate."

Walt and Francey sometimes breakfasted Sunday mornings out at the ranch, Francey supplying sweet rolls or coffee cake and whipping up omelets or German apple pancakes. Aofrasia had the day off and Zelda Marie was barely a decent cook. A couple of mornings they'd even taken trail rides back in the woods and had barbecued breakfasts that were prepared by Rafael. He always managed to get the kids involved.

Rafael asked Walt how much money one had to have to open a bank account, and one Thursday morning brought in a hundred and twenty-five dollars and seemed proud as a peacock to walk out with a checkbook in his hands. He drove Zelda Marie's pickup around town, stopping at the feed store, sometimes doing grocery shopping in the new supermarket, filling up on gas. He sported a cowboy hat now, a straw one, and he wore pointed boots. His trousers were no longer held up with clothesline but with a belt that displayed a silver buckle. A bandanna was always around his neck.

Francey was impressed by the handsome Mexican. She told Walt she thought Rafael looked like a romantic hero. "He's one of the most gorgeous men I've ever seen." She smiled at

Walt. "Except for you, my darlin'. I would never want to go to bed with any other man but you, no matter how handsome."

Walt stood up and slid out of his pants, unbuttoning his shirt at the same time. As soon as his clothes were off, he dove into the pool. When he surfaced, he summoned her with his finger. "Come on. Prove it. Come show it's only me you want."

It took Francey less than thirty seconds to join him in the warm water.

"My God," he said, stopping kissing her long enough to speak. "I'd thought we'd made love everywhere."

"Not in the greenhouse, either," she murmured, winding her legs around his waist and leaning back to let her hair fan out in the water.

"Nor the supermarket." His hands ran down her legs as he watched her, thinking her the most glorious human being ever born.

"Nor church, nor . . ."

"Well, we still have worlds to conquer," he said.

CHAPTER 48

Rafael's fame spread.

On Saturday mornings he held classes for children. Parents were allowed to attend, too, but were restricted to the sidelines.

Although by now his English was more than adequate, he did not feel comfortable speaking in front of a group, so Zelda Marie acted as interpreter.

"Breaking a horse," she would tell his students, "is based on three principles. The first is that if a horse doesn't respond the way you want, it should be punished. And opposite, if it does respond correctly you should reward it. Thirdly, it should be compelled to do what you want it to do, by force if necessary.

"We do not believe in sitting on a horse and testing your

bravery to see how many times you can survive being thrown off when the horse rears. This usually is done until the horse is made to do what it's told to do, by time and various punishments and rewards. It can then be ridden or can pull a cart. It is treated like a slave, as an inferior being who is to do what *you* want it to do.

"It is quicker and kinder for you to learn the communication, the connection. The horse understands best. *You* can talk with horses if you really want to."

The kids would stare in bewilderment, and some parents would shake their heads. Were they wasting money on this guy?

Rafael showed his students what love and kindness—what talking with horses—meant. Occasionally, skeptics would bring an intractable horse for Rafael to "break." Rafael would look at the horse and smile. For him, no horse was unmanageable. These horses, he said, either had been brutalized in some manner, or they were strong horses spoiled by weak handling. Almost all of them reared and refused to be ridden.

He liked to have one of them around when he began to teach a class. The first class lasted an entire morning. From then on, the sessions were just two hours.

"The bucking has to be cured," Zelda Marie told the children and their parents. "Rafael has to figure out why the horse is troublesome, how someone hurt or frightened him?"

One episode that led to Rafael's early fame came when a horse that had somehow been hurt behind the ears refused to be touched there. The owner claimed he could never get a bridle over its head. Rafael ran his hand up the horse's shoulder and over its neck. As his hand neared the top of the horse's head, the horse bucked, its eyes white with fright. Over and over Rafael ran his hand up the animal's neck, short of his ears. For forty-five minutes he repeated this action, then he let his hand stray above the ears, along the mane. The horse neighed and reared. But he kept repeating the action until, after another twenty minutes, he began to rub the horse's head and ears. The horse finally calmed down and let Rafael touch its ears.

Then he put a rope halter over the horse's nose, running his hand up the length of his nose and over its ears. The horse bucked, so Rafael spoke softly as he took the halter off and gently put it on again. When the horse reared again Rafael kept murmuring in a singsong rhythmic manner. The horse was not about to make anything easy for Rafael, but in another twenty minutes, Rafael was able to get the halter off and on.

"He has never let anyone do it," Rafael explained, "so he is not anxious to show that he will let me do it."

Rafael kept putting the halter on and taking it off for another half hour. Then he reached for a bridle and put the bit in the horse's mouth, a challenge to which his audience responded with close attention. He kept putting the bit in and out of the horse's mouth until he could slip it into the horse's mouth at will. He ran the reins up and over its ears. It reared again. Rafael started all over with the bridle and bit. In about ten minutes the horse let Rafael do whatever he liked. After four hours, Rafael gave the horse water and feed, and Zelda Marie told the audience a picnic lunch was waiting for them on the long trestled tables under the mesquite trees.

That was the first lesson. No one ever complained or asked for money back. Rafael's fame began to spread beyond the county.

In showing horses, Rafael concentrated on jumping and cutting, but Zelda Marie had a particular penchant for dressage. Her ultimate goal was to prove that Arabians could be marvelous stock horses. She wanted to gain her fame that way.

She had been able to buy a colt whose breeding rendered him more expensive than Rafael believed one could ever pay for a horse. She bought him at an auction in Colorado Springs when he was nine months old and began to train him for dressage. She named him Omar and thought he was the most beautiful horse she'd ever seen.

She spent hours and days and months training Omar in dressage, the highest test of ability of a trained horse.

Rafael would sit on the log fencing around the ring and watch Zelda Marie for hours, marveling at the smooth performance of Omar. He was as impressed with the rider as well as with the horse.

Omar had not been saddled until he was two and a half, and though Zelda Marie turned over the training of her horses almost completely to Rafael, she kept Omar as her own. He had progressed swiftly, his keen intelligence allowing him to perform pirouettes within the first month of training. By the second month he was doing the two-tack and side-step. Zelda Marie had kept him at the level of secondary dressage for a full year.

Then together she and Omar graduated to superior dressage. He quickly mastered the passage, after which Zelda Marie slowed him down to the piaffer. Then he easily and willingly learned the changes of leads and steps.

Rafael sat, a long leaf of grass stuck between his teeth, his hat pushed back on his head, watching the horse and rider in their varied executions. He had never seen such precision and grace.

Aside from the show in Austin, Omar won a great number of shows all over Texas and Oklahoma. Zelda Marie wanted to take him to Ontario. Rafael thought of the long drive, hauling the horse trailer behind him, sitting beside Zelda Marie and listening to the radio, taking turns sleeping and driving so that no one could steal the horses . . . taking turns at the wheel with Zelda Marie . . . seeing new scenery. He grinned with pleasure.

What really held his interest was the working stock horses with which Zelda Marie hoped to make her claim to fame. She now had five superior ones. Arabians had heretofore been considered too princely, too elegant, too beautiful to be stock horses, but it was Zelda Marie's contention that Arabian stallions could outwork other horses. She thought Arabians would perform spectacularly on cattle drives, and their famous loyalty to their owners, or riders, would stand them in good stead under a cowboy's seat.

Before Rafael had come into her life, Zelda Marie had halter-broke her Arabians when they were yearlings, and at two trained them on the longe line. After he appeared on the scene, they used different tactics but at the same ages. At three they began saddle training.

Rafael, who had never known pure-bred horses in Mexico, was impressed with the Arabians' superior intellect. They were faster than Quarter horses; as fast as panthers, really. And his horse, the one he had commandeered, Shah, was so quick in turns he whirled on his hind feet, a maneuver that not one horse in a thousand could do. This was a priceless trait in Rafael's favorite arenas, cutting and driving cattle.

Only once had Zelda Marie ridiculed him, and he thought he deserved it. He was loco.

They had attended an auction up in Tulsa. Rafael was standing alone while Zelda Marie talked to an acquaintance she'd just run into. He turned to look behind him and his eyes fastened on one of the ugliest, most spavined, skinny horses he'd seen. An Arabian, of course, or it wouldn't be in here, waiting to go into the ring. Why any owner would publicly show off such a horse, Rafael couldn't imagine.

Rafael followed it, sitting in a grandstand seat, watching it parade around the ring with the other horses. When the auctioneer indicated the bidding was about to begin Rafael searched for Zelda Marie who was still in the hallway talking. He sprinted to her, grabbing her arm and hauled her along with him to the show ring.

He pointed to the ugly-looking horse and said, "I want him."

Zelda Marie laughed. "You've got to be kidding."

"I'll pay you back out of my wages if it takes me a year," Rafael shouted.

The auctioneer was trying to get a bid, but no one who looked at the horse was willing to risk a cent.

"Two hundred dollars," Rafael shouted.

Zelda Marie stared at him as though he'd lost his mind.

"I'll pay you," he reiterated. "It's not yours. It's mine."

Once they got the nag home Rafael began immediately to stuff food down its skinny body. A week after they'd towed the horse home, Rafael took it out hunting with him. The horse loved it. Rafael named it Montezuma. Zelda Marie smiled to herself. If anything didn't look like a warrior it was this ugly horse.

When Zelda Marie awoke mornings, even at dawn, Rafael was already out with Zuma. One day Rafael announced, "I want to enter him in a race."

Zelda Marie tried not to laugh aloud. "I'd think you'd be ashamed to let anyone see him, much less try to race him."

Rafael tightened his lips. "I know" was all he said. "I shall not race him in big races, but I would like him to get a feeling of satisfaction. Just some local small races."

Zuma was his horse. Rafael would not let Zelda Marie pay entry fees, but he told her he would like to borrow a hundred dollars so he could bet on his horse. She would have to place the bet, of course.

Zelda Marie teased him. "I don't know of any jockey who's worth anything being willing to ride that skinny nag."

"I am going to ride him myself even if I am too big."

Her heart ached for Rafael. People would make fun of him. But he was determined, so she not only bet his hundred dollars, but five hundred of her own.

They went up to Nacogdoches for the race.

From the very beginning Rafael trailed behind by several lengths. The first half mile was up a hill, then there was a downturn, and uphill again. By the time Zuma reached the second hill, he was three lengths behind but was taking fences enthusiastically. They raced downhill past the finish line to the bottom of the hill and up again when, as he later described it to Zelda Marie, the horse ahead of him just sort of dropped back. They began passing horse after horse after horse. By the time they arrived on top of the last hill, there were only two horses ahead of them. Since Zuma wasn't even sweating, Rafael spurred him on, himself sitting low in the saddle.

Three fences before the home stretch, the horse in second place fell behind. Rafael indicated to Zuma that it was time for a real sprint.

It was a tie. The photo finish showed that both horses broke the ribbon at the same second.

Rafael and Zelda Marie celebrated by going to an inn with country dancing, and they danced and drank the night away. They ended up in a motel near dawn, and Zelda Marie thought she'd be willing to risk a thousand dollars, even if she lost it, to have another time like they did in Nacogdoches.

Rafael kept saying over and over, "After I pay you back the hundred I borrowed, I made one thousand six hundred dollars." It was more money than he had ever imagined seeing.

Zelda Marie laughed. She tossed her eight thousand five hundred on a table. Rafael looked at her, walked over and counted the money, and raised his eyebrows. "You had that much faith in my horse?"

"No," she said. "In you."

PART V

1982–1986

CHAPTER 49

Destin Savings and Loan, when it was transferred to the Coleridges, had eighty-five million in assets and only a hundred thousand in delinquent assets. It was one of the most stable thrifts in the state, if not the country.

Tracy VanAdder had run it as though even buying a paper clip would drain the thrift's resources. His small modest office was on the second floor of the bank at the corner of Main and State streets in the dusty little town of Destin. He'd engineered the sale to the Coleridges because he wanted to retire and fish, and he knew how sound Union Trust was. He also liked the idea that Kevin Coleridge was a Destin boy. And Coleridges's offer wiped out the one hundred thousand bad debt. The stockholders rejoiced.

Kevin Coleridge turned the reins over to Cole, whose first act as president was to inform the directors that the thrift would be moving its corporate offices from VanAdder's modest three rooms above the bank to an entire floor of an eleven-story modern glass building in Houston, a block from the new shopping mall in which his wife had an interest.

The board of directors complained that their established role was as a lender to the local people and the surrounding farmers who wanted to buy homes and farms.

Cole allowed that they could keep open a small branch to continue this practice, but from now on he hoped to lure brokered deposits and use them to underwrite commercial real estate projects, which thrifts had been forced to stay away from.

The board of directors stared at him, literally openmouthed.

Within two years Cole converted the little hick Destin Savings and Loan into a many-tiered corporation. The U.S. government published lists of high-performance S & Ls, and Destin was near the top of the list. It was, said the regulators, a glittering model of what could happen when government regulations were lifted and private enterprise led the way.

When Cole hired a new man—and he hired many—along with an elegant office, he gave each one a Mercedes or a BMW. He knew how to buy loyalty and hard work.

Carly had begged him for years to take a vacation. They never seemed to do much together anymore. Cole seldom attended Matt's school functions. He usually had dinner at home but then went back to work, never seeing Matt to bed or reading to him.

He did insist that Matt start swimming and tennis lessons at the club when he was barely old enough to join the youngest classes. He was proud that Matt took to each of these sports, but he didn't seem to know how to talk to the boy. When the three of them were at the dinner table together, there was no conversation in which Matt could participate. Carly tried to steer the talk to center around Matt, but Cole brushed aside anything that didn't concern business.

One night he told Carly the bank was going to invest in a ski community in Colorado.

"I'm flying out there next week," he said. "Plans are for eighty houses to be built in prime ski territory, houses that will sell for over a million and a half each . . ."

"Second homes at that price?"

He nodded. "I think the bank'll buy one of them so any of us can use the place when we want. They have twenty-five built already, sort of Swiss chalets, and if I like what I see, I'll have the bank buy the company. We'll earn enough selling them to at least pay for our own place.''

Carly studied Cole. "Is that legal?" she asked.

He didn't even stop eating to look at her. "You mean, the law about prohibiting thrifts to make large loans to affiliated persons? Oh, that's easy to get around. Form companies that have no stock in Destin and loans can be made to them.''

"Who owns these subsidiaries?"

He looked at her now, and grinned. "Oh, a bunch of us.''

Carly was silent.

"Don't worry your pretty head about it. It's too complex for you to understand.''

She wanted to scream. He so often dismissed her in that manner when he could sense her disapproval.

"I know real estate values. Want me to come to Colorado with you?''

"Uh uh. Colorado and Texas are different. I already think I'm going to do this deal. We're going to form a company and call it Elk Creek. The guys and I,'' he didn't bother to explain what guys, "envision this as something fantastic. When you fly in to the airport, probably Denver, we'll have chauffeured limousines waiting, serve them coffee and doughnuts or wine and cheese, depending on arrival time, and drive them home. It's about two hours out of Denver. The same limos will drive them back to the airport and serve champagne. Give them a nice buzz. In summer, there'll be tennis courts, a gym, pool . . .''

"I'd think for a million and a half each house would have its own pool.''

"Oh, they will," Cole said reassuringly, "but there'll be a clubhouse for those who want company.''

"What kind of people will spend nearly two million dollars for a Swiss chalet in the Rockies?''

Cole grinned. "Hopefully the kind of people like . . . well, like the Cabots.''

"The Cabots?''

"Or the Lowells. You know the old saying, that in Boston the Cabots speak only to the Lowells and the Lowells speak only to God? Well, we'll get the Cabots."

He must have thought Carly didn't get it. "People who want to be with others who are like them," he explained.

Carly shook her head as though to rid it of cobwebs. She could sense his impatience.

"Well, at least maybe I can get you away for a vacation."

"Maybe you can at that." He went on, "We'll lend people we approve of money to buy these houses. Some of the guys I know have already expressed interest. Jim Thornton of Regal Savings up in Dallas is going to fly out with me. He says if the scenery is as spectacular as we claim, they might sink two or three million into a retreat there. He envisions an outdoor hot tub overlooking mountain peaks."

"Oh, my."

Cole felt a thrill of pleasure; he was impressing Carly. He'd build them a place and furnish it and hire a decorator from New York before he even showed it to her. It would be like the old days when they'd flown to Acapulco and she'd been so impressed with everything. The days when he thought he'd spend his life showing her new things, introducing her to the luxuries of life. He'd thought she'd be so grateful . . .

When the chalet, or rather castle, was built, he and Carly and Matt flew to Colorado. Carly thought the furnishings heavy and cumbersome. The house itself was too big and it was not theirs, it was Destin's, though it was supposedly owned by Miramar Construction. Any one of the bank's officers could reserve it for two weeks at a time. Carly loved the scenery but hated the fast lifestyle and glitzy people.

One spring, when hardly any of the houses were occupied, she and Matt did fly out there, but Cole didn't come. She and Matt breakfasted on the porch, even though it was cold. It was ravishingly beautiful. There was still some snow and Matt took skiing lessons, taking to that as easily and gracefully as he had tennis. But late April was not a time when Elk Creek was populated.

Cole flew out to Elk Creek maybe six times each winter, always when Matt could not leave school. Carly of course stayed home with their son. In the summer they went out for a couple of weeks, but after four or five days, Cole was restless and returned to Houston. He didn't know how to relax.

Carly never got close to loving the chalet.

Cole thought Carly would be thrilled with his birthday present of a trip to England—a week in London and a week touring England and Wales.

But she frowned. "Without Matt?" she said.

"For God's sake, Carly, a seven-year-old would only get in the way. He wouldn't appreciate it at all. He can go down to your parents. They always love to have him."

Nothing seemed to interest Cole except the bank, so she had been surprised when he suggested the trip. She really didn't know what he did that kept him there late so many nights. All he told her was that it was challenging and he was making barrels of money. He did not say the bank was making money, she noted. He said, "*I* am."

If he'd been any one other than a Coleridge, she'd be nervous. She talked with Walt about it and he told her there was a great need for Savings and Loans. But he didn't like this deregulation at all. He had thought it could get them in trouble, though they seemed to be thriving.

"Reagan talks of trickle-down economics," Carly said.

"Honey," Walt said, "Reagan doesn't think. It's the men who surround him who want power and money and want others like themselves to have money and power. They don't give a rap—"

Carly's laugh interrupted him. "You don't sound much like a conservative banker."

"Can't I be interested in the have-nots of the world? Pretty soon, the middle class will be among the poor."

Carly had never heard Walt so pessimistic. Just as she was getting rich on her own.

Ben came in for the weekend unexpectedly and when he heard that Cole and Carly were headed for Europe he said, "I'll take my vacation then. Let me have Matt and we'll go fishing and—"

"What do you know about kids?" Cole asked.

"About as much as you do," Ben answered. "Which is not much. C'mon. Let me learn. We'll have a great time. I'll take him over to Verity and we'll see Francey and Walt and maybe even stay overnight."

So, Cole and Carly flew to England to recapture the romance of their early years, holding hands as they walked along the streets and sat in theaters, making love nightly, laughing together as they hadn't in years.

Carly had not traveled much, and the luxury made her feel pampered and important.

Cole ordered suits from a Savile Row tailor. He urged Carly to buy whatever she wanted, but after studying the styles she decided Paris must be where high fashion was; she couldn't find a dress that appealed to her.

The trip made Carly wonder what had happened to their marriage. When had the glow dimmed, and why? She couldn't put her finger on it.

"Let's have another baby," Cole suggested.

Carly smiled. She'd love to have more children. But she couldn't, just couldn't, do it with Ben again. Every time she saw him her heart lurched, just as it still did when she danced with Boomer at the club Saturday nights.

Meanwhile, despite the fun of the trip, Carly had changed. She was no longer the wide-eyed young woman who was impressed with prestige and what money could buy. She seemed to have lost some of her softness, her innocence. She enjoyed working, earning money. She found interests outside the home and did not wait for him to fulfill her needs. She was not the same woman he had married.

In London, and in a Welsh inn, they recaptured what they had found long ago in Acapulco, but it only lasted two weeks.

CHAPTER 50

"Take tomorrow off?" Boomer looked across the breakfast table at Alex.

She smiled at him. "Why?"

"You know. It's our twelfth anniversary. I want us to spend the day together. Just the two of us, all alone."

"We'll have to be home for dinner. Mother wouldn't forgive me if we missed an anniversary dinner there."

"Doesn't it dawn on her that an anniversary is just for the two people involved? I have a surprise, and I want you to take the day off." Boomer, unlike Cole, seldom let business interfere with family life.

"As long as we're home for dinner. How come you never forget?"

"If I were like other men we wouldn't even be married." He grinned at her and spooned a soft-boiled egg onto toast.

That was true. Boomer was still romantic, a thoughtful husband, and a wonderful father. No business appointment was more important than one of his children's requests. She wished he were stricter with them. He let them do what they wanted and usually did it with them.

He did have his shortcomings. His hair was still a bit too long. His dinner jackets were not like those other men wore. He had a plaid one and a midnight-blue one. Sometimes she loved his idiosyncrasies, but she wished he were more conventional. He didn't do things the people in their crowd did. Two different summers, they had driven in a station wagon to the Grand Canyon and to Glacier National Park. In order to placate her, yet get his way, Boomer hadn't insisted on camping in a tent. He knew her better than that. They had done all the things that tourists did, but Alex couldn't quite enjoy it. She disliked the rustic accommodations, but she'd tried not to complain too much. Next year, Boomer said, the kids would be old enough to appreciate Disneyland. Alex shivered at the thought. But she knew there were many things he did for her sake as well and kept his lack of enthusiasm to himself. He did not like the opera or the symphony, yet he went without a murmur, even though he was often asleep before the overture ended.

She dressed in the latest fashion, but never as colorfully as Carly. She had come to respect Carly so much that she even admired her dramatic sense of style. She was sure that Maude Coleridge shuddered at what Carly chose to wear.

Where other women wore black, Carly wore fire-engine red or stark white with vibrant accents of color. Emerald. Royal blue. Fuschia. Purple. Funny. The two most unconventional people that Alex knew were both from the little rinky dink town of Verity.

She and Boomer had driven down there one weekend and stayed with Carly's parents. Boomer drove her past the big old Victorian gingerbread home where he grew up. He parked across the street for a few minutes and gazed at it. Paint was peeling and one shutter hung askew. "I had the greatest childhood anyone could have here," he told her.

Carly had hated the town, but she went back more often than Boomer did, because Walt and Francey were there. And her friend Zelda Marie.

Alex had never dreamed that she and Carly would become so close. She knew the minute she'd met Tessa, but Carly? Hardly. Yet, there it was. And sometimes when the three women were together, either with or without husbands, they laughed until Alex felt a stitch in her side.

She had not been prepared for such closeness with friends.

She had not even been prepared to enjoy motherhood, but she did.

When Tessa was around, Alex and Carly avoided talk of children. Tessa enjoyed their children, as did Dan, but apparently they didn't want any of their own. Or couldn't have them. Neither of them seemed to regret it, though they were affectionate with both Alex and Carly's children. Alex hated to admit it even to herself, but she resented that her children messed up her home so. Each night when she arrived home, she compulsively straightened the magazines on the coffee table or picked up toys. Everything had to be exactly right. She knew that once in a while it drove Boomer nuts.

She loved Boomer and she loved her home, which Tessa had decorated. She began to muse on other aspects of her life when she interrupted her reverie. "Okay. What would you like to do?"

Boomer shook his head. "It's a surprise."

"I love surprises," Alex grinned weakly. They both knew she didn't. Surprises interrupted routine.

The next morning, Boomer had the cook pack a picnic lunch. "Bring your bathing suit and wear old clothes," Boomer told Alex.

Not even as they sped north did Alex have a clue where they were headed—until they turned off the highway and started up the dirt road.

"That lake?" she said.

"It's where I fell in love with you, I think," Boomer grinned.

He took his hand off the steering wheel and reached out to touch her cheek.

The place didn't even look different. The same bait camp. The same motel with peeling paint. Not even cabins, Alex marveled. "You'd have thought it'd be built up. Do you know that day we came here, I thought you'd brought me up to this two-bit motel to screw me . . ."

"Why, Alex!" Boomer laughed.

". . . and you just wanted me to see how pretty it was."

Boomer leaned over and kissed her. "I knew before that . . . I knew the day I first met you that I'd marry you if you'd have me." He went on, "I remember every detail about that day." He grabbed the picnic basket from the backseat. "Come on. Let's see if they'll rent us a boat."

It had a new outboard motor, but aside from that they decided it was so old it might be the same boat.

Boomer motored out of the cove and onto the lake, toward the inlet where they'd swum a dozen years ago.

"You know what I'd like to do?" Alex asked. "I'd like to go rent a room in that little motel and do what I was afraid you had in mind that day."

Boomer laughed. "You in a motel that seedy?"

"Almost, out in Arizona, in Flagstaff. Remember?"

"Uh unh. But I'll talk the old man into renting us a room for the afternoon. Right now I want to motor around the lake. We never did see it all, you know."

It took them over an hour. The scent of pine filled the air, and the dark shapes of the trees were reflected in the ripples of the water.

"Even though we've seen some of the most beautiful parts of this country," Boomer said, "this is still mighty pretty. Maybe not as majestic as the West, but still awesome."

"Agreed."

"I'm glad you feel that way," Boomer said, "because that's your anniversary present."

Startled, Alex turned to look at him. "What do you mean?"

"I knew even back then it'd be a good investment, so I bought it with my first million. Took a bit of doing because I had to find out who owned an acre here, a couple of acres there." He was beaming. "At the time I thought okay, great investment. But Alex, I don't want to develop it. I want to build a house up here and have it be ours. Our lake. Our hideaway." He reached into the pocket of his yellow shirt and withdrew a piece of paper from it. "Here it is. The deed. You even own that motel we're going to make good use of later."

"You've been sitting on this all these years?"

He nodded, reaching over to gather her in his arms. He stood up, pulling her with him when the old boat turned on its side.

They laughed as they swam to shore. They lost the picnic basket and the copy of the deed, but they couldn't stop laughing. They never did make it to the motel room, for as soon as they reached shore, Boomer said, "We'd better take off these wet clothes," and they made love on the sandy shore under a dark green fir tree that seemed to reach to the sky.

"This will be just ours."

"Don't be silly," said Alex. "Everyone we know will want a weekend home up here. But let's keep it separate from BB&O. It's ours. Ours to develop together. Just you and me. We can keep maybe five acres for ourselves. We could have a restaurant and golf course . . . a country club for those who buy homes here and their guests. And I had a wonderful idea for weekends. A floating restaurant with old-time music. On Friday and Saturday nights we could have dancing and an orchestra and a wonderful chef. By reservation only. And Sunday brunches. And all this less than two and a half hours from downtown Houston."

Boomer listened and started to say something, but she clutched his arm and moved close to him. "Oh, Boomer, what a wonderful surprise. A project to work on together. I'd nearly forgotten about this place. Oh, we'll make a fortune here!"

"We have a fortune. Two fortunes."

"No, what we have is not a fortune. Not by Texas standards."

Alex was afraid that her present to him would be a letdown. It was sitting in the driveway when, slightly disheveled but dry, they returned home. A claret-red Alfa Romeo with a silver two-foot wide ribbon wound around it and tied into a bow on top.

"Can't compare to what you gave me," she murmured.

"The lake or the screwing?" Boomer grinned.

"Both."

"Well, it's the thought that counts," he said. "And an Alpha Romeo is pretty thoughtful."

He wondered why he didn't feel happier. Somehow none of this had turned out as he'd planned.

"We'll insist on approval of all house plans," Alex continued excitedly. "We can tell them they have to use our architect." Dan, of course. "Maybe Dan and Tessa'll want a couple of acres up there, too. Oh, Boomer," she clutched his arm and reached up to kiss him. "What fun!"

Why didn't he think so?

CHAPTER 51

Carly sat in her silver Porsche studying the cornfield which, she estimated, was probably two hundred to two hundred fifty acres, give or take.

A map was spread out in front of her, resting on the steering wheel. She reached over, absentmindedly, and picked up the Styrofoam cup and sipped the steaming coffee.

A man named Dale McCullough had phoned her, telling her he was interested in selling his cornfield. What could he get?

She'd told him she'd meet him at nine-thirty. It was now nine-fifteen. She'd just had time for a quick breakfast with Matt and Cole. She never made appointments before Matt left for school, and she always drove him to St. John's.

McCullough knew this was the only strip of land left in this section north of Houston. Where she was sitting now, on a dirt road in front of a cornfield, had been the sleepy village of Bedford. Three months ago, it had been annexed into Houston, and now city water and sewer lines were flowing into it. The townspeople made sure they kept their own schools and didn't have to send their kids to schools in the big city, and now land prices in what had been Bedford and was now part of north Houston were skyrocketing. On either side of this cornfield bulldozers had leveled the land and there was pipe all over the place. Bare bones of buildings dotted either side of the cornfield.

It was the only empty area on this whole strip. Far away, Carly could hear cars zooming down the freeway. That meant anyone could get to downtown Houston in forty minutes max. It meant people living here would think they lived in the country, but three miles away, between Bedford and the Woodlands, an immense shopping mall was under construction, and no one living in the old Bedford would have to go into the city for any of life's necessities.

The big drawback to the plan was that all the trees were in the back half of the field. Who was going to pay a fortune for a house that had no trees? Not in north Houston, that was for sure. Unless apartments could be built here. That was a thought. Then the land would be worth more. Upscale apartments.

Her mind started to work. She could make a bundle. Not as much, of course, as she'd earned over the years from the shopping mall. Money from that was still coming in and would forever. She'd been smart to put that package together. She and Alex. That had been a grand idea. But this . . . this she wouldn't have to share with anyone.

Stop dreaming, she told herself. This McCullough just wanted to sell a cornfield.

An old pickup churned down the dusty road. It pulled up next to her and a man in his late fifties got out. He wore overalls, a ten-gallon hat, and old boots that had seen better days.

Carly opened the door and slid out of the seat, standing to look across the roof of the car at McCullough.

"You must be Miz Coleridge," he said.

She smiled at him and walked around the front of her car to shake hands. "I'm pleased you called me," she said.

"I don't trust real estate men," he said. "Someone told me about you. I see you been lookin' it over."

"How many acres are there?" Carly asked.

"Two hundred thirty-three," he answered, taking his hat off and holding it at his side. "On either side, I owned them, too, but I think I got cheated when I sold them. This is all I have left and I aim to make enough to retire on, or go on raisin' corn.''

Water and sewers were already being run to those properties being developed on either side. Carly had already been playing around with her calculator.

"What do you want for them?" she asked.

"Uh uh," he said. "That's how I got trapped before, 'cause I didn't know the value of land. You tell me. What can I get?"

Carly had done all her thinking. She gazed into the distance.

"There are no trees on your land," she said. "We could get a lot more if you had big old trees."

"I'm not askin' what I can't get. Give me a ball park figure."

She thought of Shep Lenchek and the kind of apartments he built. How many could fit here?

She thought of BB&O. They hadn't done an apartment complex since their very first project.

"Maybe three million," she told McCullough.

He chuckled. "Guess I could retire on that."

"That's twenty-five thousand seven hundred an acre." She could remember when land like this was six hundred an acre, and the seller would be lucky to find a buyer.

"I want to be your exclusive agent on this," she said.

"I'll give you six months," he countered.

In six months, she thought, this land will be worth even more.

"I'll draw up a contract and have it ready for you to sign later this afternoon."

They certainly hadn't wasted any time.

"I didn't know gals as pretty as you had brains, too," he commented.

Carly was used to remarks like that, she tried to smile graciously. It didn't take an awful lot of brains to figure out how much land was worth. The brains came in trying to make deals that would reap even more money.

She could hardly wait to get back to her office and start figuring who to contact and what to propose. She'd have to make some calls and find out what restrictions were on the land here.

But Ben was waiting in her office.

Before asking what he was doing there, Carly told him about her exciting morning.

"Going to rape and pillage more of the countryside?" he asked.

"Oh, for heaven's sake. This growing population needs some place to live. And if I don't sell it, someone else will."

"I'm waiting for the day," Ben said, "when all the lettuce fields and the orange groves in California have houses on them. Then where's our food going to come from?"

"You're such a purist," Carly said. "How can you possibly be a Democrat when what you really are is a reactionary? You want things to be like they were in the olden days. And I know you think earning the kind of money I do is immoral, don't you?" she said. It wasn't really a question. She knew the answer.

"Well, I do think money as the be-all and end-all of life is pretty superficial. What are you going to do with the money you make on this deal, my dear?"

She often thought Ben felt some sort of protective interest in her because she was the mother of his son.

She knew he would admire what she did with a certain chunk of her money, but perhaps that's why she didn't tell Ben—or anyone else—about her Friday mornings. She feared then that her motives might not be pure, that they'd become colored with wanting praise.

It had started two years ago, when she was making so much money she experienced a mixture of pride and guilt. She'd been driving to a section of the city where she made sure her car doors were locked. She had a client who wanted her to look at a piece of industrial property for the possible location of a tool and dye plant. The man thought it would be a smart idea to buy an abandoned lot in an area where there was a ceaseless supply of cheap labor.

Dark-skinned people walked the streets, staring at her and her expensive car with what she could only identify as hostility.

The car ahead of her had jumped forward when the light turned yellow. The driver slammed on his brakes and jumped out of the car for all of thirty seconds. When he dashed back into the car, he backed up so quickly he hit Carly's bumper. He stopped, jerked the car forward, but to the side, and burned rubber.

Carly's first reaction was to see if he'd done damage, but she hesitated getting out of the car in this neighborhood. Then she saw a lump in the middle of the road. Two men raced from the sidewalk and knelt next to the limp bundle.

Without thinking, she opened her car door and joined the throng that was gathering. A Mexican man gathered a girl of perhaps five in his arms. Blood already stained the pavement.

He looked at Carly, a question in his eyes.

She nodded toward her car. "I'll take you to the hospital."

She had no idea where the nearest hospital was. Nor did the man, but he knew where a doctor was, six blocks away.

Parked in front of the doctor's office, Carly rushed around to the other side of the car, opened the door for the man and his patient, and followed him up the steps of an ugly brown house.

Inside, there were straight-backed chairs filled with patients, and toys scattered around the room though only one child sat on the floor playing with them. Behind a long desk were two harried-looking women. One of them took one look at the little girl and said, "Follow me." She walked quickly down a hall, to a room, where she told them to wait. Carly never did understand why she followed the man and the little girl. No one seemed to question her being there.

Within two or three minutes a Mexican man appeared, wearing a long white medical coat, a stethoscope dangling around his neck.

Carly understood a smattering of their conversation. Dr. Gonzalez called for his nurse and instructed her to contact the hospital and make arrangements for an operating room. He told the nurse to get a Dr. Martinez on the line.

"Can you get this child to the hospital?" he asked the man.

The man turned to look at Carly and Carly nodded.

"It's fifteen minutes from here, but I want you to get there in ten. She needs an immediate blood transfusion and X rays. I'm not a surgeon, but Martinez is. Do you know how to get to St. Mary's?"

He gave Carly instructions, and the young man again picked up the unconscious child and carried her back through the waiting room and out to Carly's car.

They made the hospital in twelve minutes. Dr. Martinez was waiting for them.

Neither Carly nor the young man had any idea who the child was, but they both sat in the waiting room.

The young man disappeared and returned in ten minutes with two paper cups filled with coffee, thrusting one at Carly. After a few more minutes he asked what time it was.

Carly told him.

"I must leave," he said. "I am a bus driver and I am due at work in one hour."

"I'll wait," Carly said.

Shortly before noon, two hours after she'd arrived, Dr. Gonzalez appeared. "The child will be all right," he said, "and we have notified the mother."

"How did you figure out who she was?"

He smiled, and his thick black mustache made his teeth seem dazzlingly white. "We live in a section of the city where we must take care of each other. Thank you. Most people would never have stopped. If the little girl had not gotten to the hospital she'd have died. On behalf of her family, I thank you."

"Who are they?"

"The mother is a maid on the other side of the city. It will take her over an hour and a half to get back here. The father is a gardener. We don't know where he is working today. They will have great trouble paying the bill, but they will work to pay it off for years, if necessary.''

"Tell them I'll pay the hospital," she said.

"So there really are fairy godmothers."

Carly smiled. She reached in her purse and pulled out a business card. "Here's my address and phone number. Have the bill sent to me."

She turned to leave and started down the hall.

"Wait," called the doctor. "Let me buy you lunch."

Carly had a million things to do. She was already behind schedule. Still, she turned and smiled at Gonzalez. "I'd like that," she said.

The lunch was delicious. A little Mexican restaurant that had the best tacos she'd ever tasted. It was crowded at the noon hour, and noisy with laughter and shouting.

"I wish there were more like you," the doctor said. "You not only saved a child this morning but will make such a difference in her family's life. They will not have to get more behind than they are because they will not be strapped with a bill they can never pay."

"I'm glad to be able to help," Carly said, amazed to be enjoying herself immensely.

"If you want to see more," he said, "come to my free clinic on Friday mornings. There we work with children who would be blind without help, or crippled, and children who suffer from such malnutrition that they may never stand up straight. Some just have bad colds or bronchitis or tonsilitis. I am able to get appendix patients and others like that into a hospital, but not those needing specialists and long-term care. Come visit," he urged. "And see what you could do."

That had been a Tuesday. The rest of the week Carly told herself she was certainly not going back to Dr. Leon Gonzalez's office. He was pushing her too hard, trying to get her to give money. But on Thursday night, as she lay in bed, unable to sleep, she thought that he cared enough to humble himself to get help. Besides, she had really liked him, liked the energy and soulful tired eyes of this man who looked Mexican but was third-generation American. He had told her that he had three children but lived on this side of the city, on the second and third floor of the house. His office occupied the first floor. He sent his children to a school that he knew was inferior, because he felt he had to be there when any of his people had an emergency, in the middle of the night or weekends. There were always knife fights, sometimes even gun wounds, on Friday and Saturday nights. He was sacrificing his children, and he knew it. They would never be able to get into first-rate colleges because their schooling would not be on a par with what Matt was getting at St. John's or that the average middle class child was getting in Houston proper.

On Friday morning, she started toward her office but stopped at the first public telephone and called her secretary, telling her only that she wouldn't be in until one.

She spent the entire morning standing beside Dr. Gonzalez, watching as he examined three dozen children. "Come on," he said, when it was after noon. "Lunch is on you today," and they went this time to a much quieter restaurant. It was gaily and gaudily decorated but had marvelous azteca soup and fresh warm bolillos dripping with butter.

Carly agreed to pay for three operations, with the understanding Leon was never to tell where the money came from. He was never to mention her name to anyone. Paying for the operations was easy. All she had to do was write checks. But what bothered her was what could be done about all the cases of malnutrition.

"Buy the families food," Gonzalez said, "and shoes so they can go to school." He was very willing to spend her money. "See that they get milk and protein, though usually they get enough of that with rice and beans. Fruit and vegetables are what they do without."

For the next two years no one in her office ever knew she spent Friday mornings standing beside Leon Gonzalez. At noon, she wrote checks and had lunch with the Mexican doctor.

"I love my wife and children," he eventually told Carly, "but I think the luckiest day of my life was when you wandered into my office."

It was her secret and she held it close to her heart. She visited the children when they were in post op, and once in a while was so impressed with one of them that she asked Gonzalez to follow the child's educational progress. She fully intended to see that some of them got through college. And, if money had anything to do with it, she was going to make sure his own children attended the best universities in the country.

Only she and Leon and his wife, Rosamaria, knew of Carly's donations. The first year she was involved with the clinic, she gave away over a third of a million dollars. She didn't claim it on her income tax because she didn't want Cole to know.

Ben didn't know what he was talking about when he accused her of not helping those less fortunate than she.

"I'm really here to ask if Matt can come spend his spring vacation with me," Ben said, taking a cup of coffee from the sideboard where Carly's secretary had brewed it. "I'm going whitewater rafting and fishing in Oregon, and I thought he might enjoy that."

Ben never acted as though Matt was anything but his nephew, except now and then when he'd be visiting and Matt would curl up on his lap or ask him to read a story or reach out and grab hold of his hand. Then Ben's eyes would cross the room and meet Carly's and Carly could tell what he was feeling.

He was certainly much better with him than Cole was, who was disappointed that horses and science were Matt's only passions. He was irritated that Matt showed no propensity for math, either. How was he going to follow in the footsteps of his father and grandfather if he couldn't master basic algebra?

Matt loved the outdoors, and looked forward to his twice-a-week riding lessons more than anything else. Cole wanted to teach him how to shoot, but he said he never wanted to kill anything.

"For God's sake," Cole said. "He's so much like Ben, sometimes I think . . ."

But he didn't mean it.

Sometimes Carly thought Cole was jealous of Ben. She knew he couldn't possibly sense . . . couldn't possibly . . .

"Ben," she said suddenly, "why don't you marry and have children? Why don't you have a helpmate?"

Ben laughed loudly. "Is that what you are to Cole? A helpmate? And is he that to you?"

"You know what I mean."

"You mean what all society does. They can't stand to see someone single and enjoying life, when in reality none of them has happy marriages."

"What's a happy marriage?" Carly asked. "I think Cole and I—"

"Come off it, Carly. He can't stand your earning so much more than he does. He has money only by virtue of being a Coleridge . . ."

"That's not true now that he's president of Destin Savings and Loan. And he's always worked hard."

"I'm not denying that. But look at what you've amassed. And think if this deal of yours works out . . . Cole measures success by money and his dear wife is as successful financially as he is, if not more so. A man with Cole's ego finds that hard to take."

Carly thought about that. She hadn't realized that her making money made Cole feel inferior.

"Do you really think so? Are all men like that? Could you take it?"

Ben shook his head. "I don't think ego would be involved with me, but I'd have real trouble with a wife who earned fortunes by selling pristine land so that hundreds of homes could be built on it."

Carly thought a minute. "Do you really think I hurt Cole's ego?"

"Of course. He expected you to decorate the country club, to look beautiful on his arm when he made public appearances, to gaze adoringly into his eyes and tell him how smart he is . . . He thought he was marrying beneath him and that you'd be eternally grateful. But me? *I* could handle it, Carly," and Ben smiled. "I could easily handle having you for a wife." He laughed. "And a helpmate."

Carly wondered fleetingly why a pain shot across her chest. "Look," she said. "Cole's not going to mind if you take Matt to Oregon, and Matt will love it."

Ben nodded, still staring at her. "Carly, I even like fighting with you. And dammit, someday you, of all people in my world, are going to start thinking like I do."

"How's that?"

"Realize that money and position aren't important unless you can do good with them. Amassing a fortune has nothing to do with inner happiness. Until you know that, you'll never know happiness."

Carly smiled a secret smile. "What makes you think I'm not happy now?"

"Well, are you?"

CHAPTER 52

Carly fought with Ben often—never with rancor, though sometimes with passion. She was perfectly aware that after these arguments she spent so much time thinking of what he'd said that she began to view the world differently. These were not the same kinds of arguments she had with Cole, which were often about her working, her making all this money, her becoming a name in real estate in Houston.

The other thing she and Cole argued about was Matt. Carly wanted Cole to get off the boy's back. Matt was not a scholar. Cole had never received anything other than an A when he'd been Matt's age.

"Studying birds, for Christ's sake!" said Cole in exasperation. "A bird watcher?"

"It's a good hobby," Carly said. "No competition or violence."

"I know," he'd say. "He gets that from you. Ever since that incident with Zelda Marie's husband any violence turns your stomach. But I wish Matt didn't feel that way. I'd like a son who's a real boy."

"Does a gun measure manhood?" Carly asked, wondering how she'd gotten tied up with a family of men with such fragile egos. Would Cole feel threatened if he knew Matt wasn't his?

"Sure," Cole said to Ben over a pastrami sandwich, "if Matt wants to go, Easter vacation sounds good. Maybe Carly and I can go to Florida for a little vacation."

"Florida?" Carly blinked.

"There's a yacht I've heard about. Be a great way to entertain bank customers. Tax write-off, too."

Ben's eyes met Carly's.

Ben left to go back to Aransas Pass after lunch.

When Cole asked Carly if they had anything on that night and Carly shook her head, no, he announced, "Then I'm going to dine with Lloyd Martin. He wants to talk some business and it seems the only time I can fit him in."

"Fine," Carly said, reaching up to brush her lips along his cheek. "Matt and I'll go to McDonald's. He loves that."

Carly's mind was racing. She thought maybe she'd call Shep Lenchek instead of BB&O about that new property. BB&O always had to look at all sides of a proposition. They were very thorough and, therefore, slow. They'd have to toss the idea around for weeks. They'd debate it and maybe end up deciding they had more than enough to do. They had expanded unbelievably, taking a job for a new bank building in Phoenix, and they were on their third Mexican hotel for Señor Rosas. They had done a whole city complex of office buildings and parks in far-off Santiago, and the LaSalle clinic in St. Louis.

Their fame had spread, and they were in great demand. People came to them. They'd even turned down some jobs because Dan wouldn't go along with the proposed plans.

And, she suspected, Dan might look down his nose at a development in a little burg in north Houston. Once in a while he had accepted a commission for a million-plus home, but only if the people were friends of his. He concentrated on the big buildings.

She'd heard Shep Lenchek was looking for land to develop. And two hundred thirty-three acres in an area of homes that would cost, at the least, two hundred thousand might be right up his alley.

He accepted her call and agreed to drive out with her the next morning.

By then Carly had a plat of the land, had sewer and water estimations and knew just what kind of developments were going up on either side of it. No doubt about it, this was going to be the coming place for professionals. Men whose wives would have their hair and nails done twice a week, and who wanted buses convenient for their maids, who would arrive en masse every morning, freeing them for a day of tennis or shopping or lunch and bridge.

Shep Lenchek took one look. "What's the guy want for it?" he asked.

"Six million."

He walked across the dusty field among the even rows of cornstalks. Carly imagined Shep was visualizing roads running through it.

He made the same comment she had. "No trees."

Carly didn't respond. Shep had built enough homes that she didn't have to tell him anything about the property.

"Christ," he said in his rough voice, "that's twenty-seven five an acre. Two years ago you couldn't have gotten five hundred for it."

"And next year you won't get it for thirty-five thousand an acre," Carly said.

Shep chewed on his upper lip. "You think he'll take five?"

"I doubt it, but you can try." She could tell Shep had decided.

"Okay, let's make an offer of five, and see if he counters."

The next afternoon Carly drove to Shep Lenchek's office. "McCullough won't even counter. Six flat out or no deal. He says he can afford to sit on it for a year or two if he has to."

"He won't, though, will he?" Shep said. "Someone else'll grab it."

"And probably for a higher price if McCullough has to wait six months."

"First off, let's see if it's zoned for multiple use. If it is, I'll talk to my bankers and see if I can rustle up that much."

Carly suspected Shep didn't even have to see a banker. "I can put two hunnert ninety-seven homes there at over half an acre each, with wide avenues, bring in trees. Each house'll have a pool. Well, let's say just half the houses at half an acre and the rest at three-quarters to an acre, with room for tennis courts. Each house a minimum of . . . but then, the larger ones . . . I should gross seventy-four million plus."

Almost exactly what Carly had figured.

"I'll get back to you tomorrow," Shep said. Carly had made it clear to him that she hadn't approached anyone else about it.

She found out by three o'clock that half the land was zoned for multiple dwellings and the back half only for single-family homes. Just as she'd visualized. Homes in the area with trees, and apartments in the front half.

The next day Shep Lenchek bought the McCullough land and Carly earned $360,000 for less than a week's work.

She was so excited she had to tell Walt. She phoned him late that afternoon, while he was still at the bank.

"Come on down this weekend," he suggested. "We'll celebrate. We haven't seen all of you in close to three months."

When she broached the idea to Cole that night, he said, "You and Matt go. I'm caught up in this new project and may fly up to Washington to talk with Bill Wallace. He's one lawyer who can guide me through the intricacies of a Savings and

Loan like no one down here can. Except maybe Fred McKay, and he's in Dallas. I don't want anyone in Dallas in on this."

"Couldn't you do that during the week?" Carly asked. "You seem to enjoy yourself when we go to Verity. You and Walt talk shop for hours."

Cole shook his head. "Give you and Matt time to go see Zelda Marie and her horses. Matt'll be in seventh heaven then."

Perhaps Cole didn't want to go because Walt would be so proud of his little girl making such a deal and he would feel jealous. Maybe Ben was right. Carly wondered how much business Cole could do on a weekend with a Washington lawyer, who would probably be out sailing on the Potomac or playing tennis anyhow.

Would he suddenly take off for Washington if she hadn't made this deal? If she didn't want to go to Verity?

That night, for the first time in ten days, they made love, but Cole's mind seemed to be elsewhere. As soon as it was over, he got up and put on his pajamas and said, "I'm going to work for a while in the library."

"Cole, is something wrong between us?"

He shrugged. "No more than usual."

She leaned on her elbow and looked up at him, her blond hair cascading onto the pillow. "What's that supposed to mean?"

"I think if you were satisfied to be a normal wife our life would be easier."

"What's not easy about our life?"

He shrugged his shoulders. "We could have another child."

"That has nothing to do with my being busy."

Cole just looked at her and walked out the door. She heard him padding down the long staircase.

Nearly every real estate salesman in Houston looked like an All American, supported Texas U in all its sports, dressed in three-piece suits (even in the middle of summer), wore Rolexes and shiny boots. Carly employed seven of these men, but she had six women on her staff, too. They dressed as well as any women in Houston. Carly told them where to buy their clothes and where to get their hair cut. Not that she ordered them to do so, but she gave them the names of several places that specialized in expensive haircuts that made their customers look glamorous but casual. And that's how all her saleswomen looked. All but one were married, and she was divorced from one of Houston's leading lawyers, with at least three hundred friends who wouldn't dream of moving without consulting Binkie. Binkie told them who should decorate their new homes, where to find the most reliable nannies, even which churches to go to.

Though Baptists abounded in Houston, as in the rest of Texas and all over the south, the people Binkie advised were mostly Methodists. Houston did not have the huge Methodist population Dallas did, but the Methodists Binkie knew were all loaded.

Binkie was Carly's favorite salesperson, and she tried to lunch with her weekly. They'd known each other when Binkie was still married. Binkie and Alex were the only two women Carly knew who looked regal. Binkie was half a dozen years older than Alex, so the two women hadn't known each other in their younger years.

Binkie had gotten royally screwed in her divorce. "If he'd screwed me half as soundly when we were married," she said, "we'd still be married."

So, when everyone in Houston knew what a raw deal Binkie had gotten, Carly approached her about selling real estate. At first Binkie was aghast. She'd never worked a day in her life. But when Carly told her how much money she might earn, Binkie thought she'd give it a whirl. That was over two years ago, and now Binkie was in the million-dollar club. She could sell a house without even trying. Binkie was Carly's single biggest sales asset. When Binkie earned a million a year, that meant she also brought an equal amount into the office.

The good old boys real estate club wanted to make fun of Carly and Binkie, but they realized it would just sound like sour grapes. They usually hated successful women yet they had to admit those two gals were terrific. Aside from Carly's six female sales personnel, there couldn't have been another two dozen women realtors in Houston. Texas, after all, was a man's country.

When Carly got home the next afternoon, she changed from her pink shantung suit to shorts and walked out to the cabana, where she poured herself a glass of mineral water and added a twist of lime.

She waited for Matt. Mornings she drove Matt and three other boys to St. John's, and afternoons one of the other mothers picked them up. On a day this hot Carly suspected the first place Matt would head was the pool.

She was right. After he'd plunged in, she called out, "Want to go see Grandma and Grandpa this weekend?"

"Are we going to fly? Can we go out to the ranch? And do I get out of school early?" And "Can Uncle Ben come over?"

"So many questions. All I asked is would you like to go?"

"Sure. I'd rather be there than anyplace else."

Ironic, Carly thought.

And ironic, too, that she had to return to Verity to celebrate any success she had.

CHAPTER 53

Carly did let Matt skip the last class on Friday. Walt met them at Corpus, and they were in Verity by five forty-five. No Willows tonight. Francey had prepared her famous lasagna.

She laughed, watching Matt gobble it up.

Walt said he thought it would be nice if they all went out to Zelda Marie's in the morning. Early in the morning.

* * *

Walt watched Matt pile in waffle after waffle.

"No one," Matt told his grandmother, "makes better breakfasts than you do."

She kissed him and ruffled his hair.

Francey and Walt had never gone out to the Spencer place with her before, and Carly figured something was up.

Zelda Marie wasn't in the house, of course. Carly wondered if she ever was. They walked across the meadow to the barn, zigging and zagging between the towering mesquite trees that lent shade. Three horses were in the paddock behind the horse barn, and one had a new foal, standing on wobbly legs. Matt ran to the fence and stared at them.

Funny, she had hated Verity so, yet her son would love to grow up here. He'd like to be a cowboy, a rancher. Walt stood with his hand on the boy's shoulder, then led him to the barn. Zelda Marie and Rafael were deep in talk but looked up when their guests entered.

Zelda Marie walked quickly toward them, throwing her arms around Carly, kissing Walt and Francey, and looking down at Matt. "My heavens, you are growing so fast. Do I shake hands or can I still kiss you?"

Matt grinned at her and reached a cheek for her to kiss.

"You didn't tell him yet?" Zelda Marie asked Walt.

"Nope." Walt acted as though he might burst any minute.

"Well, come along then." Zelda Marie led them along the horse stalls. She stopped in front of one where a young horse munched hay. "You tell him. It's your present."

Walt looked at the young boy. "This here's a horse that isn't good enough in conformation to win shows," Walt told him. "But he's still a superior young animal, just ready for training. I thought, that is your grandmother and I thought if you'd like a horse of your own, well, maybe Rafael will train him for you and when you come down you can ride and . . ."

He didn't have to say more. The boy's face lit up and he

stared, openmouthed, at Walt before turning to reach out and stroke the horse's head, touching its wet nose with his forehead.

"Se llama Chazz." Rafael's voice came from in back of them.

"Chazz," Matt's voice sounded as though he stood in front of an altar. Then he turned to his grandfather and threw his arms around Walt's waist. Carly was glad Cole was not here to see the tears in her son's eyes. She had to blink quickly, and she saw that Walt did, too. Francey let a tear run down her face.

"Well, I guess that's our reward," she said.

After an hour Walt and Francey left them and said they'd drive back at five-thirty so the two girls could spend the day together and Matt and Chazz could get acquainted.

It wasn't until the middle of the afternoon that Carly said, "Are you going to keep it to yourself or share it with me?"

Zelda Marie raised her eyebrows. "What?"

"I see the look in Rafael's eyes when he looks at you."

"Oh, God, Carly. Me with a Mexican? Do you know what everyone would say?"

"Just a minute. Don't talk about others. What about *you?* Are you and Rafael a thing?"

"God, no. Well, I mean yes, we work together like . . . well, we work real good together. He can sometimes tell what I'm thinking without my even saying anything." Her eyes seem to plead with Carly.

"Does he have a wife in Mexico?"

"She died years ago."

"He's not had a woman in his life all the time he's been up here?"

"I don't know," Zelda Marie said in such a tone of voice that Carly looked at her sharply.

"My God, Zelda Marie, you're in love with him!"

Zelda Marie broke into tears. "Oh, Carly, don't say it. I haven't even let myself say it out loud. I don't want him to leave. He's winning shows for me, and I'm heading to have the kind of stable I've dreamt of all my life, thanks mainly to him. I respect him, Carly. He's the best trainer, and the finest human being, I ever met. And . . .'' Tears trickled down her cheeks.

Carly put her arms around Zelda Marie. How awful to be in love with someone and unable to admit it, even to yourself. ''I'm sorry I said anything,'' she murmured into her friend's hair.

Zelda Marie worked hard to compose herself. ''Come on,'' she said to Carly, ''all this time and I haven't even driven you over to look at the new house. Can you believe that? God knows when it'll be finished. Rafael says it looks fit for a queen.''

Which is what he thinks you are, Carly thought. I could see it in his eyes.

It was a mile away, near a small pond. The house had thirty-two rooms. Carly had to laugh out loud. Thirty-two rooms and eleven bathrooms. It was a replica of an antebellum southern home Zelda Marie had seen in Mississippi when she'd gone there once. Except it was larger.

''It won't be ready for months,'' Zelda Marie said. ''Maybe not this year at all, from the looks of it. But I'm in no hurry.''

''Do you do anything social?'' Carly asked.

When they'd been kids Zelda Marie had had a ton of friends. She still did know just about everyone, but she told Carly she didn't go to the one movie in town with them, or play cards with them anymore. She talked horses and cattle with the men. She attended the weddings of her many cousins, and she went to class nights and to little league games and to dance recitals. But she didn't invite people to dinner, though her new dining room could seat half the town. ''I'll start entertaining when I move,'' Zelda Marie said.

Who she really dreamed of entertaining were the Mexicans who came to visit Carlos and Aofrasia and Rafael. She wanted to say, ''Y'all come to my house next Sunday.'' And the cars driving down the lane would stop in front of her house, and she'd have strung colored lanterns which she'd turn on at twilight, and Rafael would reach out his hand to dance with her and everyone would watch as though it was the most natural thing in the world.

That's how she really wanted to entertain. So, when she looked at this big house she was building, she knew the Mexicans would never come dance here, and she lost interest in it. She was in no hurry at all to have it finished. She sometimes pretended it wasn't even there.

"I wonder whatever possessed me to build this," she said aloud.

When they returned to the house, Ao told Zelda Marie that Mrs. Davis had phoned for Carly.

"Ben called," Francey said. "Said he'd flown up to Houston to see you and you weren't there. He wants you to call him. He's at your house."

"Shit," Ben said when she phoned him. "No one's here."

"You should have let me know," Carly said.

"You should have told me you were coming down my way. Well, I'll get the next plane back down to Corpus and drive down to Verity. How'd you feel if I come out to your parents' overnight?"

"Is it anything special?" Carly asked.

"Sort of," Ben answered. "And I'm in a mood to see Matt. I try to fight those feelings . . ."

He'd done remarkably well. "Sure," Carly said. "Mom and Walt always enjoy seeing you." After a pause, she added, "So do Matt and I."

"Okay, see ya soon."

"Drive carefully. It'll be dark."

"Sure."

"What is it, Ben?" The sound of his voice sent shivers through her.

When she hung up, she turned to see Zelda Marie standing in the doorway. "So, it's both of us, isn't it?"

''Both of us what?''

'''In dilemmas. Me and Rafael. You and Ben.''

Carly caught her breath. ''C'mon, there's nothing with Ben and me. We're good friends. No, more than that. He's the brother I never ... Along with you and Walt, he's one of my best friends.''

''Have you ever wondered if he's in love with you?''

''Never,'' Carly said, but it was a lie. She had wondered back in those years when they made love Tuesday afternoons in the Shamrock. She had wondered when he had kissed her, when they had lain on the bed, naked, holding hands, afterward. When they were creating Matt she had wondered if they were in love. But the closeness seemed to have evaporated after their mission was accomplished. They had moved into a friendship she treasured. They were the parents of Matthew, and neither of them had ever said a word acknowledging that fact. Yet, in glances across rooms when the boy said or did something irresistible, and their eyes met, they silently acknowledged that fact to each other. The secret that only they shared.

She had often wondered, of course, if he made love to other women with the same passion that they had experienced, if he had shared those feelings, that tenderness with the women he had taken to bed. She had no doubt that there had been tons of them. Yet, he had not married. When nothing had come of his relationship with that Liz Andrews, Ben had brought to dinner that time, Carly was secretly relieved.

He once told her he was too busy, that a woman wouldn't put up with the hours he kept, with the time he needed to think about what he wrote.

Walt, Francey, and Carly were sitting on the back patio, talking of Carly's latest venture. She had earned over three hundred thousand in less than a week.

''You always have had a head for business,'' Walt said. ''Both of you women.'' He and Francey shared a swinging loveseat and held hands. It passed through Carly's mind that Cole and she never held hands.

When Ben arrived, a bit after nine, Francey fixed him a meatloaf sandwich, loaded with mustard and pickles. He wolfed it down as though he hadn't eaten in days. "Well, not since breakfast anyhow," he admitted. He gulped down two tall glasses of iced tea.

Carly thought again that he was the best-looking man she knew.

"I was miffed when I came up to surprise you and you weren't there."

Carly didn't say anything.

"I need advice."

"If you'd like to speak to Carly alone, we can . . ." Walt said.

"No, sir," Ben said, looking directly at Walt. "I'd like your opinion too. Your opinion is one I value most."

"Flattery will get you . . ."

"It's not flattery, sir. If I don't believe something, I don't say it."

Walt nodded, accepting Ben's compliment.

Ben drummed his fingers on the arms of the wooden chair in which he now leaned back. "Damndest thing," he mused. "Last night the Democratic committeemen of my precinct approached me. They want me to run for Congress."

Carly laughed.

"Is it such a joke?" Ben's look was sharp as he asked.

"Oh, no." She leaned forward and put a hand on his arm. "I'm just thinking that your family thinks of you as the black sheep. Oh, Ben, I think it's wonderful. Maybe our country wouldn't be heading down the drain if there were more people like you running it."

"But you're not sure," Walt said. Not a question, but a statement.

"I'm not. That's the crux. And I need to talk with someone. Someone I trust."

Francey stood up. "I better put some coffee on to perk," she said. "Sounds like this isn't going to be an early night."

The smell of honeysuckle wafted through the air. In the distance a dog barked. A cloud hit the moon, casting a shadow.

No one said anything until Francey returned with steaming mugs of coffee.

"Okay, what are your reservations?" Walt asked.

"I don't want to give up the paper," Ben said. "I have freedom to say what I want there. Do you know that fifty-seven papers carry my editorials? Would I ever have that much influence in Washington? I hate cities. I hate wearing ties. I hate crowds. I hate having to conform. I hate not being my own boss. As a freshman congressman, wouldn't I have to do and say and think what the big politicos want me to?"

Carly stood up and bent over to kiss Ben's forehead. "I am so proud of you."

He grabbed her hand with his good one and did not let go of it, even when she sat down. He squeezed it hard.

"It's not a matter of ideals," he said. "We don't even think alike. I know you wouldn't vote for the things I believe in."

Carly thought of the clinic. "Ben, I think I've become more like you than you realize. You're still seeing me as I was seven or eight years ago."

Ben looked at her. "But unlike most of the world, you have everything you want."

She looked up at the stars and thought. She had money. More than she'd ever imagined she would. She was accepted by Houston society. She had a son she adored, supportive parents. And yet an emptiness had been welling up in her for a long time. She had pushed it down, sublimated it, fought it.

"I don't think that's an issue," she said defensively. "If I'm as vacuous and superficial as you seem to think, why did you have to come find me to talk to?"

"You're not vacuous or superficial. I didn't mean to imply that. But you're far more a typical American than I am." Ben laughed. "I came to you, Carly, because I respect your mind and because I have no one else with whom I'd rather share this dilemma.''

They all knew he'd never consult his parents. They had never agreed on anything except that Christmas was a lovely holiday.

"Dad and Cole will have a shit fit to see me run on a Democratic ticket,'' Ben said, as though he enjoyed that thought.

"Let's look at the other side of the coin,'' Walt suggested. "There has to be another side or you wouldn't be here on the horns of a dilemma.'' Walt leaned forward. "For starters, and this isn't an argument, you'll understand. You do know that power corrupts? Many a young politician has been elected because he's an idealist. He thinks he's going to Washington to change the world, to hold out his ideals and perhaps convince the old-timers he's right. But power corrupts. I have never known of a single case where it hasn't.''

Carly had never heard Walt speak so cynically.

Ben's eyes burned into Walt's. "You're saying that if I go to Washington I shall become corrupt? I'll change?''

Walt shrugged his shoulders. "I'd be pleased if you are the one to prove me wrong about this.''

They sat in silence for a minute, and then Carly said, "But if no one with ideals goes to Congress, where does that leave the country?''

"Where it's heading. Down the drain,'' Walt answered. "I am not optimistic about the future of this country. Too much greed and too much violence. And Ben, what'll happen to the paper so it'll be yours to come home to?''

Ben shrugged. "I don't know. I really love that paper and that town. I belong there. And, I don't want to live in Washington for twenty-two years.''

"Let's take these issues one by one,'' Walt urged.

And, as they did, talking and exploring long into the night, Ben reached out with his good hand for Carly's hand and held it tightly.

CHAPTER 54

On Sunday morning after one of Francey's German apple pancake breakfasts, they all drove out to the ranch, Matt riding in Ben's red pickup with him while Carly drove with Walt and Francey.

"He's going to run, I bet," Francey said.

Neither Walt nor Carly said anything.

"Ben wants to save the world," Francey went on. "If no one else is going to do it, he's going to try."

When they arrived at Zelda Marie's, Matt hopped out of the cab, dancing with pleasure. "I want to ride *my* horse." He was jumping up and down. He pummeled into Walt and threw his arms around him. "Uncle Ben and I're going to catch big fish in Orygon."

Carly wished the day would never end. They spent the morning at the barn with Rafael who, even though it was Sunday, did not leave to join his Mexican compadres. Zelda Marie made potato salad. Hamburgers and hot dogs waited to be grilled over mesquite wood. Lemonade and iced tea, deviled eggs, tossed salad, and chocolate cake completed the picnic on the long table under the trees that shaded her backyard. The men sat in the Adirondack chairs in the shade, talking, for over an hour, but Ben's gaze followed his son constantly, smiling when he heard the boy's laughter, and searching to meet Carly's eyes.

Late Sunday afternoon, Ben drove them up to the airport in Corpus Christi. Matt sat between them on the front seat, chattering all the way up. At home, when Cole was around, the boy hardly said anything for fear of being jumped on.

"Let me know what you decide," Carly said, reaching out

for Ben's left hand as they stood at the gate. Matt pulled at his shirt and Ben gathered him in his good arm. He kissed the boy soundly.

Then Ben leaned over, still holding Matt close to him, and brushed his lips along Carly's cheek. "Thanks for the weekend," he said. "You've been a big help to me."

"Have I, too?" Matt asked.

"Yes, you too," Ben smiled at him. "You are always a help to me. Just being with you helps."

"I bet you're the greatest uncle in the whole world." Matt hugged Ben.

"Well, at least I'm the only one you've got," Ben said. He turned to Carly. "Thank you. I needed you this weekend."

She squeezed his hand, then reached up to kiss his cheek, but he moved his head and their lips touched. She was very conscious of that. She walked through the gate without looking back at him, following their skipping son.

Cole was not home from Washington, but there was a message that he would fly in tomorrow and go straight to the office. He'd be home in time for dinner at his parents' tomorrow night.

One of the best things about owning one's own business, Carly thought, was not having to keep regular hours. And so it was after nine-thirty when she pushed open the glass doors to her office. Her secretary, a good-looking woman in her midtwenties, was dressed in a hot pink suit. She always dolled the place up. Carly liked Jeannie, who not only had the knack of making those who entered the office feel at home, but ran the office with utmost efficiency.

"Shep Lenchek wants you to call him ASAP."

"I hope he's not reneging on that McCullough deal."

"Money's already been banked," Jeannie said. "It's a done deal."

"Get him on the phone." Carly walked on into her office, which was furnished with a sleekly modern glass-topped desk and tables with black metal legs. At one end of the room was a tufted black leather sofa. In front of it was a long, low glass coffee table. So different from her home with its pastel floral prints and soft graceful lines.

"Carly," Shep said. "I want to sell that land. That cornfield."

"Shep, you haven't even owned it three weeks."

"Hey, girl, I can count. I want eight million. Not a cent less. Part of it's zoned for multiple units, you know. Someone can make a bundle out of it."

"Eight million?" She calculated quickly. "That's a twenty-five percent profit in less than a month."

He laughed. "No one ever accused me of not being a good businessman. You figure it out, Carly. I'll give you an exclusive for six weeks, then it's into multiple listing."

She hung up the phone and sat down, drawing a yellow lined legal pad toward her. Whoever built on that land could make a mint. She played with figures until they covered three pages. Then she picked up the phone and called Boomer.

"How about lunch?" she asked. "You and Dan."

"God, Carly, there's no way I can get away before late afternoon."

"Well, how about I pick up some lunch and you can eat in the car. I want to take you for a drive."

"I can tell by your tone of voice," Boomer said, "that you're hatching a scheme."

"It's true."

"Every time you say that I end up making money. Okay, how about twelve-thirty. I'll make sure Dan's free, too."

When Carly had Dan and Boomer looking at Lenchek's cornfield, she said, "You haven't built apartments since those first ones you did a dozen or so years ago. I think you should buy this land." If she sold the property for eight million, she'd clear another four hundred eighty thousand. Nearly an eight hundred thousand profit. Just think.

She'd thought Dan would object immediately, since BB&O was constantly biting off more and more. They were an international firm now.

"Any of it zoned for multifamily?" Dan asked.

Carly was heartened by his question. "Seventy-five acres. The rest is zoned for single family dwellings."

Dan walked around the cornfield, and turned his gaze to the woody hill behind it. "Now, offer me that and I wouldn't hesitate."

"Right now what I'm offering you is the last plat of land along this strip."

Even at lunch hour the sound of bulldozers buzzed through the still air.

"What's he want for it?" Boomer asked.

"Eight million."

Dan and Boomer both turned to stare at her.

"Eight million dollars for how many acres?" Dan's voice sounded strangled.

"Two hundred thirty-three acres, and that's thirty-four thousand three hundred and thirty-three an acre," Carly said, her voice sounding as though that were a bargain.

"And sixty-three cents," Boomer said.

Carly turned to look at him, impressed. He'd never been that good in math in high school. "You know perfectly well with the way land is being gobbled up in this area that that's a good price," she said.

"Yeah, but what about the single-family homes?" Dan asked. "Jeez, nearly thirty-five thousand an acre!"

Boomer turned to Dan. "You're not interested in building homes, I know. So, we buy it and keep the seventy-five acres for apartments ourselves and sell off a hundred and fifty-eight acres to some developer who's dying to get a tract of homes up here."

"Who wants to build houses where there isn't a single tree?" Dan asked.

"Builders who aren't concerned with aesthetics," Carly answered. "Besides, there are trees on the back half."

"I don't know." Dan rubbed his head and studied Boomer. He smiled and pointed to the wooded hills. "Now, if we could ever get that land, why I might even consider designing houses."

"Forget that for now," Carly said. What she was thinking was that if BB&O bought these acres she'd just sold Lenchek, she'd make that commission, and then she'd get a chance to sell a hundred fifty-eight of them a third time.

Two days later, Webb Stuart, who was just starting to make a name in the construction business, phoned her before Dan and Boomer had even signed the Lenchek papers. "Hear tell you got some acreage up in Bedford," he said. "I want a hundred twenty to a hundred sixty or so. Near a shopping mall and good schools, where water and sewers are cheap to install."

Carly couldn't keep from smiling. "Mr. Stuart, I have a hundred fifty-eight acres of prime land. I'll pick you up at nine tomorrow morning."

"No," Stuart said. "I want to drive up there now."

He looked it over and asked, "How much an acre do they want?"

"Forty thousand." She had never talked to Dan and Boomer about price.

Stuart took out a calculator. "That's six million three hundred twenty thousand. Offer them six million flat and it's a done deal."

When it was all over, BB&O had acquired the land at eight million, sold off six million worth, which meant their seventy-five acres only cost about twenty-seven thousand an acre, and within a five-week period, on one two-hundred-thirty-three-acre plot of ground, Carly earned over one million dollars.

"Let's celebrate," she said to Cole. "When Matt and Ben go out to Oregon let's go to the Virgin Islands . . ."

"I can't," Cole said. "I haven't made any million-dollar deals lately."

"Don't do that to me," Carly said. "It's our money. You know that. And, besides, even if I weren't working, you earn enough so we could take wonderful trips. If you'd just take the time off."

"Let's just say I'm in the middle of some deals and don't want to take time off."

Carly sighed. "Cole. We never do anything together anymore." Including make love, she thought.

"Not true," he said. "We spend Saturday nights at the club. Half our Sundays are taken up with your cronies at BB&O. It's you who doesn't want to go to Elk Creek with me."

"Seems everyone you do business with weekends is there. And I thought you enjoyed those Sunday evenings. You and Alex always seem to have a lot to talk about. And Tessa."

Alex was pregnant again. Their eldest, David was twelve, and Diane was ten. And now, unexpectedly, a third one. She remained as elegant-looking as ever. "I never imagined having three children," she told Carly. "I really never thought about more than one. But Boomer's a great father and somehow his enthusiasm is contagious."

Carly thought if *she'd* married Boomer she could have three children by now. She'd have liked that. She'd have liked a dozen children, really. She often looked at Boomer and wondered what it would be like to be married to him, to have someone around who took an interest in his children, who obviously still enjoyed making love to his wife.

Carly sometimes sensed that Boomer's down-to-earth style embarrassed Alex. He was not a gentleman like the men Alex had been raised with. But of course that's what attracted her. But if his manners and his ebullience and his clothes had bothered Alex a lot in the past she had grown accustomed to them. Boomer was certainly a force to be reckoned with in Houston. And BB&O was known far outside the boundaries of Texas. They'd even been invited to bid on a hotel in Kuwait.

Boomer and Dan explained to the Arabs that if they had to bid, they weren't interested. Low bids were not their style. If the hotel owners were interested in quality construction, with no corners cut, then BB&O would talk business. But it never entertained bids.

They were awarded the contract and given carte blanche.

Carly sighed, trying to remember when her marriage to Cole

had stopped being what it started out to be. Ben claimed it had to do with her earning more money than Cole did. Could that possibly have ruined their sex life?

Carly thought that perhaps she could do with less money and more of a relationship.

Well, they were dining with the senior Coleridges tonight, as they did every Monday.

The phone rang. She hoped it wasn't Cole saying he'd be late. That always upset his mother.

A woman's husky voice asked, "Mrs. Coleridge?"

Carly answered, "Yes."

"Do you know where your husband was this weekend?"

"I beg your pardon?"

"You don't know, do you?"

"Who is this?"

"My name's Tricia Donovan. I spent the weekend in bed with your husband at the Mansion in Turtle Creek in Dallas. I spend a lot of time in bed with your husband, Mrs. Coleridge. I thought you ought to know."

The phone went dead.

Carly sat and stared at it. The Mansion in Turtle Creek? It was one of Dallas's most elegant hotels.

In bed with Cole? Another woman in bed with Cole?

I spend a lot of time in bed with your husband.

As she put the phone back in the cradle it rang again. She didn't answer until the fifth ring. "Hi, hon," said Cole. "Look, I'm running behind, as usual. I'll meet you over at my parents'. I'll be there within half an hour."

Carly didn't say anything.

"You there?" he asked.

"Yes, I'm here," Carly said, her voice scarcely a whisper.

"What's wrong? You sound funny."

"Who's Tricia Donovan?" she asked.

"Oh, Christ," Cole said.

CHAPTER 55

"She's nobody," Cole said, his eyes on the road ahead.

"Nobody? So, you have no taste at all?"

"I mean, she doesn't matter."

"I guess I don't, either." Carly had been furious all evening, having to force herself to smile and communicate with her in-laws during dinner. At ten she told them she had to leave, she had an early appointment.

Carly knew she'd reached the pinnacle. She was tops in her profession and likely to stay there. She should be bursting with pride. Instead, she was filled with cold, implacable fury.

It was no good telling herself that years ago she had committed adultery with Ben. She'd convinced herself she'd done it for a purpose—to please Cole. To satisfy him and his parents and to have a Coleridge for posterity.

Nevertheless, she was as guilty of adultery as Cole was.

She had no right to be as angry as she was now. So filled with rage.

"Why?" she asked.

He didn't answer immediately, and then, his voice low, he said, "I don't know. I don't know why."

"Do you want a divorce?"

"God almighty, no." He did take his eyes from the road to look at her in the darkness.

"Then why?"

He didn't answer.

They drove home the rest of the way in silence.

Carly entered the house through the garage door to the kitchen. She stopped in the hall and hung her coat in the closet, sailed up the carpeted stairway and stopped at Matt's room to gaze in at her sleeping son, to listen to his even breathing.

She sat at her dressing table in her nightgown and brushed her hair, far more than a hundred strokes. Cole still had not come upstairs.

When he still hadn't come up within half an hour she grabbed her robe and walked down the curving staircase. She found the downstairs hall dark. A light shone from the study. Cole was sitting in the high-backed armchair staring into space. He did not look up when she entered and stood in the doorway.

"Sleep in one of the guest rooms," Carly said.

He still didn't look up but he did speak, his voice so low she had to strain to hear.

"She thinks I'm wonderful. That's why."

Carly continued to stand in the doorway, her arms crossed, as though warding off some unseen danger.

"I thought you were wonderful, too."

"But she earns a hundred and fifty dollars a week. She doesn't earn more than I do. She isn't as smart as I am. She doesn't sit talking business all the time. She doesn't tell me I'm rigid and inflexible with my son."

"You are rigid and inflexible with Matt." Not with "your son."

Cole didn't respond.

"I can't help being intelligent."

"You can help working. You could be like other wives. You could let me be the breadwinner."

"And then your fragile ego wouldn't need another woman? I could be like you want me to be, not who I am, and your eye wouldn't stray? Oh, my, Cole. You certainly should have been born in the last century."

He still didn't look at her.

"I'm going to bed," Carly said.

In the morning Cole either had left before Carly awoke or he had not slept at home. There was no sign of him.

After Matt left for school, Carly sat at the dining-room table, drinking cups of coffee. She took a long leisurely bath and wished she had someone to talk with. Not Tessa. Not Alex. Certainly not her mother-in-law.

She picked up the phone. When Francey answered Carly burst into tears.

"Mom . . . I think I'm going to drive down for a few days. Maybe a week. I'm going to take Matt out of school. He's going to Oregon with Ben on Thursday anyhow, for the spring break. I need to talk with you."

"Honey, what's wrong?"

"Oh, Mom, Cole's been sleeping with another woman."

Francey hesitated. "Now, you don't do a thing yet. I'll get the next plane up there and drive down with you. You're in no shape to make such a long drive all by yourself."

"Yes, I am. I'll pick Matt up at school at noon and we'll be there by dinnertime. Call Ben, will you . . . No, I'll call him. I'll drive Matt over to Aransas Pass tomorrow night, and Ben won't have to come up here to get him. I want to get away. I just want to be with you." She burst into tears again.

Carly paused before dialing Ben's number. She certainly wasn't going to tell him about Cole. She wanted to get ahold of herself so she wouldn't burst into tears talking with him.

It turned out he was delighted to think she'd drive Matt down before they took off for Oregon.

Carly wrote a note to Cole, telling him her plans. She packed two suitcases for Matt and one for herself, not taking a single dress. Just slacks and cotton blouses. She wanted to hibernate, see no one but Francey and Walt and Zelda Marie. Maybe she'd even stay out at the ranch a night or two.

Funny, she'd hated Verity when growing up there, yet when she needed solace, that's where she headed.

"Maybe I should stop working," Carly said to her mother.

Francey studied her. They were drinking coffee in Francey's sunshine-yellow kitchen. "Maybe you better think of leaving him."

"Oh, Mom," Carly was shocked. "What I think I better do

is look inside myself. I mean, it takes two to make a good marriage, doesn't it?''

Francey sipped her coffee and looked out the back window, over the turquoise pool, at the slope of lawn.

"You know what Walt asked me?"

Carly shook her head.

"If you love him. Maybe you better think about that. You and Cole seem to have been on different paths for years."

Carly held up her hand. "And maybe that's my fault. I wasn't willing to stay on his path and play the dutiful wife. I got restless and wanted to do things on my own."

Francey leaned over and put an arm around her daughter's shoulder. "A sad commentary, isn't it, that the only way for most marriages to work is for the wife to give in."

"You didn't."

"Walt's not an average man, and I'm so in love with him that we end up wanting the same things. Once I achieved success with the Willows, I've been content to do less."

"Seems to me you still keep a finger in the pie. You run it."

"Yes, but not to the extent I did. I miss Zelda Marie. I could leave the whole place in her charge and not worry. But now that she doesn't need a job, I have to put in a couple of hours a day, anyhow. And we usually have dinner there so I can control the quality and service. But it doesn't interfere with our life together. We do the gardening and the greenhouse, and we enjoy cooking together evenings. We're enough for each other. I don't think that's true of most marriages."

"What about Daddy? Before he got killed in the war. What kind of marriage did you have?" Carly had never asked Francey that before.

"I was seventeen. Neither of us knew what relationships were about."

Carly didn't pursue it.

"People get married because they think they're in love, that love will triumph over all, but all relationships that are worth anything take work. Nothing that's worthwhile is easy."

"You and Walt look like you just glide along."

"Listen, honey, I don't think there's been a day where either of us has taken our relationship for granted. We think about what we can do to make each other happy. Every single day."

Carly held her coffee cup between her two hands, her elbows resting on the counter. She didn't do that. She never woke up and wondered what she could do that day to make Cole happy. She woke up thinking of deals or of Matt or how she was going to fit in everything that was scheduled. She never thought about what she could do to make Cole happy. She had always thought marriages just took care of themselves.

She doubted that Cole ever thought about what would make her happy, either. He probably woke up each day resentful that she wasn't thinking of him, that she headed out to work to make tons of money.

Here, all along, she thought he should be proud of her.

Ben was right. It had led Cole to another woman's arms.

"He told me she didn't matter. She was nothing."

"I'd hate to be her," Francey said. "To be called nothing. Even if you leave him, he won't turn to her, you know. She's just a way to salve his ego. Maybe what you better do is talk, if you can. Calmly."

"He says he doesn't want a divorce."

"Do you want a divorce?"

"It was the first thing I thought of. Wondering how do I get in bed with a man who's been sleeping with someone else. But then I've been thinking, maybe it's my fault. If I try harder. If I become more what he wants. I must have been what he wanted in the beginning."

"Just don't become so much what he wants that you lose your self."

Carly smiled at her mother. "How come you're so wise?"

"I'm a mother." Francey laughed.

The phone rang. It was Zelda Marie. "Will you be crushed if I go stay overnight at the ranch?" Carly asked Francey.

"Of course not. It'll be grand for the two of you to spend time together."

Before she left, borrowing Francey's Ford station wagon, Carly asked, "You and Walt must have been talking about this before I arrived. What does he think?"

Francey picked the cups up from the bar and put them in the sink, rinsing them before slipping them into the dishwasher.

"He's never thought Cole was good enough for you."

Carly laughed. "Cole not good enough for me? That's a good one. He was the catch of Houston."

"Only in the sense of money and social standing."

"Well, what else is there?"

Francey turned so that her eyes met her daughter's. "Even I was smarter than you at your age." She paused. "Matt has all that. Is he a happy boy?"

Carly's heart stopped. She had never thought to use that word. "Matt's not happy?"

"Oh, Carly. You're so blind about your own life. So blind."

All the way out to Zelda Marie's Carly studied the trees and the birds, the cattle in the fields, the soy beans growing lush. She looked at the cars that passed her, at the houses with peeling paint. She tried to look at everything with new eyes, with eyes wide open.

Matt wasn't happy? He'd bubbled all the way down from Houston on Tuesday. He'd been nearly out of his skin when she'd driven him over to Ben's Wednesday night. He'd hardly even said good-bye to her, so involved was he with the flies and the rods Ben was showing him. Neither of them had more than waved good-bye to her.

But he was seldom like that at home. Maybe she'd better give him more attention, too. She'd always worked her schedule so that she was there when he got home from school. She attended all his school activities. She took him to museums and to movies, she played tennis with him on their clay courts. She spent hours with him.

But, Francey implied Matt wasn't happy.

Carly pulled off the highway and down the blacktop that led

to Zelda Marie's dirt driveway. Zelda Marie's kids were the ones who should be maladjusted. No father, a mother who worked when they were little. They were wild Indians, always full of zest, of so much laughter. Whenever she arrived, they remembered her, welcomed her with shouts and hugs. And they treated Matt as though he were a cousin, a part of the family. Matt loved coming to the ranch. Matt loved Verity and he loved Aransas Pass.

He loved Francey and Walt, and Zelda Marie and her brood, and Ben.

She guessed maybe the problem was his relationship with Cole.

She suddenly wondered if Matt loved Cole. Boys and their fathers always loved each other, didn't they? She had taken for granted they must love each other.

Now, she questioned that. Maybe she'd better question more things.

CHAPTER 56

Carly and Zelda Marie sat deep in conversation. "Men have to be catered to," agreed Zelda Marie. She stared at her friend. "Is Cole the most important thing in the world to you?"

"Oh, God, no." After she'd blurted it out, Carly was astonished at her words. "I don't even know if I love him."

"Because of this woman, you mean?"

"No." Carly shook her head vehemently.

They sat there in silence, Zelda Marie sipping her tea through a straw, studying Carly.

Carly closed her eyes and leaned back in the chaise. "You know," she said, "I think it started those first years of marriage when he and his mother tried to tell me everything I should and shouldn't do. They decorated my house and they bought my clothes and they told me which clubs to join and who my friends should be. When I used the wrong fork at a dinner party, I could see Mother Coleridge's face down the table, her head bent to the side, letting me know I'd made a faux pas. Well, if I had it to do over again, I'd go on using the wrong fork.

"She didn't like the bright-colored clothes I wore, so for a couple of years I changed to blues and grays and beiges. Until after Matt was born. And then I went back to dressing like I wanted.

"Matt, ah, Matt. His grandparents, both sets, dote on him, but Cole. There's been some tension since Cole first looked at Matt. He was in Mexico, you know, and didn't see Matt for five days. When he did see him, it was as though he didn't even want to pick him up."

Carly was silent for a few minutes. "Cole and I have drifted so far apart I don't even know if I love him. But I've said that already."

"He must feel that," Zelda Marie said. "Maybe that's why there's another woman. He doesn't feel loved and respected."

Carly looked at her friend. "Maybe I just haven't taken time for him. When we did spend an evening together, he'd sit and tell me all about what he'd been doing, his wheeling and dealing and what was happening in the Savings and Loan business and my mind would be on deals of my own, how I could make another quarter of a million, and what property I could invest in . . ."

"Did you love him when you married him?"

Carly had to think about that. "I think so. I was flattered that someone like him would want to marry me. I'd been to bed with him and I liked it." She paused. "What about you?" she asked. "Haven't you gone to bed with anyone since . . . I mean, what about Joel Miller?"

Zelda Marie shook her head. "He never set me on fire."

As she said that, the dark face of the man who talked to her horses passed in front of her eyes. He did set her on fire.

* * *

"The first thing you and Cole have to do is talk," Walt told her. "Maybe he doesn't even know why he's done this. He says he's not in love with her—"

"He didn't say that," Carly interrupted.

Walt nodded his head. "Yes, he did. When he told you she was nothing."

Cole had phoned every day, every night. Carly refused to speak with him.

The three of them were sitting out on the patio, sipping margaritas while dinner cooked. Walt reached out and took Francey's hand. Carly liked the way they were always touching each other. She envied them that.

"It's probably a good idea to go back and talk to him before Matt comes home, isn't it?" she mused aloud.

"I'd say so," Francey agreed.

So Carly left after she'd been in Verity a week, driving slowly, not looking forward to returning home.

She spent most of the five hours it took to drive north to Houston thinking about what more she wanted from life. She couldn't think of anything. She couldn't think of a single thing she wanted that she didn't have—except a happy marriage.

By the time she reached her home, she'd come to a conclusion.

"I'm going to sell my business," she told Cole. "I'll stay home and be a wife. Do the things other wives around here do."

She never accused him of anything. She never acted hurt. She behaved as though it were her fault, and for all she knew, maybe it was.

"I've told her good-bye," Cole said.

"I take that for granted," Carly said.

They made love that night with more passion than Cole had shown toward her in months if not years, but Carly didn't feel anything. She went through all the motions, but she didn't feel a thing.

* * *

When Ben brought Matt home, complete with photographs of the fish the boy had caught, Carly begged him to stay overnight.

They sat around drinking coffee together after Matt left for school and Cole for his office. "I'm giving up work," Carly told Ben. "I'm going to sell my business and be a wife."

Ben raised one eyebrow. "You mean the two aren't compatible?"

She did not reveal Cole's affair. "You told me long ago that Cole was threatened by my success. I don't need more money. I can never spend what I have. Maybe I better concentrate on my role as a wife for a time."

"I can't see you playing bridge and tennis and shopping all day."

"Maybe I'll do good works," Carly said, smiling to herself. That was already a fait accomplio. The clinics were flourishing.

"I'm going to run, Carly. For Congress. You could help my campaign."

Carly's eyes lit up with delight. "Oh, Ben, I'm so pleased. But I'm not even in your district."

"I know. And if I were in *your* district, I wouldn't stand a chance."

"No, you probably wouldn't. But I'd vote for you."

"Because you know me or because you believe as I do?"

Carly thought about that. "Well, let's say I think you're helping me to grow. Maybe I'm willing to give up my business because I see there are things more important than money."

"There are only things more important than money when you have money," Ben said.

"Most of the people I know have plenty of money but they don't think like you."

"Yeah," Ben said. "It's why I never fit in here. I have found that generally the more money one has the less compassion."

"You're never going to win in Texas if you talk like that."

Ben grinned. "The only reason I'm going to run is to see if

I can make a difference. If I can accomplish things I believe in, it won't be wasted energy.''

"And if you can't accomplish those things you so passionately care about?''

"I will have at least tried.''

"You're such an idealist,'' Carly said. "But I suppose it's one of the things I love most about you.''

"Love?'' he asked.

"Yes, love,'' Carly said, and thought, not for the first time, that she'd married the wrong Coleridge.

CHAPTER 57

Though Cole might think she was a better wife, in the year since she'd sold Rolf's, except for the mornings she spent at the clinics she thought her life had little purpose.

She had increased her time to three clinics a week, thanks to Leon. She still spent Fridays at his clinic but two other mornings a week she went to other clinics that doctors ran for the deprived children and women of the barrios. When Gonzalez heard she was going to sell her business, he voiced his main worry.

"That means you will no longer be able to help us financially?''

"Not at all,'' Carly assured him. "In fact, I'll have time on my hands and should be able to spend more time helping you.''

Carly not only paid for all the operations for children from these three clinics, but paid for prescriptions as well. By the end of a year she had learned enough, working with three doctors, to give vaccinations, take temperatures, dispense cough medicine, and predict tonsillitis.

Even though in one morning she saw more illness than she'd

seen in her life, these days did not fill her with despair. She left the clinics exhilarated to know she was able to help.

The only person she was ever tempted to tell was Ben, but she fought the temptation, remembering a scene from *Catcher in the Rye*. Holden Caulfield said if he were a terrific piano player he'd play in a closet because if he received adulation and applause, how would he know if he was playing for the purity of the act or because he enjoyed the praise?

Saturday-night conversations at the club didn't interest her in the least. Flirting with other people's husbands, dancing the night away, having her bottom pinched periodically, being held too close were not the stuff that made life worthwhile to Carly.

But, then, she wondered, what did?

She'd sold her business lock, stock, and barrel for exactly the figure she'd decided it was worth, including its longtime established reputation. Cole invested the down payment at a pretty impressive percentage.

Her photo appeared at least monthly in the society section of the *Post*. She and Cole saw every Broadway show that came to town, heard every jazz combo. Thank goodness she didn't have to go to football games. Once in a while they went to tailgate parties, but seldom the games themselves.

She began to jog. She'd go out early in the morning, before Cole was even awake. She started running a mile, and pretty soon she was doing four miles before breakfast. Cole thought she was nuts. Matt decided if his mother could jog like that, he could, too, so he began rising early and accompanying her. It was the nicest time of the day for Carly.

Ben wrote witty letters twice a month to Matt, who devoured them.

Matt's marks in history and English improved. When Ben mentioned a book, Matt read it, even if he didn't understand it all. He answered each letter his uncle wrote to him. At least once a month, Ben phoned.

After Carly quit work, Cole spent a very attentive few months. He brought Carly flowers—nosegays of violets, sprays of gladiolas, a primrose plant, gardenias whose scent permeated their bedroom. He made love to her more often than he had in years. He couldn't understand why she didn't conceive again.

"I'm too old," she said. She was thirty-nine.

But something was wrong with their lovemaking. Carly couldn't put a finger on it. When she saw Francey, she asked her, "Do you and Walt . . . Oh, you know, Mom." They'd never really discussed sex. "I mean, do you still enjoy it? You've been married longer than I have. You're older. Do you still . . ."

Francey put a hand on Carly's arm. "Do Walt and I like sex? Honey, it's a never-ending delight. I know it's hard to think of your mother as a sexual creature. Yes, Walt and I love sex even though we've been married seventeen years. It is never, not ever, boring or dull or repetitive, and it is always filled with love. Why, is something lacking with you and Cole?"

Carly shrugged. So, it wasn't just that they'd been together so long. "I don't know. I always thought sex was such fun. But for years, now—"

Her mother interrupted. "I think everything in your life is directed to being the kind of wife he wants so he won't stray again. I think you resent him and that's why you don't enjoy making love with him."

Carly thought about that.

Carly talked with Alex. They'd never really had conversations about their personal lives, except about shopping or going on vacations or work. So, when Carly asked, "Are you and Boomer still . . . oh, I don't know. In love?"

Alex, picking at her ubiquitous Caesar salad, looked up, a startled look in her eyes. "Why, of course. Anything made you think otherwise?"

"No, no." Carly held up her hand and waved it in the air. "Nothing like that. I've been wondering lately about the difference between being in love as opposed to just loving. We're all in love, I suppose, when we get married. Then does it sort of grow into just being used to it and taking it for granted?''

Alex squinted and asked, ''Is something wrong with you and Cole?''

''No.'' But Carly's voice wasn't convincing. ''I've just been philosophizing on the nature of love lately.''

Alex put down her fork and gazed at her. ''You want to compare your marriage to others, I gather.''

Carly felt herself blushing. Was she so transparent?

''Well, I have to tell you I am still excited by Boomer. He opened up a whole new world to me. I think I'd been lonely all my life and didn't know it. I thought I relished being alone. And then along came Boomer, and he changed everything. Boomer adds excitement to my life. He is a rock of steadiness without being dull.

''However, and oh, Carly, I've never said this to another person, Boomer still embarrasses me. But, on the other hand, I look at most of the men I've known and thank God I didn't settle for any of them.''

''Including Cole?''

Alex reached a hand across the table to touch Carly's. ''I didn't say that.''

''But you've thought it?''

Alex refused to answer. But she did ask, ''What's wrong, Carly?''

''I don't know.'' Carly let out a sigh.

''Maybe it's because you stopped working. That's part of the satisfaction I get out of life. One man, no matter how marvelous he is, isn't enough to fulfill all that I want in life.''

Carly turned that over in her mind. ''That's not what we were brought up to believe.''

Alex laughed. ''I know. Once we met Mr. Right, we weren't ever going to want or need anything else, right. You know one problem we face in this day and age? We were taught our lives would only be complete if we had a man. Nothing was said about friends. Well, women friends—I really mean you and Tessa—supply me with things men just don't know how to.

And even from you and Tessa I need different things. We need *people* in our lives, not one person."

Carly looked around the dining room, at the tables filled with elegantly dressed women. Very few men. Men ate downtown, not out here.

"Of course," Alex continued, "I often wonder if we drive our husbands nuts. We're not the kinds of wives they were brought up to expect. Look what we did with the mall. We helped make BB&O millions."

"It doesn't seem to have fractured Boomer's ego," Carly commented.

"No. I'm lucky. Boomer doesn't have to have his ego fed. Well, not too often. Not like Cole." And then Alex tightened her lips. "Carly, I'm sorry. I didn't mean to say that.

"But I never figured you really sold Rolf's because you were tired of working. I think I know you better than that. You thought you'd try to be the perfect wife and that would please Cole. Am I right?"

Carly nodded.

"Is it working?"

"I guess so." But Carly didn't sound happy. "For the marriage, but not for me."

"Are you happy now?"

She and Alex had never had such an intimate discussion. "I don't even know. I just so often feel empty. The only thing that gives me real, constant pleasure is Matt." And the clinics.

"Don't rely too much on a child," Alex advised. "They grow up and leave."

Alex glanced at her watch. "I have a two-thirty appointment," she said. "Look, Carly, if you need to talk more or if I can do anything . . ."

"Thanks, Alex." Carly sat and drank coffee as she watched Alex leave. Alex always looked regal, self-contained. She looked as if she didn't need anyone else.

But Alex still found Boomer exciting.

Carly knew for certain that Cole no longer excited her. She wondered if it was partly because she had become disenchanted with him, with his beliefs, with his goals in life. At one time they'd shared goals: To get somewhere. To be someone. To make a lot of money. She'd achieved those goals. Cole hadn't gone as far as he wanted to go yet. He wanted to make more money than his father had. That would prove his success. But when that happened, would he slow down? Or would he want even more?

She paid her check and wondered, as she walked out into the fall afternoon, if she was asking questions that had no answers.

CHAPTER 58

Cole strode into Destin Savings and Loan at four minutes after two. He had had a most satisfactory luncheon meeting, exploring exactly what was legal and what wasn't on a deal he was contemplating. Lawyers could be worth their weight in gold.

He stood in the lobby surveying his domain—the marble floor, the rows of teller cages. Cages. He shook his head. Terrible word. He didn't want any of his tellers to feel . . .

His thoughts stopped. He'd never seen that red-haired teller before. Must be new, though she seemed to know what she was doing. Damn fine-looking woman, even if she might be a tad older than he. He strolled toward her cubicle. Ah, that was a better word than cage.

He stopped in front of her. "You must be new here."

She nodded. "Second week," and smiled at him dazzlingly. She didn't even know who he was.

"Your name?"

She pointed to the small brass placard. He read "Tiffany Delacourte."

"Tiffany?"

She smiled at him, her eyebrows raised. They were the most exquisitely formed brows he'd ever seen.

"I'm Cole Coleridge," he introduced himself. "I like to get to know my employees. What time is your afternoon break?"

"Three-thirty."

"Come up to my office then," he said, "and we'll have coffee and get to know each other."

"Oh, yes, sir."

Sir. He thought she was probably forty. Green eyes, greener than he'd known eyes could be.

When she arrived in his office he asked Leona, his secretary, to bring in two cups of coffee. He gestured for Tiffany to sit on the long burgundy couch that faced the mahogany coffee table. He crossed the room and sat in a matching armchair opposite her. Leona handed them their coffee, then left.

He shook his head, his eyes on Tiffany. "Is that your real name?"

"Of course not," she said. "It's Ethel. I changed it legally when I got divorced three years ago."

"Tell me something about yourself."

She sipped her coffee and crossed her legs. Cole could see the lace edging her slip. She had dynamite legs.

"I graduated from Ohio Wesleyan," she said, "where I met my husband. I worked for a year, teaching school, and then had two kids. Once they got to college I took off."

"A teller in a bank isn't a very good-paying job."

She smiled at him. "My only experience is keeping house and raising kids. I feel lucky to have this, Mr. Coleridge. I'm taking accounting and bookkeeping courses in night school, but I need some way to keep my head above water until I've finished the courses. I just moved here from Cleveland."

The next week, Cole invited her to lunch.

"I called your night school," he told her. "You're an outstanding student."

She nodded her head. "I aim to go far. Might be a late bloomer, but I'm going to make up for the lost time."

"What's your goal?"

"To be rich as Croesus."

"Well, let's see what we can do about that."

The next week he promoted her to be his assistant, at three times a teller's salary.

Within six months Tiffany Delacourte was a vice president of Destin S & L, with her own office. She proved to have a razor-sharp mind. Cole put her in charge of the money desk, which oversaw large deposits from trust and pension funds. It was a key position.

As he did with all his vice presidents, he gave her a Mercedes and a salary of seventy-five thousand dollars. A far cry from the twelve thousand she'd earned half a year before.

She and Cole lunched daily—seldom alone, always with other officers of Destin or with prospective businessmen. Tiffany was always the only woman. She spent a lot of money on clothes, and they were in good taste.

He never asked her if she had a boyfriend, or what she did weekends, and the only time she ever commented about his private life was one morning after his and Carly's picture had appeared in the paper at the opening of the symphony. "You sure do have a good-looking wife," Tiffany said.

It was three months later, when Tiffany had been in Houston nine and a half months, that she walked into Cole's office one afternoon at five o'clock, just before she was ready to leave.

"I don't know if you'll be at all interested in this," she said, sliding a key across his desk. "But I want you to have it. I take for granted you can look the address up in the phone book."

Cole understood it was the key to her apartment.

Within the week he discovered that though she might not have been born with the name Tiffany, her red hair was not dyed.

A month later he invited Carly to go to Elk Creek for the weekend, telling her a group of officers and lawyers were going to hold a meeting there. As he had anticipated, Carly declined.

So, Cole and two of his vice presidents and Hardy Wilson, the president of a Savings and Loan in San Antonio, and George Stevenson, president of an ice cream chain that stretched across the country and to whom Destin S & L had lent two and a quarter million, discussed business in the hot tub that overlooked the Rockies.

Hardy Wilson, the president of First Alamo Federal Savings and Loan, was someone Cole had known since his days at St. John's. Though Hardy had gone to the University of Texas instead of Harvard, they'd always kept in touch. Now that Hardy also headed a thrift, he and Cole talked on the phone at least weekly and lunched whenever Hardy came to Houston.

The main business they conducted was signing papers, which Cole had brought along with him. He assured them all that what they were doing was entirely legal.

Cole had asked George to acquire several old buildings, and had suggested that Hardy find a friend to acquire some over in San Antone. The first one they discussed was an old abandoned farm. George had borrowed the money from Destin to buy it for back taxes of twenty-six thousand. A company Cole had had his lawyer form, with Tiffany on the board of directors, then bought it for thirty-nine thousand, which they borrowed from First Alamo Federal. Then George Stevenson bought it with fifty-eight thousand he borrowed from Destin Savings and Loan. George then sold it to the company which Cole's other vice president fronted for eighty-three thousand. Then the original company, for which Tiffany signed, rebought it for ninety-three thousand and she sold it to one of George's other companies for a hundred and two thousand. The two S & Ls involved made money, on paper, each time they lent money for the purchase of this property.

They did this with thirteen properties that were between Houston and San Antonio. By the time they'd finished signing, three hours later, a four-and-a-half-million-dollar profit was made on paper, and the thrifts gained money in their accounts for loans due.

Everyone except Cole and Tiffany left Sunday afternoon. They stayed another three days at Elk Creek—in the hot tub, in the heated pool, and on the immense round bed in the VIP guest suite. The one that had mirrors on the ceiling.

The whole trip, of course, was a tax write-off because they really had accomplished a lot of work. Four and a half million in loans.

"You know what?" Tiffany said, sitting naked among the pillows and holding a glass of champagne in her hand. "I do like Colorado. I wouldn't mind coming out here again."

"Count on it," Cole said.

When they returned to Houston, Tiffany moved to a larger apartment, one that she couldn't have afforded, even on seventy-five thousand a year, if Cole hadn't had the bank buy it. She was entitled to live there, he told her, since she was a vice president. For Christmas he gave her a bonus for the excellent work she was doing: a mink coat.

She *was* an asset to the bank, and he never had to explain something twice.

One afternoon around four he wandered into her office. "You know as soon as we lend money we enter what we'll earn on that loan on the books as income."

"You mean," she knew what he meant, "that for every million we loan we earn five points or fifty thousand dollars and it looks like immediate income?"

Carly would never have grasped the idea so quickly. "Yup. Goes on the books as income as soon as the loan's made."

"So," she grinned and crossed her shapely legs, "the more loans we make the more it looks like we earn."

"Bingo."

"This is leading up to another of your ingenious ideas, I can tell."

Cole nodded, thinking her lips looked like cherry velvet.

"You know that loan we're making to Cantree Development for that project they're going to start in March?"

"Sure, they're borrowing a million and a half."

"Right. Well, instead of just giving them what they're asking for, I've been thinking we could lend them two million, keeping half a million on reserve in case they default on the loan, and have the use of it—"

"Who do you mean by we . . ."

Cole grinned. "Well, we'll deposit it in a fund to be available should it be needed during the next ten years."

"And invest it in that yacht you've been yearning for off the gulf?"

"Smart girl. Sometimes I think you read my mind."

He had already worked out a plan to circumvent the regulation that prohibited Savings and Loans from lending more than a hundred thousand unsecured commercial loans to employees or officers, or even directors. Tiffany had helped him with that.

A few weeks later, Tiffany suggested another way they could use Hardy and his S & L. "You know how we regularly sell parts of our loan portfolios to other thrifts?" It was a way that selling Savings and Loans raised money and fattened their loan portfolios. "I talked with Al Makerness," who was one of the bank's lawyers, "and he says it's perfectly legitimate. We have to get rid of some of our bad loans. Let's sell them to Hardy Wilson and hope he won't catch on that the loans have been made to unstable borrowers on terribly overappraised land."

"You have something concrete in mind or we wouldn't be having this discussion," Cole said.

Tiffany smiled. "Sell him about five and a half million in loans that are dragging us down. It'll fatten his portfolio, the FSLIC will think he's got a lucrative account, and we'll have cash and be rid of these deadbeats."

For just a fraction of a second Cole questioned the morality of doing this to a friend. But he figured if Hardy wasn't astute enough to catch on, he deserved it.

* * *

"Tiffany, my dear, the day I discovered you was one of my luckiest days."

"Wanna make it a lucky night?" she asked.

He picked up the phone on her desk and called Carly to tell her he wouldn't be home until eleven.

"Take me to dinner first," Tiffany said.

Cole nodded. It would have to be a place where no one knew Carly.

CHAPTER 59

"Don't you think we ought to go down to Aransas Pass and spend Election Day with Ben?"

"Whatever for?" Cole asked. "He's a big boy. If he can't stand to lose, he shouldn't enter politics."

Carly narrowed her eyes. "You expect him to lose? Then isn't that all the more reason . . ."

"Come on, Carly. I hope to hell he loses. Can you just see someone who's so off-center representing us up in DC? He and others like him are just what's wrong with this country. I'm not about to commiserate with him if he loses, that's for sure."

She stood up and walked over to the phone.

"Who're you calling?"

"Your mother. Maybe your parents would like to go down with me. Give him their support."

Cole picked up a magazine and leafed through it.

"Oh, darling," Mrs. Coleridge said, "of course not. Kevin is going to have a fit if Ben wins. He's not going to, is he?"

"Then, all the more reason to give him comfort."

There was silence, and then Mrs. Coleridge said, ''No, dear, I don't think so.''

''Well, I'm going down. Someone from the family should.''

''That's nice, dear.''

Carly didn't announce to Ben that she was coming. But she drove down, not understanding why she didn't take the plane which would have saved her hours each way. She arrived in Aransas Pass just as twilight settled in. Skies were gray and a wind bent the palm trees. Carly hoped there wasn't going to be a hurricane.

She drove to the newspaper office first, but it was closed. Ben's house, too, was dark. She guessed she should have told him she was coming, but she'd felt like surprising him, hoping it would please him.

She glanced at her watch. Might as well go get a bite to eat while she waited. Of course, he was out politicking at the last minute. Who, running for office, would be sitting home calmly the night before the election?

She drove slowly through the small town, finding it again, much to her surprise, most attractive. After Verity, she thought she'd hate any small town.

Carly smiled, thinking of her mother. She and Walt. A marriage made in heaven, that one. Carly had graduated from high school in 1963, nearly twenty years ago. That meant her mother must be about fifty-seven, and Walt maybe sixty-two? They certainly didn't seem those ages. They were so full of life and energy and love.

That hadn't been the path of her marriage. She wondered if Francey and Walt were some of the chosen or if others also had that magic in their marriages. Certainly Tessa and Dan seemed as in love as ever.

Could she and Ben have had that? Whenever they looked at each other now, there was a veil over their eyes, even when they talked of neutral things. They seldom let that invisible wall come down.

As she passed a sea food restaurant she saw Ben's car parked in front. She pulled in at the nearest parking space, half a block away, and got out. She hoped he'd be pleased to see her.

She pushed the wooden door open and had to squint in the dark. At a long table, his back toward her, Carly saw Ben. There must have been fifteen or sixteen people at the table, beer in pitchers, everyone keyed up, laughing—a celebration. Those who had worked hardest for him. His friends. All of them nervous and excited about tomorrow.

She turned before Ben could see her and walked back out into the dark, rain beginning to pelt down on her. She ran to the car, opened the door, slid behind the wheel and wondered what to do. She was hungry. It was now after eight. She gunned the motor and took off down the street, turning right, away from the gulf. She drove on slowly, looking at either side of the street until she came to the Kitchen Cupboard and remembered she and Matt had eaten lunch there once with Ben. She parked and ran through the rain, shrugging to spin the water off her shoulders at the door of the restaurant.

Inside it was warm and cozy, the rain slanting onto its windows. Candles and flowers were on each table.

She ordered onion soup, homemade bread, and a salad. She'd have liked a margarita but they only served wine. She chose red and sipped it as she waited.

She shouldn't have come. She'd thought it would be such fun to surprise Ben. Maybe she'd never realized he had a life of his own over here. He had friends, a full life. Actually, he was the town celebrity. People read his columns in New York and Omaha and Chicago and Topeka and Los Angeles.

He'd been on *Donahue* and the *Today* show. When she watched him on TV, Carly was always reminded of Robert Redford. He had that boyish charm and one just knew he had integrity. He came across as so genuine. It was clear he cared about the world.

She wished she'd looked more carefully before backing out of the restaurant. Looked to see if there was a woman beside him. Ben never mentioned women in his life. He never mentioned his life in Aransas Pass, for that matter. He sent her his editorials now and then.

Carly looked at her watch. Not quite nine. She could sit in her car with the rain beating a tattoo on the windshield until after midnight for all she knew, waiting for Ben to come home. She decided to get a motel room. She'd call and tell him she'd be there the next day. He need not know she'd spent the night waiting for him.

Her room overlooked the gulf and the beach, but she couldn't see it for the torrential rain. People wouldn't come out to vote in this weather, she worried.

She lay in bed with the TV droning, unable to find anything interesting after "Magnum P.I." was over. The TV buzzed in the background as she closed her eyes.

She wondered, as she had for all the years Matt had been alive if it hurt Ben not to be able to claim his son. She could see, anyone could see, how much the boy and Ben loved each other. Certainly Matt was far more like Ben than Cole. Mrs. Coleridge kept saying the two of them were like her father.

The next she knew *Good Morning America* was telling her something about President Reagan and she flicked the remote control off. She wasn't quite up to Ronnie so early in the morning.

She glanced out the window at sky that was cobalt blue. The water beyond the waves rolling onto the beach was turquoise and purple. She slid open the glass doors to her little patio and knew at seven-thirty in the morning that Ben would win because it was such a beautiful day. Everyone would turn out to vote.

She showered and dressed in light-blue slacks and a navy blouse. She slid the long dark-blue-and-emerald wooden earrings through her ears and smiled at her reflection. Neither Cole nor his mother approved of costume jewelry, but there was a lot of it she loved. She was still pretty good-looking even if she was thirty-nine.

She had breakfast in the motel dining room, and when she returned to her room, there, on the local news, was Ben, coming out of a voting booth, smiling. He looked like a Greek god, she thought. She thought every woman who looked at him must have fallen in love with him.

He was saying he hoped there'd be a big turnout. He was optimistic. His eyes were smiling. She felt a catch in her breathing, thought that for just a fraction of a second her heart stopped. She sighed, wondering how she was going to find him today. Maybe he'd be at the office and maybe he'd be all over town. Maybe he'd walk along the beach alone, needing time for himself. Maybe she shouldn't have come.

She flipped the TV off when Ben's image left it, took her overnight bag with her as she checked out, and went in search of her brother-in-law. She found him immediately at his office. His face lit up when she opened the door. Perhaps she'd been right to come, after all.

"Carly." He strode toward her and grabbed her right hand in his. He leaned over and kissed her cheek lightly, smiling at her. "I had a feeling you'd show up. You're here to help me celebrate if I win, aren't you?"

She nodded. Or comfort you in defeat, she thought, but he seemed not even to consider that option.

"You must have left in the middle of the night. I'd have picked you up at the airport in Corpus, you know."

"I drove," she said.

"What did you do? Start in the middle of the night?"

She just smiled.

"Come on, you want coffee? I do. I haven't had breakfast yet." He jerked his head back toward the office. "I might as well not even be working here anymore. Jay Hemphill's been doing most of it while I've been politicking." He laughed. He was full of joy today. "Hey, Hemp, I'm taking off."

When he stopped at a red light Ben turned to smile at her again. "I felt it in my bones you'd come. Carly, dear, you are the one loyal family member."

"Maybe because I'm not really family."

"You're my family," he said, his voice low as he now looked straight ahead. "You and Matt."

It was the first time in all these years that he'd mentioned anything about being Matt's father. Carly reached out to touch his arm. He couldn't take his hand from the steering wheel, for of course his other hand couldn't hold the wheel.

Ben pulled into the same restaurant where she'd had dinner the night before.

"I just want coffee," she said. "I've already eaten."

After he'd ordered breakfast, he asked, "You going to come see me in Washington if I win?"

"You seem pretty sure of yourself."

He cocked his head to the side. "Well, will you? I'll show Matt the Lincoln Memorial and the . . ."

"Of course we'll come visit you. Is there anyplace you'd live where we wouldn't come visit you?"

"Oh, God, Carly." Ben leaned over and reached out his right hand to put over her left one. "Do you know what you mean to me?"

She didn't pursue that. "I keep wondering how you'll make out in a big city? Houston was too big for you."

"I wonder too. You know, I may only last two years and be screaming to get back here."

The waitress brought their coffee and Ben's juice. "This is going to be a long day. You may be bored silly with all the minutiae."

"You may get tired of my tagging around all day. You know, I could go back to your house and stay until dinnertime."

"No," he said, clutching her hand again. "Stay by my side. I've spent thirteen years, or more . . . how long have I known you? . . . dreaming of having you by my side, you know."

"Oh, Ben."

He didn't say any more but began to eat his refried beans and chiliquiles with gusto.

"You don't look like a congressman," Carly said.

He nodded, his mouth full. "I know. I'm going to have to start wearing suits, and I don't even own one. Ah, that's what we can do today, Carly. And that's how sure I am of the outcome. Come choose me a couple of suits."

"Cole has a great tailor. You need to look important."

"No," he said. "I don't. I just have to wear a suit that fits. If I'm elected, Carly, I'm not planning on changing. If you think my job begins to corrupt me, let me know, but I'm going to be on the watch, constantly. If I have to compromise my principles to stay there, I'll come home."

"You know perfectly well you'll have to compromise your principles to stay there."

"If I was sure of that I wouldn't go. You sound too cynical."

"I've lost faith."

"How can you say that? The American Dream came true for you."

Carly thought about that. She nodded. "So, how come it seems hollow?"

Ben studied her. "Is your personal life empty, then?"

"Oh, Ben." Tears formed in her eyes. "I don't know what's wrong with me. I should be happy, shouldn't I?"

The waitress refilled their coffee cups. They sat in silence for a few minutes, and then Ben asked, "What about Cole?"

"What about him?"

"I mean, him and you?"

Carly shook her head. "This is your day. I came down here to lend you support, not to talk about me."

"There's nothing, not a single solitary thing, I'd rather talk about than you."

She shook her head again.

"Well, then," he stood up. "On such a gorgeous day when I couldn't concentrate on work anyhow, let's go take a walk along the beach."

He did win, by over two to one. The results were certain by ten that night.

By the time the celebration party ended, it was after two. Carly was so tired she couldn't see straight.

She followed Ben into his little house, where she'd changed into a dress earlier, and he sprawled out on the couch. "I know, you're pooped."

"Congressman Coleridge."

"Didja hear some newspaper guy refer to me as 'scion of a wealthy Houston banking family.' Do they think that's how I got elected?"

"Don't be touchy. The people love you."

He looked up at her, still standing. She'd kicked off her shoes.

"The people? Are you included?"

"I'd have voted for you. You know that."

"Yes, I do. But do you love me?"

"Of course. You know that. You've always known it."

"I don't mean love me like a brother. I don't mean love me like a friend. I'm both of those to you, I know. I mean, do you love me? I mean love like a man and woman?"

Fear goosefleshed over Carly.

Ben stood up and swept her into his arms. "I mean *love*, Carly. Grand passion. I love you like that. I have always loved you." His hands ran through her hair and he pushed her head back so that he stared down directly into her eyes. "Do you know why I'm not married? Because no other woman is you. Sure, I've been to bed with other women. But I wake up in the morning and have to leave. Or am sorry I invited them here. I open my eyes in the morning and the only woman I want to see beside me is you."

"Oh, Ben, don't . . ."

"Don't? I have years of words built up inside me that have been waiting to be said to you. Do you know what I feel for you? I love you so much, Carly, that sometimes it's painful. Those months we made love? I kept hoping you wouldn't conceive, so we'd go on forever."

"Ben, sh—"

"You know the most wonderful thing of my life? Matt. Living proof of us. Carly, leave Cole. You and Matt come to Washington with me."

His lips were upon hers and she felt herself on fire, melting into his arms, against him. She surrendered herself to his kisses.

"Do you love me, Carly?"

"I do," she breathed, realizing she had for years.

His lips parted hers and she felt his tongue, the warmness of it, its urgency. "Yes, Ben, I guess I've always loved you."

CHAPTER 60

"I drove down to Verity yesterday," Boomer said.

Carly was dancing in his arms at the club Saturday night. She always liked it when Boomer asked her to dance. She didn't have to pretend with him, maybe because they'd known each other forever. But, it wasn't just that. She was comfortable with him, but at the same time she always felt a sense of excitement. He was still one of the most interesting people she knew.

"Any particular reason? I didn't know you still went back there."

"I haven't been there in years, not since my aunt died," he said, smiling down at her. Boomer had the nicest eyes in the world, she thought. Brown. She'd often wondered how different her life might have been had she stayed home that Saturday to await his phone call instead of driving to Verity with Cole. "I was just in a mood. Instead of going into the office I drove down there. Went into the bank and saw Walt. We even had lunch together. At the place where Blue's used to be, but now it's called The Grotto."

Carly smiled.

"I went by the old house. Hadn't seen it in a long time."

There was still the high wrought-iron fencing around it. Even with paint peeling, it still looked imposing, especially now that there were so many little ranch houses—one story, three-tiny-bedroom houses—in town, even though the population was about as steady as it had been over twenty years ago.

He lowered his head to talk in her ear, so no one else could hear. "Remember how we used to make out in my bedroom?"

"I about died when you went off to college."

He pulled her closer. "Maybe I was a fool, Carly. I often wonder if I was."

She shook her head and frowned. "Don't say that, Boomer. You and Alex seem happy . . ."

"We are," he said. "And I'm not trying to make a pass at you. But sometimes I remember how much you and I laughed."

"No one can be everything to anybody else."

"You're pretty wise, aren't you. Why do you let Cole treat you like shit?"

She missed a step, pulled back and looked up at him.

"You don't have to pretend. Everybody knows. Why do you put up with it, Carly? You're too fine for that. He must have rocks in his head."

Carly felt a lump in her chest, a pressure so profound she had trouble breathing.

"God, the color's drained out of your face," Boomer said. "Carly, don't tell me you don't know?"

She broke away from him. "Boomer, I need air," she said and zigzagged across the dance floor, between couples, and out through the wide open doors, onto the terrace. She grabbed the railing and held on for dear life.

Boomer's voice came from behind her. "Carly. Oh, Carly, I . . . we've all thought you put up such a brave front. We've admired you so. Alex has been dying to say something to you. She's wanted to tell you to stand up for yourself. Kick him out or . . ."

Carly turned to face him and stood up straight. "Okay, Boomer, just what the hell are we talking about?"

"I feel like a cad, Carly. I wouldn't hurt you for the world. I really thought you knew . . ."

"I gather the whole town thought I knew. Knew what?"

"He's not even trying to hide it. It's been going on for months."

"Months?" She practically strangled on the word. "Hide what? Some woman?"

"Tiffany Delacourte."

"Who? Oh. The woman at his bank? Oh, Jesus." She put a hand on his arm and took a deep breath. "I must have been blind. I thought by being a wife and letting him be the head of the household, he'd stop . . ."

"They lunch everywhere. They golf together once or twice a week, right here at the club."

Hadn't he been afraid she'd see them, hear about it?

Or didn't he care?

"Boomer, I have to go home. I don't want to go back in there."

Everyone knew. Had known for months. Oh, dear God in heaven. She felt so stupid.

"Just a minute. Let me tell Alex and I'll drive you home."

"No," Carly shook her head. "I want to be alone."

"Great," Boomer said. "I'm with you when your baby's born and when you find out your husband's cheating on you. Carly, what can I do to help? Anything, just anything."

She had left him, though, sailing down the steps of the verandah, walking toward the valet parking lot.

Whether she worked or stayed home to be the perfect wife, she had failed.

She drove home, her foot hard on the accelerator. She'd phone Walt and Francey, go see them.

Maybe she'd leave Cole. Go to Ben. He'd asked, begged, her to. She and Matt. Go to where they really belonged.

The phone was ringing as she entered the house. Who would phone at this hour of the night?

It was Walt. Relief flooded over her as she heard his voice.

"It's your mother," Walt said in a foreboding tone of voice. "I've been trying to get you all night. Carly, she has cancer. Lymphatic cancer."

"I'll leave now," Carly said without a moment's hesitation. "I'll be there by dawn."

"Wait and get a plane."

"No," Carly insisted, fighting back tears. "I'll be there by dawn." Matt would be all right. The maid and the cook and his father could look out for him. His father? That was a laugh.

She began to cry. Her mother had cancer? Francey was dying?

She threw underwear and hardly anything else into an overnight bag. She knew she wasn't thinking clearly. How could she? Hearing your husband was having an affair and that your mother is dying in the same night. Maybe she was in shock.

Suddenly she decided to take Matt. She didn't know how long she'd stay. He could attend school there for a few weeks. Or months.

She didn't even leave a note. Not this time. Cole probably wouldn't even care where she was.

She shook Matt awake and half carried him down to the car. He curled up in the backseat, unaware of what was happening.

Oh, Mom, she thought.

She had never even considered a life without Francey in it.

CHAPTER 61

Carly phoned home in the morning. Carly simply said to Cole that Francey needed her and she intended to stay as long as necessary.

She couldn't stand the look on Walt's face, the pain in his eyes when he gazed at his wife. Once she heard him crying when he was out of Francey's hearing.

Carly enrolled Matt at the school in Verity. He spent Saturdays at the ranch with Zelda Marie and his horse.

Each day Francey seemed to lose strength. When they were alone, she clung to Walt and admitted she was afraid. He was, too, but he held her close and told her she had to get well. He couldn't live without her.

Carly spent afternoons sitting at her mother's bedside while Francey talked to her. "You know what, honey? I began to live when we moved to Verity. I know you've never liked it here, but my life began when I met Walt. Well, that's not true. It began the day I had you. You gave my life meaning. Happiness. Oh, but I wish you and Cole could have the kind of happiness Walt and I've shared."

Carly decided that when this was over, when she was no longer needed here, maybe she wouldn't return to Houston at all. She'd call Ben and tell him, if he still wanted them, she and Matt would come to him. Before they left Houston Ben wrote to Matt not of his frustrations but of the excitement that abounded in Washington. But there had been a letter to Carly in which he'd written of the exasperations. "Government is so goddamned big and the bureaucrats all seem to be inferior. I swear they're people who couldn't get jobs in business. They go by the book and can't make a decision on their own if their life depends on it. They're not interested in people, only in the security of their careers. It's enough to make a Republican of me, to see what a waste government is. Carly, I won't last long here."

He'd been there four months.

She thought of election night when they'd held each other close all night.

He'd begged Carly and Matt to come to Washington with him, even if it would create a scandal. His brother's wife. She wondered if she should phone him and tell him about Cole . . . and about Francey.

But she didn't have to make that decision. At ten o'clock one night, after she'd been in Verity nearly five weeks, Ben phoned her from Washington.

"Mother told me about Francey," he said. "I'm sorry, Carly. She's a wonderful woman. And I know how much you love her."

Carly nodded. "We're hoping. She's being very valiant."

"I have news, Carly."

She waited. Was he going to quit mid-term? Or had he decided to run for the Senate?

"I'm getting married."

When she said nothing, he asked, "Carly?"

She couldn't breathe. Her throat felt swollen and she couldn't swallow. For a fraction of a minute she thought she was going to suffocate, then her breath began to come in ragged gasps. She put her hand over the phone so that Ben wouldn't hear.

He continued. "She's with the EPA."

When Carly still didn't respond, Ben said, "You know, the Environmental Protect—"

"I know what the EPA is," Carly snapped.

"She's a field representative," Ben said. "We met . . ."

Carly didn't hear how they met. She put her head between her knees to still the dizziness that engulfed her.

She wanted to shout into the phone, "Just when I need you."

Ben was going on and on. "I knew you'd be happy for me. Carly, I'll never stop loving you. You've been my great love, you know that. But Meryl and I, it's time for me to start a family. Have someone to talk with nights . . ."

Is that what she and Cole were supposed to have done? Talk with each other nights? Discuss the day's problems? Ask each other important questions? Hold hands and solve their life's dilemmas?

"I need someone to love, Carly. To be loved by. And Meryl's the only other woman aside from you . . . Carly dear, wish me happiness?"

"Of course." She tried not to choke. "Ben, I want nothing for you but happiness."

"I want you to come to my wedding, Carly. I want your support. I want you and Matt and Meryl to meet."

"When are you getting married?" Carly asked.

"A week from Saturday," he said. "Here in Washington."

She bit her lip. "It's impossible, Ben. Not with Mother . . ."

"Carly, you and Matt could fly up Friday and fly back Sunday. Maybe Cole will come, too," but he didn't sound too hopeful about that. "I haven't told my parents yet. I wanted you to be the first to know. But I'm sure they'll come. Please be there, Carly.''

"I'll see," she said. "Let me see what I can do."

Go to Ben's wedding? Just when she'd thought of her own marriage to him?

She talked it over with Walt.

She didn't want to go to Washington, didn't want to see Ben marry another woman.

She fought down the temptation to call him and say, "Ben, I'm leaving Cole."

Would he toss this Meryl aside for her? She was his great love, he'd said. Matt was his son. Wouldn't he be happier with them than settling for his second choice? That's what he implied Meryl was.

But she didn't. She couldn't force herself to.

"You'll only be gone a weekend, Carly," Walt said. "Of course you and Matt must go to Ben's wedding. The boy's always adored his uncle. Of course, go."

So, she called her in-laws and arranged to fly to Washington with them. They'd meet at the Houston airport and fly north from there.

In the plane, Matt sat by the window and reported on the constant change of scenery. "Does this mean Uncle Ben won't take me fishing?" he asked.

Carly, her eyes closed, answered, "Just because he's getting married doesn't mean he's going to stop loving you."

"What about you? Will it mean he doesn't love you any longer?"

Carly's eyes fluttered open. Her breath stopped again. Her throat was so dry she couldn't swallow. Finally, in a voice she didn't recognize, she said, "I hope not."

Meryl was young, eight or nine years younger than Ben. She wasn't even pretty, Carly thought. She had straight brown hair and she wore glasses, but she laughed a lot, though Carly got the sense that she was a very serious young woman. When she and Ben met them at Dulles, the young woman was wearing jeans and a T-shirt that said, "Save the whales" splattered across her chest. Carly couldn't quite call it a bosom. She shook hands with Matt, and before long she had an arm around him, and she was gracious and unself-conscious with the Coleridges. Carly could tell that Mrs. Coleridge had to force herself to be cordial to a girl who met them at the plane in a T-shirt.

Meryl made no attempt to kiss her future in-laws, but her manner was warm. She was on her own turf and welcomed them as guests. After a flurry of introductions she turned to Carly and appraised her openly. "I've heard more about you than anyone else. I'm awfully glad you could come. I've been looking forward to meeting you. I'm sorry your mother is ill."

Carly found herself responding positively to this young woman who seemed so sure of herself, and who gazed at Ben with such obvious love.

The Coleridges thawed when they discovered her father was the president of Delta Pictures, which had produced three Academy-Award nominated movies that year. She wasn't a Hollywood type at all, but then they discovered she'd been brought up in Nyack, New York, by her mother, who had divorced her father twenty-one years ago. She'd graduated from Cornell. Maybe, Carly thought, that's what gave her that self-confidence. Ivy League type. Money.

Maude Coleridge thawed towards her by the time they finished dinner. No, no wedding rehearsal, they'd taken care of that in the afternoon. No bachelor party, either. Meryl's mother and brothers would arrive from New York in the morning. She didn't know whether or not her father was coming in, but she hoped so. She wished he'd give her away. They weren't being married in a church, but at the home of Senator Everton, who seemed to have adopted Ben. He lived in Georgetown, in a mansion that had been in his wife's family for generations, and had offered the garden for the reception.

* * *

Matt fell asleep by ten, but Carly walked around the hotel room, gazing out the window at the Washington monument, trying to analyze what she felt. She thought her insides had stopped functioning when she saw Ben kiss Meryl, but with the look in his eyes that he had given *her* at times—the look that said they shared a secret.

Was she letting him make a terrible mistake by not speaking up? By not saying, "I'm going to leave your brother" before it was too late for them?

It was after eleven when she picked up the phone and dialed his apartment. Meryl answered. Of course. They'd probably been living together. Did Carly think they were spending their last night apart? Meryl had probably moved in weeks ago. Carly hung up the phone.

She got in the twin bed across from Matt, who lay breathing regularly, and turned off the light. She lay with her hands clasped across her chest, listening to her ragged breathing, to her irregular heartbeat.

Oh, Ben, she thought. Bennett Willard Coleridge. We came close. We came really close.

CHAPTER 62

"Boomer," Dan's voice was hesitant.

Boomer looked up from his desk to see Dan and Tessa standing in his doorway. Tessa looked stunning, as usual. She wore a white silk suit with a red-and-white polka-dotted ruffled blouse. Her only jewelry was her pearl earrings and the immense diamond ring on her left hand. Dan had given it to her for their tenth anniversary over five years ago, since they'd never had time to be engaged. They had thrown an enormous anniversary party and taken their vows again. They still looked at each other as though they were newly in love, though they often had really hot arguments. Never about anything personal, but disagreements about how a project should be approached. Dan always looked at the money angle, and Tessa shot for the moon.

The spats never lasted long. Even in the office they usually went their separate ways, engaged in unrelated projects. Boomer often thought how fortunate he was to have such a fine business partnership. He and Dan had never had an argument. Even when they started with different viewpoints they'd always managed to talk matters over, compromise a bit here, search for a new idea there. Boomer wished his marriage were as harmonious. Lately that had seemed off kilter, and he couldn't quite put his finger on it.

Boomer smiled at his friends and partners. "You guys look like the cat that swallowed the canary. What's up?"

"Got a few minutes?" Tessa asked.

They took seats in the comfortable leather chairs on the opposite side of the desk from Boomer. Tessa, of course, had decorated the office and she kept comfort in mind as well as looks.

Boomer leaned forward and clasped his hands on the desktop. He waited while they looked at each other. Finally Dan said, "You know that being partners with you has been the greatest experience possible."

Boomer couldn't tell whether it was a cake of ice or a ton of lead that suddenly sat in the middle of his stomach.

"It has been for me, too."

"Yes," Tessa said, smiling at him, "we know that."

There was a moment's silence until Boomer said, "What is it you're trying to tell me?" He had a feeling he didn't want to hear.

"We want out," Dan blurted.

"Out?" Boomer's voice cracked.

Tessa leaned forward and put a hand on the desk. "Boomer, we love you. But we want to smell the daisies."

"For fifteen years," Dan took over, "we've worked our

tails off. So've you. We have more money than Tessa and I can spend in a lifetime.''

''We want to travel. See the world. Live in France for a while, then maybe the Greek Islands, maybe Majorca, see India and Australia and Spain. The fjords . . .''

Boomer waved his hand in the air. ''I get the idea. Can't you do that and work here, too?''

Tessa shook her head. ''No, we want to cut loose. We don't want to work at all anymore.''

''We're going to sell our house,'' Dan interrupted. ''Sell everything we own and just take a few suitcases each and go where the wind blows us.''

Boomer stared at them. ''You can't be serious.''

''Yes,'' Tessa said, her voice low. ''We are, Boomer. We know you'll think we're letting you down, but we just feel there's so much else to life than work. We've made our marks. We're rich. Filthy rich. And we want to see how the rest of the world lives.'' She stopped when Boomer waved his hand again.

''Buy us out for a million,'' Dan said.

Boomer frowned. ''It's worth much more than that and I know you know it.''

Both Tessa and Dan nodded. ''We do know it,'' Tessa said. ''But we don't need more. We don't even need that, but we know you wouldn't consider it any other way.''

''I'd be taking advantage of you to buy it for that.''

''No, no you wouldn't.'' Tessa was doing most of the talking. ''Boomer, darling, we don't need more.''

''You'll get more than that for your house.''

Tessa nodded.

''Christ, guys, I can't go on without you.'' BB&O without Tessa and Dan? Work without them, his supports? Life without them?

''No.'' He shook his head.

''No what?'' Dan asked. ''No, you won't buy us out?''

''No, I won't let you go.''

Tessa stood up and walked around the desk and leaned down

to put her arms around Boomer's neck. She kissed the top of his head. "Boomer, there's never been a better friend in all the world. But we have to do what we've been talking about for the last three years. We're beginning to feel imprisoned."

"It started," Dan said, "when we went to London six years ago. And then when we went to Turkey, and every year . . ."

"Yeah." Every year they'd taken a six-week trip.

"And we saw how little we knew of the world. Tessa's forty-five and I'm forty-two and we want to spend the next twenty years exploring this planet. Stay where we want to stay until we get tired of it and want to move on. We want to be free."

"I can't imagine you two living out of suitcases. Living like flower children."

Dan laughed. "I wouldn't go that far. We're too accustomed to our comforts. Boomer, we've been talking about this for a few years and now the time has come."

"BB&O won't be the same without you." Boomer told himself it wasn't acceptable for grown men to cry.

"There are a ton of good architects around," Dan said. "Some of them even on our staff."

"Not with your vision."

Tessa kissed his cheek. "We want to take off in three months." When Boomer didn't respond, she added, "How about dinner tonight?"

"Yeah, sure," Boomer said.

When he was alone he stood up and walked over to the window, staring down at his city. He wondered why his body ached so. Though the sun shone brightly at eleven in the morning, all Boomer saw was the glare. He felt a terrible headache coming on.

Exactly three months later Tessa and Dan flew off with a total of nine suitcases, to Paris, heading for Provence. Boomer couldn't believe he wouldn't see them again for years.

When he looked back, he realized that something more

was amiss. Something in Alex's reaction to the news. "Oh, Boomer," she had cried, looking up at him from across the desk in her study. "What will you do? They've made BB&O."

He bristled. "I wouldn't exactly say that."

"I don't mean you're not a good builder. Of course you are. Your reputation is international. But what's gotten you such business is Dan's designs."

Boomer had had these same thoughts, but somehow Alex's reaction jarred him.

A month before Dan and Tessa took off, Boomer said to Alex, "You know, maybe they're right. It's time to cut back."

"What does that mean?"

He looked at her, surprised at the sharpness in her voice.

"We have more money than we'll ever need. The kids'll be taken care of forever. Why work this hard?"

She stared at him. "Have you taken leave of your senses? What do you think you've worked this hard *for?*"

"Maybe so I can enjoy some of the fruits of my labor, not that I haven't enjoyed the journey. Perhaps we can sell off a lot of the company. Just do local jobs. I'm forty—"

"You don't have to remind me of age!" Alex peered in the mirror of her dressing table. After all, she was a year older than her husband.

He leaned down to kiss her shoulder, studying their reflection. "Let's *do* things while the kids are still around. Let's take trips, camp . . ."

"Oh, gawd," Alex groaned. She'd heard him talk of camping forever. "The children are going to be around a while yet. Boomer," she turned pleading eyes to him, "I want a husband I can be proud of."

He stood up straight. "You mean unless I'm earning millions you can't be proud of me? You mean you'd be the wife of a *nobody . . .?*"

"That's about it. And Alexandra Headland is not about to be a nobody."

He did not remind her that Bannerman had been her name for over fifteen years.

Alex began brushing her hair. "Don't act so silly. You know I'm proud of you. When we met you didn't have anything . . ."

"I had me," he murmured.

She ignored that. "Now, even my parents are proud of you."

"You told me you'd have married me even if they'd disapproved."

"Sure, because I saw the potential in you. I knew how far you'd rise." Boomer turned on his heel and strode out of the room, slamming the door behind him.

She sighed. Damn Tessa and Dan.

Maybe, Boomer thought, there had been a nagging awareness that day he'd given Alex the lake as an anniversary present and she'd insisted on developing it instead of making it their hideaway. Now the lake was surrounded with second homes, themselves encircled with acreage on which the owners kept horses or motor bikes which zoomed through the woods on a Sunday afternoon, along with the power boats that dotted the lake. The little bait-and-grocery store had become a mini supermarket, and Alex had talked Leonard, who owned Houston's La Brasserie, into opening a small chic restaurant up here, giving him an acre of the land and having BB&O build a Swiss chalet-type building for him.

The home Dan had designed for them was as luxurious as the one in town. Boomer was surprised Alex was still content to live in their first house. They came up to the lake every weekend in the summer, when the social life of Houston stagnated.

To his surprise, Boomer hated those weekends. He'd sit on the wide veranda that overlooked the lake, and listen to the noise. Motor boats, motor bikes, one couldn't even hear the birds. The kids, of course, loved it. And he did relish hearing the shouts of the children enjoying themselves. They all knew how to drive the boat, and they became like fish themselves, jumping off the pier.

Boomer bought a tent and set it up in the woods, and David and his brother, Rick, slept nights out there, though Diane wasn't the least bit interested in roughing it. She was like her mother.

Alex's idea of a satisfying weekend was inviting several other couples and their children, if necessary, and having Leonard cater a small elegant supper Saturday night, a long lazy Sunday morning with the newspapers and waffles that Boomer always prepared, sipping orange blossoms or just plain champagne and a seemingly endless carafe of flavored coffee—sometimes hazelnut, other times French roast or amaretto. Never just plain coffee.

Then about two, they'd dress casually, and drive to Leonard's and dine until after four. After that, the two-hour drive home, with the kids either arguing or falling asleep in the back of the station wagon. The vehicle was used only for family outings, not driven at all during the week unless it was to chauffeur the kids to games or some school event.

Diane, at eleven, fell in love for the first time up at the lake, with a boy three years older whose father was the president of a fleet of cargo planes that flew around the world. That pleased Alex. She thought her daughter had started off with good taste.

Neither Dan and Tessa nor Cole and Carly could be talked into building a home up here. Cole preferred his lodge in Colorado or his boat in the gulf off Sarasota. Carly seemed to prefer Verity. Or at least seeing her mother and stepfather and Zelda Marie. She'd been down there consistently since that night Boomer had told her about Cole.

He could kick himself for that. She had looked so vulnerable, so pained when he'd blurted it out. Despite all her success, she'd never lost her náiveté.

Alex had told him she thought Carly had sold her business for the sake of her marriage, so that Cole wouldn't feel in competition. Boomer couldn't understand that. He didn't feel in the least threatened by Alex's success. She was successful before he was. And if she'd decided to quit, or at least take it easier, he wouldn't feel . . . well, he couldn't understand how Alex did feel. She seemed to feel threatened by his desire to slow down.

He thought maybe he could arrange it so she wouldn't have to know. He could just stop accepting contracts from foreign countries, from St. Louis, Phoenix. He was so sick of Scottsdale and Tucson. Outsiders might think Texas wasn't the greenest of states, but here, around Houston, it certainly didn't look like death the way the desert in Arizona did. People told him the desert was bursting with life, life he couldn't see. There was nothing interesting about the desert to him. Always brown and lifeless.

As long as he kept up a high profile in Texas, Alex could still be proud of him. He'd let go of the other things gradually . . .

And then the bottom went out of the oil boom.

CHAPTER 63

Walt woke with a start. Francey was not next to him in bed. He glanced at the luminous hands of the clock. One-fifteen. He sat up and kicked off the covers, jerking his feet into his slippers. The first place he looked was the bathroom. No light. What was wrong? Where was she?

He padded down the carpeted hall, flicking the lights on in the living room. No Francey. He walked on through the kitchen, where the sliding-glass door was open. Then he saw her silhouetted, sitting on the chaise on the deck, staring up at the silvery moon that shone brightly on her head.

"Honey?" he asked, his voice a whisper.

"I'm out here." Her voice was tranquil.

He quickly went to stand beside her. "Are you all right?"

He could see the nod of her head. "I'm not going to die, Walt."

He pulled a chair across the wooden slats and sat down next to her, reaching for her hand. They had been discussing this since they'd learned of Francey's illness. "You going to take the chemotherapy?"

"Yes," she answered, still staring at the moon. "I'm going to lose my hair and feel sick. I'm going to do whatever is necessary, because I'm not going to die." She laughed. "I'm not ready."

The Houston Medical Center had confirmed the Corpus Christi doctor's diagnosis. Six months, outside, and two of those had already passed.

Last week they'd flown to California, to Stanford, the top cancer clinic in the country. They'd reiterated what she already heard.

But suddenly he felt hope. "I've thought a lot about it convincing myself my mind *can* triumph," she said. "I've been out here talking to myself, telling my white blood cells to behave."

He squeezed her hand.

She turned to face him. "You know I love you, darling, but go back in. Let me be out here by myself, to concentrate."

He kissed her cheek and stood up, walking back into the house, turning in the doorway to look back at her. Only the top of her head was visible. Concentrate, he said silently. Concentrate so hard that whatever has to die within you in order for you to live will do so.

The next morning, for the first time in over two months, Francey ate a hearty breakfast. Almost as much as Matt did.

Carly looked at her mother with surprise. "I'm so happy to see you could eat so much."

Francey nodded. "I'm not going to die," she said. "I'm not ready to leave Walt. And now that you and Matt are here, I'm certainly not about to leave."

* * *

After the second world war, when the United States reached the apex of its power, the U.S. dollar became the main reserve currency in the international monetary exchange. Banks all over the world used dollars as reserve assets the way they had ordinarily used gold. The international monetary system, in fact, was based on the strength of the dollar and the readiness of the United States government to exchange dollars for gold at the rate of thirty-five dollars an ounce.

By the time of the Nixon administration, the situation had changed. The U.S. was no longer the only strong economic power; in fact, the dollar was beginning to suffer. The size of the U.S. deficit, the financial policies of other countries, and the lack of confidence of foreigners in the U.S. economy strongly affected the value of the dollar.

In 1971 President Nixon, with the assent of the Congress, took the United States off the gold standard. It would no longer buy gold for dollars.

The Arab countries, which supplied most of the world's oil, were hurt by this move. For a while they removed their oil from the international market. When they subsequently formed OPEC, they emptied into the world market a glut of oil at cheaper prices than the U.S. could produce it. And even though the U.S. had invested fortunes in the Alaska pipeline, oil had been discovered in the North Sea and in Russia. All of it sold more cheaply than it could now be produced in Texas, or in Wyoming, or anyplace else in the United States.

Oil drilling ground to a halt. Producing oil wells were capped. Offshoot businesses in the petrochemical world came to a standstill.

Convinced that the supply of oil was endless and convinced the price of oil would only go up up up, the banks of Texas had the majority of their portfolios in oil. They went belly up.

Before this, anyone who had a hint of an oil strike, who had a new gimmick that was based on oil or natural gas could easily acquire loans from almost any bank in the Lone Star state.

Now, with the oil business at rock bottom, the borrowers could not repay the billions of dollars in loans the banks had lent them. People could not buy the apartments and houses and condos that companies like BB&O were building for them. BB&O and every other construction company had to leave their buildings standing, unfinished. Businesses that had been thriving suddenly declared bankruptcy, leaving the banks holding empty bags—loans for which the borrowers had no money to repay them.

"Shit," Boomer's banker told him. "Don't blame us. Nobody saw the price of crude bottoming out overnight."

In a two-year period, over ninety-five percent of the banks in Texas changed hands.

The two office buildings that BB&O were erecting remained but shells. The companies who had commissioned them declared bankruptcy. BB&O was engaged in a four-hundred-apartment complex, stretched out three-quarters of a mile along a new highway north of Houston. Construction had to be stopped. The companies who had supplied the materials were broke. The people who would have lived in these apartments lost their jobs. They left Texas in droves, hoping to find jobs in other parts of the country.

Boomer was losing over twenty thousand dollars a day. "Christ," he told Alex, "by the end of the year we'll be broke."

"No," Alex said. "*You'll* be."

"What does that mean?"

"I mean I diversified. In my business my investments in oil were only twenty-two percent. I haven't put all my investments in Texas, either."

Boomer breathed a little easier. "Thank God you're that smart," he said. "Too bad the bankers of Texas didn't have your foresight."

She looked at him strangely. "Boomer, you have to figure a way out of this. You can't let millions of dollars dribble away."

Boomer stared at her. Did she think he wanted this? He had a four-million-dollar loan on property that now was suddenly worth less than two million. BB&O had contracted for thirteen of the homes being built up at the lake, and now every single one of the buyers had pulled out.

"Got any brilliant ideas?" he asked.

"Not at the moment," she answered. "Though, I should warn you, I'm not about to be made a public laughing-stock."

Boomer cocked his head and raised an eyebrow. "You sound as though I'm purposely doing this. It's all of Texas, you know."

"There are still scads of people with millions, *billions*, of dollars."

Boomer wasn't quite sure just what she was saying. He wasn't even sure what this conversation was about.

"I'd thought this would be a fine time to sell this house and buy one in River Oaks, near my parents," Alex went on. "The Kincaids' house is going to be for sale. We can't get one-third of what our house is worth on the current real estate market, but we can pick up the Kincaids' for a song."

"I thought you'd been happy here for the last fifteen years."

"I have. But there'll never be another time to get the Kincaid house for what they're having to sell it for."

"I see this as a time to tighten our belts."

"I have money." Alex reached out to touch his arm. "I know you're not going to be content to live on your wife's earnings, and you'll figure a way out of this."

When Boomer didn't answer, she pressed his arm and said, "You will, won't you?"

Boomer had no desire to make love that night but he needed to test out a theory he had. He reached out for Alex in the dark. She pushed his hand away.

He was correct: Unless he was earning the millions he had since she'd met him, his wife wanted nothing to do with him.

He lay there, long after he knew Alex had fallen asleep, wondering if the life he'd been living had value if it was all based on how much money he earned.

* * *

There was talk of shenanigans at Destin Savings and Loan. Boomer wondered how Carly felt about that.

He phoned her at her parents' in Verity and told her he was going to drive down. Could she have dinner with him? He needed to talk with someone and he had the feeling Carly would understand. It would be a chance to talk with Walt, too. He valued Walt's advice.

It had been too long since he'd seen Carly. She'd been down in Verity for over two months.

Carly said she'd love to see him, and he'd better plan to stay overnight. They had guest rooms to spare, she told him. His visit would surely brighten up Francey, who seemed to be improving right before their eyes.

"I'll be there about five or six," he said. He liked the idea of the long drive through the wide-open spaces of the gulf country.

He wondered why he wasn't more panicked about the turn his life had suddenly taken. If he wanted anything left at all he'd have to pull out pretty completely. And start all over again.

He was just forty, after all, he told himself.

CHAPTER 64

Carly turned to Walt. "Want some iced tea?" she asked.

"Sure," he called back from the patio. They sat out there together every evening after Matt and Francey had gone to sleep. They could relax for the first time all day. Carly loved these evenings.

She and Walt talked of nothing and everything.

She brought two tall cold glasses from the kitchen and, handing him one, sat in the lounge next to him.

"That was Boomer," she said. "He's driving down to-morrow."

When Carly said no more, they sat in comfortable silence until, without even realizing, she said it aloud. "What kind of marriage is it if Cole and I each find satisfaction in other people's beds?"

Walt's head jerked to look at her, his eyebrows raised. "Are you telling me what I think you're telling me? You're *each* finding satisfaction in other people's beds?"

Carly felt tears gathering behind her eyes. "Cole's having an affair. Everyone in Houston knows about it." A tear streamed down her cheek. "And oh, Walt . . ."

She told him everything. About Ben fathering her son, about the way she felt about him the night after he'd won the election, about how she'd been ready to go to him . . . and then he announced he was getting married.

"You in love with him?"

Carly shrugged, clutching Walt's hand tightly. "He's one of the most important people in my world." Realizing that wasn't an answer, she went on. "I've been attracted to him since the minute I met him. Even on my wedding day, it flitted through my mind that I was marrying the wrong Coleridge."

Walt sucked in air and shook his head. "Oh, honey . . ."

"I talked myself into being in love with Cole. That weekend we came down here and he proposed . . . I think if he'd done it up in Houston that day, I'd have had the courage to say no."

Walt studied her. "Why?"

More tears slid down Carly's cheek and Walt handed her his handkerchief.

She sniffled. "Oh, Walt, you'll stop loving me. You'll think I've been so . . . so indiscriminate."

He didn't say anything for a minute. Then he lit one of the cigars that he knew Carly hated. He thought he needed one.

"Go on," he said.

"I'd run into Boomer again, after five years . . . and, oh, we made love. I knew then that Cole wasn't right for me. Boomer was my great love. I'd just told Cole about Joe Bob and I thought I wouldn't see him ever again. And I happened to run into Boomer that Friday night and, well . . .

"Boomer had just left Saturday morning when Cole phoned and said he wanted to meet you and Mom and somehow things got out of hand, and we drove down here and he proposed, and you all seemed to like him, and I thought of all that money and prestige. I knew Houston would have to accept me, which Verity had never done, and . . ." She began to cry again. "It took me a long time to realize it doesn't matter who accepts me or not." She was tempted to tell him about her clinic work. "It's what I accept that matters."

Walt made no move to comfort her but chewed on his cigar and stared up at the stars.

"I don't know to this day if Boomer tried to get in touch with me that weekend. Right after my engagement to Cole was announced I saw in the paper that he was going to marry Alex Headland. And, funny thing, we've all gotten to be friends. Alex and I've done some great business deals together. We understand each other. I like her a lot. Though still, sometimes when I'm alone with Boomer I really feel something, but . . . he's too much a gentleman to make a pass. He's become a good friend. We've never even talked of that time."

Her voice faded away.

"So, what about Ben? Your feelings for him?"

"I think I fell in love with him when we were trying to conceive Matt. I knew what I was doing was wrong. We rationalized we were doing his parents and Cole a favor, making a Coleridge grandchild, but I think, really, Ben and I did it for ourselves. I felt cared about when I was with Ben. I could tell him anything.

"He changed me. Sometimes he'd help my marriage, sometimes he'd make fun of my wanting to earn so much money, of caring so much what people thought of me. He accused me of being selfish and not sharing my money with those who really needed it." She paused, staring into the darkness. "But you know what, Walt?"

She decided to finally tell someone about the clinics. Walt

would understand. She told him about the clinics and how she had invested money that not even Cole knew about and gave the clinics the interest her money earned each year. She told him how she had even given her time for so long. "If it weren't for Ben, I probably would never have done any of that.

"He doesn't know about that. I've never told anyone. Until you. Ben got me interested in the Chicano problems, gave me a whole different perspective."

Walt stubbed out his cigar and sat down again next to Carly, putting his arm around her.

"Walt, do you hate me? Because I've been immoral?"

He sighed. "That's your word, honey. Not mine. Seems to me you've hurt mainly yourself. Not others."

There was silence.

Then Walt asked, "Why haven't you told Cole?"

"I thought of telling him, more than once . . ."

"I'm glad you didn't." Walt put a hand over hers. "It always seems to me that confessing helps the confessor and hurts the other one. Confess to me, but not to Cole."

Walt kissed her cheek. "For whatever it's worth, I don't consider you immoral. Carly, I love you more than anyone in the world next to your mother. Nothing can change that."

"I've killed a man. I've conceived a child with another man, I've slept with Boomer . . ."

"Adultery is not the worst sin."

"I want to leave Cole because he's having yet *another* affair. After he said he'd stop."

"No," Walt said. "Your marriage hasn't been good for a long time. If you leave Cole it's because it's time to."

Carly sighed. "I'm going to be forty next month, and I feel like my life's over."

Walt smiled. "I hadn't even met your mother, or you, when I was forty. The wonder of my life hadn't even started."

Cole was furious at Carly for remaining in Verity so long. Shit, she didn't have to stay down there for two months without even coming home for a weekend. What were people beginning to think? His mother was asking. What the hell was he supposed to do? He had clients to entertain and no wife as hostess.

How did it look her staying down there for so long? Pulling Matt out of school, enrolling him in that third-rate—hell, fifth-rate—school when he needed the quality of education only St. John's could give him.

He'd be damned if he'd go chasing her down there. Every now and then, when he lay in bed alone at night, he wondered if she'd heard about him and Tiffany. Wouldn't she have confronted him? Yelled? But she'd never mentioned it.

His mother nagged him about Matt. "Certainly he can fly up for a weekend visit. Then, just keep him here and put him back in St. John's." But what would he *do* with the kid?

He did try to remember to phone Carly Sunday evenings, acting solicitous about Francey, always ending his phone call saying, "I miss you."

It never elicited a response from Carly. In fact, in all their phone conversations Carly's voice and conversation were flat. She asked no questions and answered his in monosyllables.

Along with his anger at Carly's absence was relief. At least he wasn't faced daily with her damned judgments. After two treks to Elk Creek and three visits aboard the *Enchantress* she'd refused to participate in weekends she referred to as "just short of drunken orgies."

She wasn't impressed in the least that some of the company were congressmen, not just from Texas but all over the United States, and even a couple of times senators came along. He called them by their first names, to boot.

They even turned to him for loans, or for loans for constituents in their own states. For millions of dollars, too.

Carly didn't even act proud when this led to his being invited to sit on the boards of corporations as far away as California and Connecticut. When he'd tell her, she simply gazed at him with raised eyebrows and question marks in her eyes.

The high rollers and influential politicians who called Cole by his first name justified, in his mind, having bought that yacht. Carly might think it ostentatious but Tiffany loved it.

The *Enchantress*'s lustrous white hull, a hundred twenty feet long, dripped with the plushness of the 1920's, when it had been built. There were two levels of lacquered teak cabins, and promenade decks were enclosed by burnished brass handrails. The main salon was as impressive as his mother's River Oaks living room. The staterooms were comparable favorably to suites in five-star hotels.

Cole had paid, or rather Destin Savings and Loan had paid, a million four for it. By the time he had refurbished it and made it a floating vacation paradise, it had cost two and a half million.

A bargain, Cole and Tiffany told each other.

He was aware that federal regulators might find it puzzling why a landlocked Texas thrift found it necessary to purchase a yacht. So, with his executives and a few of his wealthiest customers, he formed a partnership called "The Enchantress Limited Partnership." So that the "partners" would not have to invest their own dollars, by overfunding a shopping center in Lubbock by twelve million dollars, Destin was able to route one and a half million to each of the eight partners so they could purchase shares in the limited partnership.

Destin S&L was able to afford a permanent crew of four, and hired others on a temporary basis. From November through April, the yacht docked in Sarasota and most weekends cruised the Gulf of Mexico with a seemingly never-ending party.

In May, Cole sailed north to Washington and left the yacht there until late October, where it was at the beck and call of lobbyists and congressmen who did not even pay the liquor bills for the parties they threw as the *Enchantress* floated up and down the Potomac. With Tiffany acting as official hostess in her position as a senior Vice President of Destin S & L, Cole was present for at least one weekend a month, whether in the Gulf of Mexico or the Potomac River.

Moving easily and gracefully through these hosts of power brokers, Cole seemed to acquire a sense of humor. At least he smiled more often than usual and began to be known for his wit.

Carly would not have recognized him.

CHAPTER 65

Carly peeled apples. She was going to bake a pie, Francey's famous recipe. Boomer loved apple pie. At least he had when he used to dine at their little house over on Gardener Street back in those days when she had been so in love with him, a kajillion years ago.

Talking with Walt had been good last night. Somehow she felt freer than she'd felt in a long time.

She decided it was time to face her situation with Cole. Even though she'd run away from him, she hadn't let herself think of their marriage. She just wanted to stay in Verity with Walt and with Francey. She hadn't even wanted to think about her marriage until now.

Maybe this thing with that woman in his office was partly her fault. She hadn't gone on those awful weekend trips with Cole, trips she felt she couldn't bear. Maybe, if she were a good wife, she would have gone and smiled and kept her mouth shut. That *was* a wife's role in life, wasn't it?

But Carly wasn't willing to be the kind of wife women were expected to be. She'd never known a role model who stayed home and baked cookies and had nothing in her life but her husband and children. Carly had inherited that will to work from Francey.

Ever since she'd sold Rolf's she hadn't felt useful, except for her involvement with the clinics.

These last two months in Verity at least she'd felt useful, had taken over the running of the house. Soon Francey would want to be running her own home again, if she continued to improve the way she had lately. Ever since she'd decided not to die. She wore a wig now that she'd lost so much hair, and every Thursday after her chemotherapy treatments she was tired, but seemed so much better, stronger.

They'd had the same cleaning woman who had kept house for Walt when his first wife was alive, so all Carly really did was the shopping and cooking. She found herself enjoying it, after so many years of having a cook. She bought a juicer and juiced carrots and celery and beets and whatever else all the cancer-diet books suggested and gave Francey glass after glass. She began to drink the juice, too, though she couldn't say she loved it. She pored over recipe books she found in Corpus and began to change the entire way the family ate. Even Matt didn't realize how much less meat they were eating. She fixed him soyburgers and used soy granules in lasagna and spaghetti, and her son and stepfather didn't even realize it wasn't hamburger. She started cooking a lot of Indian and Mediterranean food.

Everyone raved about it.

She wondered suddenly what had made Boomer decide to drive down to Verity. He had said he'd be coming alone.

As she thought of Boomer, Carly realized she missed Alex, too. There were no women in Verity with whom she had much in common. Except Zelda Marie. And in truth she didn't have much in common with her, though a gossamer thread of shared history tied them together.

In fact, now that she thought about it, Carly realized the only people she really missed were Boomer and Alex. There were more people she cared about in Verity than in Houston. She laughed. That was a switch.

Now that summer vacation was here, Matt spent most of his days out at the ranch despite the fact that Walt had built a barn and riding ring for him. As often as not, Zelda Marie phoned to ask if he could stay overnight. Carly always said yes. Since playing with her kids he was tanned and full of something that seemed new to him. Joy. He bubbled about everything.

Just as Carly stuck the pie in the oven, Zelda Marie phoned. "Couldn't you pull something out of the freezer for Walt and

Francey and come on out here for dinner? You could even stay overnight, too. God knows we've got enough room.''

"Can't," Carly said. "Having company for dinner."

"I do think in two months you've gotten to know more people than I do," Zelda Marie laughed.

Carly had to admit she'd certainly met a goodly portion of the town. There had been a steady stream of people, lugging cakes and salads and casseroles and flowers picked from their gardens, and magazines and even a gray-and-white kitten for Francey. If Francey had ever felt rejected by Verity, that time had long passed.

"It's Boomer," Carly told Zelda Marie.

Zelda Marie had had to drop out of school before Boomer and Carly started dating. She hadn't seen Boomer since she'd quit high school, twenty-three years before.

"What's he coming here for?" she asked.

Carly shrugged her shoulders. "I've no idea. I do know his business has gone to hell in a handbasket. I think the whole state is going broke."

"They've capped my oil well," Zelda Marie said, though it didn't seem to disturb her.

"I invited him to stay here overnight. Walt and Francey will enjoy seeing him."

"Bring him out tomorrow," Zelda Marie offered. "I wonder if I'll even recognize him. Well, I take for granted it's okay if Matt stays overnight."

"He's been there all week."

"So? What's one more night? I hardly know he's here. They're all out in the pool now and I hear them shoutin' and havin' a ball."

Zelda Marie didn't do a thing around the house anymore. Three of her children were grown by now, and the two who were still at home were older than Matt, but that didn't seem to bother anyone at all. Ao's two youngest were Matt's age, and her children played with Zelda Marie's as though they were siblings.

They did homework together, and they rode the school bus

together, and they attended movies together, and Zelda Marie saw to it that they received nearly as many Christmas presents as her own children did.

Boomer arrived in the middle of the afternoon. It was hot and humid. Carly thanked heaven for central air-conditioning.

Boomer told her she was a sight for sore eyes and caught her in a bear hug and then went inside to see Francey, hugging her, too. He told her she looked just like she had when he'd known her twenty years ago.

Francey said she was going to take a short nap and that Walt would be home at five fifteen.

Boomer followed Carly out to the kitchen and gratefully accepted the lemonade she'd made earlier. "Before we settle in, come drive by the old house with me. I've been thinking about it a lot lately."

"I thought you just saw it a couple of months ago."

He nodded. "I did. And it seems to me it looked real run down, but I want to see how bad."

"It needs paint," Carly said. And probably a lot else.

"Come on." He reached out for her hand. "Humor me."

They drove into town and down Main Street. "Hasn't changed much in all the years we've been away."

"Population's about the same," Carly said. "But I figure there must be a lot of different people, because I sort of like it now."

Boomer cocked his head. "You aren't trying to tell me you're going to stay here?"

Carly smiled. "It's like old times driving through these streets with you."

He reached out and squeezed her hand. "Life's been pretty good to us, hasn't it?"

"Well, I've always thought we had something to do with that."

He turned down the street where the Bannerman house stood, towering above the other houses. The tall trees shaded the street, and the lawns were green. Boomer slowed down in front of the gabled house and cut the motor, staring at it.

"Who owns it now?" It did look run down.

"I don't know," Carly said. A tricycle rusted in the overgrown grass. A wooden slat was broken on the porch railing.

"Looks depressing, doesn't it," Boomer said. "Funny, I dreamed about it the other night, and it was white and neat like when I grew up there. And Aunt Addie's," he nodded at the smaller house next door, which was still very trim and still yellow, freshly painted while the Bannermans' had peeling paint.

He keyed the motor and the engine purred. "Okay, I've seen enough."

The house was cool when they returned and Carly sank gratefully into a chair in the green-and-white living room.

"This is a lovely spot," Boomer said.

"I'm comfortable here," Carly said. "Matt loves it. I'm not going back to Houston—"

"Who are you kidding?" Boomer interrupted. "You could come back for a few days a week with your mother improving. Whether you've admitted it to yourself or not, you don't want to come back."

"I hope this isn't what you came to talk about."

Boomer shook his head and sat down in the high-backed chair across from her. "I'm not sure why I came. I guess I just had to get out of town."

They looked at each other.

"I've heard . . . I mean, I've read in the papers . . ."

"It's a mess, Carly. The whole goddamned state's in chaos. The bottom's fallen out of the real estate market, people are leaving the state in droves, I owe about fourteen million . . ."

"How much do you have?" Carly asked.

"It'll leave me with several hundred thousand."

"That doesn't sound too bad." She smiled, knowing that with the Texans they knew, that amount was next to nothing.

"A far cry from the millions I've had. I'd like to hear what Walt thinks. I'd like to . . . I don't know, Carly. It just seemed to me we're both having problems and maybe . . . I guess I don't know who else to talk with. I don't even know what the hell's happening in my life.''

Boomer leaned forward. "And I figured you don't, either.''

It was true.

"If you'll come out to the kitchen with me and talk to me while I fix a salad, I'll give you a drink," she told Boomer.

He laughed. "In a jelly glass?'' Francey had offered him wine in a jelly glass when he and Carly were dating.

He followed her and sat on a high wooden stool as she took salad greens from the fridge along with a pitcher of margaritas she had mixed.

"Have you seen Cole at all?''

Boomer shook his head. Should he tell her the rumors?

"You want to tell me about BB&O?''

"Tessa and Dan sure got out at the right time.''

"Do you feel bitter?''

"Not a bit. I don't even envy them. I couldn't stand to spend the rest of my life doing nothing but traveling around. But we're closed. The office is still there and the receptionist, but no one else. All the architects, all the assistants, all the landscape . . . the carpenters . . . everyone's gone. We're closed.''

"What are you going to do?''

He shrugged and sipped the drink she'd handed him in a very expensive crystal glass. He admired it.

"What does Alex say?''

He didn't answer but gazed deeply into the glass.

"Ah,'' Carly said. She set down the colander and walked over to him, taking his face between her hands and forcing him to look at her. "Is that it? That's why you're here? It's not the business. That you can handle. But your marriage? Is that it?''

"I don't even know.'' He tried to smile.

Just then Walt opened the kitchen door. When he saw Boomer, he stuck out his hand, "Well, well.''

"Good evening, sir.''

"Sir?'' Walt thumped Boomer on the shoulder. "Don't go

making an old man of me, Boomer Bannerman. Good to see you.''

''I'm glad you think so. I've come here for advice.''

''From me?'' Walt said. ''Don't know if I'm up to the responsibility.''

''Up to it or not, sir . . . Walt, I'd like some of your time.''

''All you want, son. Right now, I need to jump in that pool. We can talk after dinner.''

Walt nodded, and walked through the kitchen.

''I want your advice as well as his,'' Boomer said.

''You need my *advice?*''

''Maybe not.'' Boomer held out his glass and Carly refilled it. ''But I need to talk. See what you think.''

''About Alex?'' she guessed.

''Yeah. I just don't know what's going on.''

Certainly, Carly thought, Alex must be giving Boomer all the support she could.

Carly thought maybe she better talk with Walt about *her* money. Hers and Cole's. She did have one account from which she turned the interest over to the Houston clinics, but she didn't want to have to touch that. Should she be worried about her money? She'd made a fortune over the years and let Cole invest it. When Boomer left, she'd talk with Walt about that. She hadn't thought about it until now, even though she knew banks were going defunct. But somehow, down here in Verity, it seemed so far removed from the rest of the world, and Walt's bank was safe. Was Cole's?

Boomer's voice cut through her thought. ''You thinking of leaving Cole?''

''I am,'' she said, and for the first time realized that's just what she was going to do.

''Would you go back to him if he needed you?''

She closed the oven door and thought a minute.

''You aren't really asking me about me, are you? It has something to do with you. You're wondering if I were Alex I'd back you up, aren't you?''

"Oh, Carly," he said.

She put her arms around him.

CHAPTER 66

"It's just going to get worse," Walt told Boomer. "Just about every bank in Texas had their investments in oil. And now we can't drill it for what it costs to buy from the Arabs. Everything from oil to polyester is going to be affected. That and the growing slump in the economy nationwide bodes no good."

Boomer nodded.

"Some are taking what they have and fleeing. But you're not that type. Do you have enough to cover your debts?"

"Barely. I'm thinking of paying off all I owe—I mean all the people who've owed me have pulled out and I'm left holding the whole ball of wax."

"Sure," Walt said. "Happening all over. Which then leaves the banks holding the bag. I'm lucky. I've never had *that* much of our investments in one basket. I've lost some, but not enough to go under."

"That's what Alex said. She diversified."

"Well, then you should be in okay shape."

"I don't know . . ."

Both Walt and Carly looked at him sharply. "She seems to think what I earned was ours and what she earned is hers."

They were sitting where she and Walt sat every evening, on the patio out by the swimming pool. Tonight Francey had joined them, as she had the last few nights.

"I feel like a poor relative," Boomer finally answered. He'd been trying for several days to figure out just what it meant.

"It's happening to everyone," Walt said. "It's not your fault you have all these unfinished, unpaid-for buildings. People with lots more money than you are going to tumble."

"Alex would prefer you didn't pay off the debts?" Carly asked. She didn't believe that. She thought she knew Alex better than that.

"I don't know," Boomer answered.

"I think you better have a talk with her," Francey said. It was the first time she'd jumped into the conversation.

"What are you prepared for?" Carly asked.

Boomer turned and smiled at her. "What are you prepared for with Cole?"

"Touché."

"Neither of you have answers, do you?" Francey asked.

"I'm getting there," Carly announced. "Boomer set my mind straight."

Boomer raised his eyebrows.

"You asked me if I was thinking of leaving Cole. I said yes without even thinking. So I guess it's been turning around in my mind and I just hadn't realized I'd come to a conclusion."

"And then what?" Boomer asked.

Walt and Francey just looked at her, and then glanced at each other, nodding their heads imperceptibly.

"I don't know. I haven't gotten that far."

Carly suggested driving out to Zelda Marie's after breakfast. Boomer could still get back to Houston before dark if he left by noon. Francey insisted on packing a ham sandwich and a thermos of lemonade. Boomer couldn't understand why that made him so happy.

The tree-lined driveway leading up to the big house impressed Boomer. He'd known they'd struck oil, and years ago Carly had told him Zelda Marie had built a mansion, but he was unprepared for the size and opulence.

But Zelda Marie hadn't changed, so far as he could see. She looked better than he remembered, and he guessed he might not have recognized her, but she threw her arms around him and said, "Why, Boomer Bannerman, if anything you've just gotten more handsome. I'd have known you anyplace."

She showed them her barns, and Boomer commented that most people would consider it a privilege to *live* in them. Zelda Marie just laughed.

Matt came running from someplace, hay clinging to him, and hugged his mother and Uncle Boomer. "Whatcha doin' down here?" he asked.

"I grew up here," Boomer reminded him. "Came to the old hometown for a visit."

"Can you ride?" Matt asked.

Boomer admitted he'd only been on a horse a couple of times since he'd left Verity.

"Want me to teach you?" Matt asked.

"Maybe another time," Boomer said, running his hand through Matt's hair.

Matt took off.

"Verity seems to agree with your son."

"I know. Funny, isn't it?"

They had coffee with Zelda Marie and then drove back to town. Boomer didn't even get out of the car, just said, "Thanks, Carly. You don't know how much better I feel. I don't know just what I'm going to do about my life, but I sure feel more like I can face it than I did two days ago." He leaned out the car window and kissed her cheek.

"It was great to see you. Tell Alex I miss her, too."

He nodded. "Keep in touch," he said. "You have my phone number. When you come back up to Houston, let me know. We have plenty of bedrooms."

The ceiling fan whirred softly. Despite a home that had cost over a million and a half dollars, Zelda Marie had refused to install air-conditioning. "That means keeping windows and doors shut and living like they do in the winter up North," she said. "I grew up with fans. I can continue with fans."

When visitors came to look at her horses, they sweltered in

luxury in the wing of the house reserved for guests. There was a wide oak door at the entrance, opening onto a hallway that could have served as a ballroom should Zelda Marie decide to have a dance. She thought to herself it'd be a wonderful place to have her children's weddings someday.

To the right of the wide hallway was what she called the family wing. Six rooms downstairs and an equal number above them. Behind the living room, was the office, where Zelda Marie kept all her horse records. Her office smelled of leather in much the same way the barn smelled of hay. She liked to be in both these places.

The other was the family room, where they watched TV and the kids just about lived. There were three other rooms, for which Zelda Marie could never determine a special use. Stray dogs whelped in one of them. They were cluttered, even if they didn't have a special use.

In the other wing, to the right of the great hall, the kitchen could have prepared food for a small army. It contained all the latest appliances. Aofrasia was now in charge of not only maids to clean the house but a cook. Carlos supervised the many gardeners and handymen Zelda Marie employed. Walt suggested she needed an accountant, but she said no, she enjoyed keeping track of everything. Up at the college at Kingsville, she'd taken a course in accounting and taxation. She liked the details involved with figures.

She spent many of her evenings and several afternoons a week in her office. Sometimes Rafael slipped quietly into the room, and said, "It's very hot," and she would look up from her books and smile at him, her heart turning over even if she'd already spent the morning working the horses with him, and they would head to the pool.

Saturday afternoons no one worked. And then she and Rafael skinny-dipped, ending up making love on the dried grass under the mesquite trees, or in the barn in the sweet-smelling hay that clung to them. Or they'd go to her rooms, making love in the shower before heading to the bed and talking the afternoon away.

Zelda Marie was afraid. She knew something dreadful was going to happen. She was so happy she knew it couldn't last. She'd been happy ever since Rafael had climbed through her window that night, years ago. She never took her happiness for granted.

Ever since Joe Bob died, her life had been too good to be true. Sure, in those years she'd had to work just to keep their heads above water, but she thought that had strengthened her. She thought those wretched years with Joe Bob were for a purpose. So she could really, deep down, every day appreciate Rafael.

And she did appreciate him. They never talked about their relationship, but when she moved here to the big house, he had come along. He had moved his few belongings into one of the guest rooms, upstairs in the other wing, but he never slept there. The excuse was that now Aofrasia and Carlos had too many children; there was no room for Rafael, and there were all these extra rooms in the big house and she felt safer at night with a man around. She did not say any of these things but they were on the tip of her tongue if someone asked. No one ever did.

On Sundays Zelda Marie joined the Mexicans, whether at Ao and Carlos's or at one of the other houses. They did not act embarrassed to have Zelda Marie in their modest homes. And at Christmas, when she entertained them with a lavish party she was always pleasantly surprised that they didn't act as though they didn't belong in such a grand house. They had been coming to celebrate Christmas Eve with her for many years now. It had become a mixture of the kinds of Christmas Eves she'd known as a child and a Mexican celebration. Her mother and father always attended, and there was room enough for any number of guests and relatives to stay overnight.

Zelda Marie was perfectly aware the house was obscene. Suddenly having more money than she knew what to do with had affected her brain, she told her mother. Her parents, despite their equally colossal income, still lived in the little house in town to which they'd moved over a decade ago. But her father drove a Lincoln Continental and her mother a Cadillac.

Even when all five children were there, she didn't use up the rooms in that big house.

And Fate may have understood that.

Or Fate may have determined why Zelda Marie had built her obscene manor house.

One night, when she and Rafael lay entwined, the bedclothes on the floor, they were awakened by a knocking on the big oak front door. Someone shouted, calling Rafael's name over and over.

He jumped up and ran to the window, kneeling so that whoever was outside would not see that he was naked in the señora's bedroom.

"Que pasa?" he shouted.

She understood enough Spanish to know that someone was wounded and the doctor wouldn't see him because none of them could afford to pay. The doctor didn't make house calls to Mexicans anyway. He would not come to his clinic in the middle of the night, either, not for a chicano. And José Moreno was bleeding to death.

Rafael jerked his jeans on and ran, bare-chested and barefoot, down the long curving staircase to the front door.

By the time Zelda Marie dressed, tucking her shirt into her pants, the unconscious José had left a trail of blood over the tiled hallway.

Rafael, his voice colder than she had ever known, said, "You call the doctor. He will come here for you."

She did not tell Doc Clarke why he was needed. She knew she'd awakened him but told him only who she was and that he was needed out here immediately. She hung up before he could ask her why.

When he arrived and saw who his patient was, he was furious. He said nothing, however, cleansing and sewing the wound of the man whose abdomen had been ripped open by a knife. He gave him an antibiotic, saying he should rest in bed for five days and not work until completely healed. He charged Zelda Marie a hundred dollars, an obscene amount. She walked into her office, and from the safe took out a crisp new bill, handing it to him. She smiled sweetly, "Since it's in cash, you won't even have to report it to the IRS."

He pulled her out the front door with him and whispered, "What you got to do with truck like this?"

"I think it's called Christianity."

"Come on, Zelda Marie," Doc Clarke said. "Helping them only encourages them."

Doc Clarke shook his head and turned his back on her, walking down the steps. Over his shoulder he said, "Don't call me out in the middle of the night for one of them again. I won't come."

The doctor walked across the driveway to his car, shoved his bag ahead of him, and climbed into the driver's seat.

He gunned the motor, reflecting his fury, and took off.

Zelda Marie returned to the house. "Let's take him upstairs," she said. "We'll take care of him here for the next few days. He shouldn't be moved. Momma will come out and see he's okay." Her mother would give Doc Clarke a good tongue-lashing, Zelda Marie was pretty sure of that. "Tell his mother she can come visit. And that girlfriend of his, too."

One of the men who'd brought José laughed. "Which one?"

CHAPTER 67

Francey had fixed dinner tonight, and while the casserole was simmering, the two women sat on the patio, listening to details of Walt's day. He and Francey looked at each other and Francey nodded her head, giving him a go-ahead signal.

"School starts next week," Walt said.

"Where's the summer gone?" Carly asked. She must have been here over four months. She hadn't seen Cole in all that time.

"What're you going to do?" he asked.

Carly looked at Walt, the dearest man in her world, and raised her eyebrows. "What do you mean?"

"Go back to Houston or put Matt in school here?"

"I haven't even thought about that," she said.

"Isn't it time to talk with Cole?" Francey asked.

"All I have to tell him is that Matt and I are leaving. And settle the finances, of course."

Walt let that sit in silence. After a few minutes he said, "I've a proposition for you."

She laughed. "No one's propositioned me for a long time."

Walt had a kindly look on his face. "Their loss, my dear. I'd think men would be falling down over you."

"You're prejudiced, for which I'm eternally grateful."

"Francey's health has given us time to consider what we want to do with the rest of our lives."

They'd returned from Palo Alto the week before, with the incredible news that Francey totally perplexed Stanford. Two CAT scans showed no sign of cancer.

"I want to slow down and work in the greenhouse," Walt said. "Specialize in orchids and miniature roses. I don't want to work hard anymore. I want to spend all my time with your mother. Maybe even take a couple of trips."

"You want me to house sit?" she asked.

"You've always hated Verity, though, haven't you?"

"Well, I thought I did. It seems a pretty tranquil place to be right now, though."

"Carly, stay. Come live with us, you and Matt. This house is big enough for half a dozen people. You can have privacy. You can entertain if you want."

Francey giggled. "You can even invite a lover to stay overnight, for all we care."

Carly laughed out loud.

"I own sixty-three percent of my granddaddy's bank," Walt continued. "I don't want to give it up or sell it. I want it to stay in the family.

"You've got a terrific mind. Carly, I want you to be president. I want you to take my place. I've given this serious thought."

When he saw the amazed expression on Carly's face, he reached out to put a hand on her arm. "Give yourself a year's option. I'll be here to train you. To talk things over with. And you don't have to do things the way I've done them. I'll kick myself up to Chairman of the Board, but you'll be president. It's time for new blood. Young ideas. And you're what? Forty now?"

"Almost."

"I can take it easier and you can have a new direction in life. I'm not handing it to you on a silver platter. It's work, and hard work. You won't be the most popular person in town even if one of the most respected. Sometimes you'll have to say no to nice people who want loans. Sometimes you'll have to foreclose mortgages on people you know have worked their tails off. Sometimes . . . well, you get the picture."

Her face was a study in surprise. "My heavens, Walt . . ."

"No, mine, Carly. It would be heaven for me if you'll say yes."

She looked at Francey, whose face was filled with anticipation.

"Matt loves it here," he went on.

"Me?" Carly's voice was faint. "Me, the president of the bank of the town I always wanted to get away from?" She laughed. "How ironic!"

Walt held his hand up in the air. "Don't give me any of that crap that you're not smart enough or can't do it . . ."

"Hey, wait," Carly said. "I *do* think I can do it, Walt. I've been so bored these last couple of years. Sure, I can do it. If I can close million-dollar deals . . ." She laughed. "Maybe my whole life's been leading up to this. Maybe I just put in time in Houston to prepare me for . . ."

Walt smiled.

"So, you're saying yes?"

She looked hesitant but only for a moment. "I think so, Walt. But how will Verity react to a woman bank president?"

"They won't have any choice, will they?" he said.

Carly stood up and began pacing on the wooden deck, her

arms crossed in front of her. "Oh, Walt. Oh, my goodness, Walt. Forty years old and a bank president. Are you sure?"

"Honey, Francey and I have talked about this for months. I've always had it in the back of my mind, but as long as you were tied to Houston I thought it was an empty dream."

Carly walked over and knelt next to the man who had adopted her, who had been anchor to her and Francey for over twenty years. "Are you sure? Really sure?"

He put an arm around her shoulder and kissed her forehead. "There's nothing greater I could ask of life, except for your mother's continued good health."

"Well, let's ask Matt. If he wants to stay here I guess I better go see Cole."

CHAPTER 68

"Where the hell do you expect me to get that much cash?"

"It doesn't have to be cash," Carly said.

She felt nothing. Not anger. Not belligerence. Nothing, except maybe a chill, deep in her chest. She sat, legs crossed, leaning back in a leather chair in Cole's office in their house. No longer home, she thought.

"All I want is the money I earned over the years and what I got from selling Rolf's. That's mine. I don't want a cent of yours."

"It's invested. I can't get it immediately."

Carly didn't answer. She simply looked at him. Her face was devoid of any expression.

"My lawyer will be in touch with yours," she said. "Accountants will contact you through him."

"Who's your lawyer?"

"I really haven't decided. But I'll have someone by this time tomorrow. You can have the house. You can have everything except the money I earned during our marriage."

"I'll demand joint custody," Cole said.

Carly reached for her purse and gloves, stood up, and said, "I'll have my lawyer get in touch with you. I'll be by tomorrow to pick up my clothes. I'll go through the house and see if there's anything I truly want." Actually, she didn't think there was much.

"My mother will fight to see Matt."

"She doesn't have to do that. I wouldn't dream of denying Matt the right to be able to visit his grandparents, or you. Assure your mother— No, I'll go see her myself."

"Where are you staying?" Cole asked.

"With Boomer and Alex. I hope to leave the day after tomorrow."

"Where are you going to live?"

She smiled now. "I'm going back to Verity. I've gotten really fond of it there and Matt loves it."

"You're not going to let a Coleridge have a high school education in that backwater town?"

"I am going to do just that. Boomer and I both graduated from there and look what we've achieved. Besides, Matt's happy there."

"Carly . . ."

He hoped Tiffany wouldn't hear about this. He certainly didn't want to have to marry her. She'd put pressure on him, he was pretty sure. Christ, marry that broad? She might be smart and she might be a hot lay, but marriage? Maybe he could keep this under wraps for a while.

"I'll fight you . . ."

"Your mother won't allow that. And though she may not always have thought I was worthy of you, your parents have always been cordial to me. I've a feeling they won't react quite as graciously to this Delacorte woman."

This Delacorte woman, Cole told himself, respected him far more than Carly did. But he let Carly's comment pass. "What are you going to do?" he asked.

Carly smiled. "Actually, I am going to be president of the First National Bank of Verity."

Cole stared at her. He slapped his forehead with the palm of his hand and began to laugh. "That's one for the books. You, a bank president?"

Carly walked to the door and turned the handle, opening it to let in the hot September air, dripping with humidity.

"I must tell you, Cole, the first couple of years were fun. But after that . . ."

"You never gave it a chance. You were never willing to participate in my life."

"Not true," she said, wondering if it was partially so. "I just wasn't willing to participate in your high-rolling weekends with those phonies and sycophants. I wasn't willing to watch men get drunk and wind up in beds with women other than their wives."

"You're a snob in reverse. Those men are the movers and shakers of this country."

"Which does partially explain the state the U.S. has fallen into."

As she stepped out the door into the twilight, he called from inside the house, "I have one of the best lawyers in Texas."

She knew that. Well, all she wanted was the money she had earned. A portion of what she'd received for selling Rolf's was salted away in the secret account that supported those three clinics in the city. Nothing, she hoped, would put a stop to that. She turned over all the interest she received to Dr. Gonzalez and the other two clinics. She thought maybe she'd better make out a will, and leave the principal to the clinics, too.

She didn't want to make it too easy for Cole, though she'd do anything to get out of her marriage. She'd earn enough as the president of First National to support herself and Matt, especially if she wanted to continue living with Francey and Walt.

Francey'd sold the Willows, and Carly was pretty sure Walt offered a good deal on a loan to the buyers, a couple from Brownsville. Francey was feeling fine without even being tired nowadays, which continued to astound Stanford and the Houston medical centers. She knew her mother and Walt would love to baby-sit Matt.

Carly smiled at the thought. Who was she going to go out with? She didn't care about a social life right now. All she wanted was a job that made her feel worthwhile, that challenged her and let her make decisions. And that's where she was heading.

Wasn't life funny? Where would she and her mother be today if she hadn't won that valedictory prize when she graduated from high school?

Alex recommended a divorce lawyer who had the reputation for getting fantastic settlements for his women clients.

"We'll make your husband bleed," he assured her.

"No, that's not what I want," Carly told him firmly. "All I want is the money I earned that he invested as ours."

Alex met her for lunch. And it was her turn to cry on Carly's shoulder.

"I don't know what's wrong with Boomer and me," she said, picking at her wilted lettuce salad. "Ever since BB&O had to close he's not even interested in new ideas. He's bent on paying off his loans, and that'll leave him cold flat broke."

"He told me that he'd still have a few hundred thousand left."

Alex's eyes blazed. "Oh, come on, Carly, you know that's peanuts. He doesn't know how to do anything except build. And no building at all is going on in Texas."

Carly did know that.

"I'm embarrassed," Alex went on. "Everyone knows about BB&O. People tell me how sorry they are. I'm not used to being *pitied.*"

"Does it affect *your* business?"

"Of course. The economy affects all of Texas. All of the U.S. It's hit everyone." Alex paused, then went on. "I know it's not Boomer's fault, but oh, I don't know. Somehow all the little things I've put up with over the years seem like mountains now. I tried not to let them bother me because Boomer was respected by everyone because he was so successful. He made his first million by the time he was twenty-eight and I was proud of him, but now . . .''

"Don't you think he needs your support?"

"How can I give it if I no longer respect him? For God's sake, he talks of doing what *you're* doing. Moving back to Verity. Buying back that monster of a house he grew up in, I mean really, Carly, can you see me in that rinky-dink town?"

Carly had to smile. "No," she admitted. "I can't, Alex. But just because Boomer's gone under financially shouldn't mean the end of your marriage or your feelings for him."

"It shouldn't, should it?" Alex tossed her head. "But it does. We don't even seem able to talk much about it. When I want to go up to the lake, he says he's not interested. He's the one who gave that lake to me."

"But it's not what he wanted now, is it? It's all developed."

"Oh, Carly, stop. Don't sound like one of those environmentalists. Boomer's bad enough. You're the two who should have gotten married." She cast a glance at Carly. "Did you two ever . . . I mean, I know you went to the senior prom together, but did you ever date each other aside from that?"

"Oh, Alex," Carly said. "I was never sure if you knew. I loved Boomer like crazy and thought I'd about die when he went off to college. It was never the same after that."

Alex had an amazed expression on her face. "His father died his senior year in college. You mean you two went together all that time and you've never mentioned it, either one of you?"

Carly had never told Cole. "It seems a long time ago, twenty years now."

"Boomer never told me . . . and neither of you ever gave signs of having had such a major love affair."

"I don't think it was such a major love affair now," Carly said thoughtfully. "Once he went off to college he had a life I never knew anything about. I don't think Boomer ever really loved me." She stared into space as Alex studied her.

"Have you resented me?" Alex asked.

Carly reached out to put a hand on Alex's arm. "Not for a minute. I was all over it by the time we met. Boomer's my good friend now. You know that. It was just a teenage romance, Alex. We grew up to be good friends, and I love his wife."

"This is all incredible. A part of Boomer—and of you— that I haven't known."

"It was a long time ago. He used to wait for me at five, standing in the door of the bank, and I'd look up and my heart would begin to beat fast and I just knew no one ever loved anyone as much as I did Boomer." She laughed. "You know, kid stuff."

"Did you love Cole as much as you did Boomer?"

"Oh, Alex, who knows? It was different. I haven't loved Boomer in twenty years, Alex. But I do like him. And respect him."

"Funny, I don't know that I do the latter."

"I can't understand that. If you truly love someone don't you want to stand by him in times of trouble? He hasn't given you any cause to doubt he loves you?"

Alex shook her head. "No, I don't think either of us have been tempted to be unfaithful." She gave a sharp look at Carly. "Have you?"

Carly answered, "Cole's been unfaithful, flagrantly so."

"He's not subtle, is he? How strange that I dated him before I met Boomer? Well, want to go over and see the Kincaid house this afternoon? I bought it yesterday, but Boomer doesn't know yet. He says we should tighten our belts, but I've lusted after that house for years. It's time to move back to River Oaks. If we make that move people will see we're not flirting with poverty. I'll be able to hold my head up."

"Oh, my," Carly said.

"I have to do something for my self-respect," Alex said, signaling the waiter. "Carly, I must tell you how wonderful it is to have a friend to talk so intimately with."

Carly nodded in agreement. But she was feeling depressed for Boomer.

CHAPTER 69

"You'll think I'm nuts," Zelda Marie said.

"Wouldn't be the first time," Carly grinned.

Zelda Marie leaned forward. "Do you know how wonderful it is, you bein' back in town. I never thought I'd live to see the day."

"The funny thing is, I'm happier than I've ever been in my life. So is Matt. He's just blossomed here. His Coleridge grandparents are having a fit he's going to Verity instead of St. John's. They say he'll never get into an Ivy League school from here, but he wants to go to Texas A & M and be a rancher or do ecological work."

"Does he see Cole at all?"

Carly nodded. "Cole flies him up to Houston every couple of months, but they really don't have a great time together. He does see Cole's parents. I don't think they should be denied their grandchild even if Matt is bored with them. But he's sweet. He seldom complains. But his life is here, in Verity. And Walt's more a father to him than Cole's ever been. Matt thinks his grandfather and Ben are the two most wonderful men in the universe."

"You hear from Ben since he got married?"

"He's not going to run again for a third term. He says he felt more influential when he was in Aransas Pass with his newspaper. He hasn't been happy in Washington. He says it's made him lose faith in America." She looked into the distance and said, "They're expecting another baby."

Zelda Marie squinted her eyes and studied Carly, but she didn't say anything. They were sitting on Zelda Marie's porch, early on a Saturday evening in April. Zelda Marie had asked

Carly to supper so she could toss around an idea she had. An idea concerning the house.

"Cole's thinking of moving to the Cayman or the Virgin islands. He's through in Houston, of course," Carly said.

"I read that it's going to take every American, man, woman, and child about seventy-five thousand dollars each in taxes for years to come to pay off what the public lost in the S & L scandals. I don't know how he can hold his head up."

"I have a feeling he personally made out like a bandit. We won't mention *my* money." Carly swung back and forth on the wooden swing that hung from the ceiling. "Well, what's this idea you have?"

"All but one of my kids have left home," Zelda Marie began. "Sally Mae's going to get her master's in June and has a job with a newspaper in Portland, Oregon."

"Yes."

Mike was twenty-one and working on an oil rig up near Austin. Girls surrounded him all the time, he was so handsome.

Sissy, at nineteen, was the mother of a six-month-old and worked nights at the phone company in Brownsville. Her husband, Darryl, was foreman of a citrus ranch down there, and their goal was to have a ranch of their own some day. Little Joe was in his freshman year at the University of Texas in Austin, and the youngest girl was still in high school.

"After they all prove how hard they can work and get to appreciate money," Zelda Marie told Carly, "I'll buy each of them land if they want. I got enough squirreled away so's I can help all the kids whenever they need it or I want to, but not till they prove themselves to me. I have no truck with laziness."

They were nice kids. They had all turned out better than anyone had a reason to think they would.

"My idea is, I'm thinking of turning the house into a hospital."

Carly stared at her.

"Doc Clarke won't make house calls to the Mexicans, and he won't let 'em in his clinic unless they pay in advance. I was over at the Martinezes' and they were talking about how some of the Mexican women die in childbirth because they don't dare go near the hospital.''

Hospital was a poor word for the six-bed clinic Doc Clarke ran.

"They'd rather die than go to him. They *do* die. Of pneumonia or complications of old age or diabetes or lack of pre or postnatal care. And on and on.''

Carly's mind was racing.

"I got thirty-two rooms here not counting bathrooms.''

Aofrasia appeared at the screen door and announced dinner.

The table was set for two, with a low vase of yellow roses and forget-me-nots.

Zelda Marie sat at the head of the table large enough for a baronial banquet, and Ao began to serve.

"Are you out of your mind?'' Carly asked.

"Rafael said everyone would think so.''

Carly shook her head, not yet sitting down. "I'm not talking about your idea. Most people, maybe everyone except your mother and I, will think that idea is nuts. What I'm talking about is, where does Rafael eat?''

Zelda Marie's eyes widened. "Why, in the kitchen.''

Carly sank onto the tufted seat. "Zelda Marie, look at me.''

Zelda Marie's eyes met hers. She stared at Carly for a full minute.

"How many years is it now that you've been sleeping with him?''

Zelda Marie shrugged. "About ten, more or less, I'd say. But, Carly, no one knows that but you.''

Carly laughed. "Oh, Zelda Marie, everyone knows. Everyone. It's been a scandal for years, him living out here in this house with you. You spending Sunday afternoons with the chicanos. Everyone knows, honey.''

A bright pink spread across Zelda Marie's cheeks.

"I've wanted to ask you for so long why you haven't married him. And made an honest man of him?''

Aofrasia padded into the dining room and placed plates of aromatic black beans and rice in front of the two women.

"Well," Zelda Marie said, "he hasn't wanted me that way."

"What do you mean?" Carly asked, spooning Ao's home-made salsa over her food.

"Well, if he'd wanted us to get married, he'd have asked."

Carly sighed. "Oh, darling, you're so stupid!"

Confusion whirled in Zelda Marie's eyes.

"You've been in love with this man for ten years, you're forty years old, and you think he doesn't want to marry you? He has a room in your house, in your big grand mansion, he eats in the kitchen with the maid and gardener . . ."

"They're his friends. Well, they're mine, too."

"So why don't you all eat together?"

Zelda Marie looked like a little girl who's been scolded.

"Well, we've never talked about it . . ."

"What? Eating together, or your relationship?"

Carly thought her friend might cry.

"Either. I've been afraid if I brought anything up . . ."

"Zelda Marie, you just can't go on treating him like a servant."

Zelda Marie stared down at her plate.

"Do you love him?" Carly asked.

"You know I do."

"Does he know?"

"He should."

"Have you told him?"

Zelda Marie shook her head. "He knows, though."

Carly started to eat. "Oh, my, this is heavenly."

They ate in silence for a minute, and then Carly continued. "Propose to him. This has gone to ridiculous lengths. He'll never ask you to marry him. Look at all this," Carly gestured in a wide arc. "He couldn't even afford this room much less all else that you own. Most American men couldn't handle it, much less a Mexican who's born with machismo."

"Me? Propose to him?" Zelda Marie's face reflected both shock and amusement.

"Would you like to be married to him? Be partners? Be able to talk things over with him?"

"Oh, I talk everything over with him concerning the ranch, just not . . ."

"Just not your feelings? How you feel about him? Oh, honey, come on! Make him a partner. He's been working with you for twelve, thirteen years. You're never going to have more of a helpmate than you have in him. Even if he doesn't know diddly about finances and about running this spread, he has his own area of expertise . . ."

Zelda Marie had relaxed and now giggled. "And does he!"

Carly stared at her friend and then laughed, too.

"What if he doesn't want me?"

"Who else has he even looked at in all the years you've known him?"

"None that I know of."

"How do the kids feel about him?"

"They take him for granted. I don't think they know about us."

Carly had finished her plate of beans and rice and was sopping up the leftover juice with a flour tortilla. "Zelda Marie, you are one of the most naive people I have ever met. Are you afraid they wouldn't approve of what's been going on under their noses since they were little kids?"

Zelda Marie's mouth hung open. "You think they know?"

"I told you *everyone* knows."

"Does your mother know?"

Carly nodded. "Of course."

"And Mr. Davis?"

She nodded again.

"And they didn't disapprove?"

"Zelda Marie, who's to approve or disapprove? Is this what's kept you from Rafael all these years?"

"You're a fine one to preach that! Lookit all those years you wanted Verity's approval!"

"And no matter what I did, I didn't get it. It wasn't until I decided I didn't give a damn that they began to accept me.

Hey, nothing will make Verity reject *you*. Your ancestors were early settlers here and you have tons of money. I say again, nothing you do could make Verity reject you!''

"Not even marrying a chicano? They won't invite him to their homes."

Carly was silent and studied her friend. Their eyes were locked on each other. "Does it matter?"

Zelda Marie thought about that. "What if he says no?"

"Would that be the end of your relationship?"

"I guess that's what I'm afraid of. Either that he didn't love me enough or that my money intimidated him."

"Well," Carly shrugged, "there come times in life when we have to act, not wait for life to happen, and be willing to risk all."

"I'll talk to him tonight," Zelda Marie promised.

It wasn't until Carly was driving home that she realized they'd never gotten around to discussing the pros and cons of Zelda Marie's plan to turn her house into a hospital for the Mexicans. When Zelda Marie had first brought up the idea, she had said, "We could start by turning the other wing of the house over to it. Get a doctor and a nurse, and it could be a sixteen- or twenty-bed hospital if we just use even eight rooms. That'd leave rooms for operating, for consultation and examination, for a kitchen, for an office . . ."

Obviously she'd given a lot of thought to the idea. She and Rafael had talked it over, Zelda Marie had told her. In fact, Carly wasn't sure which one had had the original idea.

After Carly left Zelda Marie sat on the wooden swing on the porch staring into the darkness. She wondered if Carly was right. And how much of her happiness she dared risk.

She was happy as she was. On the other hand, she realized she'd been waiting every year for Rafael to pick up and leave.

Return to Mexico. Or tell her he was marrying some dark-haired black-eyed girl.

He had never told her he loved her.

She had known from the time she said good-bye to that Joel whatshisname that Rafael was the only man for her. That was a long time ago.

He came in from the barn. She heard him in the kitchen, opening the refrigerator door. He would be pulling out a cold can of beer. He would stand out there until he finished it and then turn out the light and silently mount the stairs. Going to his bedroom first, showering, and then walk across the hallway, across the barrier to her part of the house. He would climb into her bed. He would expect to find her there, awake in the darkness, in the heat, waiting for him.

"Rafael," she called.

Was she sealing her own fate? Would he walk away from her? Would he be angry with her?

He appeared at the screen door and peered out into the night. He opened the door, letting it slam behind him, the can of beer in his left hand. She could not see his eyes but she could see his silhouette and knew he was looking at her, a question in his eyes.

"It's a lovely night," she said.

He nodded, silent. He put the beer on the railing and lit a cigarette, tossing the match onto the grass.

She wanted to ask him why he stayed. Was it the horses? Was it because there was no life for him any other place? What she said was, "I love you, Rafael."

He did not move but inhaled deeply, picked up his beer, and took a swallow. "I know." She could see the outline of his head as he jerked around to face her, even though he could not see her face yet. "Claro. Of course."

"What do you mean of course?"

He laughed, a soft sweet sound. "What else do you call what has been between us for so many years?"

"I don't want to lose you, Rafael."

"Nor I, you." He did not sound worried.

"What do I mean to you, Rafael? I don't mean this place or the horses. I mean me. Me, alone. Just me. What do I mean to you?"

"I thought you knew."

She shook her head. "I don't."

He walked a few steps and leaned against the pillar. Now she could see the whites of his eyes, the curve of his mouth. He flicked the cigarette into the night air, its embers glowing among the grass. "The world."

She closed her eyes, thinking that might still her beating heart.

"Rafael. Marry me."

The silence was so heavy she thought maybe she could weigh it.

"I will not leave you," he finally said. "You do not have to marry me."

"Oh, Rafael." She stood up and walked over to him, putting her arms around his waist, her head against his chest. "We should have talked years ago. I don't like to think of your having a room across the hall, of our having to pretend. I do not like your eating in the kitchen, of acting like a servant. I want you to be my husband."

He cupped her face in his hands and looked deep into her eyes. "It would not be proper. People in the town will . . ."

"I don't care. Rafael, you have been more of a father to my children, you have been more of a helpmate to me . . . We'd never have won races and shows and established ourselves as a superior stable without you. We'd—"

"I do not want you to want me because I train your horses," he laughed.

"I want you," she giggled, "because you have the most beautiful body in the world, because you make me feel beautiful, and because I don't want any other woman to have you as long as I'm alive."

"I will love you as long as you live," he said, grasping her hair in his hand. "And whether we are married or not."

"Do you want a Catholic wedding?" she asked.

He looked into her eyes. "You are serious? Well, yes, then. Not because I believe, but so that all our friends will come and be happy for me and will not be shocked."

He didn't want his friends to be shocked? Zelda Marie had to laugh aloud at that.

"Let's wait until Sally Mae is home from school," she said. "Next month." She had thought the entrance hall would be perfect for her children's wedding. Well, it would be fine for *hers*. She would have Carly as her attendant, and maybe Aofrasia, too. And her father would give her away. She knew her mother would not object to this marriage, and she hoped her father wouldn't. Certainly he had had enough time, twelve years, to get to know Rafael. Or maybe the priest would demand they be married in the church. Well, they would have the reception here.

Wait until she told Carly! What if her friend hadn't come out to dinner tonight. And she'd really invited her out to talk about the hospital idea . . .

"I am going to make love to you," Rafael whispered. "Now."

He picked her up in his arms and kicked open the screen door. As he carried her up the long stairway, he said, "This could never happen in Mexico. A woman would never propose to a man. What a wonderful country. And I accept."

He had reached the top of the stairs and headed for her bedroom. "I shall marry you," he said. "I shall cherish you and love you just as I have from the first week I have been here."

"Zelda Marie Hernandez," she said. "That's a mouthful."

As he began to unbutton her blouse, she giggled, "Wait a minute. You have to promise me from now on I can eat in the kitchen with you all."

"Ah, mi corazón," he said, his eyes laughing with her. "From now on whatever we do will be together." And then he bit the lobe of her ear, ever so gently.

CHAPTER 70

Cole wasn't doing anything that Michael Milkin and other Savings & Loans weren't doing throughout the United States. But what first brought Destin S & L to light was that it advertised its junk bonds as getting two percent more than certificates of deposit. Twelve thousand retirees, most of whom came to Destin monthly to pay on their mortgages, were lured into the higher interest. The tellers at Destin assured the customers that these junk bonds were as safe as the federally insured CDs.

As American Continental Corporation told its California salesmen, "The weak, the meek, and the ignorant are always good targets." Cole didn't put it that way. He didn't even think of it that way. He thought of it as making use of deregulation, of making bucks and then more bucks, only he said dollars. Tiffany thought of it in terms of bucks. Even when the oil boom went bust, the S & Ls were sure their good thing was going to last forever.

Congressmen across the country told federal regulators to lay off investigating S & Ls. When the domino theory began to take effect, and one after another of the thrifts tumbled, millions of people lost billions of dollars in their investment in junk bonds, and the federal government was left holding the bag on deposits that the FSLIC insured up to a hundred thousand dollars each, when the Savings and Loans went defunct. The officers and board members of these thrifts had long ago deposited their bonuses in foreign countries and in places which the government couldn't, or at least didn't, touch.

Neil Bush, the President's son got off scot free, as did thousands of others who participated. Charles Keating and Michael Milkin made nationwide newspaper headlines and went to jail for a while. The average American didn't even understand what it was all about but were told that they would owe thousands of dollars for years to come. A portion of the taxes taken from their weekly paychecks went to make sure that depositors of CDs in these Savings and Loans would be reimbursed. In fact, every person who drew a paycheck in the United States of America would work so many hours a day for so many years to come to reimburse the robber barons who had gotten away with bilking the American public. This was part of what they worked for and paid income tax for.

Carly had lost all the money Cole still owed her because he had invested it in his junk bonds. She knew damn well his own money was someplace else, but she had no way of proving it.

She was angry enough about the money Cole had stolen from her, but she was furious to think she had lived for so long with a man she now found so amoral.

But she made a conscious decision to get on with her life.

She was leading the First National Bank of Verity, Texas, in a new direction.

She and Walt together had approached the principal of the high school with their idea. Carly's really.

Carly and Zelda Marie had talked over what they'd have to do to staff a hospital. They knew no doctor would want to devote his working life to a tiny hospital that catered to Chicanos in a town with only six thousand population, at least three-fifths of which was gringo. And no matter how idealistic a young doctor might be and how dedicated to helping his people, this project wouldn't hold a doctor forever. So Carly came up with the idea that if Verity High School had an outstanding student of Mexican heritage each year who was bright enough to get in the right school and who wanted to be a doctor, the bank would pay for both pre-med and med school and interning if the student would come back to practice in Zelda Marie's hospital for two years. That meant, of course, that every other year, at least, given a student of high enough caliber existed, the bank would be sending someone through med school.

The First National Bank's prize would no longer be the one Carly won—one hundred dollars for the outstanding student. It would be ten years of education.

"Nothing worthwhile is ever achieved with haste," Walt told Carly, when she felt frustrated at the time it was taking to get the project off the ground. "In the meantime, how about advertising for a couple of nurses. There must be many who would welcome the opportunity to get out from under doctors' thumbs and be able to make their own decisions. I bet nurses deliver more babies than doctors do. They can sew up knife wounds, and they're as good at diagnosing ailments, minor ones anyhow, as most doctors."

Carly and Zelda Marie had gone to Houston and found two nurses, one in her late thirties and the other in her early forties, both divorced, who did welcome the challenge. They would be arriving the first of June.

The doors of the clinic—for it couldn't be an accredited hospital—would open the first of July, after the nurses and the hospital beds and the sheets and the X-ray machine and the medicines and all the other details were in order. A doctor in Corpus Christi agreed to let them use his name and offered to serve on the board of directors so they could have access to medicines. He agreed to spend Thursdays at the clinic to handle any situations that baffled the nurses and to serve as liaison to a hospital in Corpus if a patient needed serious care.

Eduardo Luna liked what they were doing. His great-grandfather had been Sam Houston's doctor. He was a fifth-generation Texan who had received his medical training at Cornell. He was also one of the busiest men in Corpus Christi, but still he managed to make one day a week free to help the Chicanos of Verity.

He offered to send a dentist and an eye doctor over twice a month and to make eyeglasses available at cost to those in need. He also suggested that two of his friends come out to Verity and hold an AA meeting there every Tuesday evening.

"If it weren't for alcohol and cigarettes," he said, "most of us doctors would be out of business."

Zelda Marie was so involved with her new project that Rafael took care of all the horse training. Their stable was becoming known in Virginia and Kentucky and California and wherever quality Arabians were wanted. From all over the United States, vans arrived with horses for Rafael to train.

Rafael had moved his clothes across the hallway into half of the big closet in Zelda Marie's dressing room. And Zelda Marie ate in the kitchen.

When there were guests, people who had driven their horses hundreds, and once in a while even thousands, of miles just so that Rafael would train them, or men and women looking over the horses that Zelda Marie and Rafael had for sale or breeding, then Rafael and Zelda Marie sat at opposite ends of the long table in the dining room, and dined in elegance, even if she and her new husband wore jeans and boots. Rafael's boots, however, now cost three hundred and fifty dollars.

Carly marveled at her sense of contentment. "And in Verity, of all places."

To the continued surprise of the Stanford Medical Center in Palo Alto, Francey had beaten cancer. Walt took Matt fishing now and then. Carly kept telling herself she should find a house for herself and Matt, that it was ridiculous at forty-two to still be living with one's parents, but life was so comfortable here. She talked business with Walt every night, and she loved her mother's cooking, and Matt had his horse here and the riding ring, and there was the wonderful pool she dipped into when she arrived home from work. She found her job more and more stimulating with each passing day.

Walt urged her to attend banking meetings around the country, and her mind was excited by what she learned and the people she met. She felt she was living a more cosmopolitan life than she had in Houston.

She and Matt drove over to Arnasas Pass monthly to see Ben, and the more she got to know Meryl, the better Carly liked her. She felt no jealousy at all anymore, and their children were adorable. Carly had to laugh at the turns her life had taken.

None was funnier than looking up from the pool early one evening, before dinner, and seeing Boomer standing on the deck.

"You look good even with your hair dripping wet," he said, smiling at her.

"Why, Boomer Bannerman. What a pleasure."

He knelt and said, "Francey tells me there's enough to eat if I stay for dinner."

"That's an understatement. There's enough to eat if you stay for a month." Carly started swimming toward Boomer, and he reached down to help her up the pool steps. "Carly, I swear you look as good as you did when you were seventeen."

"Sure," she said, swinging her head back and forth and splashing drops on him.

Just then Walt came out the kitchen door, bringing drinks to them. "Francey says to tell you dinner in twenty minutes."

"I came down to get some advice," Boomer said, and Carly noticed his eyes traveled the length of her body even if he tried to hide it.

"That's why you came last time, about a year ago."

"This is different advice I want, though." He handed her one of the margaritas Walt had prepared, and their hands touched.

Carly smiled. "Boomer, it is ever and always a pleasure to see you." She raised her glass and clinked it against his. "A toast to old friendships. Just seeing you makes me feel good."

"I hear tell you've become about the most important person in Verity."

She ran a hand through her wet hair. "Just those who want loans think that. But I am happy, Boomer. I'm so happy it makes me nervous."

"You're a great role model, Carly. For those of us who have been hurt and see you going on. You lost so much."

In the pit of her stomach Carly knew that Boomer and Alex had broken up.

At dinner, when he announced it to all of them, he did not act upset. "It's been three months now," he said. "I'm adjusting. We have joint custody of the kids. However, I may create complications because I'm thinking of leaving Houston."

They looked at him, waiting for him to continue.

"I've bought the old house," he said.

"You're moving back here!" Carly could not hide her pleasure.

"Is it true?" Francey asked.

"Yup. Going to spend time renovating it and make it look like it did when I was a kid. It'll give me a sense of roots, not to mention I got it for a song."

Carly imagined he had. The house had been on the market a long time. No one wanted such a big house or one that would need so much fixing.

"Doesn't sound to me like you need any advice. You've already done it," Carly said, thinking how wonderful it would be to have Boomer in Verity.

"That comes now," Boomer said, but he was looking at Walt rather than Carly. "Mel Tibbs wants to sell out."

The hardware store Mel had owned for over forty years.

"I heard tell," Walt said. "You interested in that?"

"It appeals to me. I know about building and builders' supplies. I could give good advice."

Carly sucked in her breath. The man responsible for so many of the innovative buildings not only in Houston but the world over, the man who had built so many hotels and developments and malls. That man in the little dark hardware store in Verity?

He looked happy as a kid at his own birthday party.

"Do you think it'd be a good investment?" Boomer asked Walt. "Actually I'd probably gut the place and make it light and airy. I couldn't work in that dark hole. Zeb Morris is interested in continuing to work there. He was working there when I was a kid."

Walt nodded. "That'd be fine. Sure, nearest other hardware store's over twenty-five miles north. Don't know what Verity would do without one."

"I've enough money left to buy my old house and the hardware store," Boomer said, "but I have to make a living from it. I want to know if you think I can."

"Mel did for as long as I can remember." Walt kept nodding his head. "Depends, doesn't it, on what your standard of living's going to be."

"I guess it surely does," Boomer said.

"Can you afford a horse?" Matt asked.

"I think I can afford a horse." He smiled, then glanced over the boy's head and, for the first time at the dinner table, his eyes met Carly's.

"What do you think, Carly? Do you think it's a good idea?"

"Boomer, it's the best idea I've heard since Zelda Marie thought up the hospital." She sipped her decaf. "And personally I even like it a lot better."

"You do?" Now he was smiling broadly.

"I do."

CHAPTER 71

Carly's secretary said, "Mr. Coleridge on line one."

There was only one line.

Carly nodded and picked up the phone. "Ben?"

"Well." She could tell he was smiling. "And to what do I owe this pleasure?"

"I have to go up to Corpus on business and hope I can talk you into driving over and having lunch with me."

"Why don't you come on over here and stay overnight with us? We've plenty of room." She knew that Ben and Meryl had bought a four-bedroom home overlooking the ocean.

"No," Carly said. "I'd like to talk with *you.*"

"Oh, you mean alone. Why, sure, Carly, I'd love that. It's been too long."

She hadn't seen him alone since his wedding and now he had two children.

"I'm going to get an early start, as my business will take a couple of hours. How about lunch at one-thirty?" They agreed on Thursday and a restaurant.

She didn't let her heart flutter when she saw him. Even though she'd be driving back to Verity later in the afternoon, she allowed herself a margarita, something she never did at lunch. Well, she told herself, rules were made to be broken.

His marriage had not lessened the frequency with which he saw Matt, and Matt had grown to like Meryl a lot. Ben always made alone time with him when the boy visited, took him fishing. Matt had to bait Ben's hook for him and help him take the fish off the hook when he caught one. Maybe it wasn't that which anyone loved most about fishing.

Once in a while Carly drove over with him and stayed for a Saturday night. And though she liked Meryl, could understand how Ben found happiness with her, she was never entirely comfortable.

After they'd ordered their lunch, Ben reached across the table with his right hand and put it over her left one. "You look as lovely as ever. Life in good ole Verity is agreeing with you, right?"

She smiled. "Right."

And then she took a deep breath and launched into the reason she'd called him. "Does Meryl know about us?"

"About us?" His blue eyes bored into her. "Oh, you mean about Matt? Of course she knows. She knew before we got married."

"You mean, when we all came up for your wedding she knew?"

Ben nodded. "In most things, Carly, I'm tactlessly honest. Yes, I felt she had to know."

The weight that had been sitting on Carly's chest dissolved. "I'm so glad. That makes this all so much easier."

Ben cocked his head and that unruly lock of hair fell over his forehead.

"Makes what easier?"

"I want to tell Matt."

Ben continued to stare at her.

"I mean," she rushed, "not if you don't want me to tell him. Maybe you'll want to talk it over with Meryl."

"Why, Carly?" The expression in his eyes had not changed but there was a crack in his voice.

"I want him to feel proud of his father. He and Cole have never gotten along. You know that. Since all this business broke about Cole having cheated so many people in business . . . and now that Cole and I . . ."

"The kid's only thirteen. Can he handle knowing you and I committed adultery?"

"I've thought about that. A lot. I think he'll forgive me because he *wants* you for a father. He's always wanted you to be his father. He admires and respects you and Walt more than any other two people in the world."

"I've a feeling he respects you, too."

She paused for a moment, then continued, feeling awkward. "I fell in love with you, Ben. I don't think I allowed myself to admit it, but I did fall in love with you. I know that now."

"And I've been in love with you since the first night I met you," Ben confessed. "I thought you were the most beautiful woman I'd ever seen."

They stared at each other so long. It took the waiter bringing their salad to interrupt their trance.

Carly laughed self-consciously. She almost told him she'd been about to come to him when he announced his wedding, but she stopped herself. "There will be questions from Matt to which we'll have no answers. But I think he'll be so happy to know you're his father."

"So, you're asking how I'd feel and how I think Meryl will feel?"

She nodded, not yet touching her salad.

Ben began to eat. "I have a happy marriage, Carly. Perhaps

not the passion I felt for you. Meryl and I like each other and love each other. If not in the same way I loved you—and probably still do—in a way that does not make me yearn for you in the way I did for so many years. I am happy with her and the kids. I know, she is more in love with me than I with her, but the fact remains I do love her. And I am more than content with my lot in life. We are both happy to be out of Washington. Aside from bringing up the children, she works hard on environmental issues, on both our little town level and the state level. She likes Aransas Pass. We have a good life together.''

She heard him.

"That does not negate the love I have for Matt . . . and for you, Carly. It means I don't want to cheat on my wife, even though seeing you still fills me with desire.''

"And maybe I wouldn't still love you if you were willing to cheat on her.''

They smiled at each other and ate in silence until the waiter brought them their main course. They had both ordered the flounder with new potatoes and buttered carrots.

"I doubted that there was any way you could make me love you more. But this is it. Carly, I would be proud for Matt to know I'm his father. Even if at first he stands in judgment of us . . .''

"He won't. He may not understand, even when he grows up, but knowing you are his father will give him a sense of pride he never had thinking Cole was his father. It may also explain to him the distance he's felt with Cole.''

"Are you going to tell Cole?''

"I don't think that's really necessary, do you? But if the time ever comes when it seems necessary . . . I would reconsider.''

"It would be nice not to give him that blow when he's down and out . . .''

"Brought about by his own shabby morals.'' Carly's voice was sharp.

Ben nodded.

"I've told Walt. I told him a couple of years ago." Ben looked surprised. "Now I'd like to tell Mom."

"You don't think Walt has?"

She shook her head. "I think he knows if I wanted her to know I'd tell her myself."

After she let that sink in, she asked, "Got any ideas of how to tell our son?"

"It'll be a shock. Shall we tell him together?"

"Is that going to hurt Meryl?"

Ben thought a minute. "She's so secure in her sense of self and in our marriage that I think she'll feel even closer to him when the truth comes out. Give me a bit of time to talk with her, and then how about coming over next Friday and staying for the weekend. You and I'll face Matt together and be there for a couple of days to help him understand."

"Ben . . ."

He winked at her. "I know."

"You know what?"

"You love me."

She laughed. "It's true. That's exactly what I was going to say. I do love you."

"And I love you, Carly. Don't you ever forget it. You're a part of my soul. And Matt is a part of our blood."

CHAPTER 72

"Lake Como, Italy," Carly murmured as she opened the envelope. "Must be from Tessa."

It was.

Carly's eyes skimmed the pale-mauve pages. She'd reread it with more concentration later. "They're coming home for a month and hope it's okay to come down to visit for two or three days. Okay? It'll be wonderful."

Carly and Francey were in the kitchen on Saturday morning. Francey had just taken two gooseberry pies from the oven. Earlier Carly had prepared potato salad and Francey had made two ham sandwiches slathered with mustard on Francey's home-baked pumpernickel. Even though she'd been on a totally healthy diet since the cancer, she hadn't forgotten the more hearty fare. Carly was going to take a picnic lunch over to Boomer, who was painting his house. He wouldn't hire someone, even when Carly and Francey exclaimed it wasn't safe to be three stories off the ground.

"Hell," he'd grinned, "I've been much higher without as much support on those skyscrapers in Houston and Santiago." He was going to be responsible for every square inch of the renovation of his old home.

He'd spent the last two months remodeling the kitchen and now was scraping paint off the wooden wainscotings inside and wallpapering and painting. He was doing this work evenings and weekends, when he came home from the hardware store which he'd renamed Bannermans. He guessed the job would take him at least two years.

Verity welcomed him home like a conquering hero. Half the town was old enough to remember the days when Boomer had led Verity to football fame and when he'd starred on the UT team in Austin. They'd also had more than a fond spot in their hearts for his father.

Boomer seemed content. He told Carly the hardest part was not being with his kids every day. He flew them down to Verity one weekend a month and went to Houston one other weekend.

He and Alex were civil to each other, but Alex couldn't find her way out of the fast lane. She had never regained her pride in Boomer. He'd paid off every debt he owed on the unfinished apartments and on the partially built buildings, but he could no longer get a loan on a handshake because he didn't even know the people who ran the banks now. Even Union Trust had been taken over, and Kevin and Maude Coleridge had decided to live in Mexico.

Whenever the kids came to Verity for the weekend, they

seemed to ridicule small-town life yet still love going out to
the ranch. They played games with the local children with an
enthusiasm they'd never before displayed. Diane was an expert
rider and told Zelda Marie that someday she'd like to train
horses. Fat chance, Zelda Marie thought, with Alex as her
mother.

Once in a while Alex drove down with the kids, even though
it was a long drive. While the kids stayed with Boomer, Alex
spent time with Carly. Carly missed Alex and Tessa.

Alex never even talked of her estrangement from Boomer.
They were pleasant to each other, and they all dined together
on a Saturday night, usually at Francey and Walt's but now
and then at the Willows.

Carly called out to Boomer as she walked down the sidewalk
to his house, where he was twisted around a pillar, painting,
"Tessa and Dan are coming for a visit."

He looked sideways at her and grinned. "They tired of traips-
ing around the world?"

"Not a bit," Carly said, walking on into the house, through
the open oak door, and on into the kitchen where she put the
potato salad and the sandwiches in the refrigerator. She looked
around. Boomer had done a great job. All new cabinets, new
tiled floor. He'd just pulled cupboards out of the wall and sat
down and designed a whole new kitchen Carly thought worthy
of Tessa. He'd installed the wall oven and the stove top himself.
The room was a bright cheery yellow, overlooking a garden.
He'd weeded it thoroughly but had let the old-time flowers
blaze. There were two big trees at the back of the garden in
between which Boomer had strung a hammock.

"I wore old clothes," Carly said, "so give me a brush and
I can at least paint the railing."

Boomer looked at her and grinned. "Only in small towns
do friends come to help."

"No," Carly shook her head. "You and I were just moving
with the wrong crowd. Even in cities neighbors help." She
thought of the section in Houston where she was sure Boomer

had never been, where the clinics that she financially supported were. Neighbors helped there.

Boomer placed his paintbrush across the top of the paint can and stood up. "Wait'll I get some newspaper and another can of paint and a brush. You want some gloves to protect those pretty nails of yours?"

Carly shook her head. Just then the phone rang.

Carly sat on the steps waiting for Boomer to finish his call and looked across the street, at the houses with their trim lawns and big trees shading the street. A couple of kids ran down the street shouting, kicking a can, one of them waving at her as he ran by. They were all younger than Matt, who was in junior high. How time flew.

She thought how funny life was, she and Boomer having been millionaires and now ending up back in Verity, happy as could be. She liked living with her mother and Walt. So did Matt. At last a man who listened to him each night, who watched all his Little League games and made sure he cleaned out his horse stall every night. Walt bought a horse trailer so they could haul Chazz, Matt's horse, out to the ranch weekends.

They'd even gotten six chickens at Matt's urging, and he gathered the eggs before the school bus stopped each morning. Francey didn't eat eggs any longer, but she did use egg whites in cakes and even made omelets from egg whites, adding onions and green peppers, and no one even knew the difference. They were all eating differently since Francey's bout with cancer.

After about twenty minutes Carly began painting the spokes of the railing. She realized she was happy. Much of it had to do with being president of the First National Bank of Verity, of course. She liked having to make decisions. Walt had warned her she wouldn't like parts of the job—such as having to repossess cars and foreclose mortgages—and he was right. She'd been left with two bad loans, but Walt told her that was pretty good, considering she was making loans to so many people with so little income.

She usually spent Saturday evenings with Boomer. Sometimes they'd take Matt and drive to Corpus to the movies. And when his kids were down, they all had dinner over at Walt and Francey's, and they spent the weekend with all the kids, often at the ranch. The kids loved Zelda Marie's nearly Olympic-size pool.

The Bannerman children were fascinated with the Mexicans. At first they'd looked at them as though they were from another planet, or at least the other side of Houston. But when they'd spent time with Zelda Marie and Rafael and Ao and Carlos and their kids and were pulled into the warmth and laughter that always seemed to prevail out at the ranch, Carly could notice a visible change of attitude.

Boomer had a proprietary interest in Matt. "After all, I was there when he was born," he'd always say.

Boomer and Carly's conversation was often about their children and their work and Verity; they never talked of their feelings, maybe because Boomer wasn't divorced. They'd become each other's closest friend. A day wasn't complete without seeing Boomer. The bank closed earlier than his hardware store did, and though he employed two men—one of whom he inherited and had been there thirty-six years—he was always there at closing time, and most of the rest of the day, too.

"Damndest thing." When Boomer returned from his phone call, he had forgotten to bring another can of paint.

Carly glanced up at him.

"That was Alex," he said, sitting down on the wooden swing that hung from the ceiling.

Carly waited. She waited so long she began to paint the wooden posts again.

After a while Boomer said, "She asked if I wanted to take the kids for the summer or should she send them to camp?" He looked perplexed. Then, gazing at Carly, he asked, "You know the answer to that, don't you?"

Carly nodded. "Of course. You said yes."

"Carly, there's nothing I want more than to have them with me. I left them with Alex because kids need mothers and because she can give them more worldly goods than I can."

"So what's this about the summer?"

"The Republicans want her to run for the Senate."

Carly put the paint brush down and stared at Boomer. "A woman senator from Texas?" She could scarcely believe it.

"A *divorced* woman senator," Boomer said.

"I thought you weren't divorced yet."

"That was my call. She just told me it was final."

As Carly thought about it, she came to the conclusion Alex would be wonderful in the Senate. She wouldn't champion the same things Ben did, but that meant she wouldn't be as disillusioned.

"At least she doesn't have skeletons in the closet like so many politicians do. The worst thing anyone can accuse her of is being divorced, and that's a matter of public record."

"So, if she's nominated you'll have the kids for the summer. Well, that'll be fun."

Boomer nodded. "I told her if she gets elected and moves to Washington I insist on having the kids. She's not going to have time for them. Not the kind of time growing kids need. And I won't have them going to schools in Washington. It's a false environment."

"And?"

"And she said she'd think about it. I told her the only thinking she had to do was whether or not to run, because if she did I was taking the kids while she was in Washington."

"And?"

"She said she'd think about it."

Carly went on painting. Boomer walked around the house to the garage and opened another can of paint, and came back out front.

"Is there anyplace or anything more wonderful than Texas in spring?" he asked. "Isn't this a glorious day?"

Carly agreed it was.

"You ever think about us, Carly?"

Carly looked over at Boomer. "In what way?"

"Any way."

"Of course," she answered. "I've spent a good portion of my life thinking about you, Boomer."

Now his eyes met hers and he grinned. "You have?"

"You must know that."

"Why'd you run away with Cole that weekend we made love all those years ago?"

"I've often wondered. I don't know. I guess I thought I was nearly twenty-five and time to get married and . . ."

"Have you wondered? Have you ever thought what it would be like . . ." He looked at her, sitting on the floor, and reached down a hand. "Here, stand up a minute," he said. She laid down her brush and held up one paint-spattered hand. He helped her up and stood looking down at her. "C'mere," he murmured, putting his arms around her. His paintbrush still in one hand, he pulled her close.

"Boomer," Carly said, "the neighbors . . ."

"They're all probably saying it's about time," and his lips met hers.

Carly felt herself melting, felt his tongue touching hers, felt the strength and warmth of the man she'd known for so long. She sighed. "Do you know what you always did to me? I can still remember how I'd feel when I'd look up at five o'clock and see you standing in the doorway of the bank waiting for me. I'd know that in just a couple of minutes you'd be kissing me like you just did and I'd be feeling like I do right now."

"How do you feel right now?" He was grinning down at her.

"Jittery."

"You're not the only one. I've got an idea. Call your mother and tell her you're not going to be home for dinner."

"I can't go out to dinner dressed like this," she said. "In jeans and Nikes."

"Who said anything about going out to dinner? We'll get it here." He kissed her again and Carly was aware that her insides turned to Jell-o, just like they had twenty-five years ago the first time he kissed her.

"What have you got against four kids?"

Carly frowned for a minute. "You mean . . ."

"I mean, how would Francey and Walt feel about you and Matt living here? With me and my brood. You could see your folks every day." ·

Carly made a face. "You mean you're inviting me to cook every day? After a day of work, to cook for you all? Forget it."

"You can afford a cook, can't you, even if I can't?" Boomer laughed. "Do you know you have paint over your nose?" He kissed it and some white brushed off on his lips. "Carly, I've wanted to make love to you for all the years I've known you. I've wanted to make love to you every day and evening and middle of the night since I returned to Verity, but I thought I'd wait until . . ."

"Until you could make an honest woman of me?"

"Something like that."

"Well, if you're going to start courting me, which is what I gathered you were implying, let's see how good this part of it still might be. We know we're good friends. Let's see if . . ."

"Carly, there's not one chance in seventeen billion that we're not going to still be good lovers."

"Humor me."

He picked her up in his arms and kicked open the screen door, which slammed behind him as he carried her upstairs, two steps at a time.

Monday at five o'clock, as she closed her office door, Carly saw Boomer standing at the bank's front door. And the old familiar rapid beating of her heart began. Her pace quickened and she smiled when he held the door open for her.